They played us perfectly, Kane thought

His side saw it coming all the way—and Huitzilopochtli and Tezcatlipoca still had them where they wanted them.

They *had* to fight the monsters. No choice about it. The whole culture of mass human sacrifice propping up Talocan was based on the belief that only by strengthening the gods with their very lives and blood could the Valley's people ensure they would be protected from the monsters who dwelled below the city and without its walls, lusting to flood in and destroy them.

So Kane and Brigid and sundry grunts had to go out and get videoed wading through fresh-spilled monster guts.

And, of course, it had all been just one big happy trap.

Other titles in this series:

James Axler
Outlanders

SUN
LORD

A GOLD EAGLE BOOK FROM
WORLDWIDE.

TORONTO • NEW YORK • LONDON
AMSTERDAM • PARIS • SYDNEY • HAMBURG
STOCKHOLM • ATHENS • TOKYO • MILAN
MADRID • WARSAW • BUDAPEST • AUCKLAND

First edition May 2004

ISBN 0-373-63842-6

SUN LORD

Special thanks and acknowledgment to Victor Milán
for his contribution to this work.

To Big Jon Guenther
without whom this would
never have happened.

The Road to Outlands—
From Secret Government Files to the Future

Almost two hundred years after the global holocaust, Kane, a former Magistrate of Cobaltville, often thought the world had been lucky to survive at all after a nuclear device detonated in the Russian embassy in Washington, D.C. The aftermath—forever known as skydark—reshaped continents and turned civilization into ashes.

Nearly depopulated, America became the Deathlands—poisoned by radiation, home to chaos and mutated life forms. Feudal rule reappeared in the form of baronies, while remote outposts clung to a brutish existence.

What eventually helped shape this wasteland were the redoubts, the secret preholocaust military installations with stores of weapons, and the home of gateways, the locational matter-transfer facilities. Some of the redoubts hid clues that had once fed wild theories of government cover-ups and alien visitations.

Rearmed from redoubt stockpiles, the barons consolidated their power and reclaimed technology for the villes. Their power, supported by some invisible authority, extended beyond their fortified walls to what was now called the Outlands. It was here that the rootstock of humanity survived, living with hellzones and chemical storms, hounded by Magistrates.

In the villes, rigid laws were enforced—to atone for the sins of the past and prepare the way for a better future. That was the barons' public credo and their right-to-rule.

Kane, along with friend and fellow Magistrate Grant, had upheld that claim until a fateful Outlands expedition. A displaced piece of technology…a question to a keeper of the archives…a vague clue about alien masters—and their world shifted radically. Suddenly, Brigid Baptiste, the archivist, faced summary execution, and Grant a quick termination. For Kane there was forgiveness if he pledged his unquestioning allegiance to Baron Cobalt and his unknown masters and abandoned his friends.

But that allegiance would make him support a mysterious and alien power and deny loyalty and friends. Then what else was there?

Kane had been brought up solely to serve the ville. Brigid's only link with her family was her mother's red-gold hair, green eyes and supple form. Grant's clues to his lineage were his ebony skin and powerful physique. But Domi, she of the white hair, was an Outlander pressed into sexual servitude in Cobaltville. She at least knew her roots and was a reminder to the exiles that the outcasts belonged in the human family.

Parents, friends, community—the very rootedness of humanity was denied. With no continuity, there was no forward momentum to the future. And that was the crux— when Kane began to wonder if there *was* a future.

For Kane, it wouldn't do. So the only way was out— way, way out.

After their escape, they found shelter at the forgotten Cerberus redoubt headed by Lakesh, a scientist, Cobaltville's head archivist, and secret opponent of the barons.

With their past turned into a lie, their future threatened, only one thing was left to give meaning to the outcasts. The hunger for freedom, the will to resist the hostile influences. And perhaps, by opposing, end them.

Chapter 1

"Ils viennent!" shouted the guardsman wearing the maroon-and-gray tabard with the arms of the Duke of Burgundy over a mail hauberk. As he struggled with the unfamiliar bolt on top of an Uzi, a triburst of jacketed 9 mm slugs hit him in the face. Two of the bullets punched out the back of his skull and through the peaked steel helmet he wore, spraying gore across the stone passageway.

Without slowing, Kane pivoted to his left and pulsed another 3-round burst into the face of the guard's partner across the corridor.

Kane heard a yammer of full-auto fire as his partner, Grant, bringing up the rear a few paces back, sprayed fire down the corridor behind.

"Good thing this crazy duke keeps his real blasters under lock and key most of the time," Grant called. "Otherwise these medieval screwheads could get to be a real pain in the dick."

"They can do plenty harm with their quaint implements," Kane said. His wrists still bore the red marks of the ropes that bound him to the rack from which Grant had rescued him. "Trust me."

"You might at least thank me," Grant told him.

"Remind me," Kane said.

Then they ran.

THE MISSION HAD BEEN a goat screw from the git-go.
Brigid Baptiste's researches into Totality Concept archives
had turned up evidence of a mat-trans gateway having
been built in what had been France. It didn't show up on
Cerberus redoubt's display of active sites. Lakesh had dispatched his ace operators, ex–Cobaltville Magistrates
Kane and Grant, to investigate whether the facility had actually been built and, if it had, why it was seemingly in-
operable.

The pair had jumped into what proved to be a reborn
Duchy of Burgundy. As in other parts of the world they had
visited, the local authorities had responded to the devastation
wrought by the nukecaust by reviving the real or imagined
glories of the past. In this case, the local ruler had established
himself as a low-tech version of one of the North American
barons, decking out his bullyboys in mail armor and arming
them with swords, pikes and crossbows. Or his ancestor had;
the system showed every indication of having been in place
for years, possibly since just after skydark itself.

Kane and Grant didn't get much chance to appreciate
the sociology of the situation. Apparently some local serf
or gamekeeper cannier than they were spotted them in the
local woods and ratted them out to the duke's men. A party
of mounted and well-armored infantry—which Brigid,
monitoring them from back at Cerberus, helpfully informed them were once called "hobelars"—jumped them
as they crept through some wooded hills a few klicks north
of the walled city in which the old archives told them the
mat-trans gateway should be located.

Kane was just barely able to empty a saddle with a
triburst before both men had to turn and run for it through
the early-autumn afternoon. Kane stepped in a snare trap

and was snatched up ignominiously into the air, dangling by an ankle like a captive rabbit.

"Run for it!" he shouted. Grant dived down a narrow, brushy defile and managed to lose the pursuers in the rapidly gathering dark.

Kane's first thought was to hose his pursuers with his Sin Eater. His second was to try shooting through the limb that suspended him just high enough so that the fingertips of arms dangling to full extent wouldn't reach the forest floor. With his pursuers rapidly gathering about him and dismounting, he discarded both notions. To shoot would only get him stabbed or hacked to death. With the armored men already behind him, any kills he could score would be nothing but Pyhrric victories. And while part of him was definitely in sympathy with the coyote strategy of chewing his own leg off to escape a trap, his point man instincts recoiled: as long as he was alive and reasonably intact, there was a chance that his wits would spring him. Crippling himself would only reduce those odds—and even wearing his shadow suit, he stood a good chance of breaking bones in his foot if he bounced a 9 mm jacketed bullet or two off his instep.

Besides, there was always the prospect of rescue—as long as Grant remained at large.

Instead, Kane released the Sin Eater, allowing his automatic holster to snap the weapon back into place along his forearm. Then he showed empty palms to his would-be captors.

"I give," he said.

THE CAPTIVE KANE, arms bound behind him, was bundled inside the walls of the city, and thence into the keep of the citadel. Down a set of stone stairs slick with long use he was frog-marched into an actual dungeon, and on into an equally actual torture chamber. Only then was he stripped. His shadow suit and the Sin Eater in its holster were tossed thoughtlessly aside.

He briefly considered trying to take out his captors and make a break for it. He let that notion go, as well. They were too many, too big, too well armed and much too alert.

Instead he was strapped naked onto the massive wooden frame of a rack and his wrists and ankles tied to ropes wound around spools at either end. These were rapidly cranked until his limbs and body were drawn out taut by a pair of torturers who, while not tall, were broad and obviously professional. They then stepped back, the windlasses held in place by cams, while he was questioned in a thin, acerbic voice by an equally thin, acerbic man in a gray gown and tight-fitting white cowl. Obviously a white-collar type, possibly the chief torturer.

Unfortunately, he only spoke and understood what Kane took for some dialect of French. Kane tried to give appropriate answers. There was no point in dissembling, especially when the price for being caught would be *dis*assembly, of him. However, once the fact that he was called Kane was established, pretty expeditiously, the torturer in chief took all his answers as lies, and issued appropriate orders to his bare-chested underlings.

Things got interesting. Kane had a chance to marvel at the elasticity of the human body as the rack was tightened gear tooth by gear tooth. It took a long, deliberate time to become uncomfortable.

Then it did, all at once. Despite the subterranean chill beneath the low, groined ceiling, Kane popped a sudden sweat.

Questions were asked. Answers were rejected. Kane's

arms and legs were pulled to the point of agony and beyond. Another turn of the wheel would certainly dislocate Kane's shoulder or hip joints, if not both.

Eardrum-popping noise filled the torture chamber. The hooded man's sunken-chested body shivered violently. A scarlet mist formed behind him in the thick, humid air. At the same instant, three stains, appropriately burgundy in color, darkened the front of his gray robe.

He slumped to the smooth flagstones as if his bones had dissolved.

Another triburst. Kane looked down the scarred and pallid length of his body to see the torturer by his feet spinning down clutching his throat, which geysered red with the characteristic spray of a severed artery.

The unmistakable figure of Grant loomed over Kane. The remaining torturer uttered an incomprehensible screech and plunged at the erstwhile Mag, swinging a three-foot iron bar with both hands in a wild overhead stroke.

The huge black man jammed the blow with a burly forearm beneath the wrists. "You obviously—" he punctuated his words with a single shot from his Sin Eater "—do not know who you are fucking with."

He let the man fall. Sin Eater at the ready, Grant turned his head this way and that, sniffing the air. His broad, often-broken nose wrinkled.

"Smells like shit in here."

"Maybe the inconsiderate bastards neglected to put individual flush toilets in the cells," Kane said, grunting only slightly at the exertion of speaking.

HIS BARE FEET mottled blue and pink, the lower half of his shadow suit pulled up to his waist, so that the torso, hood and arms dangled down the backs of his thighs like molted skin, Kane raced past the bodies of the men he had just shot. Behind him, Grant paused to face back the way they had come, fishing in a pouch on the Ripstop harness he wore over his own shadow suit.

A knot of armed men had appeared at a T-junction behind them. Grant bowled a matte-finished gray sphere the size of the shooter marble down the corridor toward them. The microgrenade detonated right where the lead man was about to plant his lead foot.

The chain-link smock he was wearing probably saved him from being disemboweled. That may or may not have been a good thing, since the mail did nothing to prevent his legs from being torn off, one at the hip, the other just below the knee. He fell, screaming and spurting blood. Dazzled and deafened, his comrades tumbled back away over each other out of sight. They dragged at least one more badly wounded man with them.

"Is it just me," Grant demanded, "or is the world overrun with reenactors?"

Kane's only response was to keep running. Grant turned and followed his comrade around a corner, digging in his microgren pouch again. This time he came up with a couple of tiny balls of a bilious yellow-green hue. He quickly activated them, working slider switches set in the low raised belts around their middle, which were designed to be worked by feel but impossible to activate by jostling.

"Let's see how they like this action," he said. He bowled them down the corridor.

They bounced against the far wall of the crossing corridor and burst with loud pops. Instantly a fog bank of a revolting pallid shade similar to the grens themselves

walled off the whole end of the corridor. The double amputee's screams died in a choking, gagging gargle. They heard the liquid surge of puking, then strangling sounds as the injured man began to suffocate on his own vomit.

The microgrens contained a fast-acting nausea gas, with a kicker of oleoresin capsicum—pepper gas. They also contained an aerosol dye. The pair carried the gas grens in both visible and invisible models, depending on whether it would be more deleterious to their enemies' morale to see what was making them throw up or not. In this case the whole point was delay, so a visual barrier was definitely indicated.

Kane and Grant turned and ran.

The subterranean corridor took several more doglegs, apparently at random. Then the two came up against a massive oaken door, iron-bound and set in what appeared more recent masonry than the surrounding walls. The door was secured by a huge, rusty, iron lock.

Kane braced and aimed his Sin Eater at the giant ancient lock. "Stand back," he said.

"Don't you even think about that!" Grant exclaimed. "I'll shoot you myself."

Kane grinned and stepped back, lowering the black machine pistol. "Just fucking with you. You've got some minipencil charges in your pouch, don't you?"

"Yeah." Grumbling, Grant stepped forward, digging in his pouch yet again. He came out with an object not unlike an old-fashioned medical capsule, about two centimeters long and about five millimeters thick between thumb and forefinger. He crushed the end with a quick pressure, and thrust it into the padlock's keyhole.

Both men stepped hastily back. "I hope Brigid is right about this gateway being shut down on local manual over-

ride," Grant said. "Meaning, we can turn it on. Because our only other way out of here is to die a lot."

"She is," Kane said. "She's always right. That's one of the many things that pisses me off about her."

Grant gave his partner an odd look. "None of my business, but hadn't you two better get things worked out between you one of these days?"

"And why would that be, partner?" Kane asked blandly.

Grant shook his head in disgust. "Point men. They're all crazy."

Kane grinned.

The pencil charge went off with a sharp crack. The lock popped open.

Grant started forward. Kane stopped him with a gesture. "Uh-uh," he said. "Let me do the honors."

Grant scowled more deeply. "Why?"

Kane stepped forward smartly, twisted free the broken lock. "Because I'm the point man," he said. He opened the door.

Inside was another door, this one vanadium steel, still shiny despite the passage of years. The wooden door had concealed a smaller entrance. A keypad was set in the wall beside the newly revealed door. Whistling tunelessly through a taut grin, Kane tapped out a quick combination.

The door slid open with a whisper of sound.

Inside lay darkness. "Light," Kane said.

Wordlessly, Grant handed him a Nighthawk microlight. Shining it out the bottom of his left fist, which he held up by his ear, Kane stepped through the door and took a rapid step to the right to clear that fatal funnel of the doorway.

Almost immediately, lights came on within the chamber, amber and dim. "Bingo," Kane said to his partner, who was covering their back trail.

Grant peered over Kane's bare shoulder. Through the door he could see a large open chamber. In the midst of that was a smaller chamber with walls of sea-green armaglass. He could also see part of what appeared to be control consoles in white synthetic. As was usual in the case of a mat-trans gateway that had been protected from the elements, everything appeared pristine. The Totality Concept had built for the ages.

"Okay, what have we got here?" Kane positioned himself in front of the control console, pressed buttons. Display lights glowed alight in response. "Signs of life. That's a promising start."

He entered commands, typing a bit tentatively; his hands were more accustomed to gripping weapons than punching keys. That was one thing about being a door-kicking, dreg-bashing, hard-contact Magistrate for the baronies: you didn't have to screw with a lot of paperwork. Not like the Intel bunch.

Grant looked in all directions as a sudden thrumming filled the air in the chamber, felt rather than heard. "It's alive," Kane said.

At the same moment an insistent pounding sounded from the door. It came mutedly through the thick alloy.

"So the thing still works," Grant said. "After two hundred years."

Kane shrugged. "The rest of them do. Why shouldn't this one?"

He stepped away from the console and gestured grandly at the green-walled jump chamber. "Shall we?"

"You said to remind you."

"Right. Thanks for saving my ass."

"Anytime."

THE FIRST THING Grant became aware of upon returning to the here and now was a deep, ragged voice intoning "I hate this, I hate this, I *hate* this."

He realized the voice was his. He was almost phobic about jumping. This hadn't even been that bad a jump: similar to being torn apart in five dimensions at once, wound onto spools, then flushed down the cosmic crapper. Nothing special at all.

"—is he?"

Grant realized another voice was speaking. He forced himself to roll onto his back—he wasn't even aware of having fallen down—and pried his eyes open. Brigid Baptiste stood at the entrance of the mat-trans gateway in Cerberus redoubt, dressed in an issue white bodysuit, a worried look in her green eyes.

"I said, where's Kane? Didn't he jump with you?"

"Yeah. Of course he did." Still disoriented, he was irritated at being asked such a silly question.

"Then where is he?" Even in his befuddled state, he could hear barely suppressed panic thrilling through the archivist's rigidly controlled voice.

"What you mean? He's right—"

With a grunt of effort, Grant rolled over.

He was alone in the mat-trans unit.

Chapter 2

"There is no sign of him," said Dr. Mohandas Lakesh Singh, founder of Cerberus redoubt and recruiter of the ragtag band who made up the only known organized resistance to the schemes of the hybrid barons to dominate humanity. Gazing up at the big world map on the wall of the command center—and carefully not looking at Brigid Baptiste—he shook his head. "He appears to have fallen completely off the planet. I am so sorry, my very dear Brigid."

Domi, dressed in her customary shorts, middie top and red stand-ups, and Grant, still in his shadow suit, stood in the control center with Brigid and Lakesh. Brewster Philboyd was at the control console.

Brigid's face was ice. Her eyes strained toward the giant screen until it seemed to her emerald laser beams should shoot from them and make the big board smoke, as if somehow to burn through the layers concealing Kane from her.

Why am I so cold inside? It's not as if I even particularly like the man. And even as she thought the words, she knew them as hollow as the feeling inside her belly. Like or not, indeed any emotion or lack thereof notwithstanding, they were what the jump dreams had revealed them to be so many months before. Anam-chara. Soul-friends, their destinies bound inextricably together not just through years but lifetimes.

"He's not dead," she said.

"How can you be so sure?" Lakesh asked.

She looked at him stonily. "I'd know."

"Perhaps he's looped," the erstwhile Moon base tech suggested. "Caught in some eddy of the space-time whorl."

"Bite your tongue," Grant growled.

"After all, the gateway had been out of use for centuries," said Collins, who monitored environ ops. "It might well have malfunctioned."

Lips pressed together to form a thin line, Brigid turned a pale green and swayed. But Lakesh was shaking his head. "No, my very good friend, I do not believe so. After all, once friend Kane brought the station in Burgundy back online, we instantly achieved telemetry with it. We were able to monitor both ends of the jump. We recorded no sign of malfunction at either end."

"Could his biolink transceiver have gone out?" Philboyd asked.

"Impossible," Lakesh said. He shrugged. It was an uncharacteristic gesture for him—acknowledging lack of omniscience and omnipotence. "It is almost as if he has simply ceased to exist."

Both Brigid and Grant snapped their heads around to stare at him. He held up placating hands. "Ah, no, my friends. Please forgive me—this is as trying for me as it is for you. I do not in fact believe that our excellent Kane has in fact ceased to exist. Nor do I believe that he is caught in a chronon loop."

"Then where on Earth is he?" Brigid snapped.

Lakesh showed her a thin smile. "Dear lady, you have answered your question even as you asked it. In all truth, I believe him to be, in fact, on Earth."

The others broke into a babble of questions and interjections. "As to where he may be, other than on this planet and still contemporaneous with us, I cannot conjecture. Nor, frankly, can I say what leads me to believe this. As with Brigid, I simply have an intuition, which concurs with hers—I likewise believe he yet lives."

Grant had produced a cigar from his pouch and begun unwrapping it. Now he stuck it in his mouth without lighting it. "What I want to know is, what're we going to do about it?"

Lakesh held up his soft brown hands. "Exhaustively analyze the data from the jump. Run comprehensive diagnostics on our satellites and systems here that monitor the biolink transmitters. Continue to search." He shrugged again. "Pray. Under the circumstances, it can hardly hurt."

"Isn't there anything more we can do?" Brigid asked.

"I am open to suggestions, my dear."

KANE SWAM in a haze of red and pain.

Relax, a voice said within whatever fitful consciousness he possessed. *Rest easy. Give in to peace and the transformation.*

"It's not my nature to give in." Did he speak the words aloud or merely think them? Did he do anything at all? Did he even exist, or was he a mere wisp, a figment, a vacuum fluctuation transitory as any virtual particle?

You are as real as any. And of course it is your nature not to surrender. It is for this that you have been chosen.

Though there was no voice, the words seemed somehow feminine.

"Chosen for what?" he demanded.

A destiny greater than any you might have imagined. The voice was soothing oil over the raw wound that was his awareness. *Now, be at peace, for soon enough you will know strife enough to satisfy even your turbulent spirit….*

"No!" he raged, defying with every scintilla of his being. But it did no good. Gentle velvet blackness enfolded him and put him out like a light.

BLOOD. So much blood....

Unaware, Brigid tossed her head and moaned. Outside the great peak beneath which Cerberus redoubt lay buried it was night. Here within her room, it was, as well, though the corridor outside knew only artificial day. She slept. But her dreams were anything but restful.

Shards and impressions they were. Nothing coherent. Nothing that could be sorted for referent or story. Just overwhelming tidal surges of blood and fear and pain.

She felt them, but they weren't hers. Yet they seemed somehow real, and overwhelming. Faces, distorted by bursts of emotion, seen as if through a scrim—dark red, as for blood.

And the sounds. Screams, cries, wails of agony that went deeper than bone.

In the dream she pressed hands over her ears. The howls went through them like nails.

The blood ran down. Dripped down. Rained down.

Onto...Kane.

He opened his eyes and looked at her past rivers of blood.

She wrenched herself from sleep with a monstrous effort. The scream that still rang in her ears was her own.

SUN AND SAND.

"*Sol y arena,*" said the bandy-legged man in the loincloth. To his mild surprise, Kane understood—standing blinking into the one, with the other hot beneath his bare feet.

For some reason Kane was wearing a loincloth, too. Strapped to his left arm was a shield that seemed to be of hide stretched like a drumhead over a wooden framework. In the other was a sort of blunt-tipped wooden sword. It seemed an odd way to be kitted out.

If only he had a better idea who Kane was. It was him, he grasped as much. But who was that?

"So now, Tonatiuh," the other man said in the language he had spoken before. The name came as both "Spanish" and *"Español"* at once, as though piped into his brain through two channels at once. Something was out of adjustment here, but Kane couldn't put his finger on precisely what.

"So now, Tonatiuh," the man said again. "We commence our lesson. Powerful as you are, you have much to learn and little time to learn it, great lord."

The trainer raised his own small frame and hide target shield and wooden sword. Kane—that being the name that resonated most in his mind of recent usage, although somewhere, deep down, the name Tonatiuh resonated, as well—appraised him carefully from eyes slitted against the glare of the morning sun spilling over the top of the two-story wall of dressed massive blocks of stone that surrounded the circular training ground.

He was no large man, a good head shorter than Kane. The trainer was stocky, though. His bare, somewhat long arms and short, bowed legs were corded with muscle beneath bronze skin, and if he was well-endowed with belly, his shoulders were broad enough to do credit to a much larger man. Indeed, they put Kane in mind of Grant.

The trainer was no handsome man. He was clearly on the downward slope of middle age, although he carried his obvious years as lightly as he did his gut. His face could be called nothing but ugly, a mass of folds and wrinkles dominated by a great jut of nose, from which both forehead and chin receded rapidly as if in full retreat. His hair was full and coarse, as black as a crow's wing, showing not a single thread of white, and tied up on top of his head in a topknot that hung to his nape. But the eyes that watched Kane keenly from within that seamed and well-weathered face were as bright as polished flecks of obsidian, and while that face seemed as expressive as if it had been crudely hewed from a block of stone, the eyes at least seemed to attest to a substantial store of rich if rough humor.

"Let's try a few strokes, you and I together, master," the man said. "Gently at first, for I am but a mere mortal."

He stepped forward then, swinging his wooden sword slowly in an overhand blow at the crown of Kane's skull. As if by reflex, Kane stepped back with his right foot, rotating his shield upward so that the descending blow clacked upon its rim.

The trainer stepped back. "Good. Perhaps the memories return, yes?"

"Maybe." To his own ears Kane's voice sounded like a bad stretch of gravel road. He tried to moisten cracked lips with a tongue scarcely damper.

"Again."

Here came the man forward, swinging his strange yet not wholly unfamiliar sword at Kane's head as if moving underwater. Kane blocked with a certainty that argued actual training in the use of the shield, not just defensive reflex.

I'm a trained fighter. He knew that much. But when had he been trained with shield and sword of any sort, much less one as curiously shaped as these wooden mock-ups?

"And now you strike at me. Gently, if this unworthy one may presume to remind so great a warrior, yet one who, wakened recently from long sleep, may not yet realize his own strength." The black eyes danced, and Kane sensed the grin the man's face would never show, possibly could not.

The words conveyed no sense to him, other than that the man was clearly reminding him that this was practice not deadly combat. He stepped in, assaying the same kind of through-molasses cut at that topknot as the man had employed on him. The man stepped back, blocking with the certain ease of autonomic response. And so they moved back and forth in a slow exchange that was more dance than battle, one attacking, the other defending, across the thirty-yard expanse of the arena. Then they switched roles and crossed back again. Kane felt sweat dripping from his body and stinging in his eyes. Curiously this slow, deliberate mock combat—ritual almost—was somehow more draining than full-speed combat. Which was the most draining pastime Kane knew.

At last they paused. Though the trainer's burly body was now sheened with sweat, his breathing was slow and easy as if he had just wakened from a midday nap. "Let a poor old warrior rest a moment, by your mercy, Lord Tonatiuh."

Kane nodded, for want of a better response. A small brown child with an inverted bowl of black hair and a spotless white smock brought clay flasks of water. Both men drank greedily.

Though he was certain—to the extent he was certain of anything, and if he was unsure of his own name, how certain was that really?—he had never met this man before, Kane knew the type down deep in his bones. An old campaigner, one who would never rise higher than senior Magistrate in the Mag Division at Cobaltville, never come within a hundred miles of being tapped for an Admin post, but one who would serve willingly and well for decades.

And where did all that come from? Kane wondered as

he wiped his brow with the back of his sword hand. A Magistrate—a Mag. Hard contact. I was one of those, in the place called the barony of Cobaltville. In my...most recent life.

Yet he knew also that he was no longer a Mag, had not been for many long months, even in that life. And was it the same as this one? Or had he died and been reborn, yet another turn of some endless and enormous wheel?

No. He knew that much from simple reasoning: he was a mature man, not so shy of middle age himself, and from the aches and twinges in his bones and muscle, not all of which had to do with recent exercise, he had himself led a life little if any easier than what was written in splashes and striations of pale scar on the trainer's doughty hide. And his mind and muscles were alike well used to combat: whether it was true, as the question of his identity and indeed the multitude of identities schooling within his mind seemed to suggest, that he had lived before, and carried with him some baggage of memory from prior lives, that kind of neuromuscular conditioning would not follow a soul from flesh to flesh.

"You are thinking, Lord," the trainer said. "I can see it writhing on your brow. Be wary of it, if you will heed an old man's hard-won wisdom. It profits you little, and thinking instead of acting in battle's heat is death."

"Name," Kane asked. The language came readily enough, even though he knew that as Kane he had spoken no Spanish. It was speaking that came hard. And not just because of the dryness of his vocal apparatus; it was as if speech itself were a long-disused skill. "What's your name?"

"This unworthy one is known as Taker of Fifty Captives, although it may be that I have taken one or even two more since being granted that name—it hardly seems worth the bother of counting anymore." A shadow passed over that granite face, and it seemed to Kane that there was more to the tale than the trainer cared to tell, and possibly remember. "The *señor* may simply call me Fifty, if he pleases."

He bowed, then straightened. "You remember the arts of combat well. Therefore it is time for the next stage in recalling you to your rightful glory."

He clacked his broad-bladed wooden sword against the front of his shield. The noise it made was startlingly loud; echoes chased each other like rats around the walls of the arena. Before Kane could ask what the blazes he was talking about, a gate at the far side of the arena swung open. The gate's leaves were painted red with gold serpent heads, stylized in a blocky way and with tongues protruding toward one another. In marched six men clad and equipped like Fifty, but young, strapping and bulging with muscle.

"And now," Fifty said, still courteously but with an edge to it, "it shall please my lord to fight all six at once."

Chapter 3

"Any sign?" Brigid asked, coming into the control center.

Grant looked up from a steaming mug of coffee. "Not a thing."

Lakesh was not on hand. Donald Bry had charge. A couple of Moon base technicians whose names Brigid had not yet discovered were on duty with him.

"What I want to know is, what's being done to look for Kane?" Grant said.

"What would you suggest we do?" Bry asked.

Grant started to bridle at the little red-haired man, whose manner had been flippant. "Easy, Grant," Brigid said. "It was an honest question. And a good one."

Grant's huge chest expanded in a deep breath. He sighed and made a chopping gesture with his free hand. "Yeah. All right. Except...you guys are the techs. Aren't you the ones supposed to know what to do?"

Bry's face pinched. He had a large head, forehead rendered prominent by the retreat of his hairline, and little love for Cerberus redoubt's more active operatives. However, he took his job with utmost seriousness, and he was good at it.

It wouldn't break Bry's heart to have Kane fall off the planet, Brigid knew. What the little tech would find intolerable was himself being unable to find him.

Well, good, she thought. We don't have to love each

other to do what needs to be done. In fact the principal actors in the Cerberus drama often acted as if they disliked one another pretty actively…on the surface. But she, and Kane and Grant, and Domi, and even Lakesh, were all bound together by something more than mutual respect for one another's proved abilities, or even a shared, immense and possibly doomed purpose: freeing humanity from the tyranny of the human-hybrid coalition that governed the baronies.

As if to emphasize the fact, the door opened and Domi came slouching in. "Nothing?" she asked.

Grant just growled and shook his head.

"Apparently the technicians can find no sign of him," Brigid said crisply. Although she and the little plush-haired albino had acquired substantial mutual respect for each other, their relationship was frequently not unlike one between a couple of porcupines.

Or maybe it's just me, Brigid thought, a little ruefully. She was not the most social person on Earth; her archivist's training had left little space to learn the social graces. Or maybe it was that the personality type that had made her such an ace archivist ill-suited her for social contact.

Domi frowned. "Why can't they find him? His biolink transponder should shine like a beacon on our satellite coverage."

Bry muttered something under his breath.

"What was that?" Domi asked sharply.

"Nothing," Bry said.

Passive-aggressive didn't work well on the ruby-eyed little child of the Outlands at the best of times. With Kane—for better or worse, the strong backbone of the Cerberus-based resistance, as well as its strong right hand—missing in action, these were hardly the best of times. Everyone was on edge.

In three swift steps, Domi was beside the little technician. She grabbed the little wavy red wisp of hair just aft of his bald forehead, dragged his big blue-veined head back and held the tip of a knife at his throat. It was a serious knife. The blade was nine inches long and nastily serrated. It had been her constant companion since the day she used it to chill Guana Teague and liberate herself from the slavery the gross boss of the Tartarus Pits under Cobaltville had imposed upon her after the six-month live-in gaudy slut contract she had signed with him ran out. No one knew where she kept the knife in her customary skimpy attire, but she was never without it.

"I didn't hear it, but it wasn't *nothing*," she said sweetly. "Don't try to blow smoke up my ass. I'm not in the mood for kinky."

Her calculated coquetry was keener torture than the knife tip dimpling the pallid skin beside his Adam's apple, where a few grams more pressure would sever his jugular and set his large domed head to draining. Domi was not indiscriminate in her choice of sex partners—her liaison with Teague had been purely a business proposition—but her criteria were certainly her own, obscure unto the rest of the world. However, whatever her standards were—and indeed Brigid at least suspected they changed day to day if not minute to minute, as did most things about the mercurial Outlands girl—they did not extend to Bry. He was approximately the last man or even humanoid being on the planet she'd sleep with, and she had made it abundantly and indeed scathingly clear at various times in the past.

Nonetheless Bry wasn't above making snide salacious remarks to her, or about her in her hearing. He did none of that now. Mostly he sweated and rolled his eyes like a calf being abducted by experimentally inclined hybrids.

"I said he's dead! Okay? It's the only thing that makes any kind of sense. It's the only reason we wouldn't pick up his signal, if he's still on Earth."

"All right, but about this 'still on Earth' thing?" Grant asked. "Could he have maybe accidentally gotten diverted to the Moon or something? I mean, maybe Sindri snatched him. It's the kind of trick he'd pull, twisted little pain in the ass that he is."

Bry was beginning to hyperventilate. His lower lip quivered. He rolled beseeching eyes toward Brigid.

"Domi," she said quietly.

Domi made a face but stepped back, letting the panicked technician go. Her knife went away. Bry fell forward in his chair, his shiny expanse of forehead almost slamming into his keyboard.

With visible effort he straightened and pulled himself together. After a moment he responded to Brigid's green gaze, which bore on him like a spotlight. "I'm not strong on mat-trans theory yet. I'm more a hardware technician, an electronics guy. But I don't think that's likely. To snatch somebody out of midjump like that would require a technology way ahead of anything we know about."

He shook his head. "He's dead, I tell you. It's the only logical explanation."

Eyes ablur, Brigid felt herself running from the control center.

WARILY KANE TURNED to face the six newcomers. They laid their broad wooden swords across their shields and bowed to him. He stood watching. He wasn't quite tracking what was going on here.

"Of course the lord will be generous, and take care not to hurt these poor ones," Fifty said. "Begin!"

The six straightened. "Hail, Tonatiuh!" they said in unison. Then they fanned out and began to close on Kane.

Whoever else he was, all at once he was pure Kane, point man and pure hard-contact Mag, and the dregs were in sore need of a serious head-busting. The only trouble was, there were six of them. Oh, and it seemed like a sucker bet that they knew how to use their little wood trash-can lids and toy swords a boatload better than Kane did.

But the rules of the game didn't seem to include explaining to Kane what those rules were, nor even what the game was. So while he had no earthly idea of what might constitute cheating, he was going to do his damnedest to do some of it.

They moved warily and well, their topknots just dusting their spines at the top of their shoulders. Kane feinted to his right, then ran left, in order to pass the unshielded side of the man at the left end of the approaching arc. As Kane expected, rather than just whack him a good one with his wooden sword, the man reflexively spun clockwise, hastily bringing up his shield.

Kane stiffened his lead left leg with the heel digging into the sand, and slammed a hard thrusting side kick south of the swordsman's belt. Again by reflex the man twisted his pelvis and bent slightly, interposing the muscle of his thigh between Kane's heel and the family jewels. But Kane wasn't aiming for the groin, an easily and automatically defended target, and overrated into the bargain. His aim point was the pelvis itself; his kick knocked the man, off balance and stuck in midstep, sprawling backward into the man to his own left. Both went down like dominoes.

Kane darted left. The four currently on their feet had turned and were swarming two and two around either side of the limb tangle of their fallen comrades. So far, carrying the fight to the foe—trying to reduce the odds as much as he could—seemed to be working. So he'd ride that horse until it foundered beneath him.

Kane had shown himself more skill at this game than he thought he possessed during the one-on-one. But a few rounds of patty-cake with good old Sergeant Fifty meant nukeshit. So he also wanted to fight on his terms as long as possible. And that meant grabbing the initiative by the balls and twisting.

The closest opponent coming to Kane's left around the downed pair raised his shield defensively and cocked his sword back for a whack, clearly expecting Kane to play by the rules and stand and deliver. Kane rushed him instead. He put his own shield up and rammed into him with all the weight of his wiry body and all the strength of his hard-muscled legs.

His adversary wasn't expecting that. He didn't fall down, worse luck. Kane drove his shield arm back against his chest and slammed the butt of his own club straight into the bridge of the man's prominent nose. Kane felt that little satisfying snap as the cartilage broke. Red, red blood began to cascade down the startled young man's face as he fell onto his butt.

Kane noticed one of the first pair he'd put down, now on his right, trying to rise. He side kicked the man in the face. The man fell down again—and the partner of the warrior whose beak he'd busted hacked him on the fore-head with his sword.

Sparks cascaded behind Kane's eyes. He felt his knees buckle. He lashed out blindly with his left foot, more by accident than anything else catching the man who'd struck him right between the legs with a rapidly rising instep.

The guy was raised a good four inches in the air by the

force of the kick. His eyes bugged out of his head like a character in a cartoon vid. All the air blew out of him in a whoof that carried on as a voiceless scream of anguish long after he had any air to scream with. Before he reached the top of his arc, he jackknifed and fell sideways off Kane's foot as if he'd been straddling a fence rail.

Then the other two landed on Kane like a ton of rubble.

Perhaps they were fired up by the unquestioned carnage he had wrought upon their comrades—hell, he'd even surprised himself, managing to put four guys in the dirt even temporarily at the cost of only having his bell rung once. Maybe they were simply following orders to give him a good workout. Or maybe it was just youthful high spirits. Whatever, they immediately began a drumroll duet on his head and shoulders from behind.

Kane started to get pissed. At the same time he felt heat flush his body, limbs and face. He spun, roaring with anger, lashing out blindly with his oar-shaped wooden sword.

He felt a shock of impact. Then the wooden blade swept through air unimpeded.

He became aware that the two who had been belaboring him were rolling ass over teakettle away from him across the sand. This struck him as unusual.

"Enough!" Fifty clapped his hands to emphasize his shout.

Kane halted in place. He was panting as if he had just run five miles. What the hell? he wondered. He knew from long and brutal experience that there was no activity more draining then combat. Yet, intense as his battle had been, it had also been brief. Much too brief for him to be this winded, even accounting for the time he'd spent coming out second best.

He began to tremble. His knees shook, and his cheeks burned as from fever. His stomach churned as if with nausea. Am I sick? Or had one of the blows to the head busted open a vein within the box his skull, a bleeder that would eventually implode his brain with built-up pressure?

He swayed. One of his erstwhile assailants caught him by the elbow, holding him up. Fifty shouted something in a language Kane didn't recognize. Another of the loin-cloth-clad young stalwarts came to support his other arm. The others hung back as if to allow him room to breathe. And to hold up one of their own comrades, apparently the one Kane nailed in the nuts.

Fifty was in front of him, holding up a hide sack before his mouth. Becoming suddenly aware of a desperate thirst, Kane snatched the bag from his gnarled brown hands, squeezed a torrent of water into his mouth, guzzled it greedily down.

Just as abruptly he fell to his knees, his weight dropping so rapidly and unexpectedly that he instantly tore free of his upholders. It was as if one of the duke of Burgundy's horses had kicked him in the gut. He puked the water he just slammed down in a long, graceful arc that glittered in the morning sun.

He dropped to all fours, retching and shaking violently. Fifty patted him cheerfully on the back. "I tried to warn you, Lord Tonatiuh. You should first take a mouthful and spit it out. You must give your stomach time to prepare to receive the water."

Kane sat back on his heels, propped himself with palms on thighs. He felt about half past dead. "What—what happened? Heatstroke? Too much sun?"

"Ah, no. For you are the Sun. It was your aspect coming upon you. Your body is not yet accustomed to containing such power."

Kane raised his face to stare at the trainer, blinking to

clear his eyes of sweat that stung and broke the sun's rays into rainbow blurs. The fever, it that was what it had been, had passed. He was still shaky and shy on breath, but now it was more the effects humans associate with brisk exercise, not to mention throwing up.

Now his only problem was that he had no idea what Taker of Fifty Captives had just said.

He wiped his mouth with the back of his hand. His mind was still fuzzy, unfocused; he was no longer even so sure that he was Kane. It seemed a myriad of voices clamored within his skull, all different—all him.

He was trying to frame a question that might possibly make a start at resulting the maelstrom of mystery he was caught up in, when a ball of black smoke rolled into view above the stone wall of the arena. It didn't seem close by.

Kane's sudden stare, and a murmur among the six young warriors caused Fifty to turn. "Shit," he said. The hard thud of a distant explosion reached Kane's ears. "The monsters are attacking Tenochtitlán again."

Chapter 4

The former Moon base tech dashed out the door of the commissary and almost into Brigid.

"Ms. Baptiste! You've got to help. He's killing him!"

She knew with immediate certainty who was the potential killer and who the victim. She strode into the commissary.

A number of techs were present, including Farrell and various Moon base refugees. Nigel stood holding a napkin to his leaking nose; his eyes were already starting to blacken. Apparently he had received a fist in the face as the price for attempting to rescue Donald Bry, who dangled with his feet kicking madly a foot above the floor, Grant's massive hand clamped around his throat. The little technician had both his own hands clamped on Grant's wrist. His skin was bluer than usual.

Despite herself, Brigid was impressed. This was quite a feat of strength, even for a man of the shoulder breadth and chest width of Grant.

She took a deep breath and strode up to him. "All right, Grant. Put him down now, please. This isn't an intelligent solution to our problems."

"Back off, Brigid," Grant gritted. The veins stood out on his columnar neck and broad forehead, and the sweat ran down his face to drip from the ends of the mustache framing his mouth. "I'm…sick and…tired of this little prick…and his jokes about…Kane being caught in a time loop."

Brigid laid a hand gently on the elevated forearm. It was like touching carved oak. "Please," she said, "put him down. He really is one of the most knowledgeable technicians we have, and we need all the brainpower we've got if we're ever to stand a chance of getting Kane back."

"We got more techs. I'm telling you, I've had it with this little bastard."

"Grant, this is useless! What would Domi say?"

Grant frowned. For a long time after the four of them—Grant, Kane, Brigid, and the little albino wild child—escaped together from Cobaltville, the relationship between Grant and Domi had been problematic. She was almost obsessive in her determination to get him to bed her; he was equally adamant in his conviction that it would somehow be wrong to accommodate her. Grant's relationship with Shizuka only complicated matters. But then they had seemed to work the matter out.

Grant's standard expression was a scowl; now his eyes narrowed to near-invisible slits as he looked at the archivist. "She'd say it was way past time I popped his outsized head like a zit." But he set the man down on his feet with relative gentleness.

Instantly the other technicians crowded around and helped Bry to a chair. "I should have threatened you with DeFore," Brigid said. "Just be glad she doesn't have to do an emergency trache on Bry. She'd have opened you a new one. With surgical precision."

Grant made a wry face. Then he scowled again. "He just kept cracking wise about Kane being stuck forever…out there. The little son of a bitch doesn't know what he's talking about. He has no idea what it would mean to be caught in a perpetual jump nightmare."

"I understand," Brigid said, more grimly than she intended. "But Kane's not looped. He's not dead. He's alive, and he's on Earth. I…feel him."

Rubbing his neck, Bry lifted his head to look intently at her from the midst of his gaggle of sympathizers. Grant swung his great head like a war wag's main gun to bear on him. The little technician dropped his eyes and kept his lips zipped.

Grant looked back to the tall, statuesque archivist with the flame-gold hair spilling over the shoulders of her Cerberus jumpsuit. "If you say so. One thing about you—you don't say things just to hear your own voice."

He nodded toward the door. "Let's go find Lakesh. I'm going crazy sitting around this tomb."

SIRENS WAILED from beyond the walls of the arena. It was a sound that accorded strangely with the settings and the way the combatants on the sun-spilled sand were kitted out.

Another serpent door, at the far end from the one through which the six warriors had entered, swung open. Three people stepped out onto the field. One was a young man, dark skinned and black haired, with a neat beard and mustache, dressed in astonishingly normal-looking clothes: tan pants, a dark green shirt, soft boots. The second was a stereotypical whitecoat, in that he was dressed in a white lab coat over dark slacks. He was a thin-shouldered older man in round specs with a skinny neck and pointy chin tapering outward into a mushroom-shaped head. The mushroom effect was considerably exaggerated by the fact that, to judge by the wisp of white hair at his temples, the lush dome of dark hair from his ears up was a ludicrous wig that made him look like Moe in prenuke-caust Three Stooges vids.

It was the third who really made Kane stare: an almost angelically pretty young woman, dressed not unlike the young man in tan slacks and dark shirt, with rather wispy dark chestnut hair tied up atop her head except for curls dangling down her cheeks before her ears and huge brown eyes.

She was obviously a hybrid.

"Lord Tonatiuh," she said in a clear voice in English, "you must come with us, please. We need your help."

"I WANT A MANTA," Grant said in a voice as flat and hard as a steel plate.

"You wish to seek him," Lakesh said. His voice and face were mournful.

"That's right. I got to know."

"You do not believe, then, that Kane is either dead or trapped in a temporal loop, friend Grant?"

The big black ex-Mag shook his head ponderously. "Brigid says he's on Earth. I go with that."

"Even though there is no scientific verification for her belief?" He didn't look at Brigid, who leaned against a console with her arms folded under her ample breasts and her back to the wall-sized map display of the planet.

"She has a feel for Kane. They have some kind of psychic link. Some kind of soul link. I don't know what it is, but I know it's real. So do you."

Lakesh had steepled his fingers before his breast. "So I do. I am quite inclined to agree with you. Yet, to what end would you perform an aerial search? Do you think to see from an aircraft what our satellites cannot?"

"I—I don't know." He glanced at Brigid. "I thought

about taking Brigid along. Mebbe if we get close enough to where Kane is, she can feel him."

Brigid's expression showed real pain. "Grant, I'm sorry," she said. "I don't know if my...link to Kane is that strong. It's not so much that I can feel his presence, as that I do not feel his absence. If he was...gone...I'd feel that."

"But mebbe that's enough," Grant said. "Mebbe the farther away you get from him, the greater sense of absence you feel. Mebbe you can triangulate."

Brigid looked away. He was almost begging, this huge, formidable, infinitely proud man. She couldn't bear to watch it.

"I am sorry."

"And there you have it, Grant, my most excellent friend," Lakesh said, in tones so lugubrious that Brigid was tempted to believe he meant them. "I cannot risk one of our limited stock of Mantas on what I very much fear can only be characterized as a wild-goose chase. And far less can I risk you, especially with our other ace operator among the missing. We need you. Cerberus needs you. Humanity needs you."

Grant rounded on him in fury. "I could just take one. You can't stop me, little man. Nor could all your so-called security, even with all the new people from the Moon base. I could just go without your permission."

"Of course you could," Lakesh said. "You could have done so without asking. The fact you did ask reveals the uncertainty within your soul. You yourself know you have no realistic chance of locating friend Kane."

For a moment Grant glared at him. Brigid could see the former Magistrate swelling with rage, until he seemed a little tower of menace, filling the control center with his presence. Lakesh faced him unshrinking. Not for the first time Brigid realized that Lakesh possessed a substantial store of physical courage, for all his sedentary lifestyle.

Then Grant seemed to collapse upon himself. He spun and almost ran from the room.

Lakesh stood looking after him, shaking his head in sorrow. "He longs for certainty," Lakesh said, almost to himself. "And that is the one thing that, for all my genius, I cannot vouchsafe him."

Brigid turned a frigid green glare upon him. "That was cruel. I know you are unscrupulous, even ruthless for what serves your ends. But cruelty is unusual for you. And unworthy of you."

Without looking at her, Lakesh raised a placatory hand. "Peace, dearest Brigid. I intended no cruelty. I beg that you believe me.

"I see that perhaps I should not have said that. Because the one thing the heroic Grant truly fears upon this planet or off it is uncertainty. It is the one thing he can't deal with. And to touch a man that strong and proud on his one point of naked vulnerability is both cruel and risky."

He turned to stare at the big digital map of the planet and clasped hands behind his back.

"I only wish that I knew what I should do."

KANE WAS confused.

Back with the sand of the arena growing hot beneath his bare feet, he had grown increasingly sure of his identity as Kane, erstwhile hard-contact Mag and present enforcer for Cerberus redoubt as he battled the six stalwart young warriors.

Now he rode in a strange electric carriage, three wheeled and open to the elements, through a large city in which monumental stone structures mingled freely with glass-

and-steel boxes that might have come from a preskydark ville, with everywhere frozen explosions of tropical flora from parks and planters that sometimes threatened to overgrow it all. And now the hard certainty that he was Kane was receding, falling out of focus. He began to wonder if instead he might not be what the others persisted in calling him: a god.

From ahead of them came the thuds of explosions and the faint sound of screaming, like the cries of distant seabirds. Their driver, a young warrior seemingly cast from the same mold as Kane's training opponents, but kitted out in outlandish body armor that seemed to consist of gilded polycarbonate and extravagant green feathers, steered through curiously empty streets toward a column of black smoke growing into the achingly blue sky. Battle had been joined, and they were bound for the thick of it.

As outlandish as the driver's get-up were Kane's companions. They were the three who had walked out upon the sand when the distant attack commenced: the professorial type, the clerk and the winsome hybrid girl.

They were now arguing, apparently about him, as if he were not there. "But he has not yet manifested," the hybrid was saying in a voice as clear and lovely as a bell. She spoke English, which now seemed to the man who was and was not Kane as exotic as Spanish had a few short moments before, although as readily understandable.

"But he began to take his aspect upon him, Teresa," the whitecoat said. "You saw how he tossed young warriors around as if they were dolls, at the end of the mock combat."

"But, Dr. Marroquín," the young man said, "it was certainly unconscious, and incomplete at that. How do we know that he can take the full aspect upon himself? And more, how do we know that he can use it effectively?"

"Because he is Tonatiuh. We must have faith, Ernesto. And remember, the chosen vessel of the Sun god is a proved survivor, a warrior of many lifetimes' experience."

He turned his gaze upon the man he named Tonatiuh. "Listen to me. What I have to say is important. Important to you, and to humanity. It may be the most important thing you have ever heard.

"You are Tonatiuh. You are the god of the Sun. You have been called back to Earth to battle the forces of the monster gods Tezcatlipoca and Huitzilopochtli. It is your duty, and your destiny."

"I don't understand. I don't understand any of this."

"We're getting close, Doctor!" the young man exclaimed nervously.

"Be still, Ernesto." Dr. Marroquín didn't take his gaze from Kane's eyes. Reflected sunlight turned the lenses of his glasses to disks of fire.

"You need not understand what is happening, Lord. All you need know is that battle will soon be joined. You must reach deep within yourself to find the godhood there. You began to feel it at the end of the practice session—a strength beyond the strength of your body, mighty as that is. Now, look within. Feel within. Do you feel that strength?"

Kane—for that sense of identity would not go away, however it blurred, however the others assured him he was someone and something else—closed his eyes. He cast his mind back, groping for the memory of what it was that had come over him. He sensed light and warmth, but couldn't force himself back to it.

He shook his head.

"We're running out of time," Teresa said.

Kane opened his eyes. He saw the whitecoat raise a soft

hand to the young hybrid woman. The gesture reminded him forcibly of someone else—someone he sensed that it would be death to remember, for to so remember would be to turn his face away from the godhood that now seemed their only chance of survival.

"Have faith, my child," Dr. Marroquín said. "When he felt threatened before, he took his aspect upon himself without thinking about it. When the time comes, he will seize his full power and wield it to full effect. You will see."

The driver pointed and shouted in a language Kane didn't understand, although like the unnatural strength he had felt before, it seemed to hover just beyond reach of his mind's fingertips. They looked the way he was pointing.

A ball of fire rolled skyward above the tops of the buildings across the street, leaving a trail of black smoke.

Chapter 5

Dr. Marroquín turned to him. "You have doubt in your soul as to who you are. Put those doubts aside. You are Tonatiuh. You are the Sun god. It is all you are or have ever been. Yours is the power of the solar flare and the shield of the Sun."

Kane stared at him. "Then we're fucked, old man," he said. "I don't know anything about any of that. It all sounds bogus to me."

The hybrid girl shook her head. The young man gave her shoulder a quick, tentative squeeze, then jerked his hand back as if the contact burned him. She blinked. Kane saw tears dewing the ends of long lashes.

"I'm sorry," she said. "I know—forgive me, Lord. Please do not let my doubts affect you."

Dr. Marroquín laid his hand on Kane's shoulder. The whitecoat's eyes bored into his. Suddenly they seemed no longer weak and watery and swimming behind thick glasses. Instead they seemed revealed as bottomless pits of blackness…and something more.

"Listen to me," the old man said, and his voice seemed to reach deep inside Kane like spectral fingers. "You remember being someone else. You remember being others. These memories are true. But you are the Lord Tonatiuh. You are the lord of the Sun. This is also true. Look within and you will see it. But quickly, because time is short."

The eyes were suns themselves, black stars—obsidian mirrors as large as worlds. Kane felt himself falling into them.

And as he fell, he spun. Diffused. And as his sense of being dissolved, he found himself merging not with darkness, but with light.

And heat. And within that heat and brilliance it was as if he coalesced, was forged anew.

He became aware of blood and fire, and other selves. He raised his head and opened eyes strange to him. He felt the purpose and the power of a potent other, and it was as if he—the spark that still thought of itself as Kane—rode again as copilot in a curious flying war machine driven by a mighty black warrior.

His mouth spoke words in a language Kane didn't know, although somehow he grasped their meaning: *Give to me my weapons and my armor. I am ready.*

Part of him thought, So this is what command schizophrenia feels like. But that part was passive, already receding to the depths behind awareness as great purpose filled his entity.

The hybrid woman gasped. "It is true! He is the one!"

"Did you ever doubt, my dear?" the whitecoat murmured, not without a touch of smugness.

At his command the open-topped vehicle stopped. Moving as if in a dream, Kane stepped forth onto the sidewalk. They were in a district of shops, mostly one- or two-story buildings. Olive oval blurs of faces appeared in windows, hovered, fearfully withdrew as Kane extended his arms to the side. The driver helped Ernesto fit him with a suit of armor not unlike the one the driver himself wore: a harness with breast and backpieces that hung over his shoulders and protected him down the sternum, a sort of abbreviated skirt of formed plates, greaves and pieces that fit along his forearms, all looking like gilded metal but, from the light weight and feel, apparently some form of plastic—possibly with molded steel-ceramic ballistic cores, the Kane part of him supplied.

On his left arm was strapped a circular shield of similar material. It bore the stylized circular image of a sun face. An open-faced helmet with a high golden crest and green feather plumes was placed on his head and a very modern-seeming plastic fastener closed beneath his chin.

"Shadow armor," the Kane identity prodded his voice to ask.

"The black bodysuit you wore?" Teresa shook her head. "I am sorry, Lord. We cannot. It will interfere with the *prana* flow."

Last the driver strapped the lanyard of a most curious weapon to his right wrist and pressed the haft into his hand: perhaps two feet long, and obviously the pattern for the paddle-bladed wooden sword he had been wielding not half an hour earlier. By way of a blade it was inset with thin shards of what appeared to be black volcanic glass—obsidian—flaked to razor-fine edges, all along the sides and even at the tip.

"The blades are actually sandwiches, with very thin wafers of obsidian between layers of synthetic to reduce the likelihood of breakage," Dr. Marroquín said. "My own design, as it happens."

Tonatiuh's awareness tracked the progress of the battle not far away. He heard a very mundane rattle of full-automatic small arms, not unlike his Sin Eater—and where was that? Such terms as "Sin Eater" and "fully automatic" puzzled the now dominant personality no less than the current sequence of events mystified the observer Kane.

Teresa suddenly pressed fingertips behind her right ear. "Oh, dear," she said. "It's not just a giant beast we face. It is the god Tlaltecuhtli—the frog monster."

To Kane the watcher, that made no sense whatever, although it sure didn't sound promising. Whoever was actually driving the machine nodded sagely.

Ernesto knelt before him tending to the fittings and straps of his high-tech low-tech armor. "Our police are brave enough," he said. "But they're only men."

"Bullets will do no more than sting Tlaltecuhtli," added Teresa.

"How about this stick, then?" Kane demanded.

"It can help you to summon your solar flare," Marroquín said.

"How do I do that?"

Teresa and Ernesto looked at each other. "We cannot teach you," Ernesto said. "All we can tell you is that you must channel the energies that flow through our valley."

"You must seek within for your true weapon," Marroquín intoned. "When your mind is ready, the sword shall be ready."

That sounded familiar somehow, but Kane had no time to mull over how, or even to whom, for their wag driver suddenly sang out, "My lords! They come!" in that guttural tongue Kane didn't know but understood just the same.

"And what about this monster—"

The brick front of a building across the street bulged, buckled outward. Thrusting through the cascade of rubble came a vast swag-bellied frog the size of a Sandcat. It had long black dreadlocks and a mouthful of shark's teeth— that Kane observed when, upon catching sight of him standing across the way, it threw its head back on its nonexistent neck and uttered a terrifying bellow of challenge.

Their driver snatched a bulky long-arm from a rack behind his seat. Kane looked at the monster. He looked down at the Stone Age weapon in his hand. "You have *got* to be shitting me," he said.

Teresa fell to her knees beside him and clasped his sword hand in both of hers. They were small, cool and dry, but their strength was fervid.

"My lord!" she cried. "You must lay aside Kane, and your skepticism and modernity. You are Tonatiuh, lord of the Sun, as surely as that creature is Tlaltecuhtli, the Earth lord, the frog monster."

With an overt air of fatalism, the driver aimed his plasma weapon at the monster and fired a brilliant blast. The creature's outline appeared to blur; perhaps it dodged with inhuman speed, for the blazing line flashed harmlessly past to explode the front of a structure on the next street over. Then it hunched forward and flung its tongue from its mouth.

The tongue unrolled like a carpet, all the way across the street, to wrap the kneeling warrior like a net. Screaming hoarsely, he sought to struggle free, the plasma weapon falling from his hands. He was snatched from his feet, whipped back across the street into that waiting mouthful of knives.

His scream peaked, then cut off as the great jaws closed. Blood gouted from both sides of the hideous frog face. Then the jaws opened again and allowed the corpse to fall in three segments to the sidewalk.

The frog monster clasped its sides with short arms and shook, emitting croaks of laughter. Rage began to build, and as it did, it pressed Kane again into the background of his consciousness.

The tongue lashed forth again to seize him. As he stared at it, the monster seemed to slow to a crawl. He cocked his obsidian-bladed sword and waited.

When the forked tip unfolded to reach for him like tentacles, he struck. The thin but infinitely sharp stone blades bit into the great muscle behind the fork with a shock he felt in his bones.

Time sped up again. The blade bit through as effortlessly as a sharp scythe cutting grass. The forked tip fell away as reeking black blood showered Kane and the others. Geysering blood like a squid its ink, the tongue whipped back across the street to disappear back into the shark-toothed mouth. Tlaltecuhtli squealed like the brakes of an old-time loco wag.

For a moment they stared at each other, man god and monster god. Black blood drooled down the frog creature's pendulous lower lip. Their rage grew until the air between crackled as with corona discharge. Then Tlaltecuhtli gathered his enormous bulk and launched himself into a lumbering bipedal run that caused the ground to shake beneath Kane's feet.

Suddenly Kane's eyes lost focus. The charging monstrous bulk blurred almost to transparency. So did the building around him, and his companions, and the vehicle that now burned with the pallid red flames of fuel alcohol. He saw all around him arcs and loops of fire, living fire, like the filaments and prominences of the Sun.

His fury was joined by wild joy. With no material arm he reached out and clasped one of those strands of brilliance, though he knew it was horribly hot—as hot as the Sun itself. Yet somehow he knew it would not burn him.

The contact was like grasping, not something hot, but a live electric wire. The energy surged through him, pain and ecstasy commingling as did his fury and mad joy.

Roaring, he cocked his arm back. Behind his plumed helmet his sword burst into a blaze of flame beyond fire, so that his companions cried out, cowered and shielded their eyes, momentarily more daunted by the fearful radiance of his sword than the onrushing mass of malevolence bearing down upon them.

Tonatiuh flung his arm forward. A solar flare blasted from the blade of flame and struck the frog monster in the center of its gross slogging torso.

With a steam-whistle scream the vast creature was blasted backward, back to complete the ruin of the building it had run through, charring and dwindling as it flew through the air.

Onward rushed the flare. In the next street a building already damaged by the dead driver's plasma blast collapsed. Behind it the base of a three-story building exploded.

Kane became aware of a grip on his arm. He gazed down into the elfin dark-skinned face of the hybrid woman. "Please, Lord, cut it off," she begged. "You will destroy not just the city but yourself, as well!"

He realized then that the power was not coming from within him. Rather it was channeling though his body, his being: the power pulsing through those arcs of brilliance that he still saw, though ghostly now, surrounding them. And now he also sensed, as rubble crashed down and smoke billowed up along the path of his solar flare, that as it passed through him, it was eroding and consuming him.

But he was lord of the Sun. He had but to command it to stop. It did.

He swayed, dropped to his knees.

"Water," said the old whitecoat, standing up from where he had been sheltering behind the tricycle wag.

Ernesto uncapped a ceramic bottle that he had been carrying slung by his side. He raised it to Kane's lips. Kane took a mouthful, rolled it in his mouth and spit to clear the dust, then drank greedily.

"Lord—" the hybrid girl began in worshipful tones.

He ignored her. Whatever the blazing power was that had coursed through him, it was gone now. He felt spent, shaky. But he forced himself to cross the street. He'd seen lots of men get real dead by taking for granted that foes far less potent and terrifying than the inexplicable creature had been put down for a permanent dirt nap when they had in fact not been. He wanted to make sure.

He paused outside the rubble of the building into which he'd blasted the frog monster. It appeared to be a shop selling electric lamps, judging from the sprung harps and ripped shades in evidence amid the structural debris. There was no sign of activity from within.

He hefted his shield and funny volcanic-glass sword. Their weight reassured him, even though he still didn't have much faith in the good they'd do him if a pissed-off giant toad with dreadlocks was lying for him on the other side of what remained of the wall. He sensed he wouldn't be able to tap into the force-lines again before he had rested.

He peered cautiously around. A body lay there, but not the bloated pale-bellied bulk he'd anticipated. Instead, sprawled in the wreckage of a display case lay the body of a human being that, allowing for the fact that the front half had been carbonized to charcoal, eradicating the facial features, looked entirely normal.

He heard a crunch of grit under a sandaled foot, spun, raising sword and shield. His three surviving companions fetched to a halt a wary distance away.

Suddenly his head was whirling and his stomach doing its level best to keep up. His personality, which had settled back down toward the comforting presence and memories of Kane, started to fray around the edges again.

He gestured into the ruin with his stone-edged stick. "He...was a man. Just a man."

Dr. Marroquín nodded sagely. "Of course, mighty Lord. He had his aspect upon him. That gave him the appearance of the god Tlaltecuhtli, as well as the powers."

A wisp of memory spun through the maelstrom inside Kane's head: Maccan on the Moon, speaking of one of his late Tuatha de Danaan brethren who had used psychic powers of illusion to convince humans he was a true shape-shifter. Had Tlaltecuhtli done the same?

He turned to walk toward the body of the driver. It felt as if his body were lead, his feet sinking to the knees in the pavement at every step. The nausea was horrific now, unmanning. But he made himself approach the man and look down.

The warrior was dead. As Kane had first thought, his body had been severed into three parts, so that his pelvic region lay separated from torso and legs in a red lake of congealing blood. Flies were already lighting on it to feed and lay eggs.

"Poor bastard was so fooled he thought he got chopped in three pieces," he said aloud, in a voice that was crazed like a dropped piece of pottery. "Now *that's* a fucking illusion."

He was conscious of a thud and jarring impact up his spine as his knees hit pavement. It was as if he wore thick cotton kneepads. Then the sidewalk was rushing toward his face.

He never felt it hit.

Chapter 6

Brigid's moans joined the screams of the doomed as flames leaped up to engulf their bound bodies. Copper-skinned they were, and dark of hair, bare feet resting upon a pile of broken wooden weapons, to which the bearded paler men in swept, high-crested helmets had set torches.

Presiding over all, seated on a dais upon a throne, sat Kane. Except it was not Kane: the long brushed-back hair, the mustache and beard were red-gold, of a shade not too dissimilar to Brigid's own. Nor were the features, twisted in a gloating look Brigid could only describe within herself as evil, familiar.

And yet they were Kane's. As she watched, the shape and style of the hair subtly shifted, turned to black ever so lightly flecked with gray at temples and beard. The features flowed to become those of the man she had learned to know so well over the past two years. And the look upon them was a lost look, tormented itself, haunted by helplessness— and something else, something she couldn't define.

And suddenly the eyes shifted from the dreadful spectacle before them to lock on hers, to pierce them like gray icicles. And the mouth formed the words, "help me."

THE FLAMES ROSE up, mingling with the screams. Kane watched the execution of the rebellious chiefs, and gloated in their hideous agonies. They would learn what it meant to defy the power of the Holy Cross, and to lay hands upon Spaniards.

What the hell? Kane's own voice seemed like a tiny echo in a great well.

As a hard-contact Mag, he had seen a slew of scaly things, and done more than his share. Yet this went far beyond—way over the top into evil. It was horror.

More, it stank of the Archons: the game-name dynamic conspiracy of aliens, hybrids and even outright humans that had interfered in humanity's affairs for millennia, sometimes for the ostensible purpose of guiding and protecting it, sometimes for outright exploitation and enslavement.

He knew he inhabited someone else's body in the dream. It felt alien itself, like an unfamiliar suit of clothes, tailored to fit another. He had certainly not ordered this atrocity, nor had he the power to stop it. He could not even speak.

Yet he remembered having ordered it. As he still felt the sick thrill of exhilaration at seeing his orders enacted, skin blistering and burning away, living flesh charring.

And at the same time he felt something else again. Something that derived more than sadistic pleasure from the spectacle. Something that drew in the energy of pain, of the horror, the ultimate horror of knowing what was being done to oneself, that one was being ruined, mutilated, and the future held nothing but more pain and worse, until death was the most welcome release possible. Something that drew in the very life energy of those burning, living bodies. And was nourished by it.

And that something was him.

"KANE IS in Mexico."

Brigid's statement rang with the finality of a death sentence. Lakesh deliberately laid down his fork and blinked at her through the thick lenses of his glasses.

"Most likely he is somewhere in the valley of Mexico. Possibly in the ruins of Mexico City itself."

"And how do you derive such a remarkable assertion?" the scientist asked tartly. "As a trained archivist—trained by me personally—you are certainly aware of the need to possess facts before one speaks. Especially with so much authority."

Standing by the commissary table, Brigid didn't flinch from the old man's unaccustomed asperity. "I shared a dream with Kane last night," she said with calm conviction.

"How can you be sure of any such bloody thing?" demanded Nigel, who was likewise eating. Grant, who lounged with his butt propped on a table behind the tall archivist, gave him a grim look.

"We have experienced shared dreams before," she said flatly. "Perhaps you should make sure of your facts before you interject."

Nigel flushed and looked down at his plate.

"So Kane was actually able to communicate his location to you in this dream?" Lakesh asked. His tone was more curious than skeptical, and Brigid was once again reluctantly forced to confront why she had once admired the man, and in many ways continued to, despite his faults as a human being: he was a true scientist, with a genuine scientist's passion to know.

"Not precisely. However, his dream had him experiencing a previous life—as a historical character whom I recognized, by action if nothing else. The man's name was Don Pedro de Alvarado. He was presiding over the execution of a number of Aztec nobles whom he accused of fomenting the rebellion of June 30 of the year 1520, known as the Noche Triste, or Night of Sorrows, during the absence of Hernán Cortés. The nobles were burned alive upon a pile of their own broken-up weapons."

The others listening shuddered discreetly and pushed their food away. "Certainly that is most interesting, as well as thoroughly unpleasant," Lakesh said, "but, dearest Brigid, I fail to see quite how—"

"Cortés himself ordered the executions. But they were to all practical effect the handiwork of Alvarado—whom the native Meshika called Tonatiuh, identifying him with their Sun god. His proclivity for stupid brutality had provoked the assault that drove the Spanish occupiers from the capital city Tenochtitlán. There's evidence that Cortés, no shrinking violet himself and probably quite sociopathic, was disgused by his lieutenant's excesses. He certainly did not care for the results, since the destruction accompanying the Spanish reconquest of Tenochtitlán with numerous Tlaxcaltecan allies destroyed vast amounts of potential plunder. Cortés was a man who knew the true cost of war." Her finish was distinctly ironic.

"All this to the side—could it not have simply been a nightmare suffered by our friend Kane? While I am most strongly inclined toward the hypothesis—and alas I can call it no more than that—that Kane is alive and on Earth, and agree completely that this dream lends credence to it, I am not prepared to take a wild intuitive leap to derive that he's actually at or near the scene of the events you describe."

"What the hell does Kane know about this historical crap?" Grant rumbled. "He's a Mag. He doesn't know anything more about this Alvarado or this Nochay Pissy thing than he did about the Moon's bare backside till we visited it in person."

"Grant makes an excellent point, Dr. Lakesh," Brigid

said. "Also, as you are aware, Kane has previously manifested vivid memories that appear to arise from former incarnations. Never has he mentioned, to me at least, any such identification with Don Pedro de Alvarado. And while some of the men he remembers being, falsely or not, have been harsh men who had done harsh deeds—some almost as harsh as Kane himself—does the phrase 'stupid brutality' suggest Kane to you in any way, shape or form?"

Lakesh pursed his slightly purplish lips and shook his head. "No. No, indeed, dear Brigid. Indeed, if anything, a gift for a most diabolically cunning brutality is one of our beloved Kane's most salient characteristics—hence, I believe, the Lakota's bestowing the cognomen 'Trickster Wolf' upon him."

Brigid nodded. "Therefore, Doctor, if you are willing to stipulate that Kane and I share some manner of communication beyond the conventional and physical—"

Lakesh steepled his fingers before his breast and bowed. "Loveliest lady, I so stipulate."

"—then surely you can accept my intuition, along with the information supplied by Grant, as data points?"

"Assuredly I do."

"That's good enough for me," Grant said. "I'm going after him."

"It is *not* good enough for me," Lakesh said. "My very dear friends, none feels the loss of our beloved Kane as keenly as I do. For all your personal attachment to the man, please do me the favor of recalling that I myself feel no little affection for him, one might almost say kinship, which I daresay he reciprocates to some degree for all the hostility he occasionally evinces toward me. But more— I am still charged with coordinating the effort to reclaim this world for a downtrodden and enslaved humankind, and Kane is my strong right arm, as Grant is my left. His loss is an amputation for me in operational as well as emotional terms.

"Yet emotional terms are precisely what I cannot afford to think in. Nor can suffering humanity afford for me to do so."

"What do you lack to take action," Grant growled, "other than balls, that is?"

Lakesh ignored the gibe. "I have accepted what Brigid tells us. Tentatively. And yet, what then?"

THE CONTROL CENTER'S big wall display showed the most recent archive image of the valley of Mexico. The duty tech reported that no satellite with which they had contact was in position for real-time viewing.

"Even if I give you what you ask, friend Grant," Lakesh said, "with all your superb ability and tenacity, how then will you hope to find Kane? As we can see, the lake described in the Wyeth Codex has receded or been drained. Likewise the terrific devastation, wrought by earthquakes in the aftermath of the nukecaust and subsequently, has largely been cleared. Apparently a great rebuilding program has taken place. What we see is evidence of an urban area with a population of perhaps a hundred thousand or more. A mighty human haystack in which to search for the needle Kane."

He fingered his chin. "Conceivably, we should have studied the region before."

"There's got to be some way to find him," Grant persisted.

"That's what we have the biolink transponders for," Brigid said under her breath.

Lakesh beamed at her. "Precisely. And Kane's transponder has so obviously been neutralized, we are at a loss."

"Is it possible the biolink transponder has failed spontaneously?" the technician at the big board asked. She was an almost gaunt woman with metallic-seeming red hair hanging to her shoulders. Another of the Moon base refugees—Michaelis was her name, Brigid remembered.

"Hardly," Lakesh said in his most pedantic tones. "The transponder is basically a set of low-energy emitters whose radiation signature is detectable from orbit. There's nothing to break. Kane may be being kept in some confinement that screens the emissions from our sensors."

"Or the emitters have been neutralized," Brigid said grimly.

Lakesh acknowledged the possibility with a shrug and a slight languid wave of the hand.

"But we have to do *something*," Grant said, almost desperately.

"But what, friend Grant? We cannot afford undirected action. We must cultivate patience."

"I've had enough of fucking patience." Grant turned half away, then turned back.

"I'm going to New Edo," he announced. Then he walked out.

"But what if we need you?" Lakesh called in alarm.

Grant waved his hand as the door opened. "You seem to be getting along fine without Kane. Guess that means you can do without me, too."

The door shut behind him.

Lakesh turned to Brigid. "We must do something!"

"Let him go," Brigid said. Lakesh turned his head toward her with unusual speed, like a lizard on a hot rock. "He's not going to do anybody any good in his present state. And who's going to stop him?"

Lakesh sighed and turned back to his giant map display. As was often the case, he seemed to derive comfort from the nearness of large, showy technology. "No doubt you are right."

"Surely there must be some way to locate Kane," Brigid said in a low voice.

"And I am doing all that I can think to do," Lakesh said. "Anything you can suggest, I will most gratefully try."

Brigid could only shake her head.

TAKER OF FIFTY CAPTIVES, dressed in his loincloth and protective helmet, knelt just inside the doorway of the refectory in the step-pyramid dominating the great compound, on a bluff overlooking the city, in which Kane was confined. In outrage, Ernesto jumped to his feet. Dr. Marroquín held up a brown languid hand to restrain him.

"What's the meaning of this intrusion?" the young man demanded.

"Ten thousand pardons, lords, lady." Fifty nodded his topknotted head in the direction of Teresa, who had stood up from her seat on the far side of the heavy wooden table and was looking concerned. "I should never trouble you at your meal. Except Lord Tonatiuh insists he must talk to you now. He refuses to train otherwise."

Kane strode into the room behind him. He saw a long table on a raised dais that ran along the far side of the room. Morning sunlight spilled across it from high narrow windows.

He was clad again solely in a loincloth. He had a round practice shield strapped to his left arm and a wooden practice sword in his hand. He saw the pretty hybrid girl raise her big dark eyes to his and run them down his body. She looked away.

"Where am I?" he demanded in a harsh, hoarse voice. "What have you done to me? *What* am I?

"You are Lord Tonatiuh, god of the Sun," said the old whitecoat with the mushroom haircut, limping slightly as he stepped down from the elevated part of the room, approaching Kane. "As you must have proved to your satisfaction yesterday, when in heroic combat you slew the lord of the Earth, the frog monster."

Kane rocked back slightly on his bare heels. "So it wasn't a dream," he murmured, as if to himself. Then he looked at the old scientist with fierce light blazing up in his gray eyes.

"I remember being a man named Kane. A few years back Kane was the hardest of hard-contact Magistrates in the history of the barony of Cobaltville, except for…mebbe one other. If I don't start getting some answers that actually answer anything, I'm going to revert to type and start banging heads off walls until I get some responses that are more to my liking."

The three looked at one another. "I am sorry," repeated Fifty, head bowed.

"Oh, get up," Kane said. "You don't have to grovel to these people."

"Indeed he does not," Dr. Marroquín said, approaching Kane. He laid his hand briefly on Fifty's head. The trainer looked up, bobbed his head gratefully and disappeared out the door.

Kane fixed a none too happy gaze on the whitecoat. Teresa came up behind the old man as if to protect him from the wrath of the god—or Mag. And young Ernesto followed, bristling with floppy-puppy protectiveness for her.

"This is all so sweet I may just puke," Kane said.

Marroquín looked him up and down. "I see that we have

been high-handed in dealing with you." A corner of his mouth quirked up. "A perhaps not surprising occupational hazard when one is engaged in the making of gods. Yet perhaps an unwise tack to take with the gods we have made."

Chapter 7

"The valley of Mexico," Teresa said as they strode together down the corridor, "is a region of almost unparalleled geomagnetic activity. This is the secret of the gods. This is the secret of…your godhood."

Kane grunted. He still had trouble adjusting to the concept, even though he had received some pretty solid corroboratory evidence.

The corridor was paved with tiles that, while they looked like fired and glazed maroon clay, gave slightly beneath their sandaled feet: they were some kind of spongy synthetic. The walls were tiled in patterns suggestive of crude murals, white and blue and red and black and sand, depicting birds and serpents and what looked like horned toads, squat men and grimacing masks with open mouths and lolling tongues. The walls, harder stuff than the flooring, gave back muted echoes of their speech and their footsteps.

"Up until almost a century ago," Teresa said, "the seismic and volcanic activity in this vicinity was so severe as to threaten the very survival of the inhabitants, and render precarious their attempts at rebuilding in the wake of the nukecaust. Centuries ago our ancestors called themselves the 'sons of shaking earth' because of the valley's violent and incessant earthquakes. Yet these were worse, aftereffects of the thermonuclear charges set off by the Soviets along the Pacific Rim. The initial catastrophic seismic activity they sparked destroyed what was then Mexico City. The city was never attacked directly."

Kane nodded. "The Soviet earth-shakers." In the crisply air-conditioned interior he wore a robe of white-bleached linen and rubber-soled sandals of dark green synthetic weave. Over his broad shoulders was draped a short cloak of neon-bright blue and green feathers. Around his brows rode a circlet of gold. It made him feel foolish, as if he were got up like some kind of pop-culture superhero from the days before skydark. At the same time, part of him was vaguely tickled. Maybe it was one of those spare personalities floating around somewhere inside.

Teresa looked at him in surprise. She had on tan trousers, black shoes with short clunky heels, a mauve blouse and a white lab coat thrown over all. In her way she looked as if she were playing dress-up, too, a little girl trying to look adult.

"Look," he said, "I'm not a total barbarian or anything. I've actually had a certain amount of education. Also I read something about those earthquakes and eruptions here a hundred years back."

"I am sorry, Lord," the hybrid girl said. "I did not mean to impute a lack of education to you. I simply did not think that history was taught in the baronies of the north."

It was Kane's turn to look surprised. "You know about the baronies?"

She laughed. "We are not barbarians, either," she said. "We do follow events in what were once the United States. Although it is true that we are quite isolated here, both by choice and by necessity. And yes, we know of your baronies very well. After all, our civilization here is itself what you might call a spinoff of your own unification project."

Kane stopped and stared. "What the hell?"

A few paces farther along the passageway she halted and looked back. "You will have to ask Dr. Marroquín for details. Now, please, come with me if you want answers."

She pressed on to a doorway that noiselessly moved itself out of her path. Reflecting that she was a strange mixture of vulnerability and stainless steel, Kane followed—into a realm of humming power.

He stared around in frank astonishment. They stood in a great hall. To either side were arrayed rows of squat objects: massive barrellike cylinders, white metal or synthetic banded with what appeared to be gold, with beveled tops. Above them upright yard-wide rings that looked like brass rotated around their vertical axes, levitating in air. Studying them in awe, Kane realized they were subtly Möbius strips. A subliminal hum of power suffused the air and made the hairs on his nape to rise.

"*Prana* generators!" he exclaimed hoarsely.

"Not to contradict my Lord Tonatiuh," she said, "but they might more properly be described as *prana* accumulators. You are familiar with the technology?"

"Not of this design." He had encountered such devices in the chill deserts of Mongolia and the corridors bored like weevil holes through cheese beneath the Moon's gray skin, ravaged by aeons of cosmic acne. Not the same in appearance, but somehow he sensed the function of these strange squat gravity-defying machines. Indeed, it was as if he felt the currents of their power flow within him in a way that was almost sexual. "But yes. I've seen it before, anyway."

He turned to face her. "But what does all this have to do with me?" he demanded. "It doesn't answer the questions I really want answered. Such as what you want from me."

"You are a typical European-derived Westerner," she

said with a hint of reproof, "obsessed with outcomes rather than processes, driven to find answers."

"I'm a bottom-line kind of guy," he agreed amicably enough. "If you didn't think I'd want to drive straight through to the point, you don't know your man."

She smiled. "Ah, but we do. While as god of the Sun great Lord Tonatiuh is undoubtedly a great philosopher, we did not choose to invest you to debate abstruse points of sociology or cosmology with the blood-caked priests of the Black House."

He looked at her a moment longer, an odd light playing his wolf-gray eyes. He could not help noticing that for an unquestioned hybrid her dark cheeks showed an unusually healthy flush, which seemed due to something more than cosmetic intervention.

"Yeah," he said. "Well."

"Such accumulators," she said, gesturing around them, "provide power to the whole of our pocket civilization here in the valley of Mexico, have indeed fueled our return from the dark ages."

"I still don't see—"

"There are those who would plunge us back into the darkness," a familiar voice said from across the room. "Deeper indeed than ever before, perhaps."

Dr. Marroquín strode toward them across the floor, which was the same shiny maroon material as in the passageway. He seemed somehow larger and more forceful than before. He waved a hand toward a cubicle set off to one corner of the great chamber. "If you will come into the office, I can show you a sample of what I mean."

With Teresa by his side, Kane followed the whitecoat in. He stopped when he saw what dominated the far wall.

"A television?"

"It generally serves us as a monitor, but yes," the doctor said, picking up a handheld remote controller and clicking it on.

The scene presented was one of arcane and archaic splendor. A step pyramid gleamed in the liquid sun of the high mountain valley, gold and scarlet and black. At its flat top were those resplendent in feathers and gold. There were also those who were dark and strange, as if moving shadows, and something about them tweaked Kane's subconscious in a most disturbing way.

And inside him there was that which *knew*. But for the moment it was repressed. Kane was dominant, the persona that was mostly the Kane of old; as hard a man as that Kane was, he shied away from knowing.

A stairway of lesser steps, treads and risers had been carved down the front of the mighty structure. Up those steps flowed a slow torrent of humanity, naked, restrained as if in body and soul alike.

Kane sucked in a long, slow breath and set his jaw.

"A movie?" he asked, half to himself. It certainly resembled a vid from preskydark days, specifically a historical spectacle from the early days of filmmaking, when hordes of extras—aspiring actors or plain derelicts swept off the streets of a small Cific coast town, whence they had migrated because the winters were warm—were cheap. Or from right before the nukecaust, when computer-generated crowds became so popular. He had watched both kinds in—what was the mountain fastness called?—Cerberus redoubt, where those who had laid it down against the storm they knew was coming had not neglected to provide for their own entertainment any more than food, medical needs and defense.

He felt Teresa's touch on his arm. It did not displease

Tonatiuh. Nor Kane, either, whose experiences with hybrid women had been what you might call ambivalent.

"No," she said.

The viewpoint from which the strange ascension was shot slowly orbited the pyramid. In the lower right-hand corner was a logo in white, an eye in a stylized step pyramid, and the legend, Noticias Tenochtitlán. Kane didn't understand Spanish; the not-Kane within him allowed that *noticias* meant "news." Tenochtitlán was the city's present name.

That didn't pin it in time for him, affix it to the now like a butterfly on a board. What did was the object hovering at the edge of visibility, off in that bowl of blue sky formed by high-reaching mountains: a dragonfly shape with a shimmer in the air above it.

"A Deathbird?" he said. The others looked at him without comprehension; young Ernesto had joined them there.

It wasn't, he saw. It was gold rather than black. The silhouette, though similar, was subtly wrong, and the tail rotor was actually encased within the tail boom. Grant would know what kind of bird it was—he felt a sense of loss and disconnection at remembrance of that name.

And yet it was: no mistaking the tiny proboscis jut of a blaster from a chin turret beneath its nose, nor the bolt-on pods slung beneath the stub wings. Perhaps it hadn't descended from the AH-64 Apache as had the Magistrates' steeds—although these days Kane didn't ride in them, but rather fled them, or fought them when he had to—but it was unmistakably a helicopter gunship.

"This is happening now," he acknowledged aloud. "Okay. But what?"

As if in response, the screen switched to a naked young woman in close-up. Heavy black hair was bound back from her face. By the set of her shoulders Kane guessed her arms were bound behind her, as well. Yet she was serene as she spoke to the foam dildo thrust in her face.

"—opportunity to win life for my people and my community with my sacrifice," she was saying in Spanish. "Great is my honor to be granted this flowery death."

"An actress, you must understand," Teresa said hastily.

"No," Ernesto said in a stricken voice. "You do not understand, Teresa. Many do believe."

Dr. Marroquín nodded sagely. "Of course they do. Otherwise, how could the gods Huitzilopochtli and Tezcatlipoca rule? Gods, though, they are, attended by their lesser gods, their knights and of course their ranks of armed police."

"Gods." Kane moved to dampen his lips, which now seemed parched to the point of cracking, with a tongue scarcely less moist. "Rule. You aren't speaking metaphorically here, are you?"

Teresa's laugh was like a silver bell. "Surely you believe in the reality of gods, Lord Tonatiuh?"

"I'm still not sure."

The viewpoint switched back to a circling news chopper. Its vidcam eye gazed down upon the pyramid's apex. Once established, its focus bored downward with dizzying speed.

A great pedestal stood there. It was black: a single giant block of obsidian, Kane saw, veined and starred almost subliminally with milky inclusions. But from the strange encrustations dried upon it, and the dark gleaming streams that ran down its sides, he guessed it would be dark if carved of alabaster.

Above it posed a man, heroic of stature and proportioned like a steroid monster from before skydark. His skin was red bronze, almost gold; from vagrant sparkles as the light glanced off his impressive musculature, Kane guessed he had been dusted with gold powder. And golden was the radiance that surrounded him and his high headdress of green feathers and gold and scarlet as he raised a black-bladed knife high above his head.

His face was painted black, his body red and gold. Both were liberally sprayed with a fresh and liquid red.

Before him, a strapping young man writhed on the volcanic glass slab, naked, arms unbound but pinned down by the talons of creatures it took Kane a moment to realize were men. In form anyway. For another heartbeat he thought they might be burn victims, so blackened were they, backs and limbs covered with a cracking ebon crust; their hair hung in matted sopping dreadlocks from beneath strange mottled caps. Upon their shoulders rode capes of horribly suggestive shapes.

"The priests of the Black House, who serve both Hummingbird upon the Left and Smoking Mirror," intoned Marroquín; and that part of Kane that possessed knowledge Kane had never dreamed of knew that he had translated the god names Huitzilopochtli and Tezcatlipoca. "They wear upon their heads the heart cauls of sacrificed victims, on their backs their flayed skins."

"And they never wash off the blood," Teresa said in a little-girl-lost voice.

And blood they were showered in anew, and plentifully, as the great golden figure plunged his knife down and made play. Mighty were the victim's struggles and outcries, muted but clear on the audio. Both were futile.

And at the end the golden figure thrust his hand skyward, into the face of the morning sun. And it held something red and wet and pulsating.

Kane considered how unexpectedly large a thing is the

human heart. The physical one, anyway. It was not the first time he had entertained such a thought.

"They submit to this voluntarily?"

"Did that man look as if he were a volunteer...Lord?" asked Ernesto in a somewhat clotted voice.

"Some are volunteers, or at least willing sacrifices, as that young woman they interviewed purported to be," Dr. Marroquín said. "Others are criminals—cutpurses, adulterers, blasphemers—"

"Political dissidents!" Ernesto said in a hiss.

"True. But not so many. Not Huitzilopochtli or Tezcatlipoca dare move too openly against their foes, not when the party of Quetzalcoatl yet controls over forty percent of the diet. The majority of this lot, as the presacrifice show you missed informed us, are rebels from the city-state Tlaxcala. Prisoners of war."

The young man's heart was tossed carelessly upon what looked to Kane, despite being made of gilded stone, like an old-fashioned charcoal grill. As its undoubtedly stinking smoke rose toward the sun, another victim was brought forth and laid upon the altar: a young woman of striking beauty and equally striking copper-tinted hair.

"Only the fairest and strongest are offered to the gods," Ernesto told him. "At least on camera."

Kane had turned away. *I've seen enough bad things in my time that I sure don't need to see this.* "Why are you showing me this?"

"So that you might understand why we brought you here, and invested you with the person and power of the great god Tonatiuh, lord of the Sun, Mr. Kane," the whitecoat said. "To help us fight the gods, to prevent them giving up the whole of the valley to the flame and the blade—and after that, perhaps, the world."

Chapter 8

Kane reeled, spent by the effort of controlling the brightness and fury.

The wep in his hand was once more simply a sword, a sword with a blade of obsidian flakes. Yet moments before it had served as conduit for a storm of furious energy. Energy that he had drawn in from without, focused energy that had flowed through him and out again.

Energy that had burned a head-sized hole, smoking yet, through a three-inch chunk of armor plate and melted a glass channel deep into the sand and dirt mounded protectively behind it, against the stone wall.

"Most impressive, milord," said Dr. Marroquín, striding forward onto the sunlit sand. Kane hadn't seen him enter. "Yet the forces of Talocan press upon us." Talocan meant "City of the Gods." In actuality it was the central district of Tenochtitlán. "Soon they will seek to drive us under with all the strength of their gods and demons. We have scant means to stop them."

"No other gods on your side?" Kane asked hoarsely and skeptically.

The whitecoat shrugged. "Some. The rattlesnake mother, Cihuacoatl. The twins Flower Feather and Flower Prince, who rule this district of Tlillan-Tlapallan in the absence of its rightful lord, Quetzalcoatl. But it is Talocan who command the most powerful gods—Tlaloc, Xipe Totec, and of course Tezcatlipoca and Huitzilo-pochtli."

"And you expect me to make that huge a difference, huh?"

"You must."

Kane's lips compressed to a line. A neophyte god against heavy-hitting pros.

"Your training progresses well," the doctor said. "Yet we must speed it up. Understand that you are marked after the fall of the frog monster. The two will not rest easy until you are destroyed."

"Thanks so much."

"They will find it no easy task." The doctor beamed at Kane-Tonatiuh as if he had invented him. And perhaps he had. Kane had been given enough answers that morning to keep him digesting for a time, especially with a mind not altogether his own, but he would get to the truth, all of it. And if his captors/benefactors/allies thought otherwise, they didn't know their man. Or their Mags. "However, we must ensure that they find it even harder. You have yet, I believe, to master the Sun shield?"

Kane wiped sweat from his brow with the back of his hand. He was glad he didn't have to wear one of those sky-high feathery headdresses for practice, but he could have used a hat with a brim. "That's putting it mildly," he said. "I can flash the solar flare around and burn nice holes in stuff. But I can't do dick with the shield."

He raised the practice buckler strapped to his left fore-arm, which was again plain wood with a brass-bound rim like a wagon wheel to keep it from splitting.

"You do understand that the physical shield is merely a locus, a focal point for your energies?" Marroquín asked. "A crutch, if you will."

"I gather that's how it's supposed to work. I can't say I understand any of this."

"That is not needful at this time. In time understanding will come. But now you must master the shield."

"Easier said than done."

"Ah, no, my friend," the small man said, with a decidedly un-whitecoat-like grin. "It is easier done than said. Easier done, in fact, than anything. Save dying."

He raised his right hand from behind his back. It held the rear pistol grip of a Thompson Model 1928A1 submachine gun. Despite its heft, and the skinniness of his scientist's arms—seemingly accustomed to lifting nothing heavier than a beaker—he brought the piece briskly online, grabbing hold of the fore-end pistol grip with his other hand. The big muzzle brake with its slanted milled-in gas vents pointed right at Kane.

"Ho-ly *shit!*" the man doing business as Tonatiuh, god of the Sun, exclaimed in English as the muzzle brake jetted flames, pale blue and orange in the sunlight.

There was no time to dodge the stream of 230-grain copper-jacketed bullets. Their muzzle velocity was comparatively low as blasters went. But not slow enough.

By instinct he threw up the shield, as pitiful as it was.

Adrenaline exploded through his veins. Caught fire. Once more he sensed the arcs of incandescence surrounding him, like prominences rolling across the uneasy face of the Sun. They found resonance within, within the blood coursing like living flame within him, within the nerves that twined his body and limbs in nets of fire.

With the fist of his mind he grasped that flame and fashioned of it for himself a shield.

All this took place in a very short span of time.

A circle of yellow blaze sprang into being before him,

centered upon his left arm. Bullets struck it, became flame themselves. Each flared like a moth within a torch. *Vanished.*

The Tommy gun's jackhammer roar went on and on. The fat drum magazine contained one hundred cartridges; with a grin fixed to his face, clinging like a monkey to the saddle horn of a bucking bronc, the whitecoat squeezed out every last one of them.

And each turned to plasma, and then to nothing, two hand spans before Kane's bulging eyes.

"Excellent!" Dr. Marroquín lowered the hefty auto-blaster. "See? You had it within you all the time. All you need do was to believe in yourself—in the great Lord Tonatiuh."

Kane stared at the wheel of fire before his eyes. Gradually it diminished, dimmed, became a simple disk of wood bound in brass.

"You talk way too much like Lakesh," he said. He swayed and fainted.

"HAIL, Lord Tonatiuh!"

The gilded ranks stood in a sort of plaza, bordered by two angles of the rambling central step pyramid and the high compound walls. They were splendid, archaic, even barbaric in their display of feathered headdresses and shields, the obsidian-edged sword grasped in every hard brown hand.

"For an underground resistance movement," Kane remarked out of the side of his mouth, "you sure have some snappy uniforms."

But Kane wasn't fooled. These were no ancient warriors. They weren't even what Grant termed "reenactors."

Because as he stood on a stone dais overlooking the plaza, his own breastplate and back glinting golden in the afternoon sun, the helmet with its own gorgeous panache of blue-and-green plumes nodding in the all too occasional wisp of breeze to tickle his nose, were not bronze or leather or gold or even steel: they were good old polycarbonate. The shields, each painted with a blue-green serpent's head with a darting tongue and back-curving crest, were not wood like the practice ones, but rather steel-ceramic layered cores within still more polycarb: trauma plates you could strap to your forearm.

And speaking of forearms, his own keenly noted the absence of his Sin Eater nestled in its power holster, ready to slam into his hand and spew copper-jacketed leaden death at the tensing of his wrist. Nor was that simply nostalgia, because slung around each and every heroic leather-skinned neck in his audience was a strap attached to a machine pistol.

They weren't identical to his missing Sin Eater. Each had a prominent charging handle atop the receiver, which the Magistrate's trademark side arm lacked. He was not the archaic blaster enthusiast Grant was, nor did he have the encyclopedic knowledge Brigid Baptiste had gained from casting her sea-green eyes over old catalogs, but he guessed they were simple blowback machine pistols like the Ingram MAC-10 or the Uzi. For all he knew they could have been a local brew; even he, in the often vague and swirling mists that were his memories, knew it wasn't exactly hard to design and build a full-auto blowback handblaster. Exactly what they were didn't matter anyway. Instead he found significance in the picture their possession rounded out.

The several hundred stalwart men ranged facing him in sweating ranks weren't mystic warriors at all.

They were Mags. Plain and simple.

And they were saluting him. Their fervor seemed sincere. He felt at sea.

"Hail, Lord Tonatiuh!"

"They have heard how you defeated the frog monster," Teresa said. She stood just behind him to the left, Marroquín to his right. Ernesto had begged off to work in the lab. "You give them hope of victory, even against Talocan."

What have I gotten myself into? Kane wondered, not for the first time. Or rather, what he had somehow been kidnapped and dunked into. Resentment stirred within him.

He raised his arm and waved. He knew that somehow he now spoke and understood languages unfamiliar to him—or at least to Kane. But he didn't trust his command sufficiently to risk addressing the troops.

It didn't seem to matter. The golden ranks clashed swords on shields and roared their approbation.

"Okay, they like me," he said out the side of his mouth to the hybrid girl. "Just exactly what's keeping me from taking over, with them to back my play? After all, I'm the god around here."

Kane saw a seethe of emotions bubble to the surface of Teresa's face and then vanish. She seemed at once shocked, disappointed and outraged. She was unmistakably fearful—but it seemed for him, as well as of him.

"Like us," she said uncertainly, "their first loyalty is to the living god Quetzalcoatl. You would not be obeyed."

Dr. Marroquín laid a gentle hand on his shoulder. "There is more at stake here than you yet comprehend. For your sake, do not try anything hasty. Please."

"Mebbe. But this Quetzalcoatl might be a living god, but I'm the god they can see."

Teresa looked about to burst into tears. The whitecoat smiled thinly.

"Pray, make your farewells to your multitudinous admirers, Lord. There is something you ought to see."

KANE TURNED his face from the window in disgust. "A hybrid oldie in a hospital bed. I don't mean to sound callous, but so what?" He wasn't sure just what hybrids were doing there at all, but it wasn't high enough on his list of burning questions to ask quite yet.

Teresa actually gasped at his words. Ernesto, who had joined them at the elevator on the way to the infirmary somewhere in the bowels of the complex, almost stuttered, "But that is the god Quetzalcoatl himself!"

"Doesn't look like he's doing too good. Whoever heard of a god on his deathbed?"

"As I have said, Lord," the Marroquín said with a smile, "not even the gods are immortal."

"Although their essence persists," Ernesto said, "recorded in the geomagnetic flux and flow, the very living rocks of the valley."

"He suffers a degenerative condition of the brain," Teresa said. Her voice was subdued. Spots of color glowed high on her cheeks. She looked incredibly fetching, even to one such as Kane, who still felt a visceral revulsion at hybrids. "Not all his powers, nor our science, can save him."

Kane shook his head. "You say. Still hard to believe a gaunt old dying guy's a god."

"Lord Quetzalcoatl," Dr. Marroquín called. "Great Lord, attend your faithful!"

"Dr. Marroquín!" Teresa exclaimed. "What are you doing?"

The whitecoat rapped bony brown knuckles on the glass. "Lord, we beseech thee. Vouchsafe us a vision of thy true nature." He spoke Náhuatl, the tongue of the gods. Tonatiuh understood.

"Doctor, please!" Teresa begged. Ernesto laid a hand on her arm, whether to comfort or restrain, Kane couldn't tell.

Emotional subtleties had never exactly been his strong suit even when he was sole proprietor of his mind.

The elderly whitecoat paid neither any attention. He seemed to have grown in stature; his manner had become commanding, almost peremptory. At the very least, it was coming clear to Kane how the old man managed to keep charge of this rebel stronghold and its numerous personnel.

"Quetzalcoatl! Show us your power."

The dying hybrid on the bed stirred. The tubes in his nose and attached to the tap in his arm flexed alarmingly. The multicolored blinky-light displays of his vital-signs monitors did begin to dance alarmingly. Through the glass, Kane heard his moan.

Teresa tried to go to the door that led inside the hospital room. Ernesto's touch turned to unmistakable if gentle restraint. The young woman's hybrid musculature was weaker than a purely human woman's; even the youthful whitecoat, whom no one would mistake for a power lifter, held her back with ease.

The oldie began to thrash his arms, until even Kane became concerned, if mildly, that he would tear loose the needles in his veins.

The change came suddenly. It started as a shimmer, as if Kane's eyes suddenly slipped out of focus. Then it was done.

From the bed, as if thrust upward through it from the core of the Earth, sprouted the sinuous body, neck and head of a giant snake. Its head was the size of a horse's. Its eyes were fire. The juncture of head and neck was fringed with green feathers, and blue plumes of indescribable luster and beauty hung down its back in a crest.

With an inchoate exclamation Kane fell back from the glass. The eyes met his, became stars, became suns, became galaxies, blazing and wheeling and infinite. They filled his mind with white fire, and he felt that they knew him, in all his tormented persons, better than he knew himself or selves. Terror rose within him like a column of bile up his throat. He perceived benign intent within that plenum of white radiance, yet he sensed also the capacity for infinite harm.

And perhaps the taint of madness.

He felt a touch on his arm. He shut his eyes, and the spell was broken. He was himself again, whoever that was, and void of violation.

He opened his eyes. The old man lay on the bed again, moving, but gently, without apparent volition, as if unconsciously adjusting himself back to a comfortable repose. It was Teresa, freed by Ernesto, who now held Kane by the arm.

But now the blackness threatened to take Kane. He swayed, staggered. Felt the slight girl struggle to buttress his weight.

"Get a gurney," he heard Ernesto shouting to someone. "We must get him back in the vat immediately!"

And then he was lost again, and wandering in darkness.

Chapter 9

Shaking her head, Brigid prepared herself for bed. She was utterly exhausted, past the point of lucid thinking. Had she not been, she would never have been retiring. Not with Kane yet to find. Somehow.

Grant had gone off to New Edo to sulk like Achilles in his tent, muttering darkly about not returning until Kane was found—or until some means of searching for him that showed some promise of bearing fruit turned up.

There had been three fights inside the redoubt the past two days, all among the Moonies, as the refugees from Manitius had come to be known, perhaps inevitably. They may indeed have first applied it to themselves; Brigid didn't know. Neither did she know for sure what caused the disputes. But despite her archivist's distaste for intuition over evidence, she was sure in her gut that she knew what lay behind it: Domi was prowling the corridors like a white panther in heat, sleeping or teasing her way through the new arrivals, or both. She was acting strange, downright eerie, in the wake of Kane's inexplicable midjump disappearance. Her primary means of coping with stress was sex.

At that, Brigid knew they were fortunate, since Domi's other ways of dealing with emotional turmoil ran to violence and death.

Lakesh, meanwhile, had thrown himself obsessively

into research into finding Kane. Brigid knew the redoubt's ancient director better than anyone else alive, perhaps. She knew that for all his studiedly ruthless calculation and manipulation, he was, deep within, a genuinely passionate, indeed compassionate man. It was, perhaps, all that kept her from slipping lye in his morning coffee. He did care for Kane. Probably loved him as a son.

But it wasn't concern for the missing man that drove him to such prodigies of science. Or not that alone, or even primarily. Lakesh hated a mystery. Even more he hated to be outdone. He felt, she was certain, that he had been cheated of Kane. He would rampage, intellectually speaking, like a maddened bull in his labs until he had divined just who had taken Kane from him, and how, and where.

She herself passed all her waking hours pouring herself into the records and files brought back from Manitius Base. She had found tantalizing hints among the documents, especially those that treated of the near-magical technological secrets of the Danaan, who understood soulcraft and the ways of walking beyond the world better than the Annunaki or any others who had abided long upon the Earth, to Brigid's knowledge.

When she was dressed for sleep, in an old T-shirt and lime-green panties, Brigid turned a last, lingering gaze upon the computer monitor on the little shelf of the desk in her sleeping cubicle. As master archivist, she had been trained since early childhood to control, constrain, if possible squeeze emotion entirely out of her life. For her the easy emotionalism of feral-girl Domi was as alien as her promiscuity. Instead she was more similar to the stereotypical human male: uncomfortable with her feelings, reluctant to display them.

To be specific, she was in this quite similar to Kane.

She tore her eyes from the computer and could almost feel the rip. Research was her drug of choice; allowing herself to act too much the addict would naturally result in the disintegration of her intellect and personality. Indeed, she was already well past the point at which fatigue had started cutting seriously into her mental faculties, which was why she had begun the process of forcing herself to go to bed to try to sleep.

Iron discipline was no less the domain of the archivist than the warrior, and perhaps that was one reason she and Kane were always drawn back to each other no matter what sparks their contact inevitably produced. Lie down, she told herself firmly. She did.

She would've been surprised by the fact that she was asleep before her head was fully settled upon the pillow, except...

She slept. And as she slept, she dreamed.

KANE DREAMED. And as he dreamed, he wandered, lost and desperate.

Who am I? he heard a voice crying, and knew it was his. Where am I? Where are my friends? Why have they forsaken me?

Or have I forsaken them?

Urgency filled him. He ran through endless corridors that were little more than dim tunnels through fog. He had a driving desire to go someplace, but he didn't know where.

And overriding all was the sense of emptiness. Of loss, and being lost. He remembered being a child—

Somebody help me, he cried within his mind, although it was anathema to the man he was—all the men he was—to call upon another, to call out for another. Yet he couldn't restrain himself.

Please, somebody, help!

ACROSS SPACE, across time perhaps, she heard the cry:
Help me.

She came alert, though not yet awake—perhaps.
Anam-chara!

It was Kane. The cry was unlike the Kane she knew; but
it was unmistakably Kane, and so tore at her heart. How
much does he have to be suffering to drive him to that?

She reached out with all her being. His loneliness and
pain were a beacon, burning bright.

And suddenly so was triumph: I've found him!

Not in space. Nor even in time. She could not have laid
finger to a map, nor touched a point with a laser dot upon
the great wall display in the command center and say with
confidence, "He is there." Nor could she have paged
through a timeline, picked a year and said with assurance,
"He is then." She did not, could not even know whether he
remained physically within this time/space casement.

But she *knew* where he was. In emotional space, if nothing else. The bond that joined their souls was strong,
stronger than time or space or even planes of existence.
That they knew from experience. And that bond drew her
toward him now with inexorable force. If only she knew
how to follow where it led.

If only...

She rose, quickly dressed, equipped herself and left her
chamber. Whether she was awake or not was not a question
she could have answered. Nor would she have cared to.

"MS. BAPTISTE, you can't take that!"

It was Collins, who had the graveyard watch over the armory and the special-inventory room. The one locked with
an electronic lock, whose combination she had just keyed in.

So purposeful had her approach and entry been that the

tech, a long-time Cerberus staffer, had not seen fit to question either. Not until she emerged, quite promptly, with an object in her left hand was he moved to protest.

"I can," she said levelly. Her green eyes were like drills boring into his. "On my own authority."

He shook his head. "I'm sorry, Brigid. Dr. Lakesh has laid new restrictions upon those. No one can take them or even handle him without his express authorization, by comm or in person! He was real clear about this. So you can't authorize the withdrawal."

"All right," she said. She raised her right hand.

He gulped. His eyes crossed as they fixed on the muzzle of the boxy Glock handblaster she aimed between them, so close it almost touched his nose.

"Does this authorize my withdrawal of an interphaser?"

"Well," he said, swallowing hard, "technically, no."

Her knuckle whitened where it showed just outside the trigger guard. He realized he might not have made his ace-on-the-line play, here. A Glock had no manual safety to disengage by way of warning.

"No! Wait! I—I have to object, for the record. You understand. But I won't try to stop you."

She nodded sharply. "Fair enough. Object all you want. Record all you want. Keeping careful records is important."

He stared at her. "Ms. Baptiste, are you feeling—?"

She had started to lower the handblaster. Now it snapped up again, and this time the barrel prodded him right between the eyes. He held his hands up.

"All right! All right! Everybody's fine here. We're all fine."

She didn't particularly care for guns, mainly because they were foreign to the whole of her existence before her catastrophic change from senior archivist for Baron Cobalt to runaway rebel queen—unlike, say, Kane and Grant, who had been weaned on blasters, almost literally. Consequently she tended to think she wasn't very good with them.

Collins might have been a brave man, or he might not; while he didn't volunteer for missions outside, he certainly laid his life constantly on the line by living and working inside Cerberus, opposing the forces who controlled North America and thought to control all humankind—and not just on Earth. What he was manifestly not was a stupid man.

"Dr. Brigid, I won't do anything to hinder you," he said. "You got to trust me on that."

Brigid gave him a strange stiff smile and turned and walked away without a backward glance.

She proceeded to a secluded part of the armory. With no work under way here at the moment, the space was dark, illuminated only by a few amber safety lights. Awake or sleepwalking, she was confident Collins wouldn't try to follow her.

Why a degree of seclusion was important to her, she couldn't have said. Not even if fully awake. But somehow it was.

The miniature handheld jump unit was designed to allow a user to select any destination with naturally occurring vortex points, whose coordinates had been derived from the Parallax Points program and input into the interphasers database.

Brigid was no whitecoat herself, neither scientist nor technician nor yet engineer. She was an ace researcher, though. With some expertise she popped open the unit's synthetic case and began to make subtle adjustments to the microcircuitry within, according to notes saved by Lakesh, which, presumably, he had intended to be confidential....

"Brigid, wait!"

She didn't turn. Part of her mind was surprised: of all people, it was Reba DeFore, the redoubt's resident medic. It didn't take Brigid's agile mind long to solve the mystery: poor Collins feared to disturb Dr. Lakesh, much less admit that he had allowed Brigid to make off with an interphaser contrary to explicit orders—possibly he suspected she was the very person that edict had been issued to deny such access. So he summoned the one person available who might have sufficient force of personality to talk sense into the rogue archivist.

Plus, the physician was accustomed to giving orders and having them obeyed, even by the likes of the Cobaltville crew, Kane, Grant, Domi, as well as Brigid. And she had experience in dealing with the mentally unbalanced....

Snapping shut the case, Brigid glanced up. The stocky, handsome DeFore, golden braids hanging in disarray about her round but attractive face, dressed in a tatty greenish robe with pink fuzzy slippers still upon her feet, was approaching warily, backed by two Moonies, dressed in redoubt white coveralls with strap-on body armor, Fritz-style Kevlar helmets and carrying suppressed MP-5s. Apparently Collins also felt the need of something to trump her handblaster, although whether anyone within Cerberus with the barely possible exception of Donald Bry would actually *shoot* Brigid Baptiste was an open question.

"Girlfriend," DeFore began, frowning in genuine puzzlement, "what the *hell* do you think you are doing?"

Brigid smiled an enigmatic smile.

Stabbed with her thumb.

And vanished.

THE COMMOTION within the Cerberus redoubt was unlike anything known before.

Klaxons were blaring. Emergency lights were strobing. The lights throughout the underground complex went dark momentarily in a backup generator self-test, automatically invoked upon issuing of a general alert, that no one even knew about, not even Lakesh himself. Then every last one of them blazed forth in all their glory, just in case some slackards were somehow still sleeping. Or dead.

In either case, the uproar roused everyone with alacrity.

In his command center it took Lakesh only moments to bring up internal sensor data of the recent electromagnetic event that had been Brigid's unauthorized jump. He groaned aloud, which might not have been the best tonic for the morale of the personnel crowded into the center. "It is as I feared! She has blind-jumped."

"What?" asked Mariah. "Whatever do you mean?"

"It means," said Domi, "she's a self-chill." Having been blasted out of her own bed—where she was actually sleeping, alone—the young albino woman was wearing nothing at all. No one paid any notice, and it wasn't because even the recent arrivals from the Moon had begun to grow accustomed to the fact that for the wild child of the Outlands, anyplace she happened to be was clothing-optional.

"No, dearest Domi," Lakesh said in a devastated voice. "It means something far worse. It means that she is lost, alive, forever beyond rescue."

FLOATING IN BRIGHT nothingness, Brigid closed her eyes and opened her soul to the tides and torrents and images that tore at her. Anam-chara, she said with her mind. *I come. Guide me to you. Bring me, that I might help.*

The probability winds plucked at Brigid's soul down more than three axes, or even four.

Like virtually everyone else who had ever experienced it, Brigid had always before fought it with all her strength.

Now she…gave in. She let down all her defenses and opened herself to it. Surrendered.

And she was whirled apart, and away, almost lost track of who she was or that she had ever been.

Almost.

But something of Brigid, something of volition, persisted. And heard. From infinitely far away, and near at hand: anam-chara.

Kane?

Anam-chara. *I am here. Help me.*

Where are you?

I am…here.

She sensed a brightness, like a firefly in the night. *There?* she queried in her mind. *Is that you, Kane?*

Help me.

The flame brightened. She knew with a rush of gladdening that she was being drawn toward it. And she saw it was compounded of other flames: the red of Cuchulainn, the green of the man of her recurring jump dream, who died in a past life to save her, others unknown to her, yellow and blue and even, strangely, black—all compounding and comprising the white brilliance that was Kane.

Yet as she grew near, the white flame wavered, and now one, now another of the fiery colors gained ascendance. And she knew fear. For she knew Kane was in a dire place, and there was great danger that some stranger might supplant for good the man she knew. Her *anam-chara,* her soul-friend.

Kane, hold on! I'm coming!

And then in a rush she returned to being. Became flesh again in the world of substance.

She was surrounded, then, by hardness and slickness and brightness. By mechanism and disinfectant smell. But she was near Kane, hard nearby, although she could not see him.

Chapter 10

In the vast low Hall of the Gods, beneath the sacrificial plat atop the mighty Pyramid of the Sun, in the heart of Talocan, domain of the gods, in the center of Tenochtitlán, perhaps the greatest city then on Earth, the paramount god of war sat among splendors of gold and fronds and feathers with his chin in his hand and his elbow propped on the swell of his mighty bare right quadriceps. Although his face, square jawed and high cheekboned and bronze and beautiful, was devoid of the black paint with which he adorned it for ceremonial appearances, his expression was dark enough for midnight in a coal cellar.

"Hail, Great Huitzilopochtli, Hummingbird upon the Left, slayer of monsters and father of his people!" The secondary god of war approached. He was a smaller man than Huitzilopochtli, his muscles tight wound rather than bulging, face darker and narrower beneath the gold circlet he wore about his temples.

"Hail, Smoking Mirror my brother," Huitzilopochtli grunted. "Take the appropriate honorifics as given."

Tezcatlipoca smiled. It was a sly smile, which was the kind generally offered by Tezcatlipoca, except when he made grave faces to take the flowery gift or more ingenuous smiles across the negotiation table. Less mighty by far was he than Huitzilopochtli, especially in the arts of war and the particularities of combat, mortal and immortal. Yet he was a god of many aspects, unlike Huitzilopochtli, who was pretty much a narrowly focused, unconflicted war god. Which was why Huitzilopochtli was paramount god of war.

And also why he didn't trust his brother god.

"I thank thee, Mighty Etcetera." Huitzilopochtli's brow furrowed slightly at that. At once Tezcatlipoca's manner sobered.

"It is as we suspected," he said. "Our enemies raise up gods of their own against us. Tonatiuh the Sun once more walks the earth. It was he who cast down the frog monster. His aspect, it would appear, consists in significant part of a plasma weapon of great potency."

Huitzilopochtli grunted. "Small loss. I never cared overmuch for that one. He thought highly of himself for a toad. And smelled like a cesspool."

"But remember the purpose for which we raised him up, O Hummingbird—to play *rudo* to our *técnicos*. To back our claims upon the loyalty, worship and, of course, actual blood of the people—that mass sacrifice is required to strengthen us to battle the monsters who seek to overthrow the order of our valley and plunge it again into chaos—with some actual, tangible monsters. Who must, of necessity, be monstrous—as my brother god himself acquiesced."

Huitzilopochtli glowered at him. "You don't need to lecture me, Tezcatlipoca. Your pedantry wears thin. As you say, I was there when the plan to create real monsters to overawe the *plebeyos* was laid, and I concurred in your design—and our mother's, before you get too smug. I know we need monsters. I just don't care to sup with them."

"This will no longer be an issue with Tlaltecuhtli. Unless my lord cares to raise up a new lord of the Earth?"

Huitzilopochtli raised a brow at him. He wasn't stupid,

any more than Tezcatlipoca was weak. But gods have their vanity as well as mortal men. Or maybe better.

"Are you trying to plant a notion that I will come to believe is my own, Smoking Mirror? Your child psychology is if anything more insufferable than your pedantry."

Tezcatlipoca laughed. "Perhaps instead I'm trying to raise up a resistance within you to the idea of giving a new avatar to the frog monster, while making it seem your own!"

Huitzilopochtli's scowl deepened. "In any event," Tezcatlipoca continued smoothly, "no, I desire the restored company of Tlaltecuhtli no more urgently than you. Indeed, he's served his function. As god of war you will recognize that he has made himself a perfect scout."

"By making himself a dead one, causing our enemies to tip their hands," Huitzilopochtli agreed. "Well, we've smoked them out, as you intended. And now we crush them!"

Tezcatlipoca laughed. "Mightiest in feats of arms are you, O Huitzilopochtli, and capable of great cunning," he said. "But subtlety is not your strong suit."

"Whereas you are often too subtle for your own good," Huitzilopochtli said sourly. "Or at least, for *our* own good as rulers of the gods and people of the valley. So you won't let me crush these impertinent adherents of a discredited god?"

"Not yet, Hummingbird," said Tezcatlipoca, laughing a coyote laugh. "They are stronger than you imagine, and win great favor among the populace."

"All the more reason to act decisively to end their threat."

"Were that the most effective way to do so, certainly."

Huitzilopochtli regarded his brother god through narrowed eyes. "You seldom do anything without reason. So why do you tread so near to pissing me off? Not even you want that, trickster god."

Tezcatlipoca folded hands upon his breast and bowed. "Forgive me. I did not intend to give offense."

"A likely story." But Huitzilopochtli settled himself back in his golden throne, with the green feathers of the quetzal bird and the appropriately colored plumes of the blue macaw nodding above his regal head in the HVAC breeze. The system was highly developed and had been designed by Tezcatlipoca himself.

"First let us follow up the demise of the unfortunate frog monster with a veritable monster blitz," Tezcatlipoca said. "Let's see how the populace likes vampire women, carnivorous water beasts and, of course, a plague of giant scorpions."

"You interest me. Go on."

"The people of Tenochtitlán—and after all, as goes Tenochtitlán, so goes the valley—will be preoccupied with trying to avoid doing the monster mash. Our foes must act, lest the public lose faith in them and have their eyes opened anew to the benefits of the good old religion, as personified by us. We get their forces, including this new Tonatiuh, scattered across all the districts they control, fighting monster brushfires."

By way of illustration he held out his left hand, palm up, and spread his fingers wide. "And then we crush them."

He slammed his right fist into his left palm.

Huitzilopochtli rubbed his chin and nodded. "It could work. I'm impressed."

Tezcatlipoca shrugged self-deprecatingly. "It's all quite simple."

"That's why I'm impressed. This is far less convoluted than your usual plans." He frowned. "Indeed, it's so uncharacteristic that I wonder…"

Tezcatlipoca laughed out loud—a risky thing to do in

the face of Huitzilopochtli, even if you did happen to be his coequal god and ruler. "Now who risks outsmarting himself, mightiest of gods?"

For a beat Huitzilopochtli continued to glower at his brother. Then he grinned.

"You may even be clever enough to know when the straightforward beats the sly, at that," he admitted. "We'll play it your way. At first, anyway."

"HAIL TO THEE, O Lady Precious Green! Great river which gives rise to the cactus fruit, wind upon water, beauty upon shore, water goddess, giver of life and subduer of the witch queen and eater of filth!"

Brigid closed her eyes, very slowly, and opened them again. They're still there, she thought with something between resignation and disgust.

She lay in what felt and smelled like a hospital bed, in what to her brief wakening glance looked much like a hospital room: sterile, void of character as of contagion, much white and some chrome. Over her leaned a weird-looking old whitecoat, brown eyes huge behind bottle-bottom lenses. Behind him hovered an exceedingly earnest-looking young man. Both were light brown of skin and black of hair, although by the white wispy sidewalls on the older man's strange mushroom of a head she suspected the blackness of the mass on top to be the result of art, not nature.

"Where's Kane?" she demanded. "And is that a Moe wig?"

The younger man looked completely at sea. The older man straightened, smiling. "We have gazed upon the very flames of your soul. We know that you were once Brigid Baptiste, senior archivist of the barony of Cobaltville, and then again brilliant researcher and brave operative of those who resist the tyranny of the barons. And now you are given new life, new power, new purpose, as Chalchi-huitlicue, the jade skirt goddess, mistress of the waters."

"Sure," she said. "Now I'll ask again politely—once. Where is Kane?"

"He is no more," the young man intoned.

Her green eyes flashed to him like lasers. Green wrath boiled up within her, frothing and ferocious. And more than wrath—a power both utterly familiar and totally strange.

The young man's eyes bugged out of his handsome face. He hunched over himself, clutching at his sternum.

"As I am the waters that gave life to all things," she said in a ringing voice and a language she had never in her life so much as heard, "as I gave rise to the ripe cactus fruit which is the human heart, so can I send forth floods to devastate and end all life before them, and mine is the gift to stop the heart's beating I once gave rise to."

The elderly whitecoat grabbed the sleeve of what she perceived was a very ordinary hospital gown, the kind that bared your ass when you walked. "Please! Mercy, Goddess! Have mercy upon your devotees, who have joined your essence and aspect together with one worthy!"

Brigid looked at him. For a moment his outline shifted. He seemed a younger man, and then, almost for a moment—what? She had a glimpse, not before her eyes, but well behind, of a stocky jungle cat, deep russet orange and black, dappled with shadows of lush jungle growth. Then both were gone, and all she saw was a distraught old man in a laboratory coat and a ludicrous wig, begging for the life of his aide.

Which she, somehow, was in the process of taking.

"Oh," she said. She looked back at the young man, now on his knees. His face was turning black and blue like a giant bruise, and he didn't seem to be breathing, although from the rolling of his now bloodshot eyes, he retained consciousness. I hope I can stop that, she thought.

And as she formed the intent, it was as if an invisible fist released his heart. The breath rushed back into his body, the blood back to his face, and he fell forward onto his hands, panting.

"I have no idea on Earth how I did that," she said in English. "And I'm sorry—for now. However, I am going to ask some questions, and if I don't receive prompt and satisfactory answers, we may just have to start all over again."

The older man nodded gravely. "I thank you for your mercy, Chalchihuitlicue."

"Thank Brigid Baptiste," she said. "Lady Precious Green would have had your life, and that of your young friend, for your impertinence."

Whoa, she thought. And where did *that* come from? Yet she knew it was true.

The older man steepled fingers before his chest, bowed. Then he turned and stooped to help his assistant to his feet. "Are you all right, Ernesto?"

"I—I'm fine, Dr. Marroquín." Which, as Brigid could plainly see, was a brave lie. The young man looked at her, and somewhat to her surprise she saw in his mild brown eyes neither anger nor resentment. Only something she feared was worship.

He made praying hands and bowed, as well. "Forgive my presumption, Lady of the Jade Skirt. And thank you for your mercy in not killing me."

"What's happened to me?"

Ernesto blinked uncertainly at Dr. Marroquín. "All will be explained to you in the fullness of time, Lady," the whitecoat said imperturbably.

"I meant, after I…materialized in your lab."

"Ah. You were stunned by some of our security men. A regrettable necessity. But among other things, your powers of healing have been remarkably augmented. Although in truth, you should feel no lingering ill effects from your stunning."

"And the men I shot? What of them?"

"Recovering well in hospital."

"Damn," Brigid said. "I told Kane I wasn't any good with a handblaster."

She sat up. As she did she felt the kiss of cool air on her back: bare, all right. It felt good, but gave her a flash of annoyance: Why did they ever come up with such a foolish design in the first place? And why did they keep it? Do they think degradation is therapeutic?

She noticed the two men looking a little green around the edges again, realized she had to have been frowning. Then her vision did a brief whirl and she swayed.

The young man was instantly at her side, holding her up— again, a pretty ballsy act, considering. She smiled at him.

"Lady, you must not overexert yourself. You have been through much. And to take your aspect upon so soon, before you've had a chance to recover—"

"Your powers are great, Lady Precious Green," Dr. Marroquín said. "Yet even a goddess has limitations. Please move slowly until you have begun to perceive them."

"I appreciate your concern, Dr. Marroquín," she said. "And yours, Ernesto—you can take your hand back now." He did, hurriedly.

"At the same time," she went on, her voice hardening and taking an edge, "something has been done to me that I do not understand and to which I most assuredly did not consent. That does not make me happy, whatever 'powers' the procedure may have conferred on me. And I came here, in possibly not the best-considered act I've undertaken in my life, for one purpose—to find my…soul-friend, the man named Kane, and bring him home. So now, even before you make a full and convincing explanation, not just of what it is you've done to me, but what the *hell* gave you the idea it was all right to do so without my permission, you will take me to Kane. Or bring him to me. Or I'll start to explore my shiny new powers in a way you will not like."

The door blew in.

Dr. Marroquín never flinched. Instead he smiled thinly. "I believe your wish is granted, milady."

Lying on the door, indeed riding it into the room's middle in the manner of a surfboard, albeit lying on his back waving limbs in the air like an upset scarab, came a man. It was not Kane, although Brigid's first thought upon beholding him was a flash of terror: *Mag!*

But he wasn't. Quite. Despite the fact it was cast of gold polycarbonate and not the gleaming sinister black of a hard-contact suit, nor did it cover his whole body, his armor and helmet were more than slightly reminiscent of what the barons' enforcers wore when their hybrid masters felt the need to lay some serious fear upon their subjects. A device was painted upon his breastplate in blue, a curious stylized streamlined creature with a long tongue enfolding from gaping jaws and a long feather or crest extending backward from the head, ending in a sort of upward curlicue. He was shorter and stockier than Kane, but his upper arms and thighs, left bare by his curious armor, were molded thick with muscle.

The sliding door came to rest with a thud against the base of Brigid's bed. So did the top of the man's gold-helmeted head. He went limp, momentarily stunned, and

Brigid stared. Not even Grant, the strongest nonmutant man she knew, could have thrown a man that size through a door like that, and Grant was significantly stronger than—

"Kane!" The name ripped itself from her lips. Indeed, she was lucky it didn't tear them on the way out.

The man who stood framed in the doorway's unaccustomed gape paused and regarded her with wolf-gray eyes. He was tall, wide of shoulder and chest, tapering like an arrowhead to his waist. His legs, bare beneath the gold-trimmed hem of his white linen robe, were twined with wiry quick-response muscle. His black hair, just brushed to the edge of perceptibility with gray, was swept back to hang to his nape. His beard had been trimmed to a black vertical bar descending from lower lip to the tip of his chin. Embroidered in gold upon the breast of his gown was a circular device representing a face or mask, openmouthed and surrounded with curving highly stylized rays; its chin bore a bar not unlike Kane's beard.

For a moment he gazed at her without apparent recognition. Her heart threatened to collapse. But then a wild wolf-light blazed up within them. "Baptiste!"

He lunged for her, caught her in his iron-band arms. *"Anam-chara!"* She hugged him as if she had been drowning in an infinite sea of time and space, and he was the one plank, the one speck of solidity she sought for her salvation.

Which, of course, had been the case.

He looked down at her. His eyes blazed like suns; hers were bright endless seas. Almost their faces touched…

"Milord!" a voice called from the doorway. "I mean, Dr. Marroquín! Forgive it, please, we tried our best but could not stop him. What do we do now?"

"Stay back," was the dry response. "Unless you want to learn what gods are like when they're really pissed."

As if by common impulse Kane and Brigid pushed back from each other, although they continued to clutch each other's arms.

"The goat looks good on you, Kane," Brigid said.

"Thanks. What took you so long?"

She felt a stab of anger—which transmuted instantly to laughter. There was much that was strange about this man with the golden sun mask on his chest and the power of the sun—she could sense it clearly as if she could see it, taste it, hear the infinite roar of solar furnace—behind. But by his words she *knew*.

"Whatever's happened to you," she said, "you are still Kane."

She looked past him, then, and her eyes widened. More armored men stood to either side of the doorway, peering cautiously in. In their golden-gauntleted hands each bore an object, which for all its unfamiliar detail was deadly familiar in design—and origin.

"Infrasound wands!" she exclaimed. "Kane, they're hybrids!"

He shook his head and laid a soothing finger on her lips. Under other circumstances she might have tried to bite it. The impulse was absent, for just this moment.

"Look at them," he said, shaking their heads. "They're no hybrids." For they were sturdy, like their comrade who had ridden in on the smashed-down door.

"Then they're hybrid servants! Baronial Guards, or—"

She stopped cold. Because in the door, between the men, had appeared a slip of a young woman, dressed in pale gray trousers and a mauve blouse of some soft stuff. And she unquestionably was a hybrid.

The most human-appearing hybrid Brigid had ever seen, but for the barons she had encountered in the flesh, seldom to her pleasure. And, with her elfin olive-hued features, inhumanly enormous brown eyes with long black lashes, the black wisps of hair curling above a slight blush upon either cheek, she was strikingly beautiful. But... "She's a hybrid, Kane."

The woman stopped in the act of entering the room. Her eyes flashed. "Yes. I am, Lady Precious Green. And, all honor and respect to you—" she made perfunctory obéisance, which her eyes did not reflect "—please do not judge me before you come to know me!"

Brigid blinked. It wasn't a thing most hybrids of her acquaintance would have ever thought to say. But this was clearly no normal hybrid. Indeed it seemed as if the blood of the Tuatha de Danaan expressed itself in her in near pure form, to the exclusion of the lizardlike Annunaki and even, almost, of standard human.

"That seems a reasonable thing to ask," she said. "And whoever or whatever else I am now, I'm still a senior archivist, and reason is my life. So I'll certainly grant your wish, and even ap—"

A look of something like terror appeared on the ethereal face. She raised her hands. "Forgive it, great lady, but no! Please no! Do not apologize to one such as me!"

Brigid looked up at Kane. He shrugged and flashed a lopsided grin, and was so much the Kane of old she wanted to both laugh and cry. Instead, being Brigid and senior archivist, she drew in a deep breath, set her strong shoulders and the expression on her fine-boned face with a little unconscious flip of her red-gold hair.

She looked to Dr. Marroquín and swung her legs over the side of the bed. "And now, you will please us by pro-

viding both of us the explanation I suspect you have been
denying Kane. But first get me something to cover myself
with, before I stir off this gods-damned bed!"

Chapter 11

"There is nothing I can teach you about fighting, Mr. Grant," said the little Chinese guy sitting beneath a spray of wisteria captured and held in a vase in an alcove. "I can teach you about moving beyond mere fighting."

"'Mere' fighting!" Grant was outraged. "What do you mean, 'mere' fighting? That's like saying 'mere dying'!"

The man bowed. "Perhaps."

He didn't look like much. He appeared to weigh about eighty pounds, wispy white goatee and all, and was clearly an oldie, although he certainly seemed limber enough, and his eyes sparkled in his parchment-skinned face. He was apparently the real deal, though. He was flavor of the month with Shizuka's bannermen despite their brash—and to Grant's mind somewhat insecure—insistence upon the superiority of their own fighting style and their reflexive mistrust of strangers. Palace gossip said he was actually from mainland China and had turned up in the islands on trading vessels a couple times before.

Grant stood. In his own light silk robe he was an imposing figure, and subconsciously kept his head ducked to one side to prevent it encountering a roof beam—most buildings in New Edo had not been constructed with a man of his imposing height in mind. He would have towered over Master Chen had the Chinese wanderer been standing. Now it felt to him as if he confronted a child.

Still, it was a "child" who made strong claims, or allowed them to be made on his behalf. And who had just made a very specific claim that Grant found very specifically outrageous.

"You're a martial-arts master!" he exclaimed.

Chen sipped tea from a cup of deliberately rustic design. That sort of thing was currently the fashion in New Edo. "So I have been called."

"But you dismiss 'mere' fighting with—with contempt."

"Not contempt at all, Mr. Grant, if you will forgive my contradiction. Such activities assuredly have their place under heaven. But it is assuredly an inferior one."

Grant found himself near hyperventilating. He forced his massive bellows of a chest to pump more deliberately. But his eyes were bloodshot and his nostrils splayed like a bull's.

Suddenly the room came into ultraclear focus: pale buff mat beneath them, one whitewashed stone wall crisscrossed by dark wood beams, the rice-paper *shoji* panels that made up the other walls. The little man sitting imperturbably in the middle of it all, just radiating total superiority.

Grant had come to the shogun's sprawling palace with a chip on his shoulder. He was no fool, and he knew himself at least that well. He felt as if part of him had been amputated with Kane's disappearance, and the sense of powerlessness fostered by his actual inability to do anything about it ate him like a cancer. He'd half hoped that the ever fractious Black Dragons might get up to their merry pranks again, trying to undermine their scandalously female de facto shogun, Shizuka. But they puppied, and were being placid, not making any kind of nuisance of themselves at all. Whether it was all the recent alarms and threats, or Shizuka's leadership in bringing the realm through them, they appeared sated with action for the time.

And now it seemed to Grant he saw a safe outlet for the intolerable pressure of the frustration boiling inside him.

"I'm tempted to show you a thing or two about 'real fighting,' little man!"

Chen smiled at him placidly. "You must act as your nature dictates, Mr. Grant."

Grinning like a god of war, Grant struck.

From the position in which he had come to rest, with the pink soles of his bare feet resting rather comfortably against the whitewashed stone wall, his back pressed against it, and his neck bent so that his massive chin rested on his clavicle and helped buttress his not inconsiderable inverted mass, Grant said, "I humbly beg forgiveness for doubting your mastery, Master," with only the merest trace of sourness.

Master Chen smiled. "Freely given but unneeded, my friend. For were I not your master, even at 'mere' fighting, what then might I have to teach you? It was merely the part of prudence to assure yourself upon that score. Will you take tea?"

Grant grunted.

The door slid open. Kneeling, one of Shizuka's servant women bowed in the opening, her face painted white and hands hidden within the enormous sleeves of her green silk kimono.

"Grant-*sam*," she said. "My mistress bids me tell you that a call has come for you from your homeland."

"Now do I have to kill her to save face?" demanded Grant, still in his inverted position against the wall.

"It would be unadvisable," said Sifu Chen, sipping tea. "They all carry darts in their hair, in lieu of pins."

"I know."

The woman waited, head lowered so that her eyes did

not meet Grant's. "I'm not answering," he said. "Tell them I'm out or something. I'm resting. I *like* it like this."

"But they say it is most urgent."

"Same answer."

Her head raised a trifle. The almond eyes flicked toward him. "But they say they have found your friend."

Grant flexed, sprang away from the wall, landed on his feet facing it. "Later, Master," he said. "Thanks for the lesson."

Master Chen bowed.

"HOW COULD THAT old hybrid be Quetzalcoatl?" Kane demanded.

Kane, Brigid and Dr. Marroquín walked along a gallery within the giant rambling castle or mansion or whatever it was. Ernesto and Teresa followed at a respectful distance. On their right was a highly stylized mural representing a long, gory and fantastic series of events. Beneath their feet lay a catwalk made of what appeared to be bronze mesh, but was almost certainly plated steel; below them people moved slowly and spoke mutedly among lit displays and potted plants in a wider space that appeared to be some kind of museum or possibly meditation area.

On the left, instead of a wall was a huge window of smoked glass, giving a view over a great courtyard tiered with mighty blocks of stone and containing a fabulous garden of exuberant green tropical growth, elephant ears and orchids and lianas strung everywhere in profusion. Small monkeys scampered along the stems of huge leaves with yellow undersides ribbed in green. Lizards great and small crawled upon the stone blocks. A pair of globular eyes belonging to what appeared to be a dwarf caiman or crocodile protruded above the placid, murky water of a pond at the bottom of it all, with pale green algae, or perhaps tiny flowers, floating in a patch about them. Dragonflies with bodies as long as the span of the outstretched fingers of a hand drifted in the heavy air, their great wings shimmering.

"About a century ago," Marroquín said, "when the cataclysmic earth activity sparked by the nukecaust was reaching its crescendo, a party of adventurers arrived here by mysterious means.

"We know a great many things here today, not least of which is much of what goes on north of what once was the border. There are good reasons for this, which will also become clear to you shortly."

"Good," Kane grunted.

They came to the catwalk's end and into an area that might have been the waiting room for a suite of offices. Though the walls were white, the lighting was low, and much of it came from spot lights illuminating alcoves showing various artifacts of apparently ritual nature: masks, of feathers, of clay, of beaten gold; weapons, shields; cloaks of cloth and the ubiquitous brightly hued feathers. Some low, dark, leather-upholstered furniture was placed around the space, off which several somewhat better-lit corridors led. Kane looked at Brigid, as if she, as the archivist, should have the answers to the apparent incongruities. She shrugged.

"One party spoken of in documents from that time escaped from the stricken city, although grievously injured," Marroquín said, leading them across the space toward what appeared to be an elevator. "She reached a cave in the mountains to the west where she found shelter. There she made a remarkable discovery."

"She?" Brigid asked.

"Her name was Felicidad Mendoza," Ernesto said. "She was the lover of the ruler of the countryside surrounding the city, Don Hector, and daughter to his security chief, who was executed by Don Hector. She was in line to succeed her father before Don Hector was killed."

They reached the elevator door and entered when the door opened.

"As to the next twist of the story, perhaps my associate Teresa would care to recount it?"

"Felicidad Mendoza discovered an artifact of great age and prodigious power," the hybrid woman said. "Most likely it drew her to itself."

"Like the One Ring?" Brigid asked with a skeptical arch of brow.

The dark-haired woman looked briefly blank; unlike Brigid, she seemed to have no great acquaintance with preskydark literature and popular culture. Marroquín pressed a button, and the elevator descended. Teresa continued her tale.

"She was a woman of enormous potential in the use of *prana*. She had an affinity for it, a natural ability, unknown to her, to tap into and control it. Perhaps she sensed that the artifact produced a *prana* homing beacon. Her very weakness, delirious with pain and likely fever from her injuries and the stress of her escape from the city's final destruction, no doubt rendered her more receptive than she might otherwise have been. Her consciousness, her interfering self—"

"Her pervasive cynicism," Dr. Marroquín murmured.

Teresa nodded abstractedly. "—was unable to block or explain away inputs received through senses she had not previously suspected she had. In short, it called. She came."

"And what was *it?*" Kane asked.

"A great polished lens of obsidian," Ernesto said, eyes aglow. "The Smoking Mirror."

"An artifact created hundreds, possibly thousands—and indeed perhaps tens of thousands—of years before," Dr. Marroquín said. "By an alien technology, and alien hands. It derived from the folk known upon Earth as the Tuatha de Danaan, although it was quite possibly either modified or actually made by their rivals, the Annunaki."

He peered keenly from the face of one of his captive gods to the other. "I see you are surprised," he said, "but not confused. You know the referents."

"And you're not surprised that we do," Brigid said.

"No, Lady Chalchihuitlicue." He smiled. The elevator stopped, deep beneath the Earth.

Chapter 12

"Where is he?"

"Good day to you, too, Grant, my noble friend," Lakesh said as Grant entered the control center in the manner of a male bovine on the premises of a purveyor of fine porcelain.

The big great-chested black man stopped in the room's midst with feet apart, legs braced like mahogany trunks—and mostly visible, because he was still wearing the royal-blue silk kimono in which he had been taking tea with Master Chen, and it was several sizes too small for him. Eyes rolling and nostrils flared, all he needed was a pair of horns.

"Don't make me take you by the neck and shake it out of you, little man," he said. "That'd be too much fun."

"I'm kinda sorry I gave up the idea of tripping you now," a feminine voice said from behind him. "The way these Moon base women are eyeing you up almost makes me jealous."

He spun. He had charged right past the slim, slight form of Domi without even seeing her. She wore a camou halter top, khaki cargo shorts and red stand-ups. It was about as dressed as she got, unless it was cold, which it never was in the climate-controlled warrens of Cerberus redoubt.

"Where's Kane?" Grant demanded again.

Lakesh held up his hands. "Peace, my friend. I will send you to his aid soon—almost at once, in fact. But I cannot permit you to go in blind. Calm yourself to listen and I will tell all."

"That'll be a switch," Grant rumbled. But he folded arms across his mighty chest and settled himself to hear.

"They've got Brigid now, too, you know," Domi said, perching on a corner of a counter and pulling an apple from a compartment of her baggy shorts.

"What?" He glowered at her. "Damn, what have you people been doing? First you lose Kane, and now Baptiste?"

"It was scarcely our fault," Lakesh said a trifle peevishly. "She stole an interphaser—"

Grant raised an eyebrow. "'Stole'?"

"I had ordered them all secured precisely because I feared such an eventuality. She possessed herself of a unit and overrode the safety controls in a most rash, dare I say irresponsible manner. A pupil of mine!"

Grant's eyes started from his handsome heavy face. "She jumped blind?" He shook his head. "Whoa. I always knew she had some big ones on her, even if she is a librarian."

"Archivist," Lakesh corrected reflexively. "She jumped blind. Collins, whom she threatened with a handgun in order to obtain the jump unit, said she acted strangely, as if in a trance. I surmise she was sleepwalking, or perhaps more accurately, moving in a half-waking dream."

"Whatever," Domi said around a fruity crunch, "it worked. And when you said 'big ones,' you meant like, *cojones*, no? Because while I admit she has a pretty impressive set of—"

"Domi," said Lakesh, whose face had turned a shade darker and somewhat redder, as well. "That will do."

Ruby eyes flashed laser death at him. "Oh, that's right. I forget, I'm just a little gaudy slut, your contract whore, a mere slave to order me around, just like Guana Teague—"

"Domi," Grant rumbled, "shut the fuck up."

She did.

"Thank you," Lakesh said to the air. "Hardly had we responded to the alarm the good Mr. Collins had raised at Brigid's, ah, unauthorized requisition, than her biolink transponder indicated she had jumped to the northwestern quadrant of the urban concentration that has sprung up upon the site of the erstwhile Mexico City."

Grant slammed his fist down upon a console. The blinky lights of its display, red and green and amber, blinked spasmodically and went out. "Thank God for redundancy, eh," murmured one of the new arrivals, softly.

"Mexico City! God damn. I *knew* she was right. All this time. And you wouldn't let me go."

"No," Lakesh said imperturbably. He hadn't flinched when Grant's mighty fist chilled the unit. He knew Grant well and trusted that, no matter the big man's histrionics, he had total control over himself. Renegade or not, Grant was still at core the ultimate Mag. Steely self-discipline was the spine of his being. "Because even had we known for an absolute fact Kane was being held there, it's a city of over one hundred thousand, covering many hectares. At least some of whose occupants, by virtue of the fact they sequestered friend Kane without his consent, appear hostile to us. To permit you to go would almost certainly have been futile at best, and likely resulted in our losing our *other* ace field operative."

"Seems like it's your turn to pipe down now, Grant," Domi said around another gnaw at her apple.

Grant glared at her. He breathed in deep. Let it out in a sigh.

"Okay," he said. "You're right. You got the floor, Doc."

"In my own control center? How uncommonly gracious of you. We know where Brigid was at the moment she contacted us."

"You've lost her, too?"

"Her biolink stopped sending within the hour," said the bulky Nigel of the unruly hair, who was lead tech in the command center that shift.

"That's impossible," Grant declared. "Isn't it?"

"Not at all," Lakesh said. "The biolink transponders send out a signal that, however slight, can be detected from orbit. Those signals can be detected, obviously. And the transponders can then be analyzed and neutralized."

"Without killing the subject?"

Lakesh hesitated just a beat. "Yes. There are various ways."

"So we don't have to go around the planet with you able to spy on our every move?"

"We're hardly able to spy upon your every move, as well you know," Lakesh said. "And I daresay the transponder has served us, and you, well on more than one occasion. Without it, we would now be missing Brigid, as well as Kane, and little the wiser than we were before."

"Which is begging a couple questions," Domi murmured. Both men looked sharply at her. "What? I'm just part of the furniture here, just a mindless little albino outlander. You big men go back to your important man-talk the ignorant little outlaw girl couldn't possibly understand."

"Perhaps our greatest misstep in your education, Domi, my sweet," Lakesh said, "was introducing you to the concept of irony."

"So when do we go get him?" Grant asked.

"Soon."

Grant's face started to cloud over again. "Why not now?"

"It's daylight, dummy," Domi said, thwacking him lightly on the chest with the back of her left hand. "This calls for a good old-fashioned snoop 'n' poop. C'mon. Let's go pack."

IT WAS A LENS of black glass five feet across, held in a frame of what might have been polished brass. Its surface was smooth but not altogether regular, as if it had been pressure flaked into shape and then polished. A few white inclusions, one as large as a palm, glowed like a nova on its surface. White vapor streamed off it.

"The Smoking Mirror," Dr. Marroquín said. "In the ancient language Náhuatl, Tezcatlipoca."

Kane and Brigid looked at each other. The artifact was kept in a vault deep beneath the Instituto Quetzalcoatl in which they were immured as captive deities. The pair stood in an antechamber with the whitecoat and his two helpers. It was cold enough to raise goose bumps on the North Americans' bare arms.

Cold beat from the slightly amber-tinted viewport like heat from a stove. "Inside that chamber it's forty degrees below zero Celsius," Ernesto said with a curious admixture of reverence and nerd enthusiasm, "chilled by liquid helium. That is its optimal operating regime."

Even through thick insulated glass they could feel the energy it gave off, more potent than the transferred chill. It stirred something within their souls, something not altogether comfortable. As if of one accord they turned and looked down to find their hands linked. Hesitantly they let go.

Ernesto noticed nothing of the byplay. "It is a high-temperature superconductor," he went on. "Inset in the frame are SQUIDs to control and calibrate it."

"Superconducting Quantum Interface Devices," Brigid said.

The young technician looked at her in surprise. "You are familiar with the technology, um, Lady Precious Green?"

"I'm not *actually* your antique goddess," Brigid said crisply. "Although I have to admit I have memories and thoughts that are identifiably not my own…not a comfortable sensation."

"It's not that, O Chalchihuitlicue," Ernesto said hastily. "We know you are by avocation a librarian."

"Archivist," she snapped. He jumped.

"She has a photographic memory," Kane explained. "The real woman, not the fake memories you stuffed her head with. Our heads. She specialized in researching the late twentieth century. She's no whitecoat, but she's scanned a lot of technical journals. She can talk the talk."

"How did you know that I was an archivist?" Brigid asked. "That again?"

Marroquín nodded. "The mirror allowed us to read your thoughts, to a certain extent. It has many remarkable capabilities. Which, to be candid, we have only begun to plumb in almost a century of study."

"They are not false memories, Lord Tonatiuh," Teresa said.

"Are you trying to tell me there was really such a person as Tonatiuh?" Kane demanded.

"There was such a person as Don Pedro de Alvarado," Brigid said in a tautly controlled voice. "And the Aztecs did call him Tonatiuh. And he did preside over the—the mass murder of ringleaders of a rebellion his own brutal misrule provoked, during the absence of his own master Cortés."

"My dream!" Kane stared at her. "How did you—?"

She reached up to touch his scarred cheek. "I dreamed your dreams. How do you think I knew you needed me?"

"I see you have read Bernal Diaz del Castillo," Dr. Marroquín murmured.

"And Prescott," Brigid added without looking at him.

"You have most catholic tastes."

"It goes with the name."

Kane's glare turned the color of winter sky. "What the hell have you done to us?"

Marroquín smiled thinly. "Shall we repair to a slightly warmer venue?"

"ALL RIGHT. Tezcatlipoca means 'smoking mirror.' Somehow I knew before you said it," Kane said. The five of them sat in a break room in the vaults not far from the artifact's cold chamber. Several upholstered chairs and a sofa surrounded a table. Kane and Brigid sat beside each other on the sofa, not too close together. It was uncannily like something they might have found within Cerberus. "But…it was brought here by Quetzalcoatl. Or built by him."

"What makes you say that, Lord?" asked Dr. Marroquín, perched in an auditorium-style chair with legs crossed and hands clasped over one knee. His eyes were very bright.

Kane looked to Brigid. She returned his gaze calmly. Her expression gave nothing away. *I wish we could exchange thoughts someplace other than our dreams,* he thought.

"On the Moon," he said. It was Teresa and Ernesto's turn to exchange glances. Teresa sat in a chair across from the seated so-called gods, while Ernesto hovered beside her. Dr. Marroquín just sat looking vaguely pleased and bland enough for Buddha. "I was told that the original Quetzalcoatl was an Annunaki named Lam. An alien."

"You were told this by Maccan of the Danaan, were you not?" Marroquín asked.

Kane blinked. "How did you know that?"

"The mirror."

"Is there anything that…object can't do?" Brigid demanded.

Marroquín smiled thinly. "It has, as we have said, remarkable capabilities. But please put yourselves at ease. It enabled us to glean certain information from your memories that we deemed relevant to our mutual needs, yours and ours. The vast preponderance of both your memories are still private—which you may believe for no other reason than there are simply too many of them for us to assimilate even if we had any desire to do so."

She looked at Kane again. He shrugged.

"Lam of the Annunaki, as Quetzalcoatl, brought the Smoking Mirror," Dr. Marroquín said. "He initiated some of the brighter youths into a priesthood and taught them its uses. One of them or their successors might possibly have provided the historical original for the god Tezcatlipoca. Indeed, it's possible that first Tezcatlipoca might have understood the mirror better than the one who brought it. Especially if Lam stole or was given the artifact, not even he may have fully grasped its potential."

"Danaan technology is like that," Brigid conceded grudgingly. "They seem to favor a strong intuitive component in learning and making use of it. Indeed, I have come to suspect that at its most potent levels, they themselves did not—do not—fully comprehend it except through protracted meditation and exploration."

Kane noticed that Teresa, who didn't seem overly friendly to Brigid despite having helped turn her into a goddess, was listening with almost rapt intensity on her elfin, brown, not quite human features.

"You show great understanding, Lady Chalchihuitlicue," she said.

Brigid smiled thinly. "Thank you. But it seems to me you're still not telling us what we want to know, which is why you've kidnapped us, *what* you've done to us and why."

"Please." Teresa brushed back a spiral of black hair from her face. "It's…a most involved tale."

"Then you'd better move it along," Kane said, "before your captive deities run shy of patience."

Chapter 13

"Felicidad Mendoza did not die despite falling from the pyramid," the young hybrid woman explained. "She escaped, badly injured, to a cave in the mountains to the west."

"Where she found the weird Danaan toy you've got on ice in there," Kane said.

"Please, Lord Tonatiuh. Bear with us. She found something else there. She was imbued with the spirit of the goddess Coatlicue. Its powers, perhaps in concert with those of the mirror, healed her—"

Kane held up a hand. "Okay. I know I'm not supposed to interrupt. But you just lost me. You mean Quetzalcoatl wasn't the only Aztec god who was real? There really was a Tonatiuh? And Chalchihuitlicue? And why can I even pronounce that name?"

Teresa glanced at Dr. Marroquín. "Please, my lord," the elderly whitecoat said. "One's personality—yours, mine, anyone's—is among other things a self-perpetuating system of electromagnetic energy. Your thoughts, in particular, are electrochemical in nature."

He paused meaningfully. After a look to make sure the floor was clear, Ernesto, leaning forward like a dog on his leash, jumped in. "As we've said—as you've seen from the size and power of the *prana*-accumulation machines in this compound alone—this valley possesses unusual geomagnetic characteristics. Possibly unique in the world.

Historically the geomagnetic flux has been substantial. Over the last couple of centuries, since the nukecaust, it has been enormous. Certain strong personality patterns have, in effect, become recorded in the very rocks and fault lines of the valley. And the geomagnetic flux can energize them. Amplify them."

"I'm still unclear as to how all these deities can have been real," Brigid said. "We have learned that a great many legends are based on actual beings—often, of course, Annunaki, Tuatha de Danaan, and the hybrids who resulted from their having interbred to reinforce a truce. But there are a lot of gods in the Aztec pantheon alone. And there are a lot of pantheons. Are all the gods based on actual beings of greater than human powers?"

Both Teresa and Ernesto looked as if they were bursting to respond. But Marroquín wagged a languid hand. "The shortest answer is simply, not necessarily. For example, no evidence that there was ever a single individual upon whom Chalchihuitlicue, the lady of the jade skirt, was based has survived to the present day, keeping in mind that a terrific number of archaeological and anthropological records were lost in the nukecaust and its aftermath, like records of all kinds."

Brigid stared at him. Uncharacteristically sweat stood out on her high, smooth forehead. "Then…who's in my head? I have…thoughts that don't originate with me. They're in my mind but they're not *mine*."

Kane had seldom seen her so distressed. Something struck the back of his neck. He reached back and felt moisture. On his fingers was what appeared to be water. Looking up, he saw a round clear stalactite of water was stretching down from the acoustic tile overhead. "Looks as if your sprinkler system has a leak," he said.

Brigid had reasserted control, but it was clearly as brittle as rime frost. "I've just been describing classic symptoms of schizophrenia, of course," she said with a toss of her head. "Am I losing my mind?"

"Do you think so, O Lady Precious Green?" Marroquín asked. "Look down."

Droplets of water were falling from the ceiling now like light rain. As they struck the floor, they formed together in streams. The streams writhed toward Brigid's sandaled feet like transparent serpents, flowing together into a growing pool.

"You are doing that." What appeared to be sweat sheened his whole drawn elderly face now. "In reaction to your emotions you are drawing water from the atmosphere and from our very bodies. If you persist, you will begin to seriously dehydrate us. So I request that you stop."

She stared at him. "How?"

He smiled. "The power is yours, O Goddess. Command it."

She looked at him a moment more. Closed her eyes. Slightly frowned.

The rain from the ceiling stopped.

Dr. Marroquín took out a handkerchief and mopped his forehead beneath the unlikely line of his dark mound of hair. "Is anyone else thirsty?"

Teresa rose to draw water in paper cups from a cooler. "Thank you, my dear. Does that satisfy you, Lady Chalchihuitlicue, that you are not mad?"

Brigid smiled. "Not altogether. But if I am, it's one hell of a delusional system. The question remains, who's Chalchihuitlicue? And don't try telling me she's me."

"Thoughts are electric, O Lady," Ernesto said. "Emotions are electric. Belief is an emotion. Rituals involving thousands of celebrants were held for many years in worship of Chalchihuitlicue."

"Involving, let us be candid, the sacrifice of many thousands of human lives," Dr. Marroquín said. "As indeed the worship of all the gods has, save Quetzalcoatl."

Brigid's green eyes were wide pools of confusion and near panic. But her years of archivist training and self-discipline told. Kane could see her commanding herself to be calm, as she had commanded the waters to cease flowing to her.

"So the Chalchihuitlicue persona is an artifact," she said. "It has no necessary connection to any real person. It is in effect a recording of the fervent beliefs of thousands, over years."

Ernesto nodded. "Strengthened, of course, by the release of the life energies of many humans. Victims."

Brigid stared at him as if he'd turned into Tlaltecuhtli the frog monster. "And this is what you've turned me into?"

Kane rubbed his chin. The skin to either side of the vertical-bar goatee he had been left with had begun to bristle. He felt a curious fatigue beginning to creep over him.

"The key question then becomes, can you reverse the process?" he said. "For your sakes, the answer had better be yes."

Ernesto blinked at him in incomprehension. "But, Lord Tonatiuh! Think of what we've given you! The power— we have no idea where its limits lie. You are embarked upon an incredible voyage of exploration."

"Which we neglected to volunteer for," Kane said dryly.

"Which brings me to the question of why our friends have not yet attempted to mount a rescue," Brigid said.

Dr. Marroquín smiled. "Because, of course, they are uncertain of your present location. When we summoned the chosen vessel of the Lord Tonatiuh's persona to us, we drew him to a room shielded from electromagnetic emanations."

"As you no doubt understand," Teresa said, "both *prana* and the self-perpetuating system that constitutes the personality, while they have an electromagnetic component, are essentially quantum-level phenomena."

Brigid nodded. "I understand that when we jump using matter-transmission gateways we are not broadcast like a radio signal, but rather translocate directly without crossing the intervening physical distance, like an electron jumping between energy levels."

"The phenomenon the ancients called 'tunneling,'" said Ernesto, eyes agleam with geek eagerness, "to avoid the embarrassment of having to call it what it was—teleportation."

"But shoveling aside all this happy whitecoat horseshit for just a moment here," Kane said brusquely, "Brigid materialized next to my bed, or wherever you keep me when I go out. Not inside your lead vault or whatever the hell it was you used to block my transponder signal."

"To be sure. But after so stunning Brigid—and once again, I pray, permit me to express my sincerest regrets for such impertinence—we promptly conveyed her to an EM-emission sealed chamber to deactivate her biological transmitter," the doctor said. "We also relieved you both of your communicators. Which, like your other personal effects, are being safeguarded for you."

"How about returning them to us right about now," Kane said, "and turning us loose to go home, before I fire up my solar flare dingus and start burning through walls—and any other extraneous material that happens to get in our way—until we release ourselves on our own recognizance?"

The three locals exchanged a look of trepidation. "You cannot, Lord Tonatiuh," Teresa said in a measured voice.

"A barrier surrounds the valley," Ernesto said. "Erected jointly by the gods and the...others after reconstruction. It is a standing wave of probability. Anything physical that comes in contact with the barrier has, not chaos, but true randomness introduced into each and every atom of its being."

Kane frowned, not following. "Causing immediate disintegration," Brigid said.

"I'm sure there are ways out of this valley," Kane said. "Whoever built this magical force field no doubt left a few back doors and secret exits—anybody would do that. Plus I do happen to remember that there were two operational mat-trans gateways in the valley at one time. Including one in Mexico City that's not in the Cerberus database, much to Dr. Lakesh's distress. So I bet we can leave."

Ernesto and Teresa began to babble at once. They were speaking, as they had throughout most of the conversation, in English, a fact Kane wondered about but lacked the interest to pursue, since abstract information of that sort didn't seem germane to getting his and Baptiste's asses out of whatever bizarre crack they had found their way into this time. In fact, what with the other personalities jostling around inside him, including the dead red-bearded Spaniard with a taste for mass human barbecues and a nonexistent but still vocal solar deity, he felt he had even less appetite for abstraction than he had when he was plain, uncomplicated, blunt-force Kane.

Again Marroquín brought order from chaos with the wave of a slim brown hand. "You must not leave, my lord and lady," he said flatly. "For you will surely die."

"Gods die?" Brigid asked. "I thought immortality was part of the package."

"As indeed it is," Marroquín said. "As we have told you, the personality patterns for our gods persist indefinitely, insofar as we know. Their fleshy envelopes, however, do not. Which is why Lord Quetzalcoatl is stricken, and why we need your assistance desperately enough to, yes, kidnap and transform you, mentally and spiritually, as well as physically, without seeking your permission."

"Now tell us why leaving here would chill us," Kane said. "Preferably in words of one syllable or less that won't confuse and therefore piss off a real impatient Sun god."

Teresa had regained control of herself, although spots of color glowed high on her thin cheeks. "As Dr. Marroquín says, we have transformed your bodies, as well as your minds. That includes certain alterations to your metabolism. Your energy economy has changed, among other things, and markedly. It operates on an altogether higher level than any unmodified human's. Unfortunately—" her elfin face writhed with what seemed genuine concern, possibly not just for her, her compatriots and their cause "—we lack the skill to modify your bodies to support your accelerated metabolisms by themselves. Only artificial, outside support can sustain you. You and the jade skirt lady are unquestionably resourceful enough to find ways out of the valley and even back home. But then your bodies would—would eat you up from inside. Nor could the technological wizardry of your Dr. Lakesh save you. Not even the secret laboratories of the barons possess the means to keep you alive."

Kane looked at her hard. He had a feeling that they hadn't even glimpsed the iceberg to the waterline here. There was the whole issue of how these people knew so much about the baronies, yet had not been caught up in the reunification, the megalomaniac power grab by the coterie of hybrids and human traitors that masked itself behind the title Archon Directorate. Nor what the hell an obvious hybrid was doing here in the first place…

He noticed Baptiste was staring at Dr. Marroquín with a peculiar intensity in her emerald-green eyes. The whitecoat's smile had become somewhat glassy, and he swayed slightly in his seat. If looks could kill…he thought.

Then he realized that was precisely what was happening.

Or *supposed* to happen.

Brigid shook her head, as if flinging water droplets from her hair. And as a matter of fact did; Kane felt a droplet splash his cheek.

"I was chief artificer and theorist to the gods, Lady Chalchihuitlicue," the whitecoat said quietly. "Even to Lord Quetzalcoatl before his exile a generation ago. Second only to the god Tezcatlipoca himself was my lore— and I haven't exactly lost ground, since covertly stealing the mirror and fleeing to this district two years ago. So I beg your understanding that I did not fail to discern means of countering at least some of the divine powers—such as your attempt to stop my heart's beating with your gaze."

"I allowed my anger to overcome me," Brigid admitted. She seemed more puzzled than anything else. "That's not exactly like me…since from what you tell us, and I am forced at least for the time being to accept, killing you would do us no good. I was, frankly, overcome by a desire to slay you…for your impertinence."

"You realize that last sentence didn't come out in English, Baptiste," said Kane in a voice that sounded as if he'd been gargling lye, "but some weird language I don't even know the name of. Which doesn't freak me out half so bad as the fact I understood every freakin' word of it."

"It is the knowledge that the god patterns have brought

to your minds, my friends," Dr. Marroquín said. "As your response, milady, was not that of the supremely disciplined Senior Archivist Brigid Baptiste, but rather that of Chalchi-huitlicue, the lady of the jade skirt, a goddess, as is the case with most of our quaint deities, of death and life—and one who, despite a distinctly nurturing nature, has little patience with impertinence."

"Why hasn't Tezcatlipoca noticed you stole his namesake?" Brigid asked.

Marroquín grinned. It took years off him. "I left a cunning counterfeit. Almost as good as the real thing in many ways. And Tezcatlipoca pays little attention to it these days. He has other experimental devices to attract his interest."

"Let's quit walking all around the muzzle and get down to the trigger of the blaster, here," Kane said. "What do you want from us?"

"The power of the sibling gods Huitzilopochtli and Tezcatlipoca grows by bounds, as does their lust for ever more. And for blood—human blood, shed at massive rituals of sacrifice such as the one you saw on television, Lord."

Brigid said, "Television?"

"There's nothing good on here, either," Kane said, "just like the prenukecaust days back home. Trust me."

"It is possible that their lust and their ambition threatens your friends north of what once was the border, and indeed the whole world," the whitecoat went on calmly. "I would lie—and I think you would perceive it—if I stated that as surety. We really don't know what powers if any may be transferable beyond the unique geomagnetic environment of this valley. But the Smoking Mirror and Hummingbird upon the Left are using their technology and their blood rituals to strengthen their powers and those of the gods who follow them. First they will crush opposition within Tenochtitlán, then throughout the valley, and then—who knows? The divine mind is not notable for its ready acceptance of limitations."

"What's in it," Brigid asked, "for us? As individuals."

Kane looked at her in surprise. "Why Baptiste, that's real practical of you. We'll make a Magistrate of you yet!"

"Strike," Brigid said with waist-deep irony. "That's an even less attractive proposition than what these...people...have done to us."

"To answer the lady's very pertinent question," Dr. Marroquín said, "I will first overlook what we have done for you already, which is imbue you with abilities of amazing scope and potency. Understandably, you are still overwhelmed by the undeniable fact that our doing so without your leave was a violation. But laying that aside, if you help us defeat the monstrous plans of Huitzilopochtli and Tezcatlipoca, and break the back of their domination, we will give you—whatever lies in our power to provide, to your command and desire."

"You want a couple of neophyte gods to destroy the greatest, most powerful and presumably most experienced of gods?" Brigid asked. "Would that sum it up?"

Teresa shook her head, causing her little spring-shaped spit curls to lash her cheeks like the balls of a Chinese prayer drum. "Not destroy! Weaken. Help us restore Lord Quetzalcoatl to his rightful place and return balance to our valley!"

"Nor alone," Ernesto said. "There are other gods to help. Not all of the deities who rule the various *colonias* are enthralled with what the two are doing."

Brigid sat back into her cushion of the sofa, shaking her head. "This is far too confusing. And all these other people yammering at once in my head are not helping my comprehension."

"We can get the ins and outs of local politics doled out to us in reasonable doses," Kane said. He stretched out his muscle-twined arms, interlaced his fingers with the backs of his hand to him, cracked his knuckles.

"Going up against actual gods," he said deliberately, "using the powers of gods—even half-trained, beginner-type gods…forgive it, Baptiste. But this sounds kind of like fun."

A voice broke suddenly from an intercom speaker in the wall Kane and Brigid hadn't realized was there. "Dr. Marroquín! Please, you must dispatch the lord and lady at once. A terrible *cipactli* has emerged from the lake and is devouring shoppers at the Colhuacan Mall!"

"Monsters at the mall?" Brigid asked in disbelief.

Kane grinned. "Show time," he said.

Chapter 14

"Monsters at the mall?" Brigid asked again. "What's wrong with this picture?"

Kane didn't answer at once. He could barely hear her over the noise of the helicopter's engine and rotors. Besides, he was preoccupied.

The prospect of going *mano a mano*, or whatever the appropriate appendages, with a surly forty-foot-long crocodile fish that had decided to turn of all things a prenukecaust-style shopping mall into its personal people-eating food court could do that to a man. Or even god.

The chopper was a trim little blue-and-white job. A stolid, stocky woman with receding forehead and jaw, dark brown skin and raven's-wing hair tied in a bun beneath her headset was at the controls. "For a rebel faction," Kane shouted to Brigid, "these people sure don't act concerned about aerial interdiction."

Brigid nodded her head at the side window. It was something of a production, since she wore an unlikely contrivance of gold, jade and green quetzal feathers. It was her equivalent of what Kane thought of as his own god hat. She also wore a skirt of leather tabs with jade plates fixed on them, and a scrap of muslin tied around her generous breasts. The outfit was supposed to be topless, an honor that Brigid had declined, on the basis it would make her feel too vulnerable to go into battle with her boobs flopping around in the open—as she had actually put it, to Kane's surprise.

While the strip provided at least psychic shoring-up to the sometime archivist, it did nothing to conceal the fact that her nipples were standing up in excitement. Kane studiously kept his gaze from falling on them, even in passing; they were nothing to him, after all. She was just a comrade riding to battle with him.

"We have an escort," she shouted back. "They have their own local equivalent of Deathbirds, it seems. They seem to be based on the Aérospatiale Gazelle instead of the AH-64, the way ours are back home."

He leaned forward to peer out. Sure enough, he saw the distinct dragonfly shape of a helicopter gunship off their own port stub wing, abristle with chin gun and what looked a lot like IR-seeker-head missiles.

"Why don't they load it out with Shrikes or the local equivalent," Kane wanted to know, "and take out this crocofish from above with them and the chain gun?"

Brigid looked at him in disgust. "Because they want their new gods to strut their stuff for the benefit of the public. This is about politics, you know."

"Yeah." He settled back grumpily in his seat, as far as the polycarbonate backplate would let him. "Real ace on the line."

The city unfolding below was jarring to both of them. They had never known a free, open city, a sprawling *outdoor* urb brawling with life and commerce, relative health and prosperity, and Tenochtitlán was all these things. The ville in which both had been born, raised and spent their adult lives was an artificial microenvironment, towers constrained within walls. Aside from a quickie time jaunt to old New York and a few brief semihallucinatory interludes in other casements, the only referents they had for a phenomenon like Tenochtitlán were vids and images from a time that was ashes and slag over two centuries before either was conceived.

The cityscape beneath them was a strange mix of ancient myth and steaming-edge technology: steel-and-glass boxes next to stone step pyramids, surrounded by lush vegetation.

"There's the lake," Brigid said, pointing. It was a kidney-shaped patch of water glittering in waning sunlight and the lights springing on in response to day's end. It was one of a handful of irruptions of the great Lake Texcoco, which in the wake of the nukecaust had grown to cover an area greater than the present city.

"Ernesto told me it subsided," Brigid shouted. "The water table either sank or the land rose—nobody seems to know. But apparently there's now an underground lake not much smaller than what existed a century ago."

Kane grunted.

"Apparently none of the other personality patterns you're playing host to is exactly loquacious, Kane," his flame-haired comrade pointed out.

"None of us has anything much to say just now," he said, "although I guess I can now say nothing in three different languages."

He leaned his head as close to the window on his side as his helmet would permit. He could have got closer by taking off the contrivance, of course. But it was such a pain in the ass to put back on. He wasn't sure what use it might be against a giant mythical lake monster. Then again, it afforded more protection than his skull and its covering of dark longish hair.

"How the hell did they manage to build all this in less than a century?" he demanded.

"Most of the buildings in most of the cities in North America were less than a century old when the balloon went up," Brigid pointed out. "I'd guess it's actually easier and cheaper in resources to build a city on top of a bunch of rubble than to replace an already built-up urban area piecemeal, which is what happened in places like New York and Chicago."

"But these people had just undergone a brand-fresh round of war and natural disaster," Kane pointed out. "I don't know if it's possible to start out from less than zero, but if anybody can, they did."

"Is it really that much different from what preceded the building of the nine baronies?"

She had a strange expression on her face, a face he had to admit to himself, once again, that was more than handsome. "You think there might be some connection?"

"What do you think, Kane? We're shown an artifact of near magical capabilities, not just Danaan tech but very possibly a blending of Danaan art with Annunaki craft. What do we call a blend of Annunaki and Danaan? And there's the girl. She's the most human hybrid I've seen— but she's a hybrid without question."

Kane glanced forward. Even if the pilot could overhear them, he had no idea whether she understood English. Plenty of people seemed to around here. But he decided he didn't give a shit if he were overheard or not. Who was the god here, anyway?

"She's Mexican," he said. "Plainly as she's a hybrid. The Archon Directorate uses nonwhites, sure—nobody'd accuse Grant of being a paleface—but then, we're all just animals to them, all mud people. You get up to the highest levels, the ones hiding behind the Archon label, they're all lily-white and bone racists, humans and hybrids alike."

She shrugged. "Another mystery."

"I hate mysteries."

She laughed. "These last couple of years must have been hell on you."

"You have to ask?" He laughed. Then he leaned forward, suddenly intent.

"Speaking of Grant," he said, "how is he?"

"Fusing-out with worry," she admitted. "He ran off to New Edo to sulk in Shizuka's tent when Lakesh wouldn't let him fly off blind in a Manta to look for you."

"Good old Grant."

"He'll come for us, you know," Brigid said.

"That's what I'm afraid of."

Brigid pointed. "There's our *cipactli.*"

As the chopper banked into a turn, evidently preparing to land and disgorge its two-deity strike force, Kane moved to Brigid's side to peer out. He tried not to be aware of the amount of bare pale skin her outfit showed or the clean, unmistakably feminine scent of her.

A hundred yards below, the mall lay alongside the smallish extrusion of the ancient and mighty Texcoco. In fact it straddled the lake by means of an arching footbridge. Which had collapsed, no doubt under the weight of the giant scaly unlikelihood now hauling its bulk up onto a promenade which ran along the waterside by means of clublike finlike forelimbs. Or limblike forefins. Its jaws, long as a tall man and chock full of long spikelike teeth, menaced a young mother trying to dislodge her child from beneath the disk top of what looked like a table cast as one piece of concrete. The child was, not unreasonably, clinging to the central pedestal for dear life and bawling its head off. Meanwhile sec men in tan-and-green uniforms so ordinary they seemed quite extraordinary in these peculiar surroundings fired bravely if unwisely at the monster with revolvers. It ignored them.

Whether it heard the chopper or felt its down blast, it didn't ignore the whirly-wag. It raised its snout to the sky and emitted a bellow that seemed to shake the fragile skycraft.

"You have *got* to be fucking kidding me," Kane said.

Brigid swallowed and her eyes stood out very slightly from the sockets, although otherwise she maintained iron control over her expression. "How, exactly," she asked in a normal-sounding voice, "am I supposed to fight something like that?"

"Improvise," Kane said. "You're good at that."

He patted her lightly on the shoulder. "Think of it as on-the-job training in goddesshood."

She shot him an evil glare as the helicopter's engine noise changed pitch to drop the craft into the ground effect. He remembered then that her looks really *could* kill, and glanced hurriedly away.

Gods or not, the pilot did not actually land the helicopter to let them off. She brought it down to hover barely a hand span off the pavement of the promenade, leaving Kane and Brigid to jump down, clutching their unlikely headdresses in place against the rotor wash. It was quite a skillful maneuver, really, although Kane was little disposed to appreciate it, being dumped like a grunt in a rice paddy in a vid of an ancient Asian war. Then the helicopter flew away. Its gunship escort remained, but orbiting a thousand feet overhead. Obviously to forestall any attempt by the forces that controlled the city to interfere—and just as obviously leaving the god Tonatiuh and the goddess-in-training Chalchihuitlicue to deal with the beast.

"Look," Kane said, drawing his sword and using it to point. There was a slight concrete embankment here, shore-

ward of the promenade, and above that the terrace of a
restaurant, currently untenanted. Beyond that were the windows, or glass walls, of the restaurant itself, which were
crowded with diners dressed mostly like what the outsiders
thought of as normal people. "They're cheering for us."

"The more fools they," Brigid said. "Shouldn't I at least
have a weapon?"

The monster had noticed them now. The giant buzzing
dragonfly that was the chopper had definitely drawn its
gaze. And it seemed more interested in these new arrivals
than in the woman trying to pry loose her kid. As it turned
its unlovely head toward Kane and Brigid, a trio of intrepid
sec men ran out, grabbed the mom, yanked loose the kid
and ran them all back to at least relative and temporary
safety.

The crowd went wild.

"Use your godlike powers," Kane said, testing the heft
of his obsidian-bladed sword in his hand. It felt, well, in-
adequate. Indeed, not even the familiar, reassuring burden
on his right forearm was much reassurance.

"I'm a water goddess!" Brigid all but wailed. "And
that's a *fish!*"

"Do I know? Give it your mean look."

"I'm trying," Brigid said. "Meanwhile you'd better do
something, because it's headed this way."

It was. Lumbering toward them, land-swimming with
its blunt forelimbs, hauling more and more of its length out
of the water—an apparently endless process. It was no
more than thirty yards from them. They could smell an
overpowering reek of fish, and stale water, and other elements even less pleasant. Liquid drooled from its toothy
lower jaw, possibly monster saliva, but tinged pink in a horribly suggestive way.

It roared. Brigid winced and gagged at the fetor of its breath. It was almost as good as CS gas.

Kane raised the shield strapped to his left arm, which seemed, if anything, less useful than his sword. He sought for the bright lines, within him and around him.

He heard a leathery scuffling as the *cipactli* dragged its tons of bulk toward them, and a slogging of water as more of the thing emerged. It wasn't making it easy to concentrate.

"Kane," Brigid said, "do something."

She made no move to get behind him, he noticed. It was either as brave a thing as he'd encountered or simply the fatalistic realization that those evil jaws were more than capacious enough to accommodate two gods at once.

There. The fire of the Sun. Fuelled by pure adrenaline. He tapped into the lines of flaming force that suddenly glowed alive in his mind like grabbing on to a power line. And to about the same effect: a jolt of incredible searing energy blasted through both pain and ecstasy at once.

Blinding yellow radiance surrounded his sword as he sprang toward the monster. It moved at the speed of light. The monster didn't—but it still wasn't there when the hell-beam struck. Instead it had hurled its enormous mass back into the water with an even more enormous splash.

"Impressive power, there, Tonatiuh," Brigid admitted, staring at the two-yard crater with walls of white-glowing glass the blast had left in the pavement.

"Sumbitch moved," said Kane, whose eyes were wider than hers. "Did you see that? How did that sucker dodge light?"

"It probably sensed the potential energy building up inside you or around you," Brigid said, all archivist again, for at least a moment. "It may have an electrical sense, like a great white shark. But then, even I could feel it, and I don't. Unless Chalchihuitlicue does."

Kane stood staring at the murky green roil with its scum of brownish bubbles where the monster had disappeared.

"That's some nasty-looking water they got in this lake," he said, "but look at what lives in it." He still felt the fire dancing in his nerve ends, saw it shimmering the air around him.

"Maybe we scared it away," he said.

"Dream on," Brigid said. "If we were that lucky, would we be here?"

"I'm glad you're here, anyway," he said. "Thanks for coming."

She met his eye. "Anytime," she said.

The lake erupted with hurtling death.

Chapter 15

Kane grabbed Brigid and dived with her to the side. The pavement buckled and crunched as tons of flesh and water slammed down upon it. The ground was still shaking when the two landed heavily scant yards from where the horror had struck. A wave rolled over them.

The monster reared back and roared. The flame blast had scared hell out of it. That made it mad. Before it had just been hungry. Now it was hungry *and* pissed.

Its head turned from side to side. A big round mud-colored eye rolled angrily in its standout socket. Kane was reminded of alligator gar in lakes and rivers up north. They looked something like this, and Outlands rumor had it that some of them had gone mutie, were upward of twenty feet long and nowhere near averse to making a meal of human meat. If you could trust what dregs said, which as a rule you couldn't. But this thing wasn't quite like that—more croc and less fish, as it were.

These thoughts flashed through Kane's head as he scrambled back to put some maneuvering room between him and all those teeth, each of which was as long as his hand from wrist to fingertips and a good deal sharper. He would have dragged Brigid with him except she moved even quicker than he did, springing up onto a low wall and crouching there, ready.

The head turned toward him. He reached inside, found the glowing lines of force. He aimed the sword.

"All right, buddy, your head's coming right off."

And then…nothing happened.

Lots of nothing happened. In point of fact, way too much nothing happened.

Even the monster seemed to be waiting for something to happen. It might have been smarter than it looked, which wouldn't have been hard; it looked to have a brainbox the size of a beer keg, anyway. Or mebbe it was another human in disguise, somehow, like that frog monster. In any case it hesitated, head kind of pulled up and back, staring at him with its big reptile eyes.

He aimed the sword again, willed the very flame of the Sun to lash forth and incinerate the ugly thing. But no incineration happened.

"Shit!" he exclaimed. "The water's doused the nuke-raddled flare!"

The jaws gaped. A wall of practically visible stench struck him, staggered him. All those teeth homed right on him.

A large wave hit the thing upside the head and rolled it right over on its back. Oddly enough, the wave moved right along parallel to the shoreline, unlike every other wave of Kane's experience. Which wasn't that extensive, but it still didn't seem natural.

The monster wallowed and waggled its limbs in the air. Its bulgy belly was an unhealthy white, shading into an even less appealing yellow at the sides before becoming the mottled green and brown of its sides and back. It got its tail against the bottom, braced and heaved to right itself.

Another big old wave smacked it back down.

"Kane!" shouted Brigid. Her voice was strained. "Do something! I'm running short of ideas here. And energy!"

"You're doing fine," he said, as a third wave sloshed down upon the prostrate saurian.

He took quick stock of the situation. Which was all it needed: it sucked. He was wet, and the splendid feathers of his helmet hung like wilted weeds above his brow. He was still sopping wet and his loincloth was all squelchy. He knew without trying again that neither his solar flare nor his shield of the Sun would be worth a damn until he got dried out. He did know enough science to know that what made the sun hot wasn't fire at all, but fusion, and that all the glowing gas he was tossing around was basically plasma—probably superheated air. But fire or not, his power didn't seem to like the wet.

But his sword was still nice and sharp. Sharper than any steel alloy, any kind of metal at all, they said.

So he gathered himself and jumped on the monster's belly.

"Kane!" he heard Brigid scream. He was committed now. He lay upon a bellowing flesh earthquake in a sort of all-fours sprawl, halfway between crawling and lying flat on his face. The monster, preoccupied by its predicament, gave no sign of noticing his arrival.

Until he raised his sword and chopped it down into the pale leathery skin. He had a vague apprehension that it might have an armor of thick scutes. But no, the belly scales seemed fairly fine. And the black-glass blade sliced right through them, evoking a fire-hose stream of thick blood, a red so deep it was almost black in the twilight, that sprayed over the right-hand side of his breastplate.

He didn't get to enjoy the sensation long. The creature spasmed, bending itself backward and thrusting its injured underside high. Kane went straight up in the air about ten feet and fell straight back down.

Fortunately, perhaps, the *cipactli* was still there. He

landed just inboard of the creature's left forelimb, which was flailing wildly. Kane managed to wrap the forearm that had the shield strapped to it around the member's base and hung on grimly. He had a notion of trying to hack through the monster's throat. However, he had fallen with his head toward the tail. He hacked backward along his bare right leg, mincing the skin between the forelegs and hoping against hope he wouldn't sink the unnaturally sharp blade in his own thigh.

As his mad leap onto the belly of the beast demonstrated, heightened strength and speed had accompanied his elevation to godhood. He was leaving marks for certain. The problem was not knowing whether he was doing anything more than giving the creature a picturesque set of scars to impress its *cipactli* offspring with in future years.

It wasn't a happy *cipactli,* though. It was thrashing and roaring with unbelievable enthusiasm. The situation was clearly unstable.

Abruptly it broke. The monster got its long muscular tail in the proper position and rolled itself over. Luckily for Kane it rolled left over right. The very heaving impulse that started it rolling broke his grip on the forelimb and tossed him away.

Not far enough. With little time to react, he landed hard and badly. His shield was torn off his arm, and the air was knocked clean out of him.

Kane tried to spring up and dart away as the monster landed right side up right next to him. He discovered then that even gods had to breathe. He was unable to move. He could only lie there and try to suck some air into his lungs.

Something caught hold of his shoulder. It was Brigid, trying to drag him to safety. He finally got wrapped around enough air to wheeze, "Get back!" She ignored him.

Then she looked up, and her eyes got wide. Kane followed her gaze.

The monster's head loomed above them like a misshapen planet. Its huge eyes gazed on them without friendliness.

The vast jaws opened.

"Fuck this!" Kane shouted. He dropped the sword to hang on its lanyard and clenched his right hand into a half fist.

The power holster slammed his Sin Eater into his waiting hand. The blaster did some roaring of its own. A cone of flame flashed right into the gaping blood-colored maw. Blood flew in a black cloudburst as the soft tissue of palate and tongue and gullet was violated by high-velocity 9 mm jacketed hollowpoints. Kane was hoping to hammer into the brain with his snarling, ripping stream of bullets. Barring that, he hoped to get some serious internal bleeding going, either make the thing bleed out or choke it on its own blood.

Barring *that*—since he was soaked all over again by the creature lunging for him—he should get ready to die a lot. Better luck next incarnation, Tonatiuh.

The jaws snapped shut and the head jerked back and up, away from Kane. The monster had figured out it could stop the agony within its soft mouth and throat by closing up tight. Kane pulsed tribursts into the exposed throat, already bleeding dark sheets from the wounds made by his sword, and hoped like hell it wouldn't also occur to the thing it could end the agony for good and all by just slamming its head down real hard on this small offending primate.

Suddenly a wave reached up out of the lake, bore up the prostrate Kane and dumped him none too ceremoniously above the low wall on the terrace of the restaurant. As he was choking and spitting out water—really foul water, and remembering the televised rites on the step pyramid he didn't for a moment want to think about what these people *put* in it—he saw what seemed to be serpents of water reach up from the lake, twine about the giant beast like tentacles. Smaller tendrils of water, green with algae, drove themselves down distended nostrils frilled with oddly delicate pale violet membranes.

The *cipactli* shook its head frantically. Kane noted that it had no gills. Not a fish, he guessed, but some kind of fishy amphibian.

Something that needed air to breathe. Which it wasn't getting.

The mouth opened in a wheezing roar. Kane thought he heard a note of terror in it. Maybe that was wishful thinking. He popped the depleted magazine from the Sin Eater and replaced it with a fresh one from a pouch by his belt. Old habits died hard, and he gradually seemed to be becoming more and more Kane and less of those other guys as time passed.

Rolling to his side and bracing his firing hand on the low terrace wall, Kane got ready to do some more blasting should that prove necessary. It wasn't. A giant trunk-sized tentacle of water thrust its way into the open maw, down the torn and bleeding throat. The *cipactli* tried to shut its mouth but the force of the water was great, and the little water snakes were still sticking like fingers down its nostrils, blocking its air.

It tried to swim backward then with frantic limbs, into the enfolding safety of the green depths. But the water rejected it, buffeting it with waves, denying it sanctuary.

Writhing, it rolled onto its back. On its back it convulsed mightily three times as if struck by an electric current, while its belly bulged. Convulsing, it roared, despite the water's unrelenting pressure, sending a geyser toward the early glimmering stars.

One final mighty heave accompanied the roar. Then it settled back with a limp and final thump, the great head lolled to the side, the saucer eyes began to glaze and blood-tinted water began to drool from its jaws and nostrils.

A crowd had gathered. Not just behind the restaurant glass but along the promenade, along a second-story gallery inside the mall, even, Kane could see through the dusk, on the opposite shore of the little lake. They cheered madly, and as they did, Kane heard a chant begin: "Hail, Lord Tonatiuh! Hail, Lady Precious Green! Slayers of the water monster, deliverers from evil!"

That cagey old bastard Marroquín must have shills planted, he thought with admiration. His stomach and mind began to whirl and a blackness began to gather around that had nothing to do with the Sun, his totem, vanishing like a diminishing chord of music behind the jagged wall of western mountains, leaving a last trail like blood upon indigo waters. He's way too canny for a whitecoat…just like Lakesh….

The lights went out.

"THEY DEFEATED our water monster," Tezcatlipoca said.

He hung back in the darkness of Huitzilopochtli's private comtemplatorium, there beneath the apex of the pyramid, with the lights of the city outside and the sullen glow of the volcanoes fringing the valley providing the sole illumination, as if expecting his brother god to explode in anger. It was known to happen. But Huitzilopochtli merely raised a brow beneath his circlet of gold.

"It was just a mutant beast from Daraul's vats, after all, not a god. But how? I thought Tonatiuh would have a hard time singeing its waterlogged hide, solar flare or not."

"The bastards have raised themselves a Chalchihuitlicue," the smaller, more wiry deity declared, though without heat. "Together they slew the beast."

"Fire and water, then." Huitzilopochtli nodded. "Clever. Do I detect the hand of your erstwhile servant Marroquín in all this?"

"I think you do, Lord."

"You should have taken his heart when you had the chance."

"Undoubtedly." The trickster god grinned a lopsided grin that yielded nothing in savagery to even the predominant god of war. "It will make the smoke of his burning heart taste sweeter when it reaches my nostrils."

"Well," Huitzilopochtli said, shifting on the gel-cushioned throne, "this doesn't really affect our plans, does it?"

Tezcatlipoca smiled. "Hardly, Lord Hummingbird. Our opposition is proving more formidable than anticipated, to be sure. But what of that? Even if they have smuggled the plumed one back to Tenochtitlán, they can hardly hope to withstand the assembled might of Talocan."

"Indeed," said Huitzilopochtli. "Meanwhile summon up Paynal my messenger from the midst of whatever gender of adolescents he disports himself with this night, and have the two-faced one hold a press conference."

Tezcatlipoca steepled lean, competent hands and bowed, offering a grin that somehow took the submission out of agreeing to follow a command from what was nominally his co-equal god and ruler temporal.

"Wise is Huitzilopochtli," he said in a tone that skirted mockery without coming quite close enough to elicit an eruption from a temper famously as touchy as Popocatepetl's. "If any can spin the tale to malign the Sun god and the feathered-serpent faction while heaping praise upon their public-spirited deed, it is he."

"It better be," Huitzilopochtli said, transferring his grumpiness from his brother deity to his absent herald. "Otherwise I'll flay him as offering to Xipe Totec and have you make me a new Paynal."

Tezcatlipoca took his respectful leave and withdrew. Huitzilopochtli sat watching the hole he'd left in the gloom, and wondered whether his brother's *nagual,* his tutelary spirit, ought not be the coyote instead of the jaguar.

"JUMP ON THE MONSTER and hit it with your stick?" Brigid raged. "I thought I was giving you time to come up with a *good* idea!"

Such was Kane's welcome back to the world of consciousness. His head was on Brigid's thigh, and her skin was warm beneath his nape. He was vaguely aware of a circle of onlookers keeping a respectful distance under the shepherding of those uniformed sec men. As he stirred, they raised a fresh round of cheers.

"It was the best I could do on the spur of the moment," he said. "Hell, it worked."

"Sort of. And largely by accident."

"Hey, this is combat, lady. There's no such things as style points."

Brigid sighed. He made himself try to think about something other than the way her breasts rode up and down within the wisp of linen she'd wound around them. His near brush with mortality seemed to be having a marked effect on him. Affirmation-of-life kind of thing.

Catch a grip, he told himself sternly. It's Baptiste, for god's sake. Which god, he decided not to specify.

"I'm glad you made it," the woman said. Although he still felt, and no doubt looked, like a half-drowned cockatoo, she was crisp and dry as if she'd just stood up from a chair inside the lakeside restaurant and come to see what all the commotion was about. Evidently possessing dominion over the waters meant you were able to repel them. "I was concerned there after you blacked out."

"I'm back now. And thanks, Baptiste. Pretty timely intervention there. And who else would've thought about trying to drown a water monster?"

She smiled thinly. "It wasn't drowning, exactly. More a rupturing of internal organs."

A stir of motion not far away drew his eye. With effort he raised his head. Looked. Saw. Goggled.

"Tell me I'm hallucinating, Baptiste."

She glanced that way. "The half-naked woman with the head of a giant rattlesnake dancing over there and playing a drum? Sorry, Kane, she's real. At least as real as Tonatiuh and Chalchihuitlicue, and I'd hate to tell you what kind of hide it is she's using for a drumhead. I heard the spectators acclaim her when she turned up. Seems she's one Cihuacoatl—"

"Snake woman? Jesus."

"Or Rattlesnake Mother. She's patroness of Colhuacan, which is the district we're in. I think that means she's a cross between goddess and ward boss. She turned up to dance a dance of thanksgiving to us for stopping her subjects being devoured. Smile and wave," Brigid ordered.

Kane did, weakly. "I hate this place." He let his head rest back on Brigid's bare thigh.

Brigid shrugged. "Yes. Well." She nodded at the grateful deity. "And she's one of the good guys—"

"How do you know all this?"

"That premission briefing Marroquín and his elves gave us. That you didn't pay attention to."

A faint beating came to his ears. "Our work here seems

to be done," Brigid said, shifting her weight beneath him, "and the choppers really are on their way. So I guess you better get on your feet and make nice for our adoring fans."

He felt his brow furrow. "Are you buying into this whole god racket, Baptiste?"

"For now," she said, "I don't see we have much choice. Come on. I'll help you up."

He let her.

"I DON'T TRUST that one," a voice said from the darkness behind the throne.

"Then why did you make him a god?" Huitzilopochtli asked without turning.

The goddess Coatlicue stepped into the light, such as it was. She was a woman of average stature for denizens of the valley, which meant Huitzilopochtli all but dwarfed her even seated. Barefoot, nude but for her skirt of golden tablets beaten in the shapes of snakes and a necklace hung with a gold skull effigy around her throat, she managed the trick of being at once trim and voluptuous. Her skin was cinnamon, the nipples of her full and shapely breasts like chocolate, her hair a fall as of the finest copper wire, dark red, gleaming like soft metal in the lantern light. It was the red hair of the proud Indians of the ancient city-state of Tlaxcala, which long predated the arrival of the pale-skinned Europeans.

She was quite well preserved, for a century and a quarter or so.

"Because he was too gifted to kill," she said, "but too dangerous to be allowed to live, otherwise. I was not idle in the house of that gross lump my father. Growing up, I read the history of Porfírio Diaz and his earlier *científicos*. So I chose to co-opt the boy. But the price was high, and I have not failed to regret paying it, sometimes."

"Then, too," the war god said with a grin, "you wanted someone you could play off against me, Mother dear."

"That, too," she said.

She moved to his side. "Besides, the others came, the strange ones from *el Norte* with their gifts of inhuman science. I had to rush you both. Something was needed to counterbalance their might. Or else for all their fine words, they would have subjugated us, made us colonials, menials, as those from the north always have."

"But what of the third you saddled us with? Quetzalcoatl?"

She shrugged. "One gives, one must take. One takes, one must give. In making one of them a god, as well, I proved to them your might, as well as my own. And indeed I co-opted him, bound his interest to ours, for he was no longer one of his own strange half-human folk, but a god. One of us."

"Whom in the fullness of time you helped us dispose of."

She smiled. "In the fullness of time, as you say, my lord son."

"And did you miscalculate when you forbade us to kill him, but allowed him to flee into exile in Teotihuacan instead? So that now, rough beast that he is, he comes slouching back to Tenochtitlán seeking rebirth into the full power and glory of a paramount god, one of the trinity?"

She shrugged a delicate shrug. "It was all so long ago. Perhaps it was all Tezcatlipoca's idea. Or his, which he made seem mine. It seemed a trivial thing."

"And when we have crushed this interloping bastard of a feathered serpent and his miserable followers, will you connive with the smoking mirror to topple me in turn and leave him paramount? Or will it be the other way around—will you help me to seize and hold the throne of the gods in sole possession?"

His face darkened, suffused with blood—his own, this time—and he seemed to swell in stature as his aspect came over him. She stood watching him casually. As if she'd seen it all before. As of course she had.

He relaxed then, and became at least marginally less terrifying. "Or will it please you to maintain the status quo of the past thirty years, with both Tezcatlipoca and myself sharing power—and your favor—neither gaining lasting advantage over the other, and hence becoming, perhaps, too great for even she of the serpent skirt with all her rattlesnake wiles to control?"

She laughed. "Perhaps one," she said, "perhaps the other. Perhaps something else again altogether. Even the mighty left-hand hummingbird must allow the mother of the gods her secrets.

"And her surprises."

Chapter 16

"I still say we should have jumped right down on Brigid's last known location," Grant grumbled in the shadows of the alley.

It was about 2100 local time, and the cosmopolitan city that had once been known as Mexico was alive with plenty of lights for casting shadows to lurk in. Especially if you were dressed in a shadow suit from Manitius Moon base. Grant and Domi both were, of course. He carried, slung, a plasma rifle, just to even the odds in case things got ugly.

"It worked so well for her," Domi agreed perkily.

Grant gave her a sidelong narrow-eyed look. If you wanted deferential respect, he told himself, why'd you bring her in the first place? Although given the nature of Cerberus personnel—who, after all, were renegade fugitives for the most part by way of having rebelled against baronial rule—what he might actually need to do to get deference was find a dog.

Brigid's last location looked a bit on the fortified side: a sprawl of Cyclopean cubes and step pyramids, enclosing and incorporating a couple of sizable courtyards. Philboyd had remarked it resembled a militant university, a description Grant could take no exception to. Not enough, at any rate, to make him sanguine about getting dumped smack into it without any kind of recce first.

"All right," he grumbled. "But I don't know how we're going to find a way to get to them."

"We could ask somebody." She jerked her short-haired head across the street toward where diners ate and chattered amiably in a restaurant courtyard, taking advantage of the velvet comfort of the night, neither hot nor cold. It appeared to have rained earlier in the evening. The place got lots of rain, judging from the near tropical growth practically exploding from planters and small park gardens on what seemed like every block. They were well up in the highlands here, the valley being a vast irregular bowl set among mountains, and humidity didn't seem to stick around very long.

They had been making their way through the back alleys and side streets of what seemed like a populous and prosperous district of a major city for the better part of three-quarters of an hour. The people here seemed to have a pretty late bedtime—indeed a pretty late suppertime, since the folk across the way were just the latest in a long succession of diners they had seen. The streets showed a certain amount of foot traffic, some odd-looking bicycles and even tricycles with chairlike seats set low and the pedals out before the riders, and a few open-sided omnibus things filled with colorfully dressed and cheerfully chattering passengers. They didn't see any conventional wags, nor any evidence of gas engines; even the buses purred by with a hum suggesting electric power.

Fortunately the good people of the ville kept their persons and their gazes prudently away from dark alleys and byways—of which there were many. Not everybody was happy or prosperous, it seemed, not that that was a surprise. If anything, it was the happiness and prosperity they saw that shocked them both, though neither had said a thing about it out loud.

The not so happy, and the not so good, did frequent the

dark ways. But these had been disinclined to accost the wildly disparate pair, distinct from all of the locals they could see, who were for the most part short, brown and on the stocky side. Grant and Domi were very experienced at not being seen when they chose not to be, and very good at it indeed.

They were also armed up the yin-yang.

Now Grant scowled, even for Grant. "That's it, huh?" he said in a low voice that carried no farther than a whisper. "Just walk up and say, 'Howdy-do, we're new around here. What's with that big compound where you stash kidnapped former Magistrates and archivists from Cobaltville?'"

Undaunted, as usual, Domi nodded. "Uh-huh."

He exhaled exasperatedly but quietly through his nose, mouth clamped tight on a retort. It would do no good to snap. She'd either just ignore it, which would piss him off even more mightily, or it would sting, and she would do one of two things: fly up in his face rending and screeching like a nuke-red stingwing. Or be hurt. He wasn't sure which was worse. Well, on second thought he was: hurt would be quiet, at least. But a protracted sulk on his partner's part could be just as deadly.

"Do you see any black people?" he made himself ask softly.

"Uh-uh."

"Do you see any bright white people?"

She shook her short-haired head.

"Do you see *any* kind of people dressed all in skintight light-absorbent black?"

"Nooo…"

"Then mebbe we ought to kind of hang back so we don't make ourselves conspicuous."

"Then how are we going to find out how to get into where Brigid and Kane are?" she answered back.

He frowned. He wasn't used to being answered back. It wasn't in the Magistrate training, or experience, or genes. But that's what Domi did. She answered back.

"What do you mean? We know just where they are. From Baptiste's biolink."

"But how do we get to them without ending up like them?"

"What has making ourselves conspicuous got to do with getting to them?" he almost hissed.

"Somebody took Brigid out, although her telemetry said she was just unconscious, not dead, which of course we're all happy about. But that took power. Somebody snagged Kane right out of the middle of a jump. That took megaloads of power. Any kind you want to name. So the people who did so may or may not run the whole city, but it's a sure thing they run hell out of the surrounding area. So if we attract attention to ourselves, we're attracting their attention to ourselves."

"Fine," Grant said. "Then we end up like Kane and Brigid."

"Mebbe."

Grant was outraged. "Mebbe? Are you smarter than Brigid? Or mebbe you reckon you've got more moves than Kane?"

She grinned, absolutely undaunted. "Neither one. But Kane got grabbed while jumping and couldn't defend himself for nukeshit. Brigid dropped herself in the middle of unfamiliar surroundings and got jumped right away. Collins said she acted like she was sleepwalking anyway. She wasn't exactly ace to defend herself, whatever. But if we arrange to get noticed, we can pick and choose the circumstances."

He stared at her through the dark. She scared him sometimes. He couldn't exactly find anything wrong with her scheme, exactly, canny as he was. Except that it was nuts. Definitely triple stupe.

Except… He shook his head like a wet terrier. Except nothing, unless *you're* triple stupe.

"Let's try it my way first."

"First," she happily agreed.

She waited. He drew in a deep breath. "What we need most is more information."

"Agreed."

That caught him a little off guard. He had suspected she was being contrary for its own sake. "And in a strange ville," he continued cautiously, "that means only one thing…."

"Gaudies," they said in unison.

"GODDESSES," THE COYOTE said as he lapped from a heavy earthenware bowl of pulque on the tavern's hard, red floor. "You can't live with 'em. You can't sacrifice them to the left-hand hummingbird. Or he'd get way too big for his loincloth."

Seated in a booth next to the animal with his arms crossed on a knife-scarred table and his head floating like an uncertain balloon above them, Kane nodded blearily. He was drunk.

He had intended to find Taker of Fifty Captives, his sag-bellied, bandy-legged trainer, and tie one on. It wasn't a normal recreation for Kane, who didn't normally enjoy the experience of being out of control.

Since things seemed to be pretty thoroughly that way already, it seemed appropriate now.

Fifty had been nowhere to be found. Nor did Brigid find Kane to talk him out of it. His handlers were occupied. He, meanwhile, while feeling both physically and mentally exhausted, had also been wired by the fight with the *cipactli,* and he couldn't sleep. As his fatigue poisons accumulated, his focus began to deresolve, so perhaps the decision to go for a little nocturnal pub crawl in the Tlillan-Tlapallan district surrounding the institute wasn't altogether Kane's.

The institute seemed to show about the same level of activity day or night. Wrapped in a cloak, and for once without any kind of weird headdress, he managed to find his way outside without running into anybody who tried to stop him. Intimidating his way past the guards at the gate, he had set forth down strange streets, confident in his ability to find a low dive. And low companions.

The Blue Agave fit the first bill admirably. And what lower companion was there than a coyote? Even if it was a talking one—in fact, so it informed Kane, another god, Ueuecoyotl. Certainly the other drinkers in the *taverna* treated him with an odd combination of condescension and wary regard as they drank, smoked, played cards, argued and watched a sporting event on television that seemed to involve teams of guys in different-colored feather bonnets and loincloths trying to get a head-sized rubber ball through a stone hoop set high up on a wall without using their hands.

Kane shook his head, which was beginning to feel like a rubber ball itself. He didn't think he'd drunk that much. Did that mean he should knock it off? Or drink more?

"It's not that I don't like her," he told the sympathetic canid. "I...damn. It's more than that. We're bonded, like. Through space and time." *How drunk do I have to be to tell somebody something like that?* a lucid corner of his mind wondered. *Even if it is a dog.*

"It is clearly a matter of the heart," the coyote pronounced. "The only remedy is…*más* pulque."

Pulque. It looked like snot and smelled like horses. It was the perfect drink for Kane's state of mind, possibly his state of being.

Kane heard a growl. His head snapped up. He controlled with difficulty an urge for his right hand to form a half fist—waking into action the power holster for the Sin Eater he wore concealed on his arm beneath his cloak. His first thought had been that the coyote god made the sound. Then that the bar in general had.

Looking, he decided it was all of the above. All staring at the television, where the handball game, it appeared, had been preempted by an official pronouncement.

"I hate that prick," Ueuecoyotl said, glancing at the television screen over the bar, which also featured a full-length, full-frontal reclining nude of the goddess Coatlicue. She was rad-blasted gorgeous, Kane had to admit. It wasn't a painting. It was a photo.

They treated their gods differently here in Tenochtitlán.

The figure on the screen was far less fetching than the naked goddess. He was wearing a twentieth-century-style business suit. With a tie.

"If I wasn't so fucked up," Kane said, "I'd be *really* fucked up."

"Praise the god of drunkenness and irresponsible gaiety," agreed the coyote with a hiccup. "That would be me." He thumped his tail happily on the floor.

Improbably what he was wearing wasn't the worst thing about the man on the screen. That would be his face.

"Rejoice," that face said. Although the broadcast had clearly been in color a minute ago, and still was, to judge by the stylized gold sunburst in the backdrop, the face was

the utter black and white of a line drawing—a cartoon
mask of idiot glee. "A new god and goddess have emerged
to battle the wave of monsters besetting the people of
Tenochtitlán."

The picture switched to an overhead shot of Kane and
Brigid, battling the crocofish. The unctuous tones announced the heroic advent of Tonatiuh and Chalchihuitlicue. The clip showed the *cipactli*'s demise.

Kane couldn't help noticing he didn't cut the most heroic
figure at the climax. "Not my fault I did most of my fighting lying on my ass," he muttered. The crowd, however,
seemed roused by his heroic leap onto the monster's belly.

That, to Kane, now looked merely stupe. Triple stupe.

The image snapped back to the studio and the face,
identified by a legend at the bottom as Paynal, messenger
of Huitzilopochtli. The crowd moaned.

But the face had changed. Now it was a mask—literally
that's what it looked like, a mask—of despair, with the
mouth pulled down at the ends as if made of rubber, the
eyes crescents, even a teardrop static on one cheek as if
drawn there.

"Yet sadly," the hideous visage said in tones as lugubrious as they had been syrupy a moment before, "the Black
House announces that because of a weakening of devotion
to the old ways, more and worse monster incursions are
likely to afflict our blessed city of Tenochtitlán—"

The coyote turned his furry backside toward the screen,
elevated his rather handsome black-tipped silver brush of
a tail and farted noisily. Even those in direct line of fire
laughed lustily.

Someone turned down the volume as the face of
Huitzilopochtli's messenger switched abruptly back to its
happy phase, like a photon from wave to particle. Kane

stared. His eyes felt grated. Something disquieted him about the whole thing, beyond the blazingly apparent.

Isn't he on the other side? Why was he talking up Baptiste and me? He suspected the messenger was subtly trying to instill distrust and dislike for him and his fellow draftee deity, even as he extolled their deeds. The whole concept made his brain hurt. His stomach started to roll and roll, not unlike the afternoon's monster. Blackness began to encroach upon his vision from all sides, narrowing it to a tunnel.

"'Scuge me," the animal god told him. "I gotta go to the li'l coyotes' room."

"They got a facility for that?" Kane asked blearily.

"Naw. It's the alley out back. I'm just dicking with you." He trotted off unsteadily.

Kane's head dropped forward onto his arm. The blackness closed in before his head hit the receiver of his Sin Eater.

"DO YOU THINK it could be him?" Domi asked.

Grant's face fisted up so hard it just became a big X. "Who knows?" he rumbled. "I gotta tell you, I don't go in for that game too much, but if it turns out they treat you like a god here because you have light-colored skin, I am gonna be seriously pissed."

They had visited three bars, each progressively lower on the scale of elegance. The response they evoked was strangely muted, as if they were, yes, unusual, but people weren't that unused to seeing unusual things.

The last place had been pay dirt, of a sort. On a TV screen was what looked for all the world like a predark news vid of what looked suspiciously like Kane and Baptiste in outlandish clothes, fighting a big, ugly fish. Which was impossible, of course.

Except that Domi, who spoke Spanish, heard from various bar crawlers that the new gods in town were rumored to be gringos from the mysterious north, just as the young lady and her bodyguard appeared to be. Somebody had even heard the god Tonatiuh, who had just battled the *cipactli* on the eleven-o'clock news, was roistering in a bar just two blocks down....

"Look on the bright side," Domi said cheerfully. "If that's true about light skin equals divinity, they'll make me queen of heaven. If you're nice, I'll put in a good word for you."

They had left their more controversial gear bundled up and jammed into concealment behind a large garbage bin. Street people were sparse in this district. They had seen progressively fewer as they had moved toward their objective, a jumble of impressive structures set up on a height, from their jumping-in point near the waterfront. If one were unlucky enough to try to unwrap the bundle, the incendiary-microgren boobies Grant had left primed inside would dispose of the evidence and him in an instant blaze of glory.

"I knew I should have left your impertinent ass back in Cobaltville," Grant said, checking the scavvied bar rag he had wound about his forearm to conceal his Sin Eater. It wasn't terribly convincing as a bandage, but most people down here probably didn't think of the forearm as a usual place to tote a handblaster, and it would rip right through the half-rotted fabric if he needed it.

They stepped inside.

"SHOULD WE DO HIM?" Axolotl asked. He was long and lanky except for a sort of cannonball pot that pooched out the waistband of his loincloth, which was none too clean. His face, which looked as if it might have been sculpted out of wax and left out in the high-altitude sun too long, was, as was his habit, almost as doleful as Paynal's in tragedy-mask phase. His complexion was unhealthily pale. He was quick to resent any implication that he might be one of the children of Mictlán, tainted or even undead. He was just ugly.

Dragonfly Eggs, his partner in crime, grunted. "If we wait till nobody's paying attention." He was short, dark and bandy-legged, with a big nose and receding forehead and jaw, a salt-and-pepper topknot and a big jade plug through his lower lip. He wasn't much to look at, either. Which might have contributed to the fact nobody was looking.

Perhaps it was natural that they fall in together, being as each was named for one of the major Tenochtitlán food groups—some prominent others being turkeys, maize, chocolate and Chihuahuas. In normal times they were dockworkers, or professed to be. But trade was depressed lately, what with all the other valley city-states all jumping salty about paying their flowery tributes. So right now the pair mostly got by as alley bashers. And, of course, snitches.

"But what if he really is a god, like Two-Face said?" Axolotl asked.

"Then he ought to have something worth boosting, no?"

He bent down. His gnarled hand reached out and grabbed the hair at the back of the passed-out man's neck. He lifted head from cushioning arm. Black glass glinted in bar light as he brought his other hand out from concealment behind his hip.

Chapter 17

Something dark and hard smashed into Dragonfly Eggs' face. He went flying backward against a whitewashed wall, hit hard, slid down to the maroon floor.

"The universal language," Grant said with satisfaction, surreptitiously rubbing his elbow. The mugger had had a snaggletooth, and while the shadow suit had kept it from ripping the skin, it smarted.

Axolotl's eyes, protuberant to start with, practically stood on stalks as he stared at the two who had materialized as if from the thick booze-scented air of the cantina. Even for a man for whom gods and monsters were part of everyday reality, they were peculiar looking.

"A-are you a *civatateo?*" he stammered. His eyes rolled as he tried to check on Dragonfly Eggs without turning his head, which he dared not do. Plus, the tiny, unnaturally pale *chica* wearing what appeared to be a coat of light-absorbent paint would have been very interesting, if she hadn't been backed up by an improbably black giant.

And if she hadn't had the tip of a long, wicked-looking knife pressed right into the front of his loincloth in a most disturbing manner.

"Or are you gods?"

"You betcha," the white apparition said in low-class Spanish. It was clearly not low-class Spanish as spoken by the local lower classes, as so ably represented by Axolotl and his currently consciousness-impaired pal, but it was clearly Spanish, and just as clearly lower class. "He's the god of major ass-kickings. I'm the goddess of painful deaths. Lingering ones."

Grant, who didn't understand a word, smiled. To Axolotl, who once on a darkened rain-slick side street had actually beheld one of the dreadful *civatateo*, and somehow lived, it was the most terrifying thing he had ever seen.

"We were just trying to help your friend," Axolotl managed to say. "He looked unwell."

"Yeah, I noticed how your bud was getting ready to perform an emergency tracheotomy. But, funny, our friend doesn't seem to be having any trouble breathing. If you and your boy don't want to develop one, I'd suggest you grab him quick and disappear."

Heads had turned as Dragonfly Eggs had performed his short dramatic flight, as they had when, sadly unnoticed by the two thugs intent on larceny, the pair had entered the bar. When it became evident that no further action or entertainment could be expected, the patrons returned to mugs and bottles with a collective murmur of disinterested approbation.

Axolotl's prominent Adam's apple bobbed. His head did likewise. Then he did as Domi told him.

Grant seized Kane the way his would-be murderer had. "What?" the stupefied man murmured peevishly. "Can't you let a man rest his eyes, Ueuecoyotl? And when did you grow hands?"

"In my mama's womb. What the hell is wrong with you, Kane? And why are you dressed like that?"

Kane's eyes snapped wide and his head snapped up. "Grant? I'm drunk. No, I thought I was drunk. I think I'm sick…what are you doing here?"

"Rescuing you," Domi said. "Where's Brigid?"

"Baptiste? She's back—back at the Plumed Serpent House. She's a goddess, too. Lady Precious Green. Chalchihuitlicue."

"Gesundheit," Grant said. He caught him under the armpit. "C'mon, point man. We're getting you out of here."

Kane looked alarmed. "You can't. I'll die."

"If you leave the bar?" Domi asked.

"No. If I try to leave the valley. We can't leave. Baptiste and I. If we do, we'll die."

"That's just great, Kane," Grant said, hoisting his comrade aloft without apparent effort. "How you get yourself into these situations I'm damned if I'll ever know."

Kane tipped a groggy finger off his nose. "It is a classic one-percenter," he slurred.

"What are you doing to Lord Tonatiuh?"

Grant and Domi looked at the speaker. "All right, this is getting strange even for one of your one-percenters," Domi said. "A dog is talking to us, Kane."

"Oh, that's not a dog," Kane said. "It's okay, Ueuecoyotl, these are friends. No worries."

Grant was staring at him, and his eyes were wide. "When did you start speaking Spanish?"

"Same time I learned Náhuatl," Kane said. "When I woke up I wasn't just a god—I could speak Spanish, too."

"What's this rad waste about being a god?" Domi demanded, munching on a taquito she'd helped herself to from a bowl on the bar. "You've always had a high opinion of yourself, but up till now you haven't shown many signs of delusions of grandeur."

"He is a god," the animal said. The other bar patrons were watching sidelong now. "The latest and greatest. Well, mebbe not the greatest. But great enough. All hail

Lord Tonatiuh, god of the Sun, slayer of the *cipactli* and the frog monster! He most definitely is a god."

"And you're…well, a coyote," Domi said. She was taking this better than Grant. The big man's face had acquired a greenish cast that didn't go well with his complexion.

"We all have our limitations," the animal said. "But I'm not always a coyote. But I'm drunk," he finished, apparently thinking that was helpful. Or news.

"He's my pal Ueuecoyotl," Kane volunteered. "That means, 'old, old coyote.' They call him that because—"

"Please don't tell me," Grant said.

"It's been great talking with you, Old 'Yote," Domi said, "but I think we'd better get our friend somewhere he can be seen to." She placed one of Kane's arms around her neck so that she and Grant could both support him.

The creature bobbed his head and wagged his tail. "Of course. The pleasure was mine, my friends. Ta." And he turned and trotted out the door, magnificent brush of tail high.

Domi looked at Grant over Kane's sagging head. The big man just shook his.

AS THE THREE OF THEM proceeded down the alley behind the cantina, which reeked of beer and puke and piss and rotting fish, a small figure slipped into the mouth behind them. It had four legs, a tail, a lolling tongue and very bright black eyes. It watched them go with those keen eyes: two disparate figures in black, the cloaked one between them limp as a sack with his sandaled toes digging furrows in moist muck.

The coyote trotted a few paces into the alley. Then its outlines blurred, shifted, became those of a man wearing a hooded cloak. He slipped quickly into a dark niche behind a waste bin and was lost to view.

AXOLOTL AND DRAGONFLY EGG emerged from the shadow of a jut of structure. With their ubiquitous buttresses and elaborations, the buildings of Tenochtitlán were rich in hiding places. The pair moved down the alley the strangers had taken moments before. Dragonfly Eggs leaned surreptitiously against his friend, although there was no one else in view to notice his unsteadiness.

"The two should know about this," he rasped. "We must go to the Black House at once."

"Why?"

"There's war in heaven," he said. Actually he said "Talocan," but to the same effect. "Everybody know that. Here's this upstart god palling with strange gringos. Who knows what might be afoot?"

He laid a finger alongside his fleshy tuber of a nose. "I'll bet the smoking mirror will know what to make of it, though. And he will see us rewarded!"

"Indeed," a voice said.

Their heads snapped around. From behind the trash receptacle stepped the man into whom the coyote who called himself Ueuecoyotl had morphed. But it was not the broad, fleshy form of the god of partying hearty that confronted them, but a lean, taut-muscled frame; the face was not bloated with dissipation, but as keen as a blade.

Tezcatlipoca held forth his palm. Into it an obsidian lens, rough flaked but wondrously smooth between sharp ridges, fit nicely. Nothing happened, visibly or audibly. But the two men's eyes turned red as a small, focused wave of probability swept from the tiny replica of the great Smoking Mirror, producing the tiniest of effects, merely causing a few key atoms in their capillary walls to slip the surly bonds of their attendant molecules. The wave passed through each man's skull, setting loose a flood of blood within each brain.

Dragonfly Eggs and Axolotl dropped down to the alley muck. Their eyes stared without seeing into each other. Dead red.

"Indeed," repeated the god of temptation and judgment, who attempted to seduce men to wickedness and then paid them out according to their deserts. "Great Tezcatlipoca is most interested, and has given you the reward you have earned, my friends."

"FOR SUCH A LEAN GUY," huffed Domi, "who'd ever think Kane would be so heavy?"

There was no pretense now that Kane was carrying any fraction of his own weight. He was flat unconscious. Grant and Domi gingerly carried him and the gear they had recovered from where Grant stashed it, through the back alleys toward the great compound sprawling on the heights to the northwest. He had gasped out a sort of psychedelic stream-of-consciousness explanation of what was going on before subsiding totally. It left them feeling as if they knew less than when they jumped from Cerberus earlier that evening.

"Deadweight," Grant grunted. Then looked as if he regretted that choice of words.

They made their way toward what looked like a major canal. The root of the promontory with the fortified-looking structures up top rose right across the blackly glittering water. A broad avenue lined with palm trees crossed between them and the canal.

"Are there really supposed to be palm trees here?" Domi asked. "I thought Mex City was supposed to be high, dry and polluted."

They had been given a quick premission brief by Philboyd, including overhead imaging.

"Weather patterns changed after the war," Grant suggested. "After skydark. Who the hell knows? Mebbe we can ask Brigid…."

A shadow crossed his long, harshly handsome face. He had bitten down hard on a first impulse to slam Domi for yapping about palm trees at a time like this: it came to him that any distraction was probably better than wondering what the hell was happening to Brigid, what the hell had happened to Kane, if it could be fixed and them gotten safely out of here. And then I had to go and bring up Brigid.

"Quit bugging," Domi advised. "Brigid's fine. Kane told us that much. Whatever they did to her—whatever they did to *them*—it hasn't killed them yet, has it?"

"There's always that 'yet.'"

"Yeah." She grinned at him. "There always is. And not just for our deified friends."

From ahead of them a scream pealed like a bell.

The brief whine of a small but powerful motor was followed by a ripping sound as Grant's Sin Eater sprang into his hand. His plasma rifle was slung on his back, not easy to reach with Kane's limp arm across his shoulders.

A bleeding figure staggered into the alley from the canal-side street. A woman, who might have been handsome if her hair had not been a cloud of disarray, her eyes wide with terror, three parallel tears across her left cheek turning a quadrant of her face to blood. The shredded remnants of a feathered cape fluttered about her shoulders. One side of a lustrous blue gown had been torn open; one bare dark-nippled breast bounced as she ran.

She wore improbably high clogs of carved jade, with rubber pads glued to them to prevent them slipping on

pavement. It was still no more a practical arrangement for
running for one's life than prenuke high heels, as she came
around the corner she turned an ankle and went down with
a wail of despair and sudden pain.

Domi's Detonics blaster was in her hand. Neither she
nor Grant stirred to help the woman. She was none of their
affair, and while in abstract terms they wouldn't mind lend-
ing a hand they first intended to see what it was she had
been running from.

From both sides of the alley mouth figures appeared.
They were women, to judge by the shriveled dugs hanging down over their hollow bellies. They seemed little
more than skeletons, with parchment skin stretched taut
over them. Lank hair tangles, streaming with algae as if
straight from the canal, hung in gaunt faces tattooed with
white skulls. Crudely stylized skull glyphs had been whitewashed on the figures' chests, as well, so that their breasts
seemed to hang out the eye sockets; these glyphs had begun
to run and stream with water.

And blood. The half-dozen creatures who staggered
first into view had red smiles painted fresh over their skull
tattoos, red chins, black-taloned hands and bluish-green-
ish forearms twined with blood as if they had dunked their
hands in it.

They moved as if uncertain of balance and stiff of joint,
but with alacrity nonetheless. As the fallen woman struggled to rise, three fell upon her. One straddled her back like
an evil monkey and sank its teeth, perpetually bared by
withered lips, into her neck.

A jet of blood, black in the lights reflecting from the
canal, sprayed the creatures and the nearest wall. "Carotid,"
Grant commented. "She's fucked now anyway."

He raised his Sin Eater and hosed a blast into the

writhing group. The vampire women were knocked sprawling from their victim by a stream of 147-grain hollowpoints. By chance none of the slugs appeared to strike the victim; she struggled to her feet and reeled about clutching her neck. As Grant had said, she was already beyond hope. She fell. The blood spray already weakening, she clutched spastically twice, fingers plowing furrows in the alley mud, then went still as Grant took the creatures remaining in view down with surgical tribursts.

Domi, who hadn't fired, lowered her stocky little .45 autopistol, which she held in a two-handed modified Weaver stance. "What the hell are those things?"

"Charming local fauna," Grant said. "Dead now."

He glanced at his partner, who still hung limp between the pair. Kane hadn't stirred even with the Sin Eater blasting away inches from his ears. "This isn't natural," Grant said. "He's not just drunk, and isn't this far gone just because he isn't used to getting plowed under. Let's get going, see if we can find him some help—and us some answers."

"Oh, shit," Domi said softly.

More chalky skull-marked figures appeared, filling the alley mouth. That wasn't the focus of her attention. The figures Grant had blasted down were slowly, jerkily, raising themselves to their bare black-nailed feet once more. And heading toward them with gore-dripping claws outstretched.

Chapter 18

"Kane," Grant said out of the side of his mouth. "Kane, wake up. We got a situation here. We could use those god-like powers of yours."

Unfortunately, whatever powers his point-man pal may have had did nothing to enable him to rouse from his near death torpor.

Domi raised her handblaster, hesitated long enough—a fractional second—to pick up a flash picture over the corpse-glow of the tritium insert in her front blade sight, squeezed off a compressed surprise break. The little blaster roared and bucked in her white hands. The recoil was fierce as it puked up a 180-grain Triton hollowpoint at near a thousand feet a second but the triangle of her braced arms and angled torso transmitted the shock to her ribs, down through hips and legs into the dirt. The gun rose half a hand span and came right back to level as the heavy slide cycled and spit an empty brass case. It hissed as it landed in moist mud.

The lead creature stopped. It had a new hole right between the dark glaring pits between the sockets of its own skull and the holes through the white tattoo impressed upon its facial skin. Then it spasmed like a Tartarus Pit alley cat goosed by a Mag's Shockstick. It dropped straight down into a melted-seeming puddle of skinny limbs and torso.

"Just like the old zombie vids," she commented in sidelong satisfaction. The Detonics' blocky muzzle never wavered. "Head shot takes 'em right down."

"They went down before," Grant said, pointing his Sin Eater from one to another. While the pair had seen them move pretty briskly, the creatures now advanced deliberately, as if enjoying the stalk. "They got up."

"That one isn't. Acted just like any human taking a ninja mask hit."

Grant had to acknowledge that it had responded like a human to a round through the medulla oblongata, all the CNS circuits tripping at once, and it definitely appeared that whatever force it was that motivated the pallid horrors had fled the one Domi shot.

He hesitated just an instant. His thumb flicked the selector switch. His Sin Eater spoke once, twice. Two more creatures, barely fifteen yards away now, jerked and fell as if their strings had been snipped.

But the alley was crowded with a score or more of the filthy things now. Grant could smell their stink, like the reek of a big cat's breath—rotting meat. Quite possibly that on their bones, as well as their victims' flesh stuck in shreds between their foul black teeth.

He remembered then how fast they could move, and that a normal human could charge you so fast once he got within about twenty-five feet that he was sure to tag you with a knife or ax whether you shot him with a handblaster or not. "Fuck this," he said, spraying a shattering full-auto burst to take the nearest rank of creatures down, slowing them and hopefully those behind. "Let Kane down easy and then grab my plasma rifle."

Domi did so, although had he been conscious Kane might not have described the tooth-jarring landing as "easy." Domi slipped the big gleaming rifle off Grant's shoulder and snapped it up to her hip as three creatures wove past their rising sisters and blurred into death-silent charges.

She caught a flash impression of hands splayed like the claws of striking beasts, and mouths opened unnaturally wide. Then she triggered the plasma rifle.

A sun-bright line of not-quite-gas lanced from the barrel and struck the middlemost of the charging trio dead center of the skull smeared on its chest. It exploded, limbs and head and racks of zombie ribs flying in all directions, burning with a blue flame and prodigious stench.

Domi didn't wait to admire her handiwork. Knowing the beast kicked like a six-legged mule, she had been braced. She fought down the muzzle, twitched left, gave the monster on that side a flash to the groin region that blew it in two.

The third was nearly on them. Grant yelled in surprise more than pain as he felt the brilliant plasma jet burn within inches of his short ribs. It caught the final horror in the side, blew open its torso and turned it into an instant inhuman torch. What it didn't do was *stop* it.

"Fuck!" Grant exclaimed. He launched a brutal front thrust kick into the center of the flaming mass that still bore down on him as if intent upon dragging him with it to hell in its fiery embrace. He rolled his hips as he struck to put the full force of his substantial mass into the kick.

It struck the blazing monster in the upper thigh and knocked its legs out from under it. The creature grabbed as it went down. Burning claws traced trails of flame down the front of Grant's shadow suit. They danced briefly, blue, went out. Lying at his feet, emitting clouds of choking horrific smoke, the creature tried to rise, then collapsed, its own pyre.

"Sorry," Domi said.

Then they got busy as the bizarre creatures rushed them. Grant waved his Sin Eater back and forth like a sporadic torch—squirting out bursts of variable length, since just holding the trigger back made his mag go empty way too fast, and basically guaranteed a malfunction, from overheating if nothing else. Because the creatures were packed together he violated the combat-pistolcraft rule of aiming for the center of mass and instead held it head high for most of the female creatures, shoulder high for him.

The spavined blood-drinking beings went down in windrows, flaming or being blasted apart when hit by plasma strikes. But it took a pretty dead-center brainbox hit from Grant's handblaster to make one of them stay down. And the plasma rifle, terrifyingly potent as it was, had no penetrating power: when the pulse hit anything, it gave it all up right then, doing massive damage to what it touched but nothing to the monster right behind.

Still, the pair managed to strew the alley floor with humped or smoking corpses, and filled the air between the moist stone walls with reeking steam and smoke that smelled like a barbecue gone horribly wrong. Their eyes were streaming and the seemingly endless supply of monstrous attackers had almost run dry.

And then Domi's plasma blaster *did*.

Because the energy rifle had nothing like a conventional handblaster's slide lockback to clue the shooter it had run out of juice, Domi pumped the firing button three times at the last lunging horror before she realized she was holding a paperweight. She tossed the big shiny useless rifle away and reached for her Detonics, knowing she'd never get it clear in time. Grant was finishing off the last two other monsters still on their feet; there was no way he could track his Sin Eater to bear before the being sank teeth and talons into Domi's milk-white skin.

The creature spread its arms wide for the kill stroke.

A hand reached up from the ground right before it and pressed to the skull-painted sternum, right between the flopping dugs. For a moment the hand shone as if the bones glowed through muscle and skin. Then a wave of intolerable white light pulsed outward from it.

None of the hideous night beings had made the slightest sound, even as they burned. But this one, perhaps with a residue of air or even water trapped in its lungs, flashblasted into steam by plasma, put back its horrific head and screamed. Then it blew apart into flaming, reeking fragments.

Kane sat up, shaking his head and holding his hand up in front of him. Grant and Domi knelt quickly beside him, expecting to find a calcined claw at the end of his arm.

But no. Aside from the familiar network of white scars, remnants of a thousand battles and just hard living, the hand was intact. Unmarked by the terrific heat that had just emanated from it.

"All right," Grant said, "you're a god. Don't let it go to your head." He straightened and changed magazines.

"Dunno what happened," Kane said, his speech slurred. "Just…woke up. Felt some kind of…energy rush."

"My plasma rifle," Domi said. "Must've recharged your batteries."

Blue-white light struck them with an almost physical impact. Grant cursed and shielded his eyes with an upflung hand. A spotlight blazed at them from the canal.

Voices shouted to them. Grant started to raise his Sin Eater.

"No!" Kane shouted, struggling to rise. "Local…patrol boat. Let me talk."

Domi helped him up. He held up his hand and strode

forward with amazing steadiness, considering. He shouted something in a language neither of his companions understood. They both caught the name Tonatiuh.

A down-blast hurricane beat down on them as a helicopter drifted over the alley, and another million-candlepower spot pinned them to its noisome floor like bugs.

"MY BROTHERS AND SISTERS of Talocan," Huitzilopochtli declaimed in a voice that seemed to shake the walls of the Hall of the Gods, "the time has come for us to destroy the weakling Quetzalcoatl and his deluded minions once and for all!"

The first rays of the rising sun turned his bare chest to gold and made his eyes seem to glow like mirrors in his black-painted chest. He had his full aspect upon him, and the power beat from him like heat from a stove.

This was a tough house just the same. After all, his hearers were all deities themselves, if none so potent as he. They stood gazing at him with varied expressions, not responding.

Most of the key deities currently incarnated were there: Tlaloc and Xipe Totec, mightiest of gods save for the ruling two and their mother, Coatlicue, who was as was her custom absent; the fire gods Xiuhtecuhtli and Camactli, who was also god of the hunt; Chicomecoatl, whose name meant "seven snakes," in her guise of a young girl carrying a water lily; Micapetlacalli, the box of death, duly wearing the box, painted with snakes and skulls and flowers, which concealed his head and hence his visage, which was death to gaze upon; the twisted obsidian god Itzcoliuhqui, tittering in response to the gyrations of his insanity; the scorpion woman, Malinalxochi; the pestilence god, Chalchiutotolin, with his faceful of suppurating sores.

Others were conspicuous by absence. Some, like the rat-

tlesnake mother and the flower twins, Xochipilli and
Xochiquetzal, because they had thrown in openly with the
rebels. And some, like Mictlantecuhtli, lord of the realm
of the dead, did not attend for reasons of their own, which
might mean much or little.

Paynal, wearing his black-and-white happy face, ap-
plauded furiously from Huitzilopochtli's left hand and en-
joined the assembled deities to join him. They ignored
him. Talocan's gods held him in even greater contempt than
did the people of Tenochtitlán. He did have power to ma-
nipulate human emotion, potent enough to work on a god
or goddess. But not gods or goddesses.

Nothing happened until a cheer was raised by Tezcatlipoca, who stood at Hummingbird's right hand with his
jaguar head and cape on. Then the rest consented to join
halfheartedly.

Huitzilopochtli smiled. It wasn't a pleasant sight, against
the backdrop of his face, and his eyes were disturbing even
in the sight of gods. "Do you doubt me?" he asked.

"We feel constrained by the presence of your servitors,
Lord Huitzilopochtli," said Xipe Totec, lord of the west,
god of agriculture and the cycle of death and rebirth, sender
of plagues. Out of consideration for his peers he did not
have his aspect upon him. His divine semblance, of a flayed
man wearing his own skin over his shoulders, was gross
even in the sight of gods.

He gestured at the walls, which were lined by eagle
knights with plasma-projector units strapped to their forearms, and swords at their waists. "One traditionally minded
might ask, as well, when mortals are bidden to share the
counsels of the gods?"

Huitzilopochtli's big jaw set. The flayed god was, with
Tlaloc, among the most conservative gods in Talocan, the

seat of the gods in the center of Tenochtitlán. Winning the backing of those two during the god war of thirty years before had unquestionably sealed its outcome. For one of the keenest supporters of the power structure, and of Huitzilopochtli himself, to question the hummingbird was not a propitious sign.

"These are parilous times, noble Xipe," Tezcatlipoca murmured. "Traitor gods have joined our foes, have they not? Others may harbor secret doubts about the current order, or secretly hanker after their own advantage...ultimately to the expense of all. Lord Huitzilopochtli has no intention, brothers and sisters, to asperse the loyalty of any here. Yet we cannot afford to take aught for granted."

More a rustle than a murmur ran through the dozen deities. To have Tezcatlipoca implicitly endorse the mortal guardsmen's unspeaking presence indicated, at very least, solidarity in the face of present threat with his brother and rival Huitzilopochtli. It was seldom forgotten by the other *teotl*, the fear- and awe-inspiring ones, that what power was wielded by Huitzilopochtli was denied to Tezcatlipoca, and vice versa. It was presumed never to be forgotten at all by the keen, incisive mind of Tezcatlipoca.

That the two showed a united front did not mean their fellow gods were pleased to have the eagle knights on hand. Few gods could suffer a direct hit from a plasma beam and remain in this incarnation. Even Huitzilopochtli's skin-conforming *dorado* force screen could theoretically be exhausted by repeated blasts.

Not that anyone expected the Huitzilopochtli's handpicked elite to shoot at him.

"Let us attend the real cause for urgency," Tezcatlipoca said. "Our foes have incarnated new gods."

"How is that possible?" Malinalxochi asked. Like Xipe

she had left her aspect off for this gathering, in her case by way of the unwieldiness of the form she shape-shifted into. The other deities gave her a wide berth, though, owing to the venomous serpents, spiders and scorpions that tended to coil about her arms and crawl through her hair even when her aspect was off. "I thought only Smoking Mirror had the power of imbuing godhood."

"It is the traitor whose name I will not speak!" snapped Huitzilopochtli, eyes flashing at Tezcatlipoca.

"But I will," his fellow ruler of gods and men said imperturbably, "even though it was me personally whom he betrayed—Dr. Marroquín, the defector. He was, after all, one of the original outsiders. He understood their alien technology as well as any, even Daraul. Even I. He has clearly discovered the secret."

"Enough!" Huitzilopochtli made a horizontal chopping motion with an arm across his broad, bare chest. "The time has come to act, not speak. The first phase of our operation has begun—monsters are attacking various sections of the city."

"By some coincidence," Tezcatlipoca said with a quiet smile, "predominantly those districts that are most favorable to our enemies."

"They must respond, or forfeit support in their areas of greatest strength," Huitzilopochtli said. "Thus we draw them out. And now we shall fall upon them and destroy them."

"What about parliament?" asked Xiuhtecuhtli. "Will they back decisive action against the plumed-serpent faction?"

Huitzilopochtli barely suppressed a sneer, and didn't totally suppress the effort it took. The fire god, who had not been particularly young at the time of his investiture, was showing definite signs of physical aging despite the rejuvenative effects of godhood—and the alien medical and genetic treatments that sustained it, and its bearers. Some gods, including Huitzilopochtli, had begun to harbor the opinion it might be time for fire to seek a new avatar, or go into remission.

"We should have the votes to approve any action we take," Tezcatlipoca said dryly, "provided, of course, that we win."

"And the people?" asked Camactli. Youngest of the gods in chronological terms, he seemed sometimes to feel compelled to back up the elderly Xiuhtecuhtli, although since fire was the domain of both they might be expected to be rivals as much as allies. "Quetzalcoatl gains strength among them. Will they support us, or rise for the serpent, or engage in a general strike?"

"Leave that," said Paynal through his painted-on grin, "to me."

Saturnine Tlaloc rubbed his heavy, handsome face with his hand. "I don't like this," he said deliberately. "It is not meet that gods should dance to mortals' tunes."

That brought a moment of less than comfortable silence. Though none knew to precisely what extent, not even the subtle and cunning Tezcatlipoca, all were aware that more than their political position as ultimate ruling class depended upon their merely human subjects. Ultimately it was the power of belief, or worship, that sustained them in their godhood. If the public ever really lost faith, their own powers would fade and die.

"Then let us seize the day!" Xipe declared in a ringing voice. "Why stand and talk more? Let's go out and make our foes a flowery tribute to ourselves!"

"Hail, Left-Hand Hummingbird!" cried Tlaloc, who was not easily roused. "Hail Tezcatlipoca! Hail Talocan!"

Huitzilopochtli smiled in satisfaction. "Hail yes," he said.

Chapter 19

A waterfront warehouse district, idled by the current emergency. The refreshing smell of wind over water, the cries of seagulls drifting overhead.

The rattle of small-arms fire. The stink of burning hair and flesh. The feel of substances even Tonatiuh didn't care to think about, drying on skin left exposed by greaves and breastplate and skirt of armor strips, splashed there by the hot hard work of monster slaying.

Morning in Tenochtitlán.

"Kane! Look out!" Brigid's voice shouted in the Sun god's left ear. In her guise of Chalchihuitlicue she led her own monster-mashing detachment of Quetzalcoatl knights and sec men along the big canal's far bank, in sight of Kane and his.

At the frantic radio warning Kane turned and dived behind some bales of what looked like dried water weeds piled on the dock. The ripping-cloth roar of a chain gun hard nearby overrode even the turbo whine as an attack chopper came in low on a strafing run. Exploding 25 mm shells kicked up divots of concrete that had been under Kane's sandals a heartbeat before.

A khaki-uniformed Tlillan-Tlapallan sec man had time for one hoarse scream as miniature blasts tore him in two. Then the aircraft was past, while the bisected man's comrades blasted after it with submachine guns and M-16s.

Kane jumped up as quickly as he could, more to try to get a fix on the chopper than out of concern for his divine dignity. By the flash he got of his sec men and the pair of knights in view, nobody thought it out of the ordinary that a Sun god might dive out of the way of a strafing Deathbird.

Not really Deathbirds, Kane reminded himself—mostly to remind himself who he *was*—as he watched the chopper bank left and vanish behind a big yellow-brick warehouse. But close enough. And if these gunships were armored anywhere near as well, the district cops' small arms would be dead-ass useless, and even the .50s on the patrol boats would need luck to do any damage at all.

He peered over the bales. Just ahead a crane rose from the canal side, angling out over the algae-green water. To the left rose big blocky warehouses.

They played us perfectly, Kane knew. His side saw it coming all the way—and Huitzilopochtli and Tezcatlipoca still had them where they wanted them.

They had to fight the monsters. No choice about it. The whole culture of mass human sacrifice propping up Talocan was based on the belief that only by strengthening the gods with their very lives and blood could the valley's people ensure they would be protected from the monsters who dwelt below the city and without its walls, lusting to flood in and destroy them. Keeping that spirit of sacrifice alive, at least on a scale sufficient to support the ruling two's ballooning appetite for human blood and life energy, required from time to time actual monsters.

So Tezcatlipoca, with the aid of the shadowy hybrid superscientist Daraul and a slew of Black House priests and whitecoats, maintained a ready supply of horrific beasts, created by gene engineering and less straightforward means, and cut them loose in ones and twos from time to time to rampage when the piety index got a little low.

Now they'd opened the gates and turned out the lot. If Quetzalcoatl and company couldn't protect their own people against the monsters, all Tenochtitlán would reject them. The triumph of Huitzilopochtli, Tezcatlipoca and the shadowy and sinister Coatlicue would be secured. So Kane and Brigid and sundry grunts had to go out and get videoed wading through fresh-spilled monster guts.

And, of course, it had all been just one big happy trap.

Watching for the chopper, Kane started to get pissed. He felt the lines of fire twine round and around him.

He smiled.

When the helicopter swung back into view—skidding sideways, almost certainly lining up for a shot at him with its fat underwing pods of Shrikes or whatever the locals called their free-flight rockets—he met it with flame. He fancied he could see the eyes of the gunner down and front go wide in horrified amazement, even though those eyes were hidden behind two layers of smoked polycarb and sunsplash on the windscreen besides.

Sadly, the sunbeam wouldn't core the chopper end to end. Happily, Kane knew that already. He aimed under the helicopter's snout, for the chin turret containing its Gatling gun—and many, many rounds of extremely explosive ammunition.

Which extremely exploded right away. A great blazing ball of wreckage dropped onto the dock a hundred yards from him. Some of it slopped into the big canal, raising a hiss and a huge cloud of steam to join the black pillar of smoke stretching into the blue high-valley sky. White smoke streamers corkscrewed out of the blaze as rounds cooked off.

"Kane! Behind you!" Brigid called again through the bone-conduction phone of his communicator.

Before he could turn he heard a spine-freezing scream.

ONE REED, one of Kane's knights, had thrown away the blaster in his hand and was performing a wild and spastic dervish dance. As Kane stared, the man quit capering and began to bend backward.

Impossibly far. Until his head was past the level of his butt and going toward his heels. Kane heard his vertebrae groan and grind. Heard his teeth splinter.

A thin scream hissed out between locked jaws as the man's spine snapped. He fell.

Perched on a crate behind him, clutching it with three pairs of legs, a bloodred scorpion a yard and a half long twitched its sting tail above its back. Its pincers opened and closed excitedly.

Its clustered eyes registered Kane as his registered it. But Kane moved faster. As it started to flow toward him, he skipped forward two steps. His sword was a blur of glittering black.

The poison-fat sting leaped from the tip of the horror's tail as the incredibly sharp volcanic glass sliced through it. The creature continued to scuttle down the crate and toward Kane, reaching with its claws.

Kane whipped his weapon up and around and buried it in the creature's thorax, crushing it to the pavement. Green ichor squirted from its ruptured shell as air squealed out its dying spicules.

"Lord Tonatiuh!" yelled another of his bodyguards, Diego, standing up from behind a bale pile beyond the crate the scorpion had stood on. The knight threw a laser rifle to his shoulder and sent a blue-green pulse skyward as two more enemy choppers swept in low.

"This shit's getting old," Kane remarked.

One aircraft, flanks blazoned with a bizarrely stylized hummingbird, fired its chain gun. Kane heard the screams as exploding shells ripped apart a squad of his sec men advancing in file along a pink-stuccoed building front.

Smoke gouted from beneath the other bird's stub wings. Kane invoked his solar shield—and ducked. Because he doubted even it could absorb a direct hit from a .57 mm rocket.

White flashes danced in the disk of yellow radiance he held angled upward and toward the blast—whether high-velocity frags or merely chunks of debris, he didn't know. He was just as glad not to get hit by either.

The choppers slashed overhead. The trailing ship, painted with a rampant jaguar and spilling black smoke from somewhere, continued on, curving back south toward the center of town and presumably a home base in Talocan; one of his people, probably a knight with an energy weapon, had clearly tagged it. The other ship ducked behind the yellow brick warehouse.

He heard shots from behind him, shouting. He half turned so he could scan both directions along the canal side by simply swiveling his head. Foot soldiers were attacking along the canal. They looked like Talocan sec men: grunts with their shades-o'-gray camou blouses and trousers for armor, machine pistols or the ubiquitous M-16s held across their chests.

Blasterfire crackled from his own men on street and quayside, ducked down among piled cargo, behind the pedestal of another big crane, from doors and alley mouths. Men in mottled gray went down. Some voluntarily and returning fire, others lying still and staring at the sky.

Kane rapped quick orders over his command channel. His knights really were pretty sharp, and the grunt-level cop types didn't seem to resent him ordering them around. The survivors of his bodyguard squad—now nearer one hand of knights than two—had done a fine job holding the sec men to good fire and movement patterns, keeping near cover. So the surprise Talocan infantry assault hadn't caught them dangling their parts in the breeze.

Ah, but the clever bastard in the remaining gunship had notions. The chopper swayed out sideways, fired a burst from its chin gun, then let its momentum carry it behind the boom of a crane even as Tonatiuh's flare seared the sky through which it had just passed.

A quick radio check and glance confirmed that the chopper's fire had torn up nothing but pavement and assorted trade goods. Kane, who had learned more than he was comfortable with about valley culinary habits in his few days here—gods had to eat as well as drink, it appeared—didn't want to speculate on what the little caviar-like globular things in goo strewed over the pavement were.

The pitch of the chopper's noise changed as the jock twitched his collective. Kane unleashed a second blast. But the pilot had feinted. The bolt sizzled harmlessly by, and then he swung out into clear view, unleashed a volley of rockets and whipped behind the warehouse.

Kane tried to launch a follow-up shot—and blackness crowded his vision down to a near pinpoint as a reward. He sat down, gut and cranium spinning, as screams and blasts behind him told him the rockets hadn't struck as harmlessly as the explosive bullets had.

Got to let my batteries recharge. He'd already learned that playing with the monsters.

The cagey prick pilot had Kane's men sandwiched. Firing them up from front and rear simultaneously, he and the squaddies on foot could pick them to pieces. Long before that happened, of course, the sec men would have broken and gone streaming away in rout—proving to all, especially the TV choppers drifting high overhead, that the rebel gods' might was as nothing to that of Talocan.

Welcome to the PR war, Kane thought as his vision cleared and his stomach ceased its slow rolls. He'd read about it but had little experience of it; when he was a Magistrate, "public relations" consisted of reminding the denizens of the Tartarus Pits what happened when you crossed a Mag—or even looked crosswise at one. Whereas what he was fighting for now, he had been told over and again by his hosts-captors-allies, was first and foremost the hearts and minds of Tenochtitlán's fickle voters. And worshipers.

Screw that, he thought. Right now what I'm fighting for is my own inadequately covered ass.

"Baptiste," he called. "What's your status?"

"I just washed a squad of foot soldiers into the canal," she reported. "We've also got unfriendly wildlife coming out of some offices. I'm a little busy."

"We're pretty well sandwiched over here between a helo gunship and some foot-mounted coldhearts," Kane said. "Can you lend a hand?"

"Love to, Kane. All you have to do is tell me what a water goddess can do about a flying machine from half a klick away."

Kane crouched, keeping his sword in hand. He had to be judicious with the flare. He couldn't just spray 'n' pray, or he'd pass out, and this was not the time to be out of the fight.

The chopper jock was smart. Way too smart. He seemed to understand the limitations of the Sun god's powers far too well.

"Fuck," Kane said aloud in English. "I bet Tezcatlipoca briefed his flyboys on us, what we could likely do."

"Could be, Kane," Brigid's voice came. "And by the way—"

The gunship darted into sight, up and over the warehouse. Kane brought his sword up to flashblast the helo, knew already it was going to trigger a volley of Shrikes right on top of him, even if he did zap it successfully….

It blew up.

As he blinked at the big blooming green balls of afterimage, he realized he had seen something dark and elongate flash into his field of view just before the explosion. In fact, his mental replay told him, it had been streaking like an arrow right for the chopper's big engine exhaust….

A missile! he realized. That meant…

"First I got to fly your ass to fight some monster," a laconic female voice said in his ear. "Now I got to save your ass. Some god, huh."

Kane blinked. He was ducked down now with his solar shield on and over his head as assorted helicopter parts rained on him. He hadn't even known his commo unit got this channel.

"Thanks. But who is this? Our pilot from yesterday?"

The voice grunted affirmative. "My name is Poncha."

"I didn't know that."

"Didn't bother asking. I'm just an Indian. A chauffeur. Not important to a big gringo god."

"I'm sorry. I'm new to this. I was distracted."

Poncha the pilot grunted again. "Don't shoot," she added.

Kane radioed his bodyguard to tell his men to hold fire

from the whirly-wags. A Gazelle painted with the plumed-serpent insignia promptly hove into view, a hundred yards farther along from where the Talocan gunship Poncha had splashed was lurking.

Thirty or forty enemy sec men were still trading bullets and blasts with Tonatiuh's command down the street the other way. A plasma bolt seared Kane's vision and blasted a chunk out of the stained brick corner of the building right across the street from him. Some of Talocan's finest had come out to play.

"Want us to send 'em packing?" Poncha asked.

But the Sun god was getting fed up with ducking and running. So Talocan would show the folk of Tenochtitlán how weak and pathetic the deities in service to the plumed serpent are?

Very well. Tonatiuh will fill their bellies full.

As the Tonatiuh persona rose up, so did rage, combined with a strange sensation, a keen, suction hollowness like hunger. The rage took flame. Yellow fire flickered around him in a hellish halo.

"No. Tonatiuh thanks you. You may keep watch for enemy flyers." He was speaking Náhuatl. Thinking in it, too. He was no longer Kane.

The pilot came back with some impertinence that Tonatiuh might have felt bound to punish. Had he attended. He did not.

It was time to take the fight to the foe.

He straightened. The shield strapped to his left arm became a yellow-white sun. "Cover me!" he commanded.

He charged.

Bullets sought him. He ran in a quick serpentine with his legs pulsing quicker than they ever had in his life. He was a poor target for excited men whose pulses weren't slowed by the spectacle of a gigantic gold-armored figure, bearing a shield of flame, racing right at them with infinite aggression.

They shot at him. They missed, or their bullets turned to incandescence themselves within the circle of the sun shield.

The master tactician who was Kane might not have exactly been driving the machine—the killing machine he had become—but he wasn't asleep. They can't miss forever, he reminded the primal urge, the living fire that was Tonatiuh.

The enemy skirmish line got closer fast. It seemed as if Kane could feel their muzzle-blasts on the exposed skin of face, arms and thighs. Tonatiuh's response to his warning was to extend his right arm and flame three Talocan infantrymen lying unwisely close to one another out in the middle of the street. They barely had time to scream before the sudden boiling of the moisture in their tissues blew their bodies into smoking, flaming chunks.

Hadn't we better watch the fuel gauge? Kane cautioned.

The god's amusement was feral, his hunger a blaze. The table is set. Now we dine.

He was in among the enemy troops. He split the skull of the first man he overran without breaking stride, then wheeled to chop in two the longblaster a second tried to swing on him from the hip. The same stroke severed the arm beneath, so that the front half of the rifle, hand still clutching the foregrip, sprang away. The man reeled back shrieking and spurting as Kane spun the other way, whipping his hand around in a flat backhand arc. A thunk and the least tug of resistance, and a head popped free of its torso atop a geyser of scarlet.

He was a whirlwind of flame and sharpened glass—and

blood. His sword went around and around, over and down and back around, drawing black and crimson arabesques in air. Limbs leaped from torsos, heads sprang from necks. Souls sprang from bodies.

And into Kane. Or the entirely inhuman creature he had become. The god Tonatiuh could feel the life energies of the slain flow into him, drawn into the net of blazing filaments that were his inmost being, and he exulted.

Throwing down a machine pistol, a camou-clad man turned to flee. It did no good. Kane slashed his spine in two. Blood jetted from his back and hit Kane in the face.

He smiled. Licked his lips. Enjoyed. "Your blood and souls are mine!" he shouted.

His demon rider sensed danger: a flux of lethal energies. He swung the solar shield around and up—just in time for it to flare to nova brilliance as it absorbed the full blast of a plasma rifle.

The edges of Kane's vision blackened as if charred in sudden fire. Yet this time it wasn't because his energy was drained—the opposite in fact. The plasma jolt all but overloaded him, came within an ace of burning out his neural circuits.

But Tonatiuh was all in control. He instantly leveled the sword and a solar flare leaped out in light-speed response.

His enemy, a tall, strapping warrior whose helmet was molded in the likeness of an eagle's head and hooked ferocious beak, could no more dodge a beam than Kane could. But like Kane he could read his enemy's body language in time to anticipate the shot. He saved himself from incineration. But the front half of his plasma rifle vanished into a puff of metal steam.

He cast it away and snapped a lanyard-hung sword into his hand with a flick of brawny wrist. For a moment they stood there eyeing each other across a space little more than two yards in length. The eagle knight's eyes were like obsidian mirrors themselves with a face painted red on one side and white on the other.

The sun shield's glare faded, died. No point burning *prana* to maintain it now. This was man to man. Or man to god.

The knight screamed a wordless raptor cry, then threw an overhand slash at the crown of Kane's head. Almost abstractedly the outlander wondered how the fight would go. Despite his cursory training from Taker of Fifty Captives, he had little skill in the particularities of sword-and-shield combat. Whereas this guy carried himself and moved like a stud, and presumably did.

But it wasn't Kane fighting this fight. He was only along for the ride.

Tonatiuh stepped up with his right foot, thrusting forward his own shield with all the strength of his legs. The round shields clashed; the eagle knight was driven back before his stroke could land.

He was good, though, and nothing daunted. He recovered instantly and aimed a brutal follow-up cut toward the bridge of Kane's nose.

Kane's shield came up at an angle, shed the whistling blow like water to his left. The eagle knight never tried to check the stroke, but looped it around and up for yet another overhead strike.

But Kane wasn't content merely to defend. His own sword lashed out in a blow that was almost a straight-right like a punch, a wrist flick at the end driving the sword with savage force.

The other was good. He got his shield in the way.

Kane's blow smashed it dead center. The metal-sheathed polycarbonate simply shattered. So did radius and ulna of the left arm strapped behind; Kane felt agony twist the other's life force before hearing the grunt which was his only physical response.

The eagle knight didn't cease to fight; he didn't even slow. But Kane's shield easily parried his counterstroke.

His sword split the eagle's beak. And the face beneath, and skull behind. The knight's eyes rolled inward as if to stare at the blade embedded between them. A trickle of blood ran down the left side of his aquiline nose.

Kane roared with orgasmic pleasure as the life force flowed up his arm and into him.

The fight was done. The common troops of both sides, even the fully human knights, had ceased their firefight to watch the duel. At the outcome the Talocan forces broke and ran, fleeing the wrath of the lord of the Sun.

Kane yanked free his sword, shed blood and brains with a snap of his wrist, then held it up and roared triumph after the receding backs, clad in armor or gray, white and black mottled cloth. From behind the cheers of his men flew up like a flock of startled birds.

"Bravo, Sun god," said Poncha's irony-heavy voice. "But enemy flyers come. It's about to get hot down there where you are."

"Thanks, Poncha. Keep 'em off best you can," Kane said. He was all Kane again, and poignantly aware that he had just slaughtered a brave, doomed man.

So what else is new?

"Everybody, time to pull back to Tlillan-Tlapallan. Chalchihuitlicue—Baptiste?"

"I'm here. We've got choppers hitting us, too, and a lot of great big crawly venomous things."

"Then you'd better come with us. We'll cover you as best we can."

"General Excildo won't be happy."

"Screw him," Kane said. "We can't fight every animal in the Talocan zoo and a combined air and surface attack.

"Not without a plan. And better deployment."

Chapter 20

"How goes it with Lord Quetzalcoatl?" asked the man in the silken suit. He was sleek, his hair slicked back from a classically handsome face, and if the line of the jaw had begun to grow a bit puffy, his enormous personal magnetism drew one's attention from the fact, as the excellence of his tailor made up for the thickening of his waist.

Marroquín inclined his head to the side. "A dying god. With all that both conditions imply."

The other man of consequence—both the doctor's visitors had brought aides to hover discreetly—in the room high up in the institute's main structure snorted. "Can you replace him?"

He was a big man with a frankly big paunch, but solid seeming within a khaki uniform blouse. The face above the collar, which bore stars, was a big dark Indian slab.

They stood near a smoked-glass wall looking out over the compound and ramparts, across the city spread below. Little stalks of smoke sprouted here and there, marking where the morning's action had occurred. Beyond them, hazy with distance and smoke, were visible the three great central structures of Talocan: the Palacio del Parlamento, the Black House and the Pyramid of the Gods.

"That would be a most unfortunate extremity, Don Excildo," the silk-suited man murmured.

"If we restore him to his rightful place," Dr. Marroquín

said, "the facilities of the Black House might well in turn restore his health, and spare us such expedients. But that will depend as fully on your own efforts in parliament, Don Hilario, as upon the excellent General Martínez's actions in the field, or those of our brave new gods."

The politician smiled. It was a practiced gesture, and perhaps too overtly meant nothing. "A masterstroke, Dr. Marroquín, to employ gringo barbarians from the semi-mythical *norte* to house the essences of our ancestral deities. They are more—how would one say?—readily disposable than our own people."

"They are truly extraordinary individuals," the doctor said. "Nor just in skill, training and experience. At least two of them were purpose-bred to excellence. And our newest addition, though something of a feral child, nonetheless managed to win a place in their company through her own abilities."

Don Hilario performed a gracious gesture. "Of course, of course."

"Brave, huh," Don Excildo said. "This Tonatiuh of yours just ordered our forces to withdraw, without consulting me."

The whitecoat suppressed a smile. He had monitored comm traffic during the battle, and knew that the general had called Tonatiuh to demand to know by what authority he had ordered the pullback. "Divine right," the reply had been. "If that doesn't suit you, wait till I get back, ram my sword up your ass to the hilt and give you a quick plasma enema. Then we'll check the chain of command."

Dr. Marroquín still found that immoderately amusing. General Excildo Martínez wasn't incapable, and fanatically devoted to the cause, albeit his own interpretation and for his own reasons. But he was also a self-inflated old horned toad, and no mistake.

"The Sun god's host is a man of great tactical experience," Marroquín settled for saying now. "And he possesses some of the memories and abilities of Don Pedro de Alvarado, an accomplished captain in his own right. But I have little knowledge of such matters, General. You must consult him upon his return."

"I will," the officer huffed.

The door opened. A naked woman walked in. A black giant followed her like a shadow.

She was small, slim and paper-white, from short-cropped crown to sole, not omitting the trim patch of hair between her slender, well-muscled thighs. A gasp rose from the aides.

Don Hilario's face oscillated so wildly between outrage and lust that he put Marroquín in mind of Paynal, Huitzilopochtli's flack. It was the general who found voice first. "Young woman, what is the meaning of this? It's disrespectful."

"She's not a woman, General," one of Hilario's aides said, sneering. "Can't you see? She's obviously a mutie."

"I'm a bit more than that," Domi said in a ringing voice. As she walked forward, she changed. Her skin turned black as though she were a clear vessel poured abruptly full of ink, as did her hair—everything but her eyes, which remained bloodred. Small, faint white rosettes bloomed on her glossy body, like inclusions in obsidian—or the spots of a jaguar.

Suddenly she moved aside in a blur, lashing out with one arm. The aide who had called her a mutie yelped in dismay and jumped back, raising a hand to his cheek. Four thin red parallel lines tilted across it, grew fat with red droplets that ran and mingled to become scarlet hatchwork.

"And I'm not a mutie," she said, resuming her stalk to-

ward the important men. "I'm an albino. That's different.
And now you've made me a goddess."

She rolled over her hands and held them up before her
to reveal the black needle talons that now tipped her fingers in place of nails.

Dr. Marroquín pressed hands together before his white-
coated breast and bowed. "And to what do we owe the
honor of your presence, divine Itzapapalotl?"

"I just started wondering," she said. She stopped before
them and looked up at the two visitors, tiny yet defiant.
"What exactly does *victory* mean here?"

Don Excildo's face, already the color of an old saddle,
turned purple. "You presume to question our judgment?"

Suddenly a single claw was pressing up under his chin.
He lifted his head, looking surprised. "I presume as I damn
well please, fatso."

From behind came an unmistakable metallic sound as
one of the general's aides hauled out his slab-sided model
1911 .45-caliber handblaster, snicking off the safety with
his thumb.

A black blur. Before the aide could fire, something dark
flashed before his eyes. The points of his collar fluttered
as to a wind.

The handblaster fell in clattering pieces to the polished
hardwood floor.

Domi was back with her talon poking up under the general's big jaw.

"Brigid and Kane have some issues with the…entities
you've saddled them with. They're decent people. They
were brought up nice, in a ville, with walls and a roof and
running water. Even though Kane's a trained enforcer, a
blaster born and bred, he's no true coldheart. He has his
limits. That's why he's on the run from his former em-

ployers. And much the moreso with Brigid. She was a librarian, if you can believe that.

"But me—I was raised pure Outland scum. I grew up by the rules of the desert and the *monte,* where the coyote and the hawk and the rattlesnake rule. I got no trouble being one of your nasty Aztec gods. Itzapapalotl and I are one. I *am* the obsidian butterfly."

She dug in the talon. A single red bead appeared beneath the general's chin. "Drinking my sustenance straight from your vein gives me no problems at all."

Don Hilario had recovered his professional composure. *His* neck hadn't been punctured. "Perhaps Don Excildo might condescend to answer the…goddess's questions?"

"Ask," Excildo said in a strained voice.

She lowered her hand and let his head down. He refused to rub his neck. After brief hesitation, an aide bustled up and dabbed at the blood with a kerchief.

Throughout all this, Grant had stood by like an idol, with his arms folded.

"What I want to know is, how do we know when we've won and can go home?"

"But did you not know what we were doing when you agreed to undergo the conversion?" Don Excildo asked.

"I did that for my friends, to help them," she said. "Also, I wanted to find out what it felt like to be a goddess. Turns out I could get to like it too much. So answer the question."

"When we restore Lord Quetzalcoatl to his rightful place in the triumvirate, of course," murmured Don Hilario. "When balance is brought back to Talocan, and to the valley."

She cocked a skeptical eye at him. "'Balance brought back'? Not after we cut Huitzilopochtli's and Tezcatlipoca's hearts out and sacrifice them to each other? I thought they were the serious bad guys here?"

Don Hilario paled slightly. "But that would mean chaos! Anarchy! It would totally disrupt everything—"

"Are you trying to tell me," Domi said, dangerously low, "that you might want us to die for a tie?"

"By no means," Marroquín put in hurriedly. "We must decisively defeat the enemy forces. It's simply that our goal is to compel their submission, not exterminate them, Lady Itzapapalotl."

She looked him over appraisingly. "I'm not a lady, either. But you can call me that anyway."

"Democracy must be restored," the general said fervently. "True democracy, not merely parliamentary theocracy."

"Democracy, to be sure," Don Hilario said unctuously. "But suitably managed. The people's very acquiescence in the sanguinary excesses of the two show they cannot be trusted with full self-government."

"There must be a plebiscite!" general raged. "The Estados Unidos Mexicanos must rise again!"

"Gentlemen," Dr. Marroquín said, "this is neither the time nor place for this particular debate." His tone suggested gently, gently, that Hell, hard frozen, might fit the bill.

He turned to Domi. "Have your questions been satisfactorily addressed, Lady Itzapapalotl?"

"For now," she said. "But if you even *think* of trying to shaft us…"

She turned and stalked out, leaving the words hanging behind her like a guillotine blade.

"KANE?" THE YOUNG HYBRID woman asked almost shyly. She spoke English, the language of the *científicos*—scientists, scholars and the educated middle classes—as Spanish was the tongue of the common folk, and Náhuatl the speech of the gods and their elite servants, the knights and Black House priests.

The man who stood gazing out upon the lake of lights that was Tenochtitlán and the distant wall of volcanoes casting a sullen cherry glow upon the underside of a storm front moving in from the east turned and smiled.

"Thanks for coming, Teresa," he said.

It was the place of the morning's meeting, another of the many spaces devoted to contemplation, study and quiet conversation dotted throughout the institute's immense sprawl. Aside from a few amber lights glowing at the bases of planters upholding slow explosions of green, and the light spill from outside, it was dark.

She began to cross to him. Halfway she stopped. Slowly she turned.

There were three of them. One stood at either end of a low settee placed against another floor-to-ceiling window of polarized glass. The third lounged upon it.

With the gasp Teresa turned back toward Kane, elfin lovely features accusing.

"Don't blame him," said the tall, statuesque woman with the hair of flame and eyes like the sea. "We all ganged up on him and made him ask you to meet him here."

"Just wanted a chance to talk to you without Marroquín or that floppy-puppy Ernesto hovering around," said the enormous black man with the *bandido* mustache, who against all reason had refused the gift of godhead when it was offered freely to him.

"So you think I am so inconsiderable next to the doctor?" she flared.

"Of course." It was the unnaturally pale woman, no bigger than Teresa herself, with the short hair the color of sun-bleached bone and the exhibitionistic streak, rising from the couch. She wore a short square-cut smock embroidered with stylized images of butterflies and jaguars, totems of the entity with which she had been imbued. Grant had persuaded her to put it on to reduce friction with the locals. "Get real, *chica*. You're not in his league."

She skinned the smock off over her head and tossed it aside, putting its wrinkle-resistant qualities to the test. Her nude body glowed like a pale white flame, as though with light of its own. She sat again. "Ah, that's better. We're all friends here, right?"

"No disrespect to you, Teresa," Grant rumbled. "We've got an old snake of our own back home, name of Lakesh. We can't get anything over on him, either."

Teresa turned to Kane. His scarred, handsome face was grave. She felt her cheeks burn with fresh outrage. "What use will you make of me, then?"

Kane shook his head. "Sorry if you feel I've taken advantage. Then again, just think how Baptiste and I feel about what you've done to us."

He cut off her flood of expostulation with an upraised palm. "We want answers. Nothing else."

"But we'll settle for nothing less," the naked albino woman said.

Teresa sighed, felt her shoulders slump. "All right. Ask."

"Why don't you go ahead and sit, child?" Chalchihuitlicue said. Teresa hesitated a moment, then did as she was bid.

The god Tonatiuh came and sat across from her. "You've been watching us for a while," he said gently, "with that Smoking Mirror of yours."

"It isn't mine!"

"No," Domi said, "your doctor pal swiped it from Tezcatlipoca when he defected."

"It belongs to all the people of the valley."

"Whatever," Kane said. "The important thing is, you know plenty about us. You know our history with hybrids is not exactly pleasant. So mebbe you can understand why it strikes us as important to find out just exactly what they—and plenty evidence of their technology—are doing down here where there aren't supposed to be any."

"You despise me, then?" Her long eyelashes fluttered to sweep her huge eyes clear of a sudden glaze of tears.

The tall woman crossed to her. Teresa made herself look squarely at her, although she was at least as intimidated by the woman's size and striking looks as by the divine powers she herself had helped confer upon her. "May I?"

"Of course, Lady Precious Green."

Brigid sat beside her. "We don't despise you, dear. Neither Kane nor I are entirely happy about being kidnapped and…violated, but we understand your reasons, and we have agreed to help you against a very dangerous common enemy. But there's just too much we don't know."

"And in a game like the one you've pulled us into," Kane said, "not knowing can be lethal."

The hybrid woman sat a moment, looking down at the floor with its tiles polished hardwood in various shades. Then she raised her head.

"Very well. I will tell you what I can. You know the tale of your reunification."

"Only since we were schoolkids," Grant said.

"But there is more to the story than you know, Señor Grant."

"Now, that's a surprise."

Brigid sent a green eye-dart at the big man. "Don't pay any attention to him. He's in his growly-bear mode."

Grant growled.

"What you may not know," Teresa said, "is that there existed factions within the group responsible for the re-unification scheme—the conspiracy of hybrids and humans that cloaked itself behind the name of Archon Directorate."

Brigid glanced to Kane in surprise. "Oh, so?" he said.

Teresa nodded. "The original intent truly was benign—to rescue Earth and what was left of humanity from anarchy and desolation. Only after reunification was accomplished did it become clear there was a hard core within the Directorate whose only aim was domination."

"You mean," Domi said, stretching like a cat, "that there were really hybrids who thought of us humans as something other than livestock?"

Teresa nodded. "Oh yes, Lady Itzapapalotl. They believed that hybrids and humans should live and work in total harmony. As some of us who came after do still."

"In short," Grant said, "your side lost."

"Yes. And fled here."

"Where they somehow hooked up with Felicidad Mendoza," Brigid said.

Teresa sighed. "And her twin sons, Pablo and Pedro. A bitter error. Under the mirror's influence she had already fused her identity with that of Coatlicue. And her son Pedro, elder, weaker and more studious of the pair, had already begun to plumb the mirror's secrets with an understanding beyond his years."

"So Pedro Mendoza became Tezcatlipoca?" Brigid asked.

"And Pablo, of course, was invested with Huitzilopochtli. But this came later, after the mother had made common cause with the hybrid exiles."

"What was the basis for all this cheerful cooperation?" Kane asked.

"Felicidad had the powers of the goddess, and had built a power base of worshipers among the survivors of the city's final destruction. But she was only one, her sons half-grown. Her status, even her survival, was far from assured.

"For their part, the exiles were fascinated by the phenomenon of an actual goddess—a true human, not a Danaan. And she was in possession of an obvious Danaan relic, or a Danaan-derived one. The hybrids and humans were fugitives, strangers in a strange land, fearing they might be hunted down and exterminated by those whom they had helped make themselves overlords of all North America. Alliance was the natural course for both sides."

"And offered a shot at the social engineering the exiles had tried up north," Brigid said.

The hybrid woman nodded.

"Let me guess," Grant said. "They got screwed again."

Teresa nodded again. "But please, Lord Grant. You are getting ahead of the story."

He waved a huge hand at her. "Sorry. Go right ahead on. And it's just 'Grant.'"

"Thank you, sir. They joined together, the exiles and the nascent gods, making use of the still very powerful remnants of ancient technology the exiles possessed, in conjunction with the Smoking Mirror. Even as the villes of the Nine Baronies were built in the north, so the rubble of what had been Mexico City was leveled and the new city of Tenochtitlán built upon it.

"The newcomers had trained the Mendoza twins in all the arts they knew—thinking, I suppose, to bind the boys more closely to them." The young woman's voice was tinged with bitterness. "Yet in the end they were fully their mother's sons. When they entered adolescence, during the reconstruction, Coatlicue, with the full cooperation of the exile leader, Morall, and his chief scientists Daraul and Dr. Marroquín, invested each with godhood. They became, each in accordance with his nature, the Hummingbird on the Left and the deity named for the Smoking Mirror itself.

"But more was needed still. Even with their superhuman technology, the task of rebuilding was enormous. As were the threats they faced—lethal earthquakes and eruptions, marauding monsters, raiders from outside the valley. So Coatlicue raised up still more gods and goddesses, with the acquiescence of the exiles—Xipe Totec, the flayed god, Tlaloc, Chicomecoatl, the goddess of maize. They helped rebuild the city, and to make agriculture thrive within the valley, with the help of climatic change that brought unprecedented levels of rainfall, and the volcanoes whose ashfalls enriched the soil with nutrients."

The naked young woman rose, and as she did took her aspect upon her like a glass filled suddenly with night. The roseate efflorescences glowed faintly, like distant galaxies.

"Where does Quetzalcoatl come into to all this? Brigid says he's a hybrid, too."

Teresa pressed her lips together momentarily. "The new gods were not sufficient. A matter as much of politics as power—the people longed for a god who would truly represent their interests and with whom they could identify. At the same time, friction increased steadily between the exiles and their allies. The outsiders sensed the balance of power slipping away from them—and began to sense in Coatlicue and her brood tendencies similar to those within the Archon Directorate who had driven them forth in the first place. The gods wanted more than just paranormal powers. They wanted to *rule.*

"A compromise was struck—or so it was presented by Tezcatlipoca, who by then had often interposed himself as peacemaker between the exiles and his volatile sibling and mother. What was needed was nothing less than to incarnate the life god Quetzalcoatl. Morall the exile leader was himself an early specimen of what became baronial-class hybrids—his abilities and nature were appropriate to that deity. It was agreed that he should assume the mantle and personality pattern of the feathered serpent.

"He underwent the same process to which my lord and ladies were subjected, involving, among other things, stimulation of the pineal gland with converging beams of slow neutrons, in order to stimulate certain faculties latent within the human, and hybrid, brain. It is not a protracted procedure, but takes hours to recover from, during which time the subject is unconscious. Tezcatlipoca had laid a clever plan: while Morall was indisposed, the gods struck. They seized total control of Tenochtitlán and the surrounding valley. The exiles who resisted were killed out of hand, the rest secured under guard. All except Daraul, who was in on the plot.

"When Morall awakened, he was presented with a fait accompli. He was offered a choice—to join a triumvirate as coruler of the valley and the gods themselves, or see his remaining comrades sacrificed to Huitzilopochtli and Tezcatlipoca."

"Which I think is what they used to call a no-brainer," Domi said, "back before skydark."

"The plumed serpent saw no choice but to accept the devil's bargain. He did what he could to contain the lust for blood power of Coatlicue, her sons and their followers. Then, about thirty years ago, the brother gods—who had long since become deadly rivals themselves—combined against him, toppled him and drove him out. Since then the only thing that has grown faster than their power has been their greed for more—and for blood. And *prana*."

She rose. "And now you know the story of how hybrids once dreamed they could live in harmony with humans—and were twice betrayed. By, ironically enough, humans and hybrids working in concert. So I suppose in the end they proved their point, didn't they?"

The foreigners sat or stood in silence for a few moments, while the story sank in. "One question," Grant said. "If you don't want to answer it, don't."

Teresa bowed her head. "Ask it."

"How do you come into the picture? The—what?—hybrid-supremacist types we've got back home don't much object to using darker-skinned folks as servants. After all, we're all just livestock to them. But when it comes to breeding themselves, they always seem to work on the principle that white is right."

"The exiled hybrids harbored comparatively little prejudice against humanity in general," Brigid said. "That may account for a lack of more specific forms of racism."

"Lady Chalchihuitlicue is correct that the exiles tried to free themselves from prejudice in all its forms," Teresa said. Her words rang with bitterness now. "But that benign impulse isn't where I spring from.

"Among the hybrids who fled el Norte was a woman named Tyana. She too was a prototype of what became the barons. She was exceptionally human in appearance, and likewise exceptionally attractive to pure humans. Or so it would appear, since it pleased the god of the Smoking Mirror to seduce her. But the breeding plan that produced her was not entirely successful. Her hips and birth canal could not accommodate the size of a half-human child. She died in childbirth.

"Mine. I am the daughter of Tezcatlipoca, Lord of Hell."

Chapter 21

Kane paced his bedchamber. Despite, or perhaps because of, his status as a god the room was austere: a bed, a table, a lamp. Doors led to a small closet and bathroom with shower.

He passed out here at night, unless the terrible weariness overcame him somewhere else. He woke here in the morning. He doubted that he slept here in between. Brigid told him that when he drew her to him through quantum space she had arrived in some kind of clinic, beside a sealed cylinder. She believed he had been inside.

Tonight he was filled with strange, uncomfortable energy. The day's battle had brought unpleasant revelations about what he was—or what he was becoming. Nor was Teresa's tale exactly soothing. It proved how much more was going on, layers beneath layers, than he had any clue about or hope for getting to the bottom of. And not just here in the valley of Mexico.

Eventually he threw himself down upon the thin mattress. What came over him was more like a delirium-laced drowse than true sleep.

And then she came to him.

At first he thought she was a dream: a beautiful young woman, black hair hanging heavy and straight past her shoulders, clad in a gown of sheer white fabric that accented as much as it concealed of her ripe form.

Warily he sat up and swung his legs over the side of the bed. He was almost as surprised to find himself still here as her.

"Who are you?" he asked. He spoke the ancient tongue of the valley, so alien and familiar.

She smiled. Her lips were wide and full, her cheekbones high. Her eyes were almonds, little white showing to either side of black disks. She tipped her head back and let the gown drop from her broad shoulders.

She was nude beneath. He'd figured that out already.

Her breasts were large and heavy, the nipples were broad and dark. Her pubic hair was dense jungle.

She held wide her arms, inviting. She had as yet spoken no word.

"What's the angle?" Kane asked in English.

"Do you not want me, Lord Tonatiuh?"

To his chagrin he found he did. He was glad a fold of the thin gray blanket had come with him and hung across his lap; he slept naked. His response was so immediate and emphatic that he wondered if it was more his demon riders' reaction than his own. Or if it had something to do with the strange electricity that had seemed to prickle in his nerves since he had killed those men in hand-to-hand combat that day.

Not knowing made him feel vulnerable. The raging hard-on began to diminish.

Still...

He smiled lopsidedly. "So my hosts see fit to reward my efforts on their behalf? About damn time."

He stood. The blanket fell away. She waited. Her lips parted. He reached for her.

From the communicator on his nightstand, Brigid's voice spoke: "Kane! Don't touch her! She's death!"

BRIGID SAT PERCHED on her own bed, sipping chocolate. It came in two flavors here, alkali bitter or as sweet as week-old death. She was opting for sweet. Either brand carried a jolt of caffeine guaranteed to make your heart start beating after it had been cut in four pieces.

She knew even that wouldn't be enough when the nervous energy jag wore off and the dreadful lethargy overcame her.

You'll die if you leave the valley. Their hosts' warning tolled like a carillon bell in her skull at such times, when she dangled between hyper and comatose. What had been done affected their metabolisms; Marroquín had admitted that much. There was a risk of literal burnout. Quetzalcoatl, once Morall, now the chosen vessel of a god, was about to toss that god back in the pantheonic pot to await re-reincarnation because, for all his own healing powers and the bastard science of Danaan and Annunaki, Archon and hybrid and the mad genius-god Tezcatlipoca, he was sick unto death and could not hold body and souls together much longer.

What will happen to us? Her hosts had assured them the treatment they had been given could be reversed. Brigid had her doubts: how exactly did you reverse bombarding the pineal with slow neutrons? Bombing it with fast ones?

Her bedside communicator spoke.

"Lady Precious Green," Dr. Marroquín said. "You must get to your friend Kane's room at once. He is in great peril. I fear he has received a visitation by Chicomecoatl—the goddess whose embrace is certain death."

AT BRIGID'S WORDS Kane rocked back. "Do not listen to her," his visitor said in a voice of infinite seductiveness.

"She's only jealous. Come to me." She reached to enfold him in her arms.

He blocked her with his forearms. "Not so fast," he said. "There's something about the prospect of sudden death that just makes it hard to keep a charge in the Shock-stick, if you catch my drift."

"The sweetest mystery awaits."

"That's what I'm afraid of, lady."

Suddenly she was a woman of middle years, her hair a tangle, stocky but not, so he noticed, altogether unattractive. She leaped back, and a disk of intolerable yellow brilliance blazed abruptly in her hands. He felt the heat of it three yards away, so intense he smelled the bedclothes begin to smolder.

"Then die!"

She threw the flaming disk at his throat.

He caught it in his right hand. It grew brighter, glowed with intolerable fury. The bedclothes caught fire with a whoosh behind him.

The awful radiance dimmed, went out. The flames streamed toward Kane's bare legs as if sucked by sudden vacuum, and vanished.

Then his hand was clamped on nothing. The fingers were intact, the skin unblemished. Or no more than they had been before they gripped the sun-hot disk.

"You're Chicomecoatl," he said. " 'Seven Snakes.' They told me about you—one of your aspects is that of a mother with the Sun for a shield."

He smiled then. It wasn't an attractive expression.

"I begin to think Talocan can be had," he said. "How smart was that—sending an assassin with a solar shield to slay the Sun god?"

He raised his arms. And then his whole body blazed

forth with a terrible brilliance, brighter than the sun disk she had hurled at him. She threw up her arms before her face—and changed again.

A little girl stood there, dressed in a white smock and looking scared, clutching a sunflower in her hand. "Please, mister," she said in English in a child's voice. "I'm just a little girl. I wouldn't hurt you. I was only joking."

She began to cry. The light that shone from Kane's body dwindled, went out. He lowered his arms. He felt disoriented, foolish.

"I couldn't hurt anybody," she sobbed, shaking her head. Her tears struck Kane's bare chest like drops of rain. "I'm frightened, mister. Please hold me."

She held out her arms again.

The door opened.

The little girl spun to face it. Brigid stood there, tall and terrible, with a look in her green eyes Kane had never seen there before. The child Chicomecoatl looked her in the eyes.

Stiffened.

Fell dead.

"Baptiste!" Kane roared. "What the hell do you think you're doing?"

Still staring intently at the now lifeless child's body sprawled upon the floor, Brigid held up an imperious hand.

The outlines of the child's body blurred, changed. The woman Kane had first seen lay there now, naked, beautiful. And still dead.

"You men," Brigid said, shaking her head. "You're so easy."

DR. MARROQUÍN SUPERVISED as technicians in pastel lab coats collected the late maize goddess and trundled her off on a gurney. Teresa turned up briefly, too, wrapped in a red silk housecoat, but only cast Kane a hot-eyed cryptic glance and whirled away.

"Mighty fortuitous how you happened to know I had a nocturnal visitor, Doc," Kane said slowly. He had on a lightweight smock. "Not to mention who she was."

He smiled. "Not fortuitous at all, Lord Tonatiuh, but rather a trifle of twentieth-century technology," the white-coat said. "A fiber-optic video pickup embedded in a corner of the wall."

"You bugged my room? A god's own private sleeping chamber?"

"It eliminates a good deal of guesswork, don't you think?" Marroquín was totally unfazed by Kane's vehemence. Kane thought about giving him a quick hotfoot, dismissed it. He wouldn't give the sneaky little shit the satisfaction.

"Besides," the doctor added, "we require it so that we know when you've gone to sleep and may commence your life-support treatment. It is essential to your survival, although we make it as painless and unobtrusive as we can."

"How did she get in here?" Brigid demanded.

Marroquín shrugged. "We will conduct an investigation and attempt to tighten our security, but who can foresee results? Chicomecoatl was a shape changer, as you both can attest. In all events, we must all be on our guard from this point on."

A BURST OF 9 mm slugs chewed yellow dust out of the corner of the building as Grant ducked back.

Domi crouched atop a trash bin, nude body glistening in the sun that filtered down through thin overcast like a fetish carved from black volcanic glass. "Why don't you just use your plasma rifle and fry their asses once and for all?" she wanted to know.

For answer Grant ducked down, then whipped around the corner—just his shooting arm and half his face—to fire two quick tribursts. Then he snapped back into cover as a fresh furious volley replied.

"Two more down," he said. "I hate to waste joules on pissants like this. With all these gods and goddesses and monsters on the loose, you never know when you're gonna need a lot of plasma in a hell of a hurry."

"Superficially plausible," Domi said. "But bullshit. You just like the challenge."

Getting ready to pop out and shoot some more, he checked himself and swung back to her with an outraged expression. "Where'd you learn to talk like that?"

"Dunno. Mebbe Brigid. Mebbe Lakesh. Mebbe even the obsidian flutterby." She smiled impishly and shrugged a glossy shoulder.

Then she shouted, "Hey!"

An especially bold eagle knight dodged sideways into view, an MP-5 held at waist level. Grant yelled and knocked the blaster's barrel up as the man triggered an ear-splitting burst.

Domi sprang. It was a long spring, maybe twenty feet, arrow fast. As she flew past the knight, now wrestling with Grant, she reached out a claw-tipped hand, hooked the flesh on the right side of his face and used her hurtling body weight to yank his head around. His neck broke with a crack like a handblaster shot.

She landed on all fours in the middle of the street, facing a squad of Talocan sec men who had crept up in file behind the knight with their backs to the wall. She snarled. They turned and fled.

"Nyah, nyah!" she called after them. Then she bounced back under cover as some of their buddies up the block fired her up.

"Now who's showing off?" Grant wanted to know.

She stuck her tongue out at him. It was still pink. "Nyah to you, too."

He sighed. "Let's roll. We got things to see and people to do."

They checked cautiously down the street from which the attack had come. It was empty of enemies as far as they could see. They moved on, seeking more concentrations of enemies, more trouble to get into. Grant padded along on foot, acutely aware of the fact that although it was fairly cloudy his shadow suit was anything but inconspicuous out here on a daylit street. Domi kept pace leaping from ledge to cornice a story or two up like a naked ape. When no hand- or footholds offered, she made her own, sinking the needle claws on her fingers and the similar set on her toes into brick or stone or concrete as if it were tree bark.

They heard nearby shooting; here in this cubist jungle of Colhuacan business district, deserted by reason of the battle in progress, sound generally traveled short distances and unpredictably at that. Domi scampered ahead and peered around a corner from twenty feet up. Then she came back to where Grant waited and dropped lightly to the sidewalk beside him.

"Our guys in a firefight with a bunch of their guys," she said, hitching at the shoulder-rig harness that supported her Detonics handblaster. It was the only thing she wore. She reasoned that since, fast as she was, she couldn't outrun bullets—and an overtly lust-struck Ernesto had told her that her reflexes and twitch-response musculature were faster than any deity's yet measured—none of the bad guys was likely to be able to, either. In any event she hadn't yet felt a need to shoot anybody.

Maybe she just enjoyed ripping people open and having their blood run all over her naked skin. The notion did little to lighten Grant's mood.

"Let's sneak around and jump the bad guys from behind," she suggested with a predator's happy eagerness.

"It's what we're here to do," Grant conceded.

In spite of himself, his eyes trailed down her body. He shook his head. "Girl, sometimes I worry about you."

Domi glanced down at herself. "What?"

Grant gestured halfheartedly—a rare thing in itself, for him to do anything without total commitment. Her pubic hair was shaved into a stylized skull. It wasn't especially visible. But Grant was all too aware it was there.

"What's wrong with that?" she demanded. "I'm just trying to blend in with the local culture. It's the least I can do—I am one of their goddesses, you know?"

"This is all too strange for me. I thought I'd seen strange before, running with this bunch. But this all is really strange."

From somewhere ahead came peals of wild laughter.

Which at once changed into screams.

Chapter 22

Lightning split the lead cloud ceiling over Kane's head in a seam of intolerable brilliance.

"The gods Tlaloc and Xipe Totec come, riding the thunder!" the radio blared in the command center on the roof of the Agricultural Products Distribution Combine building in midtown Colhuacan. "You must aid us, Lord Tonatiuh! Please—"

The end was drowned in a peal of thunder like the earth cracking open.

"It is a general assault," One Arrow said, looking up with an earpiece pressed to the side of his head by his fingertips. He was an intel officer detached from Don Excildo's staff. "A mixed force of sec men and knights. They're hitting us at the Parque Vicente Fernández."

"How far?" Brigid asked, shouting to be heard above the reverberations of a second thunder roar, fading in a grumble.

"Just under a klick, Lady Chalchihuitlicue."

She looked at Kane.

He shrugged. "Here's where we earn the big bucks," he said.

TWO MEN DANCED past them down the street, each intent upon strangling the other. One was laughing wildly, with lips skinned so far back from his teeth blood started from his gums. The other's eyes wept blood.

A knight of the Blue Macaw staggered toward them, shrieking hysterical laughter. His helmet was gone, his topknot disarrayed, his eyes blood road maps. As he neared Grant and Domi, he raised his right hand to his temple and fired his laser armlet. His head exploded in a cloud of black steam. The body took three steps more toward Grant and Domi, fountaining blood with each of the heart's last convulsive beats.

The spray ebbed, dwindled. The corpse fell almost at their feet.

"This is bad," Domi said. "As in, the opposite of good."

"Caught you the first time," Grant said sourly. He checked the magazine on his Sin Eater to make sure it was full. Then he checked to be sure he had a round chambered.

Around the corner strode a figure. It was tall and clad in a cape of green feathers. On its feet were stone clogs four inches high, so that it clacked when it walked. Its head was covered by a box perhaps a foot square. It looked made of wood, or stiff fabric stretched on some kind of frame, of an off-white parchment color. On it were painted various highly stylized figures: serpents, bats, distorted human figures, the ubiquitous skulls, all in different colors. Its very gaudiness was somehow sinister.

The being stopped and regarded them with hands on hips. "Ah, outlanders," it said in better than passable English. Grant sensed it just meant foreigners, without the connotations the word had up north. But then, who knew, in this fused-out place?

"Micapetlacalli," Domi murmured from behind Grant's left shoulder. "Careful with this one, Grant."

A squad of sec men with longblasters at port arms trotted out of the alley behind the bizarre apparition. "Got him scoped," Grant said. "You go play with these boys."

"Done," Domi said, and became a blur, which soon intersected with red and screaming.

The tall figure had continued to move toward Grant, balancing on his tall clogs. Despite them he moved with sinuous, sinister grace.

"I am called the box of death," the figure said, voice echoing slightly from within the eponymous object. "Look now into my box of death."

He reached up, almost delicately, and swung open the front of the box.

But Grant never saw. He didn't need to. The man was inside seven yards now, classic combat-handblaster range. After Grant's decades of practice and experience, indexing his body into two-handed shooting stance was so automatic he didn't need to see his front sight to know the muzzle of his Sin Eater in its perforated shroud was aimed right into the opening.

"I'm Grant," he said. "Look now into my box of nine." And held the trigger back.

OUT IN THE PARK blasters were crackling and grens thumping as the two sides slugged it out in a conventional firefight. The Parque Vicente Fernández was huge, half a klick across here where they faced the attackers coming from the east, half a klick deep, narrowing slightly in a vague wedge shape toward the broad promenade fronting the local irruption of Texcoco on the Quetzalcoatl forces' right. Kane, Brigid and an escort of knights crouched inside the blown-in window of a bistro fronting the park, staying mindful of the broken glass.

Firebird, ranking survivor of yesterday's bodyguard, filled the gods in quickly on the tactical situation. Originally the good guys held the whole park. Fifteen minutes ago a large force spearheaded by at least two of Talocan's most powerful, the flayed one and the rain god, had smashed them hard and sent them reeling. The defenders had managed to rally and hold around a concrete bandstand and a miniature lagoon just this side of the middle of the park, backed by shooters hidden in some woods.

After butchering a few windrows of sec men, the enemy gods had kept their own heads down. As Kane was way too well aware, the most potent god could be laid low by a stray energy beam, if not bullet. They had achieved their initial aim: tossing down a challenge to the feathered serpent's interloper gods.

He switched channels on his comm unit. "Grant. Domi. Come in."

"Yee-ha!" Domi's combo rebel yell and panther screech almost took the top of his head off. "Grant just chilled a god! A whole god! By himself."

"He's just the man to do it. You there, Grant?"

"Grant here."

"You sound sour. Deicide doesn't agree with you?"

"It was a fusie with a friggin' box on his head, Kane. Whoop-te-do."

"It was Micapetlacalli," Domi said breathlessly. "Mebbe not the biggest or baddest. But he had only just zeroed-out a whole platoon of knights and sec men by his lonesome, is all. If you saw his face you went whack and self-deathed, or your brain hemorrhaged and blood bubbled out your ears and eyes, that kind of thing."

"Hence the box, I guess," said Kane.

"Not much of his ugly mug left now, after I dumped half a mag into it," Grant said, this time with an air of gloomy satisfaction.

"Good job. Looks like we're about to mix it up with a couple of the biggies."

"All right!" Domi shouted. He winced again. "We're there!"

"Back off the trigger, Butterfly. Don't you two charge over here. What I need you to do is circle around east, swinging well north of the lake, see if you can work in behind them."

"Spoilsport!"

"Negative. If you bring it off, you're on their backs with them looking this way. Then you can murder them all you like."

"Are you hosing us, Kane?" Grant asked.

"Big time. But you know this really is the best way, Grant."

"I hear you."

"Yeah. But will you play it my way?"

"Affirmative. So will the iron butterfly or whatever the hell she is, here. Grant out."

A line of yellow-white radiance bright as a thousand searchlights jagged down from the clouds. A whole squad of sec men duckwalking toward the gazebo screamed as their bodies abruptly went incandescent and the hair stood out from their heads and took fire. Then the lightning bolt winked out, leaving huge purple afterimage balloons swimming in Kane's dazzled eyes and charred bodies smoking to the ground.

Ducked down below the sill, Brigid looked up at Kane. Her face was greenish-pale. But her strong jaw was firm. "I think they know we're here."

"Right. You men skirmish forward toward the middle of the park. I'm right behind you." He turned to Brigid. "And you're right behind me."

"Like hell I am! I'm sticking right at your side."

"Like hell you are." He held up his left arm. His buckler blazed into a disk of yellow brilliance. "Unless the rain shorts it out, the solar shield will cover both of us."

The knights charged out, screaming war cries and firing bolts and beams. Brigid fell in behind Kane's left shoulder as he clambered out to follow the warriors out into the park. Their guard advanced by fire-and-movement fits and starts. Most of the action was far out front, but the occasional bullet cracked past. Kane thanked the gods, or the Tenochtitlán city fathers—same thing, come to think of it—for the abundance of solid concrete park benches. Not that it befit the dignity of the Sun god, Tonatiuh, to cower behind cover, but just in case. The solar shield was all good and well, but only sheltered so much.

The air was thick with the smell of rain and tart with ozone—and the barbecue smell of seared flesh. Burned propellant and lubricant had begun to add their bouquet to the mix.

White sparks danced in the glare circle of the solar shield. "Kane! What's that?" Brigid demanded.

"Bullets."

They were taking fire from a garden patch several hundred yards away to the left, planted with shoulder-high but great-leaved plants. Excellent concealment but no cover—no capacity to stop return fire—to speak of. Kane pointed the spot out to his escort. Several knights went prone or took a knee and fired. Laser beams and a plasma blast flared in the gloom, shockingly bright.

Though he heard screams as the beams hit flesh—or as steam flash-boiled from the lush vegetation scalded enemy fighters—Kane had lost interest. That problem was tended to; he was into Tonatiuh mode now, looking for worthy opposition: Xipe or Tlaloc. Am I crazy? wondered the Kane who was still all Kane. But it was a cry from the cheap seats.

Suddenly men were running toward them from the middle of the park. "This is it," Kane said, waving his sword over his head. "Let's shake it loose."

"You sure this is a good idea?" Brigid asked.

"No."

They trotted toward the gazebo. The fleeing men threw away their blasters and started screaming and clawing at themselves. One of the knights approached the advancing group at a wild sprawling run, then collapsed, tumbled and lay still on the damp thick grass.

Kane paused to crouch beside the man. Dead. He looked burned, but with no charring: the skin on his head was discolored, bubbled in places, peeled back away from yellow bone in others. The eyelids were puffed shut, with a foam reminiscent of salted slugs oozing out between.

"The breath of the flayed one!" one of the escorting knights exclaimed.

"What did this?" Kane asked. "Some kind of radiation?"

"I think gas, as the name implies," Brigid said. "It looks like characteristic effects of an extremely powerful blistering agent."

"Blistering agent?"

"Mustard gas." She glanced up dubiously. "I'm not pretending to be a tactician, but if that's what Xipe's power amounts to, it doesn't seem too smart pairing him with the rain god. Rain cancels out most aerosol agents."

"Mebbe the Talocan gods are only too human. Like us."

"Xipe Totec!" another knight called. "The flayed one comes!"

Kane and Brigid looked to the gazebo. A figure had appeared there. It was the size and shape of a tall, athletically proportioned man. But it was red. Not like any kind of skin.

But the red of an open wound. It wore a strange, shriveled-looking cape about its wide shoulders.

"Xipe Totec appears in the guise of a flayed man," Brigid said almost absentmindedly, "wearing his own skin upon his shoulders."

"That's really lovely, Baptiste," Kane said.

Their escorts pointed blasters at the figure. They seemed reluctant to fire on the person of a god, even an enemy god who had just subjected a number of their comrades to horrible death. Colhuacan sec men fled at sight of the being.

In his right hand Xipe held a mace with what appeared to be a round stone head. On his left forearm was strapped a circular shield like Kane's. He reached his arms out to the side and raised them.

Even at this range Kane and Brigid could see that his ribs seemed to open outward like louvers, or the breathing slits of a shark. A maroon-colored gas issued from his sides.

"All right. How does he do that?" Kane demanded.

"Perhaps poison sacs inside the rib cage. Except how is that possible, if his aspect is just a Danaan shape-changing illusion?" She shook her head. "This is really incredible. If only we could study what's actually going on here!"

"I'll try to bag him so Lakesh can study him," Kane said. "Marroquín probably has all the answers already, if he'd give them to you straight."

He straightened. "Watch Lady Precious Green and discourage any mortals who try to interfere," he ordered the knights of the Blue Macaw. "This one's mine."

He aimed his sword, summoned the power of the Sun. The glowing arcs seemed uncharacteristically dim and weak, but they were there. A lance of plasma sizzled toward the flayed god, who sidestepped. The blast shattered a pillar of the gazebo, causing part of the roof to sag.

"Kane," Brigid said urgently, "lightning—"

He smelled ozone. Hairs stood at his nape. With his own enhanced reaction time and speed he darted to Brigid and held his shield up over their heads, summoning the Sun's power to defend them.

"Wouldn't plasma be more a conductor than an insulator?" Brigid wondered.

"We'll find out."

The world whited out around them. Kane felt as if a sledgehammer had struck his shield arm. The impact drove him to one knee. Brigid, who carried no shield or weapons other than the Glock strapped under her arm, helped brace him.

Within Kane's brain, whiteness and blackness warred. Overload! he thought. With sudden insight he forced himself to concentrate on feeling the horrific energy surge, on channeling it into the fiery arcs that sprang out through the surface of the earth from its very innards and twined around them both like solar prominences. The lightning bolt was heading for the earth anyway; the question was whether he could shunt it safely around the two bifurcated bags of protoplasm huddled beneath the shield, frail despite the *prana* powers with which they had been imbued.

It worked. They lived.

Kane stretched his length upon the ground as the terrific blinding whiteness winked out. He was whirled away into blackness. Before he gave himself up to it totally, he heard a voice within him say, "Well done, mortal. Not even I knew that could be done."

"GAH!" LIKE A SCALDED CAT Domi jumped to the top of an outsized block of yellow stone that made up one flank of the broad staircase of what looked like a public building of some sort, maybe a library or museum. She crouched there, her glassy skin quivering. "Bugs!"

Still planted firmly on the pavement of the street, Grant grunted. Domi wasn't squeamish. It was the rare Outlander who survived to adulthood if she was. Pressed by hunger she would eat bugs, as well as other items that made even Grant queasy.

But there were bugs and then there were *bugs*. As in a mad profusion of the things, thousands and tens of thousands, a living river flowing toward them across a broad street and over curbs and planters. It reached him. He could feel the big beetles and scorpions and foot-long millipedes crawl across his shadow-suited feet. Not exactly a pleasant sensation, but these small creepy-crawlies, venomous as some of them no doubt were, couldn't bite through the armor, woven as it was of spider silk, Monocrys and Spectra fabrics.

"Grant!" A cat scream of warning from above. He looked up. Itzapapalotl was reaching a taloned hand down for him. "Jump! *Now.*"

"What do I care about a bunch of—"

Her eyes blazed like bloody fire. "Jump or die," she said in a low voice.

It wasn't that Domi didn't have it in her to fuck around. But not when the hammer came down. Without further thought he leaped. Her hand caught his burly forearm; his hand caught her slimmer bare one and looked pale against the black of the shadow suit and Domi's obsidian skin.

"Wait a minute!" he exclaimed, feet dangling above the vermin torrent. "You can't—"

Domi straightened, yanking him up and setting him on his feet atop the block.

"—lift me," he finished lamely.

"Enhanced musculoskeletal efficiency," she said. "Comes with divinity."

"Why'd you want me up here so bad?"

She inclined her head.

The arthropods had been joined by rattlesnakes. Sidewinders, diamondbacks, prairie rattlers. Their needle-like fangs, an inch long and more, would penetrate his shadow suit, like as not.

And if they didn't, the fangs belonging to their king-sized cousins, not to mention the stings of the yard-long and up scorpions, all following the smaller creatures like a cresting vermin tsunami, assuredly would.

KANE'S FIRST GREETING on return to the world was a stench of charred meat, as thick and cloying as fog. Shot through it was the smell of ozone.

"—answer me, Kane," Brigid was saying. She knelt over him with her face set in a mask of concern. "Come back to us. We haven't got much time."

"We're alive."

"For the moment."

He sat up. His head was clearing quickly. Around them were strewed half a dozen bodies, carbonized to greater or lesser degrees by the lightning strike. Most looked dead. Two, stirring and moaning, were evidently not that lucky.

She handed him his sword. "Trouble," she said.

He got to his feet pretty quickly, looking around. Xipe Totec strode toward them, staring at them with huge lid-less eyeballs and a skeletal smile. He was less than forty yards away. The Blue Macaw knights were backing away from him, blasters leveled, still not firing.

A couple of hundred yards off to the right, just this side of the lake, stood a figure in a resplendent headdress surrounded by a substantial retinue. Tlaloc, a voice said in Kane's mind—and it seemed to know what it was talking about.

Brigid turned away and wrenched a round shield off a dead knight's outflung arm. "What do you want that for?" Kane asked. His mind felt for the burning filaments again, but didn't get much. Warding the bolt seemed to have emptied him. "It won't stop lightning."

"Bullets," Brigid said. "Better than nothing." She looked at Xipe. He began to raise his arms. They looked as if they had raw cuts of meat fixed to them with invisible tape.

"My turn," she said. She frowned in concentration.

The Parque Vicente Fernández had a thoroughly modern underground sprinkler system buried beneath its lush sod. Apparently the local rainfall wasn't enough for the landscapers. The cap blew off an outlet right before Xipe's stepping right foot and sprayed him with water.

He sprang back with a hiss of dismay. "Bet that stings, Skinless Boy," Kane said, hefting his sword in his hand.

"I shall melt your skin and your eyes, outlanders!" the flayed god screeched. He crouched. His ribs began to do their opening-gill trick.

Four sprinkler heads blew. Five streams of water converged on the god. The maroon fog wisping from between his ribs vanished, washed down his sides and spindle shanks. He looked down at himself in consternation.

Kane felt the hair of his nape rise once more.

Chapter 23

Kane caught Brigid in a flying tackle and bore her five yards through the air as a violent white discharge vitrified the spot where they had stood.

He jumped to his feet and reached the hand of his shield arm to help her up. She seemed to be having trouble breathing. He realized he might have hit her a little hard with that godlike speed and strength of his.

"Sorry," he said. Except he couldn't hear the word. He couldn't hear anything. Indeed it occurred to him he didn't remember hearing the thunderbolt caused by the nearby hit. Hope we're not deaf, he thought.

Brigid finally grasped his hand and allowed him to pull her upright. "Take Xipe," she said, moving her lips quickly but clearly so he could read them. "I'll handle Tlaloc."

He nodded. The rain god now stood behind a hedge of eagle knights, just watching. Like Kane, he evidently needed to recharge between shots.

Kane's solar flare was still tapped. He rushed Xipe Totec. As he did, he saw from the corner of his eye a mass of water rise from the lake behind Tlaloc and stream toward him like a blast from a fire hose. It blindsided him, stretched him on the grass and scattered his guards.

Xipe faced Tonatiuh with a terrible skinless leer. His shield was unadorned except for the mandatory stylized representation of himself. His mace was an egg-shaped chunk of milky jade, beautifully polished.

Kane bore down on him full speed. It was a safe guess a homegrown deity would have a lot more training and experience in this kind of fighting than good old Taker of Fifty Captives had gotten a chance to instill in Kane. Kane figured pressing his opponent hard would increase the odds of his making a mistake, giving Kane an opening.

When he came within a few feet, the flayed thing countercharged him. Shields clashed with a bang. With both shields pinned between their bodies, Xipe swung his mace at Kane's skull with the speed of a striking rattlesnake.

Realizing he couldn't stave the blow with his sword Kane pushed off with his shield, throwing himself back and to his right. The gleaming glabrous-green mace head whizzed an inch shy of Kane's nose and smashed against his shield rim.

The shield made a weird gobbling sound as it vibrated. It hung together. But the blow drove it downward, opening Kane to a follow-up stroke.

But Tonatiuh seized his own advantage. Allowing the blow's force to torque his body left, he aimed an overhand blow at the crown of Xipe's raw hairless head. The enemy god had to jump back himself to escape a skull-splitting.

"You don't fight half badly," the hideous red visage said. "For your valor I will take you alive, strip the skin from your body myself and offer it with your heart smoke on the pyramid—to myself, of course!"

He laughed hugely at his own joke. It figured he'd be the type. Kane recklessly flung himself forward as if enraged by the flayed god's hideous threat—as Xipe Totec so clearly expected. The creature parried his flailings with contemptuous ease.

Waiting for me to wear myself out, Kane thought. He noticed the flayed god kept his mace in constant motion, rolling his wrist over and over.

He can't stop it. Or not readily. Xipe was very good at twirling it in fluid patterns without exposing himself or leaving the wep long out of position to strike should an opening arise. But the kilo or so of smooth stone at the end of a half-yard haft had momentum that gave it in effect a mind of its own.

From the depths of Kane's skull a voice spoke to him. In the early sixteenth century when Don Pedro de Alvarado had been raised and trained as a soldier, fancy rapier play was all the rage. But a well-rounded fighter also got schooled in broadsword and buckler work—basically, this. And Don Pedro had a trick.

Kane allowed his blows to flag. He panted like a winded dog—no acting job, that. His shield began to droop.

At once Xipe launched a looping overhead blow. Kane just barely got his shield up in time. The mace connected with an impact that numbed Kane's arm to the shoulder.

The impact had two effects. It stopped the mace's forward progress, rebounding to allow Xipe to cock his arm for a follow-up killing stroke. And it added velocity to a clockwise spin of Kane's body.

Xipe's arm drew back. As it cleared his neck, Kane spun through with a horizontal backhand cut of his sword.

The obsidian blades struck the exposed muscles of Xipe's neck with the sound and feel of an ax hitting green wood. A moment's hesitation and then the wep, driven by the inertia of Kane's whole body and the power of his legs, cut through. Kane followed through to face his foe again as the hideous flayed head sprang free of the human-skin-caped shoulders in a geyser of scarlet.

As the head tumbled off the blood spray it changed, becoming the brown-skinned head of an altogether normal-looking man of early middle age. The body that toppled headless to the grass was likewise normally covered in skin, dressed in a kirtle of jade-inset metal strips, with a heavy cloth cape around the shoulder, white rapidly being dyed red.

Wild energy surged through Kane-Tonatiuh. He raised shield and sword overhead and exulted as he drank in the life essence of a god.

A cry arose from somewhere, from everywhere, "Xipe Totec is slain! The flayed one has fallen."

Tonatiuh faded, although the energy lines blazed up so brightly Kane could almost see them with the eyes of his body. The battle had come to a complete halt. Most combatants on both sides wanted to watch Tonatiuh and Xipe go godhead to godhead.

The exception was the duel between Tlaloc and Brigid in her guise of Chalchihuitlicue, which raged on unabated. Brigid and her surviving guards were obscured by a miniature squall; a young waterspout marched in from the lake toward the rain god and his retinue. The meeting of hydrodynamic deities seemed mainly to have had the effect of drenching both contestants, if Brigid, ducking out of the localized downpour with her hair a matted tangle like bronze seaweed to get a bearing on her foe, was any indication.

It all was pretty comical. Except Kane had seen Baptiste finish off the giant *cipactli* with her water tricks, and she was holding her own against a much more experienced player in the god game. And she had held Tlaloc off from dropping another of his lightning strikes on Kane's inadequately covered ass.

Speaking of which, his own solar flare was recharged

and more than, now that he'd absorbed Xipe's life energy. He grabbed hold of one of those live wires of geomagnetic force and raised his sword, preparing to fry Tlaloc to a crispy critter.

A blast of icy water hit him from above. He yelled in surprise and shock. His plasma bolt died unborn.

As quickly as it had come, his own personalized cloud-burst ceased. But a swirling bank of rain, or anyway air-borne water droplets, obscured the place where Tlaloc had stood a moment before. All across the park Talocan troops retreated hastily, yelling at one another about Xipe's demise.

"They're going," Brigid said. The squall had quit. "Are you all right?"

He nodded. Then spoiled the effect by swaying and grabbing her shoulder for support.

THE SCORPION WAS DARK BROWN with a weird Rorschachy pattern of yellow down its back. It was a good two yards long, leaving out the sting, which hovered above its body at the end of another yard of tail. A big dewdrop of venom, glistening toxic-waste green, hung from the sting's evil curved tip.

It stared up at Grant with a cluster of bloodred eyes. He gave it a faceful of jacketed 9 mm slugs from his Sin Eater.

The loathsome creature splashed satisfactorily into big gleaming shards, viscous green fluid and assorted white-and-yellow globs of internal organs.

"Great," Domi said, crouching at his side. Another scorpion tail lashed at Grant's back. She snatched it out of the air with her talons, bit it through, then casually tossed severed sting and writhing erstwhile owner off the block. "Only leaves two, three thousand more of our little friends. Why not use your plasma rifle and burn 'em back a little?"

"Saving shots for big game." He danced back and riddled a man-length millipede that swarmed up over the edge at him. "Damn, I'm getting jumpy! Thing probably couldn't even hurt me."

"Speaking of big game," Domi said, "I think we've a target for you."

She pointed a talon. Grant looked across the street. A bizarre creature had appeared—bizarre even by comparison to the giant vermin flood. It was basically a giant scorpion with the bare torso, arms and head of a beautiful woman in lieu of its own head, centaur style.

"Behold Malinalxochi, the scorpion woman, with her aspect upon her."

"Now where'd you learn to talk like that? Don't say Brigid this time."

"Old vids."

The Sin Eater slammed back into its holster on Grant's forearm. He began to unsling his plasma rifle.

The vermin goddess advanced toward them, wading through the torrent of her devotees. There was something almost entrancing about the way her arthropod legs worked, like an array of cranes working all at once.

She opened her mouth to laugh. Worms writhed around the rotting stumps of teeth. A bottle-green beetle crawled up her flawless cheek.

Grant looked pained. "Now that's just disgusting."

The goddess called out something Grant didn't understand.

"Y tu madre también," Domi shouted back, which he did understand, mostly.

What he said as he leveled the plasma rifle was, "Time to die."

A flicker of motion caught the edge of his peripheral vision. He started to swing toward it. Which meant the jaws of the striking giant rattlesnake clamped on the barrel of his plasma rifle instead of his arm. He roared in surprise and tried to shake the creature off. In response it whipped itself twice around his midsection and squeezed. It felt as if it weighed as much as a small human being.

"Rattlesnakes don't constrict!" he yelled.

"Argue with him," Domi said, and sprang lithely down from the block.

As a Jesus lizard runs upon the water, so did the goddess Itzapapalotl run upon the backs of the bugs. And the serpents and other unpleasant creeping things, straight toward their mistress. Malinalxochi hissed displeasure and struck at her with her sting. Domi darted aside, clung for a moment three yards up a streetlight pole with her talons sunk into its verdigris-covered bronze and then leaped down onto the goddess's scorpion back.

"You've delivered yourself up to me, obsidian butterfly," Malinalxochi said. "Now taste my sting!"

The tail whipped forward and down. "You first," said Itzapapalotl, twisting sideways.

Malinalxochi shrieked as her own sting sank into her back like a needle-tipped spear. The great fat poison sac pulsated as reflex pumped it contents into her.

Probably she was immune to her own venom. That sting had to have hurt like a bitch, though, and blackish-red froth bubbled from her nostrils, indicating it had pierced a lung. It held all her attention for the tiny sliver of time it took the jaguar goddess to wrap herself over Malinalxochi's human shoulders and slash the muscles, veins and cartilage of her throat to the neckbones. Bathed in gouting blood, Domi seized the scorpion woman's half-severed head and wrenched it free.

The headless body went into convulsions. So did the vermin carpet. Domi sprang free as the sting tore itself out of the headless trunk's back and lashed air blindly.

Clinging again to the light pole with Malinalxochi's dripping head tucked under one arm, Domi looked to check on Grant. At that moment his Sin Eater snarled and the snake he'd been wrestling with fell into two writhing segments. Its jaws relinquished their grip on his plasma rifle, which Grant had been hanging on to by the sling with his left hand. The head whipped about on its half of body, still gamely trying to gore him with its lancelike fangs, until he destroyed it with a triburst and kicked the remnants over the edge.

"If you're finished playing with your new little friend," Domi called to him, "we should probably think about motivating out of here. I don't think these things are hurt, just sort of confused."

She leaped from the pole, touched down precisely in a patch of pavement momentarily free of writhing bodies, jumped toward the next. Grant holstered his Sin Eater, raised the plasma rifle and turned the still thrashing body of the scorpion goddess to a flaming, reeking wreck.

"Looks like a napalm attack on a crowded dock," he observed with interest.

Domi bounced up beside him from seven yards out. He still had trouble adjusting to her speed and strength.

The head was still tucked under his arm. It rolled wild eyes at him and opened its ghastly mouth. No words came out, only maggots.

"Get that thing away from me," Grant said.

"If you say so." Itzapapalotl pivoted and hurled it deftly at the pyre that had been its body.

Grant's Sin Eater hissed into his hand. A triburst blew the head apart like a cantaloupe in midair.

"Why'd you do that?" Domi said. "Going soft in your old age?"

"Prove I could."

He looked around. The crawly things had mostly quit having conniptions and begun righting themselves. They weren't moving with anything like purpose yet.

"Let's get out of here. Kane, do you read me?"

A moment, and his partner's voice came back. It sounded weary. "Kane here. You all right?"

"Affirmative. We just had a little hold up, but we should be getting near to position to hit the forces you're up against from the rear."

"No need. They're pulling out to the south of you, along the lakefront. They lost interest after Baptiste and I chilled Xipe Totec."

"Xipe Totec?" Grant asked, stumbling a little over the pronunciation.

"Agriculture god, looks like he's skinned, wears his own skin," supplied Domi, who could only hear his side of the conversation. "One of the big ones. Nasty."

"Was," Grant told her. "They wasted him."

Domi pumped a shiny fist. "Yes."

"What now, Kane?" Grant asked.

Before his friend could answer, a voice cut across: "Lord Tonatiuh! If you're there, please respond! Huitzilopochtli himself has led a raid on our forward command post north of you. We have lost many killed and taken captive. The flower prince and Cihuacoatl among them."

Chapter 24

Taker of Fifty Captives died bravely, as befit a hero.

Neither Tlaloc nor Huitzilopochtli could do anything about the weather, thus endorsing the ancient joke. Clouds squatted not far above the city's roofs, which by divine decree and ratified by vote of parliament could be no higher than two yards shy of the three central buildings of Talocan, Tenochtitlán and the valley itself: the Palacio del Parlamento, the gleaming glass Black House and tallest of all, the mighty Pyramid of the Sun, set upon the western side of the great paved plaza to greet the Sun when it rose above the mountains. The dawn light was sullen gray. No shaft of sunlight fell upon the rites being enacted at the pyramid's apex, nor did so much as a patch of brightness peek through the leaden ceiling to show the Sun's approval of the flowery sacrifices being offered in his name.

Perhaps the Sun god could have helped. But he, alas, was on the other side.

The thousands packed into the great Plaza del Sol around which the three mighty central edifices stood at the points of an equilateral triangle mirrored the heavens with their mood. The sacrifices, their hosts had told the outlanders, were generally popular events. Well, not popular, perhaps, in the usual sense. But the public by and large accepted their necessity—for they had only to look upon the chaos and unimaginable devastation that had racked the world the past two centuries to see the terrible cost of denying the gods their due. The ritual killings induced in the watchers a blend of unease, horror mingled frankly with blood lust, a sense of communion with tens of thousands of other souls and the gods themselves, a thrill of sympathy for the victims and vicarious participation in their destiny, which was glorious. The end result was a sort of mass ecstasy, in which all attending, even those who hated the sacrifices and thought them cruel barbarities—as many did—were caught up, uplifted, purged.

Like a cross, Brigid said, between a predark religious revival and the Roman games.

But today the throng was sullen, not exalted. Tens of thousands quietly endured the sporadically spitting and uncustomarily chill rain. Why they did, no one watching on big-screen televisions at the Instituto Quetzalcoatl could really say, although of course opinions abounded. Marroquín, who might have had the keenest insight, kept his own counsel, as did Teresa. Ernesto bubbled over with speculations, bouncing around as imbued with the excitement so conspicuously absent from the crowd.

It wasn't hard to resent that, and some of the other staffers in the meditation area cast him hard looks. Because the sacrificial victims, though paltry few by the normal standards of a great Talocan *chisguete,* were a score and a half of their comrades, taken alive in today's battle. Mostly in Huitzilopochtli's commando-style raid on the Colhuacan field HQ, which had been situated in a bank building a mile from the battle at el Parque Vicente Fernández.

Kane, who had not seen his instructor since his first couple of days in the Tonatiuh harness, yet still felt a bond to him that was hard to explain even to himself, expected the stocky sergeant major to fight to the end. But when his turn came to mount the final dais, he walked with stolid dignity upon the blood-slippery steps. And then Kane understood—by accepting the inevitable without display he won a victory of sorts.

Huitzilopochtli himself made play with his obsidian blade. The Black House priests stepped in, their skins and matted uncut hair caked with the dried blood of a hundred sacrifices, heart cauls of victims pulled over their skulls like shower caps, there to stay until they rotted off. Only when they pressed the noses of pry bars between the raw ends of his ribs where Huitzilopochtli's blade had chopped through the sternum and wedged open his chest to expose his beating heart did that strong old man cry out.

Then the god, his face painted black, reached a gory hand into the gaping wound of Fifty's chest, seized the heart, made more swift cuts. Fifty's body convulsed hugely and was still, his torment ended, although his heart pulsed several times as Huitzilopochtli brandished it toward the missing Sun.

Kane felt his face, his being go stiff and cold.

"Kane?" Brigid asked. "Are you all right?"

She moved toward him. Domi, in her normal guise and dressed in a white smock that was perhaps not quite long enough to do all that was asked of it, moved with uncharacteristic gentleness to intercept her. Laid a milk-white hand on her arm. Brigid looked down at the little albino, looked at Kane, then nodded and stayed where she was.

The prize sacrifices were the two gods who had been taken in the raid. Cihuacoatl was ward boss of Colhuacan, a handsome if somewhat stocky woman. She sold herself dear. When they stretched her full length upon the obsidian slab with the groove running longitudinally down it, she suddenly took her aspect upon her. Her neck elongated, her head became that of a giant rattlesnake and she sank six-inch fangs into the shoulder and chest of an unlucky Black House priest. He thrashed and shrieked louder than any of his victims, writhing against the fangs as they pumped venom into his body.

Another priest took up a club reserved for just such incidents—albeit usually less dramatic—and smote the great serpent's flat bead-scaled skull. Stunned, the rattlesnake mother subsided into fully human semblance. Huitzilopochtli drew his sword and struck off her head.

The crowd made an ugly sound. A bruise of a sound, rising from ten thousand throats.

Beneath his second skin of blood and other organic residue the stricken priest's face and limbs and body erupted in great bubbled bulges as the hematotoxin from the rattlesnake woman's bite exploded his blood cell by cell. His screams rose to a high-pressure squeal. Then he ruptured. His corrupted blood spewed all over Huitzilopochtli and his fellow priests and the exsanguinated body of Cihuacoatl.

The crowd cheered.

The last to offer flowery sacrifice was the god Xochipilli, the flower prince. With his twin sister Xochiquetzal, Flower Feather, he ruled the district next to Tlillan-Tlapallan, and had accepted stewardship over Quetzalcoatl's own ward when that god was exiled thirty years before. God of beauty, of flowers, singing and dancing and games, he was known as a gentle bon vivant, a lover not a fighter, although his aspect did hold a human heart impaled upon a maguey spike. Despite that he was greatly loved throughout Tenochtitlán and the valley.

A slim, youthful-looking god, of an almost effeminate beauty, the flower prince went to his own death without a

sound, lips curved in a quiet half smile that didn't flicker
when Huitzilopochtli butchered him alive and tore the
heart from his chest. This time when the primary war god
displayed the excised organ, the audience erupted in pro-
longed hissing, an outpouring of condensed hate and fury,
heedless of the god's whole corps of a thousand eagle
knights confronting them in phalanx at the pyramid's base.
Only the knights' own numbers—and free play with shock
batons—kept the mob from surging forward up the pyramid steps.

Huitzilopochtli stood on the edge of the topmost platform holding the flower prince's heart and staring down at
the throng. His face was unreadable under paint and blood,
but his whole body bespoke fury of its own. When it came
clear his knights would hold, he turned and strode back toward the small stone structure housing the entrance to the
guts of the pyramid, tossing the quiescent heart on the bra-
zier with a contemptuous gesture.

Kane released a long, shuddering breath. Then he
turned, too, and stalked out of the meditation area without
word or glance to the others.

HE LAY IN A FITFUL DOZE, in that place he stayed before he
was taken to where he really spent the night. His dreams
were shot through with screams.

He heard the door open and was instantly awake. He
reached for his Sin Eater beneath his mattress.

"No." A low voice, soft and feminine. "I am no threat,
Lord Tonatiuh."

"Teresa?" He half sat.

"Yes." She closed the door quietly behind her. She wore
a lightweight robe that fell to just below her knees. Not exactly normal garb for the institute's corridors, but not too

unusual if one felt the need to be abroad at this hour. Outside crickets and nightbirds sang to one another. Moths made soft occasional plops against the open window's screen. The smell from outside was green and gravid, just brushed with brimstone from a distant eruption.

Kane settled himself on his elbows and regarded her. His mind was muzzy; he still sank gradually toward that deathly torpor that he knew was not sleep, although what it really was he didn't know. But something stirred within him.

She slipped the robe from her thin shoulders. She was nude beneath.

It wasn't his first sight of a naked hybrid female. She was different, somehow, and not solely because of the color of her skin. It might have been that her hips were a trifle wider, her breasts a trifle fuller and the feathery wisp between her slim thighs was dark. But she was still elfin, graceful in that hybrid way, and completely beautiful.

Kane found he wanted her. It wasn't unnatural, considering. Yet something about the quickness and ferocity of what he felt troubled him.

He didn't like the thought that murder turned him on.

She came quickly to him. She was so light that she seemed to float, feet barely touching the floor. He threw off the sheet that covered his body. Beneath it he was naked, and hard.

"Teresa—"

She pressed a child-slim finger to his lips. "Don't talk, my lord. Please."

She sat astride him. She was already wet as she slid herself down his stiff penis.

She was virgin-tight. Whether she was actually virgin, or just small, he didn't know.

His body ached with the desire to ram into her like a hydraulic press on jolt. He clamped down hard on that impulse. He knew how fragile hybrid bones were; even his normal Kane strength would snap them if not controlled. He had no real idea how much stronger he was enhanced. Easily two or three times, at least as much faster. Since he had interrupted his own training, he had had little but on-the-job experience of his powers. Which gave him a rough notion of his capabilities, but no standard by which to truly pin them down.

So he made himself simply sit, let her set intensity and pace. His hands trembled with the exertion of self-control. He put them on her buttocks, felt the warm satin-smooth skin, the play of muscle and bone beneath as she worked her hips up and down and around.

. Their lovemaking became delicious torment. She was unskilled but wildly eager. He laved her small breasts with his tongue, gnawed lightly on her pale nipples. She squealed her pleasure—just a hint of the mewling, bubbling hybrid speech in it, not enough to tamp his ardor— and grabbed the hair at the back of his skull with a tiny but surprisingly strong hand.

At last his fever became too great for him to maintain the passive role. Still keeping her well impaled, he swung his left foot up and around onto the bed. Then he rolled over so that she lay on her back with her head on his pillow. Her hair was still caught in a conservative bun at the back of her skull; a long strand had come loose and lay curled across her throat.

"Take me," she whispered. She had been speaking English to him, as the outlanders' captor-hosts normally did. Now she spoke the tongue of the gods. "Take me hard. Don't hold back!"

But he did. Despite his lust, which burned as brightly

as the energy strands that enveloped them both and even coiled within his belly and spiraled down his arms and legs, he measured carefully the speed and force and even depth of his strokes so as not to do her harm. Despite all, the fact that she had connived at kidnapping him and Brigid, subjecting them without their assent to some kind of monstrous transformation that none of them came within light years of understanding even now, he felt the strange enormous tenderness toward this lovely, ethereal, yet delightfully flesh-and-blood creature.

But there was a limit even to his self-control. He took his hands from beneath her churning buttocks and pressed them to the wall above the bed's head. The madness grew within him. The pleasure and the fever burned like miniature suns as she drove her own pelvis rhythmically up to meet his strokes, with frenetic energy if what seemed to him now thistle-down strength.

Mustn't let go. He screwed his eyes tight shut. The energy was wild within him, threatening to explode. He concentrated on dumping as much excess as possible into the bright lines he saw so clearly in his mind.

It seemed the room grew bright around them. He could see the tiny capillaries in the lids of his eyes, silhouetted in yellow glow. Teresa cried out once as if in alarm. Then she was screaming with a different urgency, clawing at his back and sides like a drowning child, driving herself onto his hardness again and again. The muscles of her vagina began to clutch his cock, milking it with silken fury.

He put his head back and roared. His fingers dug into the wall with the effort of stopping himself from slamming into her full force and smashing her pelvis to powder. He came like a volcano, and then it was done. He let the last of his breath shudder out of him. He opened his eyes.

The first thing he saw was that his hands had closed. Both fists were all but buried in the pits he had gouged in the adobe in the fury of his climax. The second thing he saw was that he could see them clearly. The lights had somehow come on.

Yellow, flickering light.

The room was on fire around them.

In alarm he looked down. Teresa's head lay framed by the white pillowcase. Her huge amber eyes were gazing up at him with a combination of worship and childlike trust. They occupied a pool of cool darkness, surrounded by flames as the curtains, the bedposts, even the bedclothes farther than a hand span from their naked bodies burned.

Kane laughed then. He reached out with his mind to take hold the flames, draw them into him. Drained, he felt his own energy renew; at the same time the dancing yellow fire diminished, dwindled, guttered, was gone. They were left again in darkness and the smell of smoke. Kane was glad that the window was open and the castle's HVAC system blowing air out into the night.

"The institute's fire-control system leaves a little bit to be desired," Kane said with a smile as he lowered himself beside her. As he rolled off her, she cocked her leg around his buttocks and kept him clasped to her, as if to keep his softening penis inside. "Still, I'm just as glad the sprinklers didn't come on."

She smiled. "The floors and outer walls are steel and concrete," she said, pedantic even in the dreaminess of afterglow. "These inner walls are adobe. Not much to burn in this part of the building, my lord."

He kissed her, lightly, on her lips. During their frenzied lovemaking they had not kissed more deeply; not made mouth-to-mouth contact at all. He suspected she found

such distasteful. He was just as glad; had he kissed her as
fervently as he would a human woman during sex he might
have done serious hurt to the delicate perfection of her face.

He looked at that face, composed and serenely beautiful beside his on the pillow. Truly, it was as if the best features of Danaan and true human had been distilled in her.
But he felt dizzy, felt blackness close in, as if in spending
his passion he had spent his life force, his *prana*...which,
he realized with the last of his waning lucidity, was most
likely true.

"I'm just Kane," he said, voice husky with more than
the residue of passion. "The other—others—they're just
riders. They'll get off, sooner or later. One way or another."

She smiled beatifically. "I know," she said. "And this
body, your genes, are Kane. It is you whom I have come
to...admire. You yourself, Lord Kane. And you whose
genes will be blended with my own, to become the hope
of a new generation...."

She sounds awfully sure of that, he thought. He wondered why. He felt no alarm that he had impregnated her,
if he truly had; it wasn't as if she would press him for child
support, when he had gone home...or was lying cold with
dirt hitting his eyes.

He wondered, though, as he slipped away, just how he
felt about fathering the grandchild of Tezcatlipoca.

Chapter 25

Kane's soul writhed in a dream of blood and fire.

He felt the spirits within exulting as he relived the slaying, felt the warm blood of men and a god spew over him, felt their life force, their very souls flow into him, subsumed.

"I'm not you!" he screamed. "I'm not like you! I'm not a vampire!"

Diabolic laughter greeted his desperate cry. A dream face appeared floating before his dream eyes: a circular mask like a human face flattened beneath intolerable pressure, grotesquely stylized, with a vertical bar of beard beneath the gaping club-toothed mouth.

"Mortal fool," said the voice of Tonatiuh, the transplant Mayan god of the Sun. "What do you think sustains you? The same that sustains all the gods—the blood of human cattle."

"No!"

The eidolon lips smiled a ghastly smile. "Open your eyes and see."

Kane did.

Wetness pressed against his eyeballs.

Wetness filled his nose and mouth, warm and salt. Drowning! Panic flashed through his mind.

But no. Though his chest didn't expand and contract to the rhythm of breathing, he felt no physical distress, no urgency. Instead warm softness suffused him. My lungs are full of liquid, he knew. That fullness assuaged his body's reflex fear at protracted emptiness; as far as his body knew, lungs had drawn a breath, yet felt no need to exhale.

I'm dead, he thought next. At once he knew that wasn't true. He didn't know if he credited the legends told about those who came to the very brink of death and felt themselves being drawn toward white brightness at a dark tunnel's end. But he was pretty sure whatever being dead was like, it wasn't like floating in an amniotic bath.

He blinked. He felt the fluid squeeze away from his eyeballs, then flow back when the lids opened again. There was no sense of abrasion or discomfort; his reflex to shut eyes firmly against any contact with the sensitive lenses had been suppressed. It seemed, then, that he could see a hint of glow, as if light shone through the liquid that surrounded him from without.

Shone red. Ember dull, but red.

Panic blasted through him. What is going on? He lashed out with hands and feet.

Tried to. They were bound.

Adrenaline dump added to the god strength they had given him. He strained with all his might. The bonds parted. Hands and feet flew in slow motion outward through liquid, struck a curved hardness like glass. Retracted. Struck hard.

The cylinder was molded from polycarbonate. You could have emptied an arsenal of bullets from a high-powered longblaster against it and done little more than scuff its clear surface to milkiness. Yet it couldn't withstand Kane's strength and the fury of a god—or perhaps vice versa.

The sealed tube shattered. Kane sat up shedding fluid, half exhaled, half vomited his lungs and gut clear. He drank in a protracted breath of cool air that smelled of disinfectant.

He blinked his eyes free. He was in some sort of clinic-looking chamber, perhaps ten yards by seven. There were half a dozen seven-foot tubes in the room including his, in a two-by-six matrix. The two others in his longitudinal row were filled with what appeared to be....

"Blood?"

He realized his mouth was rank with the taste of blood. He spit. Then he looked down.

His dark chest hair, just touched by gray, was a red straggling mat. Fluid trails ran down his bare belly to meld with the pool still obscuring his genitals, the tops of his thighs and his feet and lower shins. Red fluid.

He had been bathed in blood. Suspended in blood. Suffused with blood.

Drinking blood. Eating blood. Being sustained, healed, recharged with blood.

As the fluid stirred to the motions of his partially submerged body, he could tell it was not pure blood; it was slightly thicker. Yet blood was the greatest component; no amount of horrific loathing could deny that.

He jumped free of the shattered tube in a single bound and scarlet spray. "What have you done to us?" he screamed at the walls. "What have you filthy slaggers fucking *done?*"

He smashed open the next tube with a jackhammer series of fist blows. He had just lifted Brigid, naked and with blood, none hers, streaming from mouth and nostrils and ears and her tied-up hair when he heard the door slide open behind him.

Gently he laid the semiconscious woman upon the cold synthetic tiles of the floor. Then he turned, wrath blazing in his heart and his eyes. The fire of the Sun played like coronal discharge around his raised fists.

A block of men faced him, institute sec men in blue-and-green jumpsuits, holding Shocksticks in their hands. The electric wands trembled like dowsing rods. He was undoubtedly the most terrifying thing any of them had ever seen, even in god- and monster-haunted Tenochtitlán: a figure half a head taller than the tallest of them, muscled like a wolf, scarred like a pit-fighting dog, blood-drenched, gray eyes mad with rage, fists raised and literally wreathed in yellow fire. But they faced him.

He saw two figures crowd in behind them and prepared to slay. Then one figure squeezed between two of the sec men.

Had it been the other—Marroquín—Kane would have cut loose or charred him down. Or tried; the results, he discovered somewhat later, would likely have been interesting indeed. It was Teresa, clutching a fuzzy robe around her slight form, who confronted his fury.

He didn't lack the urge to cinder her. Hadn't her betrayal been the most intimate possible? Yet he couldn't bring himself to burn the flesh he had so recently pressed to his own, worshiped with his mouth, penetrated with his maleness…possibly even impregnated.

He let the solar fires die.

"Please, Kane," she said in English. "Hear us, at least."

"What have you made me?" He gestured at Brigid, who lay curled on her side gagging and spitting up the bloody fluid. "What have you made us?"

Now Marroquín stepped forward. The sec men parted to let him pass. "Leave us, please," he said to them.

"But, Doctor—" one began.

"You are most brave, gentlemen. I salute you. You are true men and worthy Sons of Shaking Earth. But these are Lord Tonatiuh and Lady Chalchihuitlicue, in all truth. They have slain gods. You can do nothing here but die. Leave now, please—we are in no danger."

Kane smiled a gray wolf's smile. "Don't be so sure of that last part, Marroquín."

"As may be. Go!"

The sec men went, trying hard and unsuccessfully not to show their relief. The Mag part of Kane doubted there was a dry pair of skivvies among them.

"Kane," Brigid said. She coughed.

He turned. She was trying weakly to sit up. He bent to help her stand, then held her body pressed to his to hold her up. He was abruptly conscious of the warmth of her skin pressing his. With fluids from the vat running down her firm, voluptuous body, she was like a statue carved from red-veined marble. She was at that moment, incongruously, the most beautiful woman he had ever seen. More beautiful than the dainty, treacherous Teresa—had it been but hours before? Yet he felt no desire for her. Only a fierce and vast protectiveness. She looked up at him and smiled defiantly, and their arms tightened around each other's waist.

Kane looked around, then, to see Teresa's face frozen to a mask.

"You understand, now, why we felt it necessary to hide the whole truth from you," Dr. Marroquín said matter-of-factly. "We were shielding you."

"It's a nutrient bath," Brigid said, her voice raw from coughing. "The same as the barons have to bathe in periodically to heal and rejuvenate themselves."

The archivist in her triggered the whitecoat in Teresa. "Not exactly. It's—"

"A serviceable enough explanation for now, my dear," Marroquín interposed. "For all practical intents, yes, Dr. Baptiste. It is the same."

"So you've turned us into the same kind of human-blood-drinking vampires they are?" Brigid's voice rang like a battle bell.

"Yes. Except as you have experienced, you are now as superior to them as friend Kane found the Danaan, Maccan, to himself. Who, by the way, you could both break in two without invoking the more esoteric of your powers."

"We did not ask," Teresa said defiantly. "But we made you gods. You have both seen for yourselves how great our need truly is."

There was a commotion at the door. Then Grant appeared, heroic frame clad only in a pair of white briefs, Sin Eater in hand. He was shedding sec men the way Kane's and Brigid's naked bodies shed the dense red fluid.

"Let him in," Marroquín said, with a touch of weariness. The sec men vanished, none too reluctantly.

Grant stepped inside the room. Keeping the barrel of his handblaster elevated, he looked from Kane to Brigid, then to the others. His eyebrows rose.

"It's all right, Grant." Kane said. "Or at least it's not code red."

"We found out where we go at night," Brigid said bitterly. "And what they feed us, now that we're gods."

Grant blanched. "Domi—?"

"I was interrupted before I could rouse her," Kane said. "Doesn't seem to be much urgency now. She's okay—better than that, I'm afraid. And my point man's instinct tells me she'll probably take this lots better in stride than Baptiste and I are."

Grant lowered the handblaster. "Yeah," he said.

Kane turned back to the whitecoats. "Where does the blood come from?" he demanded. "And the other tissue?"

"From the newly dead. By nature or misadventure, not

our hands. And—" the hybrid woman's voice dropped to a whisper "—from those sick and injured beyond healing."

"You mean you euthanized them, instead of cutting them open atop a pyramid?" Brigid asked. Stricken, Teresa nodded.

"So you're kinder, gentler vampires than the guys on the other side," Grant said.

"With your indulgence," Dr. Marroquín said, "yes. We are. If you wish to see it that way, we are kinder, and *much* gentler than the gods of Talocan. That fact remains."

Kane sighed. "The bitch of it is, he's right. You saw what happened on the pyramid yourself. The Talocan gods had their own pet television station broadcasting that. It's the whole base of their regime, as well as their superpowers. And they intend on doing a whole lot more of it. And mebbe not just here in the valley."

"So what happens now?" Grant demanded. "Do we exact payback here? Or do you and Brigid just get back in your nice warm baths and pretend you don't know what's in 'em?"

"What would you have us do, Grant?" Brigid asked. "What will you do? You didn't undergo the change. Nothing ties you here."

"Nothing except the thing that brought me here in the first place," the big man said. "That being you two. And little Domi, now, the iron butterfly or whatever the hell she's let them turn her into. I'm not so sure I can rightly see the distinction between our devils and theirs. But I don't leave you. Or Kane. Or Domi."

Kane raised his arm to enfold Brigid's strong shoulders.

She looked up at him. *"Anam-chara,"* she said huskily, "I can see no good choice here."

He laughed bitterly. "And what's new about that, Baptiste?"

He looked at Marroquín. "Screw it," he said. "I'll stick. Because I think there's a chance you could be right—this fused-out divine family of Talocan, Tezcatlipoca and Huitzilopochtli and their delightful mom may pose a danger to us up north. To Cerberus, and what we're trying to do. And also… Taker of Fifty Captives was my friend. Not for long, mebbe, but there it is. What they did to him shouldn't be done to a Snakefishville Mag. So I don't stir from here until I rip that bastard Huitzilopochtli's chest open the way he did Fifty's."

Marroquín's mouth pinched and his olive skin turned parchment color. Then he laughed shakily. "You are most ambitious, my friend. Remember, our aim is to restore balance to the valley."

"And I don't say the books are balanced until I've paid the blood debt for my friend," Kane said in a voice of steel.

Marroquín shrugged. Slight as he was, oldie that he was, it was the closest Kane had seen him come to acknowledging powerlessness in any situation.

Teresa had mastered whatever emotions had been rippling through her slight body. But her voice still trembled just on the edge of perceptibility when she said, "What do you choose, then, my lord, my…lady?"

Kane looked at Brigid again. For a moment their eyes met and held. Then she smiled. Acid etched, but a smile.

"They've still got intact tubes free," she said. "So I guess we better go back to bed."

Chapter 26

They woke to find the world a very different place.

All were back in their chambers when technicians came to fetch them, just as dawn spilled into the great bowl of buried wreckage that cradled Tenochtitlán—except Kane, who had been moved while yet unconscious to quarters that had not suffered smoke damage. They were summoned to the meditation area high in the institute's admin pyramid, where Ernesto, Teresa and Dr. Marroquín awaited them, watching the giant flat-screen television.

A buffet had been set up. The smell wafting from the covered dishes made Kane's stomach rumble. After what he'd experienced—not to mention learned—the night before, he was amazed his appetite would come back within the week. But he was ravenous, as he had been on every awakening since being drawn here through chronon space via the black mirror. Evidently the hell-broth bath recharged his *prana* but left his gut empty and his human physical form in need of its own sustenance.

"What's the situation?" Grant asked, dumping scrambled chicken eggs and then chopped green chili onto a flour tortilla. For some reason he steered well clear of the dragonfly eggs, and even the fried axolotl strips. "Looks like something's happened."

"Much," Marroquín said.

The screen was split into windows. One showed a street

full of what looked like normal people battling with sec men backed by a handful of jaguar and eagle knights. Another showed what looked like an auditorium, with a herd of men and a few women in both traditional and what the outlanders thought of as "modern" garb huddled disconsolately under the blasters of a score or so mixed Talocan knights.

"The people have risen against Talocan," said Ernesto. His cheeks were flushed, his words stumbling over each other in their eagerness to get out. "There's rioting everywhere, even in districts that have been loyal to the two."

"They can't just call out the Magistrate Division and bust heads until everybody gets their minds right?" Grant asked around a mouthful of his impromptu burrito.

Marroquín smiled. "Much as they would like to, such a course is not without risks, my friend," he said. "Political considerations are paramount—the gods are powerful, but as your friends can attest, Señor Grant, their powers are not infinite. Like all rulers, even the most dictatorial, their political power ultimately depends upon the consent of the governed. Yet there is more to it than that—the gods' very existence depends in substantial part upon belief."

Brigid looked at him thoughtfully over a cup of sweetened *chocolatl* with mint. "But you told us that the entities we've been...saddled with...are self-perpetuating, recorded in the minerals and rock crystals of the valley."

"That's true, Dr. Baptiste," Teresa said. She seemed subdued this morning, even for her. She didn't look at the foreign-born woman who had been made a local goddess. "But we don't very well understand the nature of the entities we call gods. What we do know is that the more popular a god is, the more potent its powers—the more *prana* available to him or her. And it is a more enduring energy source than sacrifice."

"Receiving human sacrifice can be compared in many ways to taking a stimulant drug. Like that which you call jolt," Marroquín said.

Kane put down his own burrito, which had fried potatoes in it, as well as chili and eggs. He knew too well what it felt to *take* a life, in a sense in which he'd never conceived it before.

"I hope it's not as addictive," he said.

"It can be," Marroquín said. "Indeed, that appears to have come into play with Huitzilopochtli and Coatlicue. And Tezcatlipoca, of course."

Kane raised his head and with eyes like steel mirrors stared at the elderly whitecoat with the absurd two-tone tonsure. "Assume—just for argument's sake here—we survive our stint as gods and the transition back into our real selves. Does that mean we'll never be free? Or will we be perpetually jonesing for—for blood and souls. Will we stay vampires, Dr. Marroquín?"

The scientist faced the angry god squarely. "The Smoking Mirror enabled us to read your souls, as well as your minds. Part of what rendered you attractive—irresistible—to us was the very strength of character you displayed. By all four of you. Mr. Grant is certainly worthy of that which he has refused."

"Don't compliment me," Grant said flatly.

A chime sounded. Marroquín stepped to an intercom panel set into a wall of polished red-brown stone, spoke quietly, listened momentarily. Then he returned to the group dividing its attention between buffet and television screen.

"We have just received a call from Don Hilario. As you

may recall, he is the political leader of the coalition supporting the return of Quetzalcoatl in parliament. He has naturally been arrested with the seizure of parliament by Talocan forces."

"Those criminals!" Ernesto exclaimed. Teresa looked uninterested.

"He has been sequestered in a room in the basement levels of the building," Marroquín said. "Apparently his guards neglected to relieve him of his personal communicator. Our enemies seem quite disorganized by the turn of recent events—which should not surprise us too greatly, since none of us foresaw that Talocan would be mad enough to sacrifice two established and respected gods, nor that public response would be so immediate and severe. Don Hilario suggests—I suspect that's an insufficiently emphatic verb—that we contrive to rescue him."

"You want us to get him?" Kane asked. His tone made it clear he wasn't volunteering.

"Not you, Lord Tonatiuh. Nor Lady Chalchihuitlicue. You are our most potent weapons, physically and, may I say it, politically. We need you to remain here to respond quickly should either our opportunity or our need become great."

He turned to look at Grant, who was back at the buffet. Grant scowled back.

"Which means you want us spear-carrier types to do it," he grumbled.

"Oh, come on, Grant. Lighten up," Domi said. Although she was in human guise, and dressed in her smock even if she went to no great pains to conceal that she wore nothing under it, she sat in a sort of a cat squat on a low table, her knees wide and hands resting before her on the glass. It actually seemed to suit her, and Kane had a horrible feeling she'd never quit doing it, if they ever came out the other side as themselves again. "It'll be fun."

Grant looked at her sourly. "Haven't you learned by now never to say a thing like that?"

THE RESCUE WAS a piece of cake. Though the threat of alligators in the Tenochtitlán sewers was anything but an urban myth—or of lesser *cipactli,* anyway, escaped or deliberately released from Daraul's biofact vats—they encountered no creeping or swimming unpleasantness sufficient to cause concern. Nor did they have to spend much time making their way through the sewer system, since the subway trains were all halted for the duration, like most of the city's commerce. Nor could the manpower be spared for patrols of the subway tunnels. The guards on the platform at the parliament station, meanwhile, they circumvented by using a combination of sewers, subway and service tunnels beneath Talocan itself to hit the main subway line a hundred yards the other side of the parliament station from Tlillan-Tlapallan and backtrack. Just that side of the platform a little quiet work with a cordless nut driver unfastened a panel that gave onto a passageway into the maintenance and utility passageways beneath the parliament building.

A quick look from a side passage showed the guards outside the room where Don Hilario was being held were a pair of jaguar knights, Tezcatlipoca's finest. They weren't particularly tall but strapping and impressive in their gilded breastplates and jaguar-head helms. Each was armed with a bullpup semiauto or possibly even full-auto riot shotgun of a design unfamiliar to Grant.

In the interests of keeping the alarm nice and unraised Grant ignored Domi's hissed insistence she could take the throats out of both before they even knew what was happening. Instead the two knights watched in puzzlement as a microgren bounced before the toes of their sandals. By the time they spotted it, it had already released a surprising volume of colorless, odorless and very fast-acting narcogas. The sentries fell with a chord of thumps and clatter that made Grant wince.

"Shoulda let me take 'em," Domi said smugly. "I'd've let 'em down without a sound."

Don Hilario had not been introduced to the newest additions to the feathered serpent's menagerie of outlander divinities and heroes. The apparition of Itzapapalotl almost scared him into arrest of a different sort altogether than what he was already under. The obsidian butterfly was not known for her mercies, even by the standards of Aztec gods. His first terrified assumption was that she had been freshly incarnated by Talocan and dispatched to execute him with tooth and talon.

The apparition of Grant did visibly little to soothe his nerves. Mexico City, prenukecaust, had been a racially diverse little ville of twenty million or so. The few survivors of the not altogether natural disasters in the wake of the general thermonuclear exchange had bred out as mestizos, admixtures of Amerindian and European, and while far from uniform fell largely in a spectrum of shades of brown. Few, however, were as emphatic a brown as Grant, and fewer still were his size. And very, very few of them looked as pissed off as he did this morning.

Domi got things sorted out quickly in her slangy north-of-the-border Spanish. The handsome politician showed his own kind of resilience; he was bitching about dirt and discomfort before they were halfway through the basement on the way back to the tunnels.

KANE AND BRIGID cooled their heels in the lounge area, from which discreet institute staffers had cleared the buffet, leaving a small service for coffee, tea and *chocolatl* available in a niche in the wall clearly dedicated to that purpose. The lounges, or meditation areas, or conversation zones, whatever they were, turned out to be equipped with computer workstations providing presumably restricted access to the institute's vast archives. So naturally Brigid was happy as a baby with a morphine pacifier, sucking all available lore into her permanent memory through her eyes.

Kane just sat feeling grumpy and disaffected. He couldn't even go train somewhere—pang at the memory of Fifty's loss—to distract his mind and bleed off nervous energy: Marroquín wanted his heavy hitters Tonatiuh and Chalchihuitlicue immediately available for when, not if, the situation broke in some unpleasant way. Kane may have been totally adrift in the turbulent seas of Tenochtitlán theology-cum-politics, but the streetwise, door-busting Mag he remained at core wholeheartedly agreed with the weird old whitecoat. The big three, Huitzilopochtli, Tezcatlipoca and Coatlicue, were *not* going to sit back and passively wait for the Quetzalcoatl faction's next move, or the public's. They would make a play, hard and big, and no doubt sooner rather than later.

The problem was, being alone with his thoughts—he was too proud to try intruding on Brigid in her senior archivist's trance, which would earn him a stinging rebuff if she even deigned to notice—tended to bring his demon riders bubbling to the surface. He had taken to keeping them suppressed by whatever amount of conscious will it took except in hot-blood combat. Tonatiuh and his various prior incarnations, especially the red-bearded sixteenth-century conquistador Don Pedro de Alvarado, were not nice playmates. Even by the standards of the playmates Kane had known.

They whispered things to him he would have chilled them for, had they had bodies to chill—had he been able to chill them without self-death. It was a lot like old tales of demonic possession.

Erase that. It *was* demonic possession. Even if those who'd inflicted it on him called it divine.

He was so involved in trying to quell those voices—you like it, you know you like it, you crave the act of killing like a woman's flesh—that he actually jumped when the wall communicator bonged for attention.

"Lord Tonatiuh! Lady Chalchihuitlicue! Are you there?" It sounded like Ernesto, having trouble breathing.

It was Brigid who answered. "We're here."

"Lord Quetzalcoatl's sickroom. Please! Come at once!"

WHATEVER SECURITY MEASURES the elevator employed to keep the random and not so random curious from sensitive areas, Kane and Brigid were recognized and allowed to punch up the infirmary level on which the dying god was kept. Fortunately his room was located within the central pyramid of the immense complex on its bluff overlooking the city, which Brigid said she suspected was what decades of earth upheaval had left of someplace called the Hill of the Grasshopper.

When they hit the designated floor they set out at a brisk walk, each being too proud to run to the summons unless the coldhearts were coming over the wall. It was not long before they reached the observation window into Quetzalcoatl's room. The door stood open.

Within were gathered Marroquín, Ernesto and Teresa,

with a wild-eyed med tech sitting on a counter. Two other med techs lay asleep on the floor.

"What is it?" Kane asked.

Teresa's face was slightly green and her little jaw was set. She nodded sideways at the wasted figure on the bed. The ancient hybrid's body was rigid. His clenched fists had torn their way through the bedclothes into the mattress beneath him. His lips moved, and Kane became aware of a slight murmur.

"He's manifesting," Teresa said. "He's gone over the edge."

"What exactly does that mean?" Brigid asked.

Marroquín nodded to the med tech. "Lord Quetzalcoatl's vital signs indicators went berserk," the attendant said. "Alvaro and Ocotillo ran in to check on him. I happened to be passing outside in the corridor. Through the window I saw the feathered serpent rise up, as though issuing from the body of our lord. Alvaro and Ocotillo fell. I was overcome with a wave of blackness, but before I succumbed, I saw the serpent dive into the floor and vanish. It seemed he grew in size even as he went."

Kane looked again at the two people lying at his feet. "They're not sleeping."

"They're d-dead!' Ernesto exclaimed. He seemed exalted, as much exhilarated as scared and unhappy.

"I thought Quetzalcoatl was the good guy god, the life-giver," Kane said. "The one who wants to ban human sacrifice."

"You thought correctly, Sun god," said Marroquín.

"In our mythology nothing nurtures which does not also have the capacity to destroy," Teresa said. "You should know that well, Lady Chalchihuitlicue."

Brigid rocked back slightly, then nodded. "The jade

skirt, the precious green—water, which gives life, but can just as easily take it away."

"What's he doing?" Kane demanded.

"Ocotillo said he's been muttering about parliament all morning," the med tech said.

"Among Quetzalcoatl's attributes are degrees of clairvoyance and clairaudience," Marroquín said. "Evidently he became aware of the morning's events in parliament—and misunderstood them."

He had taken something from the pocket of his lab coat and, holding it down and before him at arm's extent, was frowning into it with evident concentration.

"He shouted something about traitors right before the serpent appeared," said the tech.

"He goes," Marroquín said gravely, "to slay parliament. Killing all in his wake."

Chapter 27

"Grant! Domi!" Brigid exclaimed. "We've got to warn them to get clear." The institute's internal instant-messaging system had apprised Brigid when Grant and Domi checked in by communicator to announce they had secured the package and were exfiltrating the palacio.

Dr. Marroquín squinted at the object in his hand: a black disk, just greater than palm-sized, which appeared to be of exquisitely polished volcanic glass. A mirror, to every appearance.

"It will do no good," the chief whitecoat said. "The lethality radius of his black field is approximately one hundred yards in all direction."

"He's killing everything inside a hundred yards of him?" Kane almost shouted. "That's mostly his own people!"

Marroquín shrugged. "Sacrifice, as you well know, is a concept not exactly foreign to our belief system. And—" he nodded down at the now-sinister figure straining on the bed "—he is not himself. Not lucid. I fear he is in his final extremity, expending himself in this one last effort, deluded as it is."

Kane moved to the bed, reaching a hard hand for the age-mottled throat. "Then I'll just hurry him on his way."

Teresa seized his arm. "No, Lord Tonatiuh! You must not!" She seemed scared more for him than of him.

"Quetzalcoatl is rendering his own flowery sacrifice,"

said Marroquín, "expending the last of his life energy, as well as the life forces of the hundreds—thousands—his projection has already slain. His power is immense. If you touch him, we will all die upon the instant."

He looked down again at his miniature Smoking Mirror. "Your friends, I fear, have entered the last minute of their lives."

"SUCH INDIGNITY!" Don Hilario complained in English as Grant's none too gentle hand pressed down on his shoulder from behind, doubling him over and propelling him through the low hatch. "I shall let them know at the institute how carelessly you handle the *voz del pueblo!*"

Grant kept pushing, then bent low to follow the politician out into the subway tunnel.

"That means 'voice of the people,'" Domi supplied, sticking out her shiny head with its short furze of hair, which resembled Velcro to an almost comical degree.

"Like I care," Grant said. He glared at Hilario. "If you don't amp the voice of the people right down, big boy, I'll *really* give you something to bitch us off about when we get back."

Domi frowned. Then she sprang past the two men into the middle of the track. "Mind the third rail, there," Grant warned.

"Power's off," she said absently. She crouched, looking more jaguar than woman, head cocked in an attitude of acute concentration. "Something."

"What?"

"Something." She shook her head. "A rumbling. A vibration. Low."

"Damn," Grant said. "I hate these earthquakes. They just go right up my back."

Domi's eyes had narrowed to crimson slits. "No. Not a quake."

She raised her head and stared along the tunnel in the direction of the Institute. "It's coming. Fast."

In the dim distance a giant serpent head, as big as a subway car, came into view. Blue-and-green effulgences streamed around and back from its gaping toothy maw like flames as it bore down on them with terrifying speed.

"WE'LL SEE ABOUT THAT," Brigid snapped. "Quetzalcoatl! Lady Chalchihuitlicue demands your attention! Wake up!"

"English?" Kane asked.

"He's American. Quetzalcoatl! Pay attention. You must stop now!"

"It's no use, Lady," Ernesto said. "He cannot hear."

"Or will not respond," Teresa said in a leaden voice. "He's gone beyond this world."

The head flew off the faucet in the sink by one wall of the hospital room. Water jetted up to drench the ceiling's dropped acoustic tiles as everybody jumped and stared. Everyone but Quetzalcoatl—and Chalchihuitlicue.

She frowned. The water stream bent until it struck the supine figure full in the face.

"Lady, no!" screamed Teresa.

Quetzalcoatl's eyes snapped open. In his life as Morall they had been the blue of a clear spring sky.

Now they were pits of darkness as black as Hell.

They turned toward Brigid. The water stream unbent to splatter the ceiling again. Teresa grabbed Kane's arm as if to drag him outside in desperate flight.

The black eyes hit Brigid's green gaze. And stuck.

Kane stood as if his feet were glued in the floor. The

dying, killing life god's eyes opened wider. He strained, then, as if trying to break their contact with Brigid's gaze.

He could not.

Kane looked to Brigid. His *anam-chara's* face was white and strained into an expression he'd never seen on her face or anyone else's. A look of fury, and concentration—and just a hint of something he could only think of as lust.

THE RUMBLING was at least as loud as an onrushing subway train's. "What is that thing?" Grant shouted. "It can't possibly be real. Right?"

"It's real," Domi shouted back. "Real enough, anyway."

Don Hilario had fallen to his knees in the middle of the track. He stared at the apparition with a look of total devastation. "It is the projected essence of Lord Quetzalcoatl. He comes in wrath, slaying as he comes."

"That's not good. Let's get out of here."

Don Hilario laughed a mad laugh. "You cannot flee the black field!"

"I think he's right," Domi called.

"Fuck a bunch of this, then." Grant turned toward the behemoth and straightened his arm. His Sin Eater slammed into his hand and filled the tunnel with shattering noise and flickering light.

QUETZALCOATL RELEASED the torn mattress and sat up. He raised shriveled, supplicating claws to the goddess Chalchihuitlicue. The force of her gaze was almost palpable. Kane felt his mind and stomach twist just from looking at her eyes from the side. Death stare!

Quetzalcoatl opened his mouth and emitted a croak of pleading or dismay.

Which turned into a rising, whistling scream, a roar, a great wind that whirled loose papers and bits of mattress stuffing and even random medical utensils left on the counter around the room's occupants like a tornado. Kane found himself gripping Teresa with one arm, holding the other outstretched as if to fend off the flying debris. Which it didn't do.

He couldn't take his eyes off the tableau: Brigid standing rigid, the being on the bed, staring at each other with ultimate intensity. A milky stream, seemingly radiance rather than substance, spewed from Quetzalcoatl's open mouth. It flowed straight toward Brigid's eyes.

And vanished.

Kane watched Brigid drink the soul of Quetzalcoatl. Then the shout ended, and the wind. And the empty husk of an old dead hybrid flopped limp back on the bed.

DOMI WAS at Grant's side, hugging him around the waist with both arms. "It's been a good run," she said.

The blaster noise and flashing ceased. The Sin Eater's slide locked back. "It's not over," Grant said, letting the spent mag drop free as he fished another of his Rip-stop harness and slammed it home, "till it's over."

He let the slide slam shut on a fresh cartridge and raised the handblaster again. The monster was a scarce hundred fifty yards off and closing fast. Grant could feel blackness rush toward him in a wave. He took aim. At least I die fighting.

The great gaping snake head came apart in a million brilliant motes. A cloud of polychrome scintillation seemed to billow toward them, then vanish.

The vast rumbling had ceased. The silence seemed to echo.

Grant lowered his handblaster. "Did I do that? I probably didn't, huh?"

"Probably not," the obsidian butterfly said. But she jumped up and wrapped her legs around his waist and hugged him with all four limbs, heedless of the fact she was bone naked.

It didn't even faze him.

ERNESTO AND TERESA had fallen weeping to their knees. Marroquín, as calm as always, pressed hands before his sunken chest and bowed. "Hail, Lady Chalchihuitlicue. You have slain the mighty Quetzalcoatl."

Brigid turned and vomited into the sink.

"YOUR GODS REGRET the tragic necessity that compelled them to employ the as yet secret means by which so many died this morning," the almost comically sad black-and-white mask declared from the television screen. "But the message is clear—those traitors who would destroy our valley and admit the chaos and monsters that have devastated the outside world for centuries into our midst cannot escape the retribution of Talocan."

Kane, Grant and Dr. Marroquín stood in the lounge watching the big TV. Brigid sat in a chair by the workstation, absorbing information out of the institute's files—in this case her drug of choice, Kane knew. Domi slept on a couch with her head on her arm, snoring softly.

"They're taking credit for the deaths?" Kane demanded in disbelief. "Why?"

"Evidently to cow the populace with their power. And ruthlessness," the doctor said.

Don Hilario had been brought back intact and was under sedation. Grant had been compelled to stun him with his fist and tie him up with Domi's shoulder-holster rig, then carry him—the politician had departed controlled flight and might well stay that way.

Ernesto and Teresa had retired for the moment. Witnessing the death of their god had traumatized them. They had both abandoned prestigious positions in the Black House itself to serve Quetzalcoatl against his ruling rivals. Chalchihuitlicue's action had unquestionably been correct, and on balance no doubt merciful to he who had been Morall. But it had twisted their psyches way out of shape.

Paynal ended his press conference. He was replaced by a blow-dried male and female pair of newsreaders who broadcast an appeal for the citizens of Tenochtitlán to return to their homes and trust in their gods. Marroquín used a remote control to switch to scenes of milling street mobs, apparently broadcast real-time by institute surveillance choppers.

"What was that thing you were looking into," Kane asked Marroquín quietly, "back in Quetzalcoatl's room?"

Marroquín shrugged and smiled thinly. "A miniature Smoking Mirror. A communicator, primarily. Perhaps a dozen exist, allotted to the foremost priests and technicians of the Black House. And Tezcatlipoca, of course. He figured out how to make them."

Kane grunted. Marroquín had been the Black House's leading scientist after Daraul and Tezcatlipoca himself. It made sense he would have been issued one, and been able to escape with it. Still, something about his explanation rang false in Kane's mind.

He didn't get time to contemplate it. Because right about then the good citizens of Tenochtitlán decided to vote with their feet. And their voices and hands and objects such as trash cans and street signs and anything else they could pick or pry up.

As if from nowhere they just surged into the Talocan sec men monitoring them. Ten or twenty of the local police vanished at once beneath the mob.

The communicator yammered. The on-screen view changed as the pilot or cam operator moved to bear on a four-wheeled armored car half a block from the riot, which opened fire on the crowd with a light machine gun in its little pimple of cupola. People fell, their screams audible over the chopper's pickups. Then a human wave flowed down the street, surrounded the light armored vehicle and began to rock it, trying to turn it over. The gun continued to fire, and people continued to fall—but it wouldn't bear on the people attacking it directly.

A new phase of the battle of Tenochtitlán was under way.

Chapter 28

"You may approach me, Paynal," Huitzilopochtli said to the figure cringing in the shadows of his personal audience chamber. He sat upon his gold throne with the concealed gel cushion in his own semblance, which he always liked to think was more than impressive, what with his hard-muscled frame and square-jawed handsomeness and all.

Bobbing his head, Paynal stepped out into the light from behind the large fern. The foliage was Coatlicue's idea. For his part Huitzilopochtli was pretty indifferent to green growing things. He had sneered at his brother Tezcatlipoca's suggestion that the plants might conceal assassins: why should he the primary war god concern himself with such, when at the least flicker of his own intention any assassin's blade would shatter on contact with his divine skin?

But then, Tezcatlipoca always chose to walk the coward's path, as he had shown these past few days, hanging back from the forefront of battle, keeping his own precious jaguar knights safe as drops of his own blood. Of course he always had some plausible and even resounding explanation: he labored around the clock on some new twist of science that would confound their enemies; one of the two must remain behind to guard Talocan itself against the rebels' treacherous schemes; and was it not meet that the honor and glory of taking the field against the usurper

Quetzalcoatl should go to the primary war god, Hummingbird upon the Left?

That last, of course, wasn't even a rationalization. As Paynal came forward, Huitzilopochtli cast a covert glance at his brother god, standing upon his own left hand. How like Tezcatlipoca to twist even the most resplendent truth to his own dark ends.

"Master," the chief propagandist said, making washing motions of one paper-white hand against the other. "Master, forgive your humblest servant! How was I to know the people would be outraged by our claiming credit for the deaths today, in the city and parliament? Should it not have made them tremble in their hearts for fear of your divine retribution for treason and heresy?"

Yes, it should. Which was why Huitzilopochtli had demanded his voice propound that line. Or was it Coatlicue's idea? No matter—what reason to give divinity to creatures of Paynal's ilk, if not to absorb blame that might otherwise tarnish the luster of the great Huitzilopochtli?

Speaking of luster, he told himself, after I slay that gringo whelp of a Tonatiuh, I'll proclaim myself sole and primary Sun god, as well. Am I not a solar deity, too? Then let's see them reincarnate that crappy little Mayan import!

When they expanded their sway beyond the valley the first thing to do, he resolved, was go and wipe out those Mayan maggots in Yucatán. The very names were practically the same: Mayan, *mayate*. Maggot. They were ugly little pricks, anyway. They looked like muties before there were any. Probably by-blows of some damn Annunaki experiment or other. Not really human at all…

Behind him the war god heard a soft step. Paynal, now groveling on his knees before Huitzilopochtli, looked up. His face locked into its tragic aspect.

Huitzilopochtli turned his head. His blessed mother stood there. He hadn't known she was lurking behind the throne. Even to him, who was literal minded, it seemed *too* literal minded. Not for the first time he wondered if she had the ability to autoteleport; Coatlicue jealously guarded the true extent and nature of her powers, even, or perhaps especially, from her own offspring. Or maybe she had just had another secret passage built into the pyramid.

Or was it Tezcatlipoca? He had designed the structure himself on computers brought by the exiles, overseen its construction while Huitzilopochtli perfected his skill in the manly arts of war. Coatlicue had always favored Huitzilopochtli, yet it did not mean she and the clever Smoking Mirror might not share secrets withheld from him. There was no doubt that Coatlicue was assiduous that neither son, no matter how strong he became, grew so strong he might think to do without her.

I'll show her, too, he told himself. I will. Someday.

"Paynal," she said in silken tones, "you have served your lord and master ill."

She was really quite beautiful, with her dark red metallic hair, immense glowing green eyes, the skin cinnamon-hued velvet on her ripe bare breasts and flat belly. Not even the baby's skull she wore as a pendant detracted from her beauty.

Paynal all but melted into the polished granite floor in self-abasement. "Please! Please, O Mother of the Stars of the Southern Sky! Spare me! I atone! I atone!"

She reached two fingers, tipped with nails painted the color of fresh blood, and with the tips of the curving nails touched him beneath the chin. With slight insistent pressure she first drew up his head, then brought him to his feet.

"There, there, dear Paynal," she said in a honeyed voice. "Am I not the mother of all the true gods, not merely the paramount pair who sprang from my own loins? How can I not nurture and cherish you as my own child?"

His face became the idiot's mask of joy. "Then you forgive me, great Coatlicue? You will spare Paynal?"

She smiled. "No."

The beaten-gold rattlesnakes with garnet eyes that hung from her belt to make up her skirt became flesh, lived, reared up and hissed, showing miniature but fully venomed fangs.

With a cry of terror Paynal stumbled back away from the throne. His patent-leather shoes got tangled and he sat down hard, holding a splayed hand up before him in a futile bid to ward off doom.

Coatlicue spread her arms. Her large and flawless breasts rode up on her rib cage as she raised her arms, the chocolate-drop nipples becoming hard. Her perfect teeth parted between red lips. A low tone emerged from the golden-brown column her throat, rising in volume and in pitch. Rising. Rising.

Even sitting to the side, out of the direct path of her cry, Huitzilopochtli's teeth were set on edge. He ground his jaw, dissatisfied with this turn of events. He risked a sideways look at his brother. Tezcatlipoca stood with arms folded, wearing a disdainful smile, the same as always. But it seemed he leaned forward with just an extra glitter to his eye.

The cry rose to the point of pain and beyond. The throne quivered with sympathetic vibrations beneath Huitzilopochtli's divine fundament, and the leaves and fronds of some of the plants began to wither and droop. Face once again a parody of sorrow, Paynal reared back, holding out both hands.

Given that he seemed no more than an animated pen-

and-ink cartoon, with his black-and-white face and black-and-white suit, what happened next was in a way appropriate: the stuff of him seemed to be smeared this way and that in lines undulating from high to low, as if some giant eraser were attempting to rub him out. His own voice rose to a scream as shrill and wild as Coatlicue's had been before it passed the threshold beyond which human ears could not pass.

And then he simply came apart. Into nothing. As if he had never been. Leaving nothing behind except, inexplicably, his shoes.

"*That* I call atonement," Coatlicue said in satisfaction.

Huitzilopochtli felt his lips press into a pout. "Why did you have to do that, Mother? I liked that Paynal."

A velvet caress on his bare shoulder. "There, dear," she said soothingly. She did not point out that Huitzilopochtli had been the only one who did. Truth to tell, the late Paynal had been a lousy propagandist, his power of influencing, while it could sway even gods, not extending beyond range of his voice and, worse, not lasting longer than he spoke. "I will make you a new one. When we rebuild Tenochtitlán in our own image."

"When we rebuild the world in our own image, no?" murmured Tezcatlipoca.

Huitzilopochtli glanced at him, his sorrow for the loss of his pet almost transmuted to floppy gratitude. Even the cynical Tezcatlipoca showed solidarity with their grand design now! It almost made his deprivation worthwhile.

He reached up and patted his mother's hand on his shoulder, and reminded himself sternly that big gods didn't cry.

"SIR," THE TECHNICIAN said, "we have a problem."

The departing sun's slanting rays turned all within the

room to fire. Even in its orange glare the young man who had spoken closely resembled a raccoon. It was not an aspect, nor sign of taint. It was just that none of the institute's intel analysts had gotten more than the rare fifteen minutes' sleep since a day or so after Kane's arrival, monitoring the complex situation in Tenochtitlán and the actions of Talocan.

"I'll say," remarked Domi. The contemplation-conversation lounge had become the outlander gods' squad room more or less by default. The buffet had been set up again and left. In human guise the albino girl crouched on a table gnawing a roasted chicken.

She nodded at the television. It was switching from scene to scene of combat. After the crowd turned on Talocan, its surviving sec men had battled their way back to the city's ruling center. Hundreds had been lost, but the ruling gods commanded thousands more. These had broken forth half an hour earlier in a concerted thrust toward Tlillan-Tlapallan and the core of Quetzalcoatl resistance behind a phalanx of eagle and jaguar knights.

With their polycarbonate armor and shields, the knights were ideal riot-control troops. Not that they troubled with any softhearted nonlethal crowd-control weps or tactics; instead they flashblasted everyone in their path with autoblasters and a leavening of lasers and plasma rifles, and anyone who managed to come within arm's reach got the chop from the resin-reinforced obsidian blades of a sword.

That cleared out the congestion in the streets quick enough. The people of Tenochtitlán were feisty and fully pissed off, but neither bulletproof nor stupid.

But a city fight was a slow fight. The sec men of the districts now friendly to Quetzalcoatl—most of them now— had upon consultation with Don Excildo deployed in hardened positions within and atop buildings to defend in depth against just this sort of assault. And while no one was going to confuse General Martínez with a military genius, he wasn't a duffer, either; he had not omitted to sow sniper teams liberally in the path of a possible breakout. Since their armor wasn't full body, even the Magistrate-like knights were vulnerable to very well-placed shots, and the sec men following them had no armor other than their shirts.

So the battle went. Inexorably the Talocan forces advanced towards the institute. But it was progress yard by yard, and each one bought with blood. In time, of course, the thrust would become a salient subject to being pinched off—but so far Talocan had committed none of its gods.

As far as Kane could see, it all amounted to a kind of dynamic stalemate in which none could gain a clear advantage. It reminded him of ancient vids he'd seen of the team sport called soccer, lots of running around, but nothing actually ever happened.

Losing interest in the newcomer and his news, Domi went back to trying to describe certain facets of the local scene to Brigid. "So, like, Xolotl, he's the lightning god, and Chantico, she's kind of a volcano goddess. They're on our side."

She nodded toward the screen. "They're out there now, although they won't show themselves unless some of Talocan's big guns turn up."

Seated at the computer, her face shaded from the light of the falling sun and hence illuminated by the pallid glow of information, Brigid. "Very well, Domi, dear. What about them?"

"They're lovers."

"Lovers?"

Domi shrugged artlessly and waved her half-eaten

chicken. "Well, see, they both have dog's heads. So it's kind of natural, if you think about it—"

Brigid stopped her holding forth her palm. "But I don't want to," she said firmly. "Domi, child, thank you. You have helped me discover, belatedly, that even for a senior archivist, whose very life is to know, there's such a thing as too much information."

"Whatever."

"What is our problem, then, Two Chuckwalla?" Marroquín asked the technician softly. Kane shook his head. The local names still took some getting used to.

"The people are calling out for Quetzalcoatl," the young intel tech said. "Reports flood in from every district. There is even murmuring in Talocan itself. If Quetzalcoatl appears, he will be acclaimed. The two will find it very hard to resist coming to terms."

Marroquín sighed. "Thank you very much. You may go."

The young man steepled his fingers and bowed a quick, shallow bow. Then he turned and walked back to his unit, his clogs clicking softly on their nonskid pads on the polished stone floor.

"But we're fresh out of Quetzalcoatls today, aren't we?" asked Grant, sprawled on a sofa.

"You're taking this all mighty easy, you know, Grant," Domi commented, tossing her skeletonized bird toward a trash receptacle ten whole yards across the room and getting nothing but the bottom of the bin. The powers of Itzapapalotl, the obsidian butterfly, were making her insufferable in ways.

Grant chuckled—a shocking thing in itself. "Sweetheart, this is all so far off my radar scope I can't even see it. So why work myself into a state? Me, I'm just a Mag at heart. Tell me where to go and who to shoot, and leave everything else to Admin and the whitecoats."

Kane was trying to scratch an itch deep inside the cavity of his left ear with a pinky and failing utterly. It was a real piss off that being a god did not spare you the frailties of mortal flesh. "You got more sense than any of us," he said.

"Took you this long to figure that out?"

Brigid turned in her swivel chair. She had taken to wearing a thigh-length green smock; if she had to dress up like a gaudy slut on duty, she said, she could at least dress the way gaudy sluts did on downtime. "What do we do now?"

"Looks like you need to make yourselves a new Quetzalcoatl," remarked Domi, who was running her finger a few inches above the buffet trying to decide what to eat next. As Itzapapalotl her already considerable appetite really was insatiable, and she would now eat only various forms of meat, poultry or fish.

She picked up a whole roast axolotl on a stick and bit into its belly. Brigid stifled a gag and turned away.

"What's with you people?" Domi demanded. "You should give these things a chance. They taste just like chicken."

"Gah," Kane said. "Where are you going to get a new Quetzalcoatl, Marroquín?"

Marroquín was fingering his chin. "A most incisive question, Lord Tonatiuh," he murmured, casting his eye about.

"Don't go looking at me, Doc!" Grant exclaimed. "I am not getting turned into a ghoul—sorry, guys. And anyway Teresa told me about Quetzalcoatl. He's a fair-skinned dude. In case you haven't noticed, I am not."

Marroquín's top aides were absent again. Though their primary current duty appeared to be foreign-god wrangler, they had other responsibilities, as well.

"Of little import," Marroquín said. "Your aspect would be a tall, light-skinned man with pale eyes and a fair beard."

"Definitely not me," Grant reiterated. "Sounds insipid, with due respect to my friends, here. Anyway I thought his aspect was that freight-train-sized snaky thing with the feathers."

"That's a psionic projection," Marroquín said. "Different phenomenon altogether. But put yourself at ease, friend Grant. While you definitely possess a sufficiently emphatic character to be invested with godhood, your personality type is far from compatible with Quetzalcoatl. Despite the manifestation you saw, which after all constituted his own flowery sacrifice and nothing typical of him, Quetzalcoatl truly is foremost a healing god."

"Also highly intellectual," Brigid said. "Which, while you're a highly intelligent man, Grant, you're most definitely not."

"Thank you," Grant said fervently.

"And also," Brigid went on, "from my studies I get the impression that the feathered-serpent persona is, well, more than a little self-important."

Dr. Marroquín nodded. "True enough. So you see, most highly esteemed Grant, you are in no danger of being selected for the role."

Grant's characteristic scowl came back. "Careful with all that 'esteemed friend Grant' noise, Doc," he said. "You're starting to sound *way* too much like Lakesh."

Suddenly three sets of eyes, gray, emerald-green and red, turned to stare intently at Grant.

"What? What'd I say?"

Chapter 29

The blue eyes opened. The four Cerberus exiles gathered around the clinic bed sighed in unison.

The eyes moved from one to another. "Why, my very dear friends, you seem relieved I have survived!" Dr. Mohandas Lakesh Singh exclaimed. "This is an unlooked-for honor, on top of my elevation to godhead!"

"Well, don't let it go to your head, Doc," Grant muttered.

"Dream on," Domi said.

"It would appear that your sojourn in the valley of Mexico hasn't diluted your comedic talents. Is it safe to sit up, Dr. Marroquín?"

"Of course, great Lord Quetzalcoatl." Marroquín pressed his hands together and bowed. So did Ernesto, Teresa and the crowd of techs hanging in the background.

"Go lightly on that action, will you?" Kane said.

Lakesh sat up. He was wearing an open-backed hospital-style gown. "But why, friend Kane? I could easily grow used to such treatment."

"That is why."

Marroquín consulted his wrist chron. "Do you feel well, Lord? The sun will be up soon. You must appear to the people as soon as possible. We need to prepare your speech."

Lakesh blinked aggrievedly. "Dear me. Where have my spectacles gone? I shall be quite no use without them."

"You won't need them for the duration, Doctor," Brigid said. "As I've found out myself."

"Ah! Well. Unlooked-for benefits of deity. I feel quite well, thank you. Invigorated. Still, my good Dr. Marroquín, I had expected to receive at least some kind of course of instruction and dare I say, a breaking-in period before I commenced my godly duties."

"You got it," Kane said. "Good half hour at least."

"You get the same treatment the rest of us did, Doctor," Brigid said crisply. "Which is, thrown into the deep end to sink or swim. The only god training is on-the-job."

"With great power comes great pains in the ass," Kane added. He looked around at the assembled institute med staff. "Speaking of which, somebody cover the new Lord Quetzalcoatl with a robe before he stands up, or learn about the wrath of the Sun god firsthand."

AT SUNRISE the new Quetzalcoatl made his public debut from the ramparts above the institute's main gates, which despite being painted with festive plumed serpents and other traditional images, were stressed concrete and would bounce a tank. Although armed goons were kept out of sight—everybody in Tenochtitlán knew Quetzalcoatl had his own elite cadre of knights, as well as conventional sec men, but the open display of guns did not suit his persona—Tonatiuh and Chalchihuitlicue discreetly backed him up on the podium, ostensibly to show respect to the returning savior of the city.

Grant, meanwhile, was happily ensconced behind the scope of a Barrett .50-caliber sniper's rifle—guaranteed to shoot even a god up to at least Tlaloc if not Huitzilopochtli himself inside out—up on the rooftop of a nearby office building with a commanding view of the gate and immediate environs. Itzapapalotl prowled nearby to provide him security while he was lost in the glass. And not all the helicopters circling a discreet distance overhead were news birds.

In security terms it was a frost. The Tlillan-Tlapallan throng, never a hard house for the feathered serpent anyway, turned out to shout *¡viva!* and offer up many *gritos,* as if it were Cinco de Mayo, still a favorite holiday hereabouts. A raid out of Talocan was feared by Don Excildo and the other paid worriers on the institute's staff. But the combat action stayed where it was, crunching gamely through the streets klicks away toward city's center.

Although the sun did shine a friendly red eye on proceedings, beneath a fairly serious pall of overcast, a desultory drizzle trailed down. It did nothing to dampen the occasion. Quetzalcoatl in aspect, looking not that different than Lakesh had when he'd enjoyed rejuvenation compliments of Sam the imperator, spoke fluent electronically amplified Spanish at the masses. Neither Kane nor Brigid knew whether he actually spoke the language before his investiture.

Kane tuned out the speech. Brigid assured him it was mostly Gandhi warmed over, with a few touches of Martin Luther King. Kane, who scarcely knew who either man was, just grunted.

Having opened to rave reviews, Quetzalcoatl then did pose a problem to his security detail: the crowd had laid eyes upon the returning god, as had anyone in Tenochtitlán with a TV tuned to the institute's broadcast band. But he still needed to get out *among* the people.

"And commit miracles?" Kane asked Brigid.

"You've got to quit thinking like a Magistrate, Kane."

"I *am* a Magistrate."

"You don't 'commit' miracles."

"You got that right."

"I don't mean you *you*. I mean 'you' as in 'one.' Forgive me for speaking colloquial English."

He showed a crooked grin. "At least it's English. How are we supposed to keep him alive if he's wandering around pressing flesh and kissing babies? What if somebody shanks him?"

"Do not forget Quetzalcoatl has formidable powers," said Marroquín, appearing behind them in a pavilion that had been set up by the wall just inside the gate, to which Quetzalcoatl and retinue had repaired when his initial speech was done. Marroquín and Lakesh had mixed like water into water, much too well; they lashed the speech together between them in fifteen minutes. "Although he is a god of peace, he can defend himself against minor attack—and of course he has his knights, who will likewise accompany him when he issues forth. We need you to secure him against assaults on a higher energy level."

"That's what I really love to hear," Kane said.

Brigid moistened her lips with her tongue. "I have to admit I've been wondering, just how does Quetzalcoatl feel about the person who, well, was responsible for him having to find a fresh incarnation?" Such hesitation was unlike the usually forthright Brigid. Kane put it down to her relative lack of experience as a deicide.

"He feels on the whole profound relief," a familiar voice said from right behind her shoulder. "Indeed a measure of gratitude to you, for releasing his former associate from the torment of irreversible dementia—not to mention preventing substantial loss of life."

Lakesh looked like himself, though dressed in a skirt of green quetzal feathers, with a cloak of the same held over his shoulders by a gold chain. "Of course, even though I am sharing my mental space with this other entity at the

moment, nothing he could do could ever hope to diminish
the esteem and affection in which I hold my beloved
Brigid. And you, too, to be sure, friend Kane."

"That's easy to say," Kane said, "since you drew one of
mebbe about two Aztec deities who aren't vindictive sons
of bitches." He wondered how his drinking buddy Ueuecoyotl was doing. He hadn't seemed the vindictive kind,
although he was arguably a son of a bitch.

Lakesh laughed. "You might be surprised—so we shall
pray you aren't. And Brigid, may I say how lovely you look
in your guise as the lady of the jade skirt? Divinity quite
becomes you, although I regret that you have not chosen
to be altogether authentic in your garb."

"Doctor, I'm frankly shocked that you of all people
would attempt to sleaze a look at my breasts."

He flushed. "No, no, you misunderstand me. Good
heavens! It is only that it seems out of character for one of
your meticulous training and inclination."

"Uh-huh."

Kane patted his shoulder. "Let it go, Doc. This is not an
argument you can possibly win. Trust me on this one."

THE MIRACLE TOUR WAS another smashing success. They
made a triumphal procession toward the center of town,
although Marroquín told Kane they would not try to force
entry into Talocan unless the two caved completely—a
contingency the whitecoat didn't foresee. The knights of
the Quetzal and Blue Macaw were out in force for this
one, riding in the forefront of the motorcade on their
powered trikes, marching front and back and all sides of
Quetzalcoatl's vehicle, a long white open-topped wag
with red upholstery and strange fins swept up from the
rear corners. Kane was riding just in front in an open-

topped Hummer sporting a .50-caliber machine gun on a pintle mount.

Brigid rode in an open wag right behind Quetzalcoatl's astonishing ride, and Grant and Domi perched on a four-wheeled armored car behind that. The idea was to spread out the heavy hitters so that a lucky strike wouldn't nail them all. Pretty much all the Quetzalcoatl faction's fleet of gunships orbited back over Tlillan-Tlapallan, ready to respond to any Talocan play. Indeed, it seemed to Kane that Marroquín, possibly in cahoots with Lakesh, was positively begging the loyalists to attack.

Which meant that Lakesh was acting with a not particularly characteristic boldness. Unless he had a lot higher estimation of Quetzalcoatl's gifts than Kane did. Kane was decidedly unimpressed with the feathered serpent's demonstrated ability to kill everybody within a hundred yards, especially since Kane and just about everybody he cared about on Earth were within a hundred yards of ground zero right now. He didn't think Lakesh would be willing to waste his ace operatives if things got dicey…but then he had never in his most fevered imaginings envisioned Lakesh riding through the streets of an old-fashioned spread-out ville, waving to cheering crowds and pausing now and again to heal the sick.

Yes, and even raise the dead. That was in Quetzalcoatl's job description, too, it turned out, although it only worked on reasonably fresh and intact chills. Given how hipped everyone was on death hereabouts, Kane was a little surprised that would even be considered desirable.

He displayed that particular ability at an aid station in a storefront a little over half a klick from the forward edge of the battle area. Way too close, especially since the fighting kept trudging slowly but inexorably closer. A circle had been cleared around a bier made out of sandbags, upon which was laid the body of a young Tlillan-Tlapallan sec man who had taken a round through the heart. He looked very young and mostly asleep, clad only in his urban-camou pants and boots. While media types flashed pictures past the cordon of knights holding them at bay, Quetzalcoatl strode grandly up to the dead kid. He was in his tall, vaguely Aryan-looking aspect, and wearing a garish feather headdress.

From near the front of the store Kane leaned his head toward Brigid's, being careful not to entangle his own goofy headdress with hers. "You think this is a setup?" he asked sotto voce. In English, for what it was worth, although everybody in the middle and professional classes spoke the language.

She shook her head slowly. "I have no idea what to believe at this point," she said. "I don't feel confident saying anything is impossible at this point."

Quetzalcoatl laid hands on the boy's chest. The hole healed as if by itself. A breathless moment, and then the young fighter's eyelids fluttered once and opened. Several people screamed as he looked around. Quetzalcoatl helped him sit up—and everybody in the place dropped to one knee with heads bowed to hail the plumed serpent.

Except Kane and Brigid. "Screw it," he murmured sidelong. "We're gods, too. Plus I am *not* bending the knee to Lakesh. As it is, it's going to take the lifetime of the solar system before his ego shrinks back to its normal inflated proportions, once he gets back to human."

"If he ever does," Brigid said.

"What's going on?" Grant's voice asked in Kane's ear. They had their regular trans-comms on now.

"Nothing much," Kane said. "Lakesh reanimated a dead kid, is all."

"Hoo." Domi breathed an exclamation that was half whistle. She and Grant were keeping watch out in the street. Somebody had to, and Domi being a naked kind of goddess had not been deemed precisely suitable to attend the great event itself. Although she was highly popular with the crowd, despite looking like a living statue.

"There'll be no living with him now," Grant said. "Can we go home?"

To everybody's relief, they did just that. Not back to Cerberus, of course. But right back to the institute to take stock and let the Quetzalcoatl propaganda machine make what it could of the god's return to the city.

A great celebration had been laid on in a dining hall on the ground floor of the compound's central step pyramid. There were banners and food and drink and musicians in big floppy hats and pants with shiny buttons down the legs who couldn't seem to quite agree on key. Everybody knew it was premature to be celebrating final victory, but consensus was that the corner had been turned. The plumed serpent had returned in triumph to the capital, to the acclaim of the multitudes, and Talocan would have to swallow its pride and treat with him.

Even Kane and Grant started to unwind. Just a little. After all, they had dared their enemies to take a poke at them, and those enemies had passed. "Mebbe the optimists are right this time," Kane said, drinking from a bottle of altogether acceptable local beer called Tres Equis. "As Baptiste told me at the resurrection today, anything's possible."

Which was when a heliborne strike force smashed down from the clouds onto the institute grounds, right outside the window.

Chapter 30

"Okay, I'm wrong," Kane said.

Celebrants screamed as a gunship made a pass right at them, its chin gun winking flame. The windows bulged and *booped* at the impacts, but actually held.

Watching from the great window Kane felt very cold. He sensed warmth beside him, looked down to see Brigid. "Correct me if I'm wrong—we just left most of our own troops out in the city, right?" she said.

"You nailed it."

Several inbound choppers blossomed into flame, oddly colorless through the glass and against the gray sky. The institute mustered some potent antiaircraft, judging by the sound full-dress Vulcan-Phalanx minigun turrets. Given the rough-and-ready nature of valley theology, as well as politics, it was small surprise.

Grant took a bite from a sticky bun. "Not enough," he observed. "And most of our birds are planted on the ground getting serviced and refueled after our little extravaganza earlier."

"I'm no strategist," Brigid said, "but if those choppers are filled with, say, Huitzilopochtli and Tezcatlipoca and the rest of Talocan's heavy hitters backed up by their knights—"

Helicopters began to land. Kane sighed. "We die a lot, looks like."

"Friends," Lakesh called from behind them. They turned. He strode toward them with Marroquín by his side. "It would appear we have been caught off guard."

"That's one way of putting it," Domi said. "I bet I can take down twenty of their knights before they chill me. What're you guys in for?"

Marroquín said, "All might not be lost."

Brigid said, "He's right. We still have two interphasers, the one that brought Domi and Grant and the one Lakesh used. We can get back to Cerberus with...well, a few of the key Quetzalcoatl people—"

"No," Kane said softly. "We're still stuck in god mode, remember? Cerberus can't sustain us and can't put us back the way we were."

Enemy knights leaped from the assault craft. Energy beams stabbed back and forth. Men fell. Many more charged, mouths wide in unheard warcries.

"I think I'll take Domi's bet," he said, "except I don't care about twenty. I only want to take one with me—Huitzilopochtli."

Grant rolled his head on his neck. "Let's ride," he said. Domi phase shifted, tore off her smock as if it were wet paper towels and flexed her claws.

"Wait."

Everyone turned to look at Marroquín. Ernesto and Teresa now stood with him, looking like fawns caught in headlights. Most of the hall had cleared out now as people ran, some to battle stations, others for the most secure hiding places available, or looking for covert ways out of the doomed institute. "You were selected for battle wisdom, as well as prowess," the whitecoat said waspishly. "Is suicide the best counterstroke you can come up with?"

Kane's cheeks burned, and for a moment Tonatiuh flared forth in full rage. "You dare to contradict—"

Brigid's touch was cool on his arm. "Easy." Like him, she spoke Náhuatl. He looked at her and saw her aspect was upon her.

"Any chance of reinforcements?" Grant asked, checking the load on his Sin Eater.

"I fear not," Lakesh said. "We have reports that the Talocan forces, including many gods, have launched an all-out ground assault led by Tlaloc. Our whole strength is engaged."

One entire five-yard-long armaglass panel emitted a musical-saw note and sagged in as a plasma bolt struck it. A rush of warm air flooded in, heavy with the smell of diesel fuel and burned bodies and incipient rain. Outside the defenders were being pushed back. Those who weren't already looking up at the sky.

Domi suddenly laughed, a bright and bell-like tone. The others looked at her, fearing to see madness in her blood-hued eyes.

"Don't you see?" she demanded. "They're going for the throat. But they've left their own asses flapping in the breeze!"

"HOLD TIGHT," Poncha's voice said through the earpiece Kane held clamped to the side of his head. The heavily laden Gazelle lurched upward from the yard.

Sitting across from Kane in the rear of the bird with four knights in battle regalia, Domi literally snarled like a jaguar as an eagle knight appeared right in front of them, just beyond the sweep of the main rotor, hoisting a bulky plasma rifle to his shoulder. Despite adrenaline fever and immediate awareness of the burning force lines winding around him and through the meridians, the *prana*-channels of his body, Kane could do nothing; his solar flare would flash-blast cockpit and pilots alike.

The 20 mm cannon's answering snarl was oddly muted by turbine roar and rotor chop, although the blaster was lighting off barely a yard behind where Domi sat, with only the thin aluminum curve of fuselage intervening.

This was a utility Gazelle, not a Deathbird-like dedicated gunship. But a minigun was bolted beneath the portside stub wing, and a strap-on ammo pack counterbalanced it to starboard. Unlike the Deathbirds' center-mounted guns, its recoil tried to twist the bird counterclockwise, opposite the spin of the main rotor overhead. A skilled pilot could keep the ship pointed the right way by easing off the tail-rotor pedal when firing, allowing recoil torque to compensate that of the main blades—but had to keep the bursts short or they would spin the ship the opposite direction.

Poncha was very skilled indeed. Her burst was very short.

The effect on the elite Talocan warrior was as if a plastic bag filled with blood and assorted chunks had been dropped to the concrete apron from a very great height. Muddy red droplets splayed across the windscreen, and then the bird was up and away, curving north and west and low as if running for the mountains.

Behind them five or six choppers burned on the apron, only one a Talocan. A dogfight roared and tumbled overhead. At least a few Quetzalcoatl jocks had gotten their birds up to rumble with the attackers.

And some were clearly bugging out. Kane felt a red flash of fury at the cowards, and it wasn't all Tonatiuh or Don Pedro.

Domi gazed at his face and read it like a computer screen. "Be grateful. They're covering us and the rest."

But not well enough. Looking out the viewport in the

port-side door above Domi's left shoulder, he saw another Gazelle rise up, start away, shudder to shell impacts. With smoke erupting from the big single exhaust nozzle it rocketed straight upward fifteen yards. Then the main rotor broke into whirling black shards. The chopper dropped like an anvil and vanished into a balloon of yellow flame.

"Grant! Lakesh!" Kane shouted for the benefit of his own trans-comm. "Baptiste!" He didn't need to shout, of course. He did anyway. Domi was doing likewise.

"I'm fine," Brigid replied at once.

"Still with you, Kane." Following hers, Grant's voice flooded Kane with relief like a drug. "About half a klick east, over a little patch of lake. Already clear of the swarm, looks like."

A pause. "That was Marroquín's ship."

Kane traded grimaces with Domi, who was hearing the same on her own unit. "Nobody's getting out of that incinerator," Kane said. "But he told us what we need to know."

"I hope the crash killed everybody instantly," Brigid said.

Kane shrugged. That wasn't usually how it went down, although they had free-fallen almost a hundred feet. No point telling her how likely it was the occupants burned alive.

Not when the chances were really good it would be them frying and dying in their own grease in just a couple short minutes. Kane doubted even Tonatiuh could dump that much heat into the energy-whorls in short enough order to do more than prolong the pain.

The Talocan warcraft showed no interest in them. They had the upper hand, but way too much on their plates to bother anybody who was clearly running. Marroquín had just gotten unlucky. Either his bird had been overkilled by somebody else's sky-fight, or a Talocan Deathbird driver had caught a shot and decided not to risk letting a possible foe get airborne; like the other two Gazelles, the chief whitecoat's bird had mounted a bolted-on Gatling.

"We're clear," Poncha reported.

Kane held the intercom headset near his head; he only just heard her words, tiny and tinny. He could still tell her tone was dead calm. Combat chopper drivers were like armor-wag jocks in that regard; they ran with the certain knowledge that whenever you took your machine in harm's way, you stood the chance of being cremated without the luxury of dying first.

"Roger that," Kane said. "Let's go downtown." The bird pitched forward and accelerated.

Domi was naked but for the harness of her shoulder rig. The four knights crammed in with them took no notice. They had more urgent things on their minds. Baptiste had told Kane that back in the heyday of the cult of psychotherapy people calling themselves scientists actually believed no human drive was stronger than sex.

Yeah, Kane thought. Try, "not dying."

Taloned black hands clutched a scoped laser rifle to Domi like a teddy bear. She wasn't Earth's best rifle shot, and Itzapapalotl had little patience with a style of chilling that didn't get an enemy's guts all wound around her in the process. But even Grant's plasma rifle didn't have a great range, nor did the knights' small arms, and they needed somebody to discourage snipers. The laser wep was easy to hit with, anyway: no recoil, no bullet drop. Just point 'n' click.

Poncha had curved the bird around the stricken institute in a wide arc and lined out for Talocan. The three main buildings of valley church and state already looked huge through the front windscreen. Craning to peer out the port on his own side, Kane could just see the institute compound. A whole lot of smoke was drifting skyward from a whole lot of places. But the institute was a big place and more than somewhat slightly hardened. It would take Talocan days to pry out all of even the rump force of defenders, even if they threw in everybody they had, gods and mere humans alike.

He felt a twinge for Teresa. The hybrid girl was such an odd blend of spiky competence and childlike vulnerability. But she and Ernesto had their own bodyguard of knights, and if they had followed their now-late leader's firm instructions, they were locked in a vault deep beneath the institute where the invaders might never even find them. Complete with easy access to subterranean escape tunnels that would let them get clear even if the two dropped the whole place on top of them with demo charges. The prior Quetzalcoatl—Morall, the exiles' hybrid leader, betrayer and betrayed—had been well paranoid, peace god or not.

Which of course was why he'd escaped to spend the past three decades in one more exile.

Kane sat back in his seat. "Huitzilopochtli," he said, as if it were a curse. "Bastard. I never even laid eyes on the puke."

"Good," said Domi, who had produced a sautéed axolotl strip on a stick from somewhere that didn't bear thinking about and was chewing it happily. "You'd have gone for him then and there. Blown the whole damn plan out the window. Men."

She seemed less stressed or fatigued by wearing her aspect than the others, even though it changed her body more. The obsidian-butterfly persona fit the feral girl like skin, her lethal appetites in flawless accord with Domi's own; and of course she got to drink down the life force of those she slew far more up-close and personal than the others, thus recharging faster.

But she still has to spend her nights in the same vats we

do, Kane reminded himself. Or her nervous system will burn itself out, her own metabolism run into overdrive and consume her body from within. He hoped again the whitecoats weren't lying when they claimed the process was reversible.

Then he laughed. As if we're likely to live long enough to find out. In its way, it was a reassuring thought.

Several choppers floated in the sky above the vast central plaza. Just one or two could possibly be gunships. Between the strike on Quetzalcoatl HQ and the streetfight passing below Kane's ship even now, Talocan had shot its whole wad this afternoon. The other craft were no doubt TV birds whose crews were hoping something newsworthy would happen that *didn't* require them to fly into a sky filled with flaming death to capture it.

"Get ready to jump," Poncha said over the intercom. "Taking fire already."

Their route took them past the parliament building from the north. Kane could see figures on the roof who seemed to be shooting at them. Just small arms, it looked like, subguns and longblasters. Nothing hit the bird, which was good, because nothing was exactly what the thin hull would stop.

The pyramid's top was crowded with knights, plumed dignitaries and the loathsome priests of sacrifice in their rotting-blood body paint and human-membrane do-rags. Evidently the two planned a major blood-letting to celebrate the downfall of their foes.

Which there was in plenty, on and around the altar of the gods. Just a little ahead of schedule. Kane and Domi both laughed aloud as Poncha's minigun belched repeatedly, scouring the pyramid's apex like a firehose. Vectoring in from the northwest, the chopper carrying Grant and the new Quetzalcoatl—or same old Lakesh—added its cleansing fire to theirs. The thirty or so men waiting on the pyramid died with no chance to defend themselves or escape.

"Rest in pieces," Kane said, as Poncha dived the ship toward its objective.

"Wish it was napes," Grant said. He meant napalm.

"You got that right."

"But then it'd be too warm for us," Domi pointed out.

Lakesh's bird got there ahead of Poncha's. She said nothing, and Kane couldn't read much body language from the back of her helmet and the slice of shoulder he could see. But the chopper-jock in him could feel her irritation in the way she waved off and flew a holding pattern around the pyramid, not circling, but serpentining and juking up and down. Making it hard on bad-guy gunners.

Who were no doubt shooting at them even now, but Kane couldn't see anybody actually doing it. The other ship flared into hover with its skids a yard or so above the black altar. The knights hopped out. One put a foot on a loop of greasy purple gut, slipped and fell. Grant jumped next, more cautiously, then reached up to help Lakesh down. The aging whitecoat had his aspect upon him, and looked and moved like an athletic young warrior god. Albeit a peaceful one. Mostly.

Once its divine cargo was clear, the chopper shot straight into the air to quickly clear the way for Poncha.

And a hammerblow struck her chopper with a noise like the sky breaking open.

Chapter 31

The cabin filled with dark choking smoke and a blast of cool air. Waving his hand before his face, Kane saw the windscreen was gone. The copilot slumped in his seat. Something in Poncha's posture wasn't right, although her hands gripped the joystick and her feet were working the pedals—hard, to judge by the way the craft obviously wanted to drift in air. The instrument panel was a blaze of red emergency lights.

"SAM," Poncha's voice said from the headset. Kane had never seen it. "*Out*. Now!"

Domi and Kane opened their doors, then as one sat back to let the knights egress first. They had merely human powers to preserve them if the bird gave up the ghost.

When. Kane wasn't half the Deathbird driver Grant was. But he was a seasoned pilot. The damage was visibly bad, and that much red on the board meant a mechanism as intricate as a helicopter was already dead. It still flew, under control of at least a sort. But it was clearly just looking for a place to lie down.

The humans jumped free. Baptiste and Grant both clamored for Kane's attention, but he didn't absorb their words. Beneath him he felt the chopper begin to rise, slowly, inexorably.

"*Go now*," Poncha screamed. "For the love of God!" She crossed herself. She was a closet monotheist, who still held to the valley's other old-time religion: Roman Catholicism. The ruling gods neither tolerated nor suppressed it; they just ignored it. It was just there, like the lake and the quakes and the smokies all around. And a whole lot less bother.

Kane registered none of that now. Standing in the open door, what he did register was that the pyramid top was a good ten yards below and falling.

Nukeshit. He and Domi were dead if they stayed in the bird. But how much good could they do, with ankles shattered to powder and thighbones driven like impaling stakes up into their bowels?

Domi tackled him from behind. They both shot right out into space.

"Stupe!" she screamed in his ear. "We're—"

He got his legs beneath him. The girl let go. The pyramid rushed up and smacked him in the soles of his sandals. By sheer trained reflex he let his knees buckle to the impact, dropped, tucked a shoulder, rolled. He lay on his back to see Domi crouched on the altar above him.

"—gods," she finished.

He lay still. He felt as if a mule had kicked him up under the jaw. He felt as if a mule had kicked him all over. It took the full awful majesty of Tonatiuh's will to suck even a molecule of air back into his body. But he was alive, and he could still feel his legs and feet. They hurt. But he could feel them.

Gods. Right. Superhuman strength and all. Evidently structural, too.

Grant loomed about him like a black colossus in his shadow armor. He reached down a giant hand.

"No time to take a nap." Their hands clasped, forearm to strong forearm.

An engine whined overhead as Grant hauled his partner to his feet. Poncha had got her bucking, swaying, dying bird pointed the way she wanted, two hundred yards above the pyramid. Its motor was sheathed in flame and orange hellglare shone out the open door.

She tipped the whirly-wag's snout down and into a long shallow power dive right toward the roof of the Black House, on which small humanoid forms could be seen. The shot that killed her had come from there, or so she seemed to have judged.

She was probably right; two more backpack antiaircraft missiles streaked toward her, sprouting long tails of white smoke from pinpoints of blue-white fire. Both shot harmlessly past the chopper to explode somewhere over the city behind the watchers' backs. They didn't have enough flight distance to guide on the chopper, even though their IR seeker heads had a huge fat target to look at; by the time it hit, right beyond the edge of the roof, the machine was nothing but a raging orange comet of fire.

Which splashed clear across the roof of the Black House, engulfing dozens of defenders. The lucky ones were crushed instantly thereafter by hurtling wreckage or ripped asunder by shredded blades. Several fell or jumped, miniature meteors themselves, the black glass facade reflecting the light of their downwardly mobile self-contained pyres.

Kane drew his sword from its loose leather sheath slung across his back. It was undamaged despite the fact he'd landed on it. The resin-impregnation of glass blades and flat hardwood handle definitely performed to spec. He held the wep up in salute. "Goodbye, Poncha," he said.

"Ave atque vale," Brigid added softly. Her contingent had debarked while Kane lay stunned.

Lakesh had organized the twelve knights with them into a defensive periyard around the sacrificial platform. He hadn't done a half-bad job. The warrior who had fallen down had not managed to injure himself.

Behind the altar itself stood a stone pavilion, which served as backdrop to the festivities and also concealed an entrance to the pyramid's hollow innards. Domi swarmed up onto its flat roof with her scoped laser rifle and a pair of 8 x 21 microbinocs.

"You're exposed up there," Grant called, meaning something other than the obvious.

"I also have a three-sixty view," she said. "Or do you think the only threats will be coming from the direction of the institute? I'm fast and I have quick reflexes."

"She's right," Kane said. "It's not as if we're not all just a little bit at risk here."

"Gentlemen," Lakesh said, "ladies, if I may direct your attention to the Black House."

Burning fuel from Poncha's Gazelle was still smeared down the front of the Black House for maybe twenty yards like luminous graffiti. A few bits of wreckage lay beneath it on the plaza, but most of the debris had stayed on the roof.

Men poured into the plaza from the Black House. They wore black uniforms that included black hoods or ski masks—impossible to tell at this distance. They carried machine pistols in gauntleted hands.

"Wouldn't you just know the priests and whitecoats would have their own sec men," Grant said.

Some regular Talocan sec men and even a handful of knights were in the plaza below. Presumably a new security contingent had been posted to the charnel house that was the parliament building. Also no doubt there were various fighters securing the interior of the pyramid beneath their feet, including gods, so Kane had to assume.

"Allow me." Lakesh strode to the front of the topmost level, toward the Black House. He raised his hands. "Priests and scientists and warriors of the Black House," he declaimed in a voice that seemed to fill the whole huge plaza, "hear me. I am Quetzalcoatl! I have returned to reclaim my rightful place in the ruling councils of Tenochtitlán and the valley!"

"Whoa," Grant said. "I didn't know he brought a loudspeaker with him. How do they get that kind of volume out of a little hideaway unit like that?"

"I'm not using a loudspeaker," Lakesh said over his shoulder in a normal voice. "Nor did I in my inaugural address. It turns out this is one of my new powers."

A red line suddenly appeared, slanting just above his shoulder downward into the mass of black-clad troops. A crack as displaced air molecules rushed back into the temporary vacuum left by the laser beam assailed their ears.

"Some wannabe blood-drinker down in the plaza shouldered a longblaster," Domi called down. "Double sorry."

Quetzalcoatl raised his hands high. "Cease! Let there be no more contention! I will not be denied, but I wish no more blood to be shed within the precincts of our holy city. Lay down your weapons, and you will not be harmed, my children."

A whole volley of gunfire crackled from the black mass. No bullets came near them. They were much too far for accurate shooting with submachine guns firing handgun loads, and people blasting at an upward angle almost always shot low. Obedient to the orders implicit in Lakesh's words, Domi held her fire.

"So be it!" Quetzalcoatl's voice boomed out. He made

a sweeping gesture of his hands, as if gathering something and casting it toward the Black House.

The great building's glass front exploded in a shower of black razor snow. It fell with deceptive slowness onto the sec men who had streamed into the plaza. The watchers on the pyramid could hear the screams as fast-falling fragments sliced through bodies, limbs, heads.

"I willingly harm no one," Quetzalcoatl declaimed. "But if my hand is forced, I will raise it to defend myself."

"Impressive," Kane said.

For the moment at least no more shots were fired. Even the surviving Black House troops had more interesting things to do than worry about the interlopers, such as bleeding and howling. However, plenty of enemies remained down there who hadn't been within the glass-fall footprint.

Brigid stepped up to the front of the platform. "Allow me."

At the base of the broad steep stairs leading up the pyramid from the plaza—the *via dolorosa* trodden by tens of thousands of human sacrifices—a wisp of white appeared in the air. It rolled, roiled, grew, like smoke from a fire. Brigid's hands were raised and eyes tight shut.

"Now, that's just spooky," commented Grant, peering over. He held his plasma rifle at the ready.

"What's she doing?" Domi called from her station atop the housing. The white cloud began to radiate outward across the plaza. Some of the sec men fled its approach, back toward the parliament building. "They're afraid it's a Xipe Totec kind of trick," Kane commented. "Poison gas, mebbe."

"It would appear she's causing atmospheric moisture to condense in the form of fog," Quetzalcoatl said in his Lakesh voice. It was peculiar hearing it emerge from the bearded lips of the tall and handsome god.

The white stuff now filled the great plaza and surrounded the bases of the three cyclopean buildings to the height of a couple of stories. Brigid opened her eyes and smiled as she looked upon her handiwork.

"Voilà," she said. "Instant smoke screen."

"Good job," said Kane. "Now they'll have trouble shooting at us."

"Now we got trouble shooting at them," Grant pointed out.

Kane shrugged. "Plenty more of them than us. I don't think there's going to be much of a problem unless they try a bum's rush up the pyramid. Or try to snipe us from one of the other buildings. Domi—"

A line of ruby brilliance split the sky with a crack. "There's a third eye open for you, dog ass," Domi said. She moved her obsidian face from behind the scope of the laser rifle, which was supported in front on a bipod. "What were you saying down there, Chief?"

"Keep up the good work."

Kane turned to Quetzalcoatl. "Why don't you and Brigid kind of drift back under the overhang, there, just in case. And you two back there, Ocelotl and Ant-Bear—" they had been in his personal guard previously, during the bug hunt and the fight in the park with Xipe and Tlaloc "—keep a real close watch on that door."

Both knights of the Quetzal and Blue Macaw were armed with plasma rifles, which ought to give a good jolt to even Tezcatlipoca poking his snout out. Kane hoped.

"Right now," he muttered, "this plan's got more holes in it than a slagger's skivvies."

"Sucks," Grant agreed. "Only it sucks less than anything else available."

Kane laughed and tipped a one-finger salute off a scarred eyebrow. "Classic one-percenter."

Grant returned the salute with a deepened scowl. "Again."

"Time to stir up the ants," Kane said.

He unlimbered his shield, also strapped around his back. Then he drew his sword, which he had thrust through his belt. He looked around the bottom of the dome of cloud.

"Deathbird," Grant said, pointing out a sleek back shape flying formation with a little white-and-blue chopper that was evidently a newsie ship. "Couple of good rockets takes us all out in a blaze of glory."

"I don't think they'll choose to play it that way," Kane said. "But let's reduce the element of chance."

He aimed the sword and felt for the fiery lines of force. White brilliance drew a line across the sky, culminating in a bright yellow sphere wreathed in black smoke where the gunship had been.

"Whoa!" Grant exclaimed. "I could never've made that shot with this thing." He slapped the plasma rifle's receiver for emphasis.

"Why it pays to have a god on your team. Let's see how good the news crew's telephoto lens is."

He let the obsidian-edged sword swing from a leather thong around his wrist and pointed to the TV helicopter. Then he rolled his hand palm up, extended his forefinger, curled it back toward his palm in a come-hither gesture, thrice repeated.

After a moment in which Kane considered sending a solar flare across the civilian helo's bows, just to get its occupants' minds right, it turned, dipped its nose and descended toward the pyramid. Then it stopped.

"Domi!" Grant said sharply. "Don't be pointing that thing at him. We *want* him to come this way."

"Damn!" she said. But she aimed the laser longblaster elsewhere.

"Perhaps if you could muster a bit of a halo," Lakesh said. "It might show to advantageous effect on the viewing public's screens."

"Full-body radiance," added Brigid. "Like a medieval painting."

"What, everybody has a suggestion now on how to run the god business?" Kane said.

"Just your fellow gods," Brigid said. "And goddesses."

"I'm an action god, not a public-relations god," Kane said. He concentrated briefly and was rewarded by the air immediately surrounding his body, and even the extravagant feathers atop his helmet, beginning to glow yellow.

"Little blinding, here," Itzapapalotl said.

"Oh." Kane reduced the output. He gestured at the news helicopter again. It resumed its wary approach.

"Doesn't anybody else think this whole thing, with the clown suits and all, is just a little silly?" he asked.

"If you hadn't just zapped a gunship out of the sky a klick away with a wooden sword," Grant said, "I'd be laughing harder than anybody right now."

The helicopter descended to hover somewhat above the apex and about a hundred yards away. "Can you hear me?" Kane said, concentrating on projecting rather than shouting. "If so, flash your landing lights."

Flash.

"Are you broadcasting this?"

The lights winked again obediently. "Then hear me, Tenochtitlán—and Talocan. I am Tonatiuh, god of the Sun. With me is Lord Quetzalcoatl. He has returned to restore peace and freedom to the people of the city and all of the valley. I am his champion. Should Talocan wish to contest the plumed serpent's right of return, I, Tonatiuh, do hereby challenge the war god Huitzilopochtli to personal combat to vindicate that right!"

He let the sword, which he'd been brandishing with what he hoped was appropriate theatricality, hang from its thong, and folded his arms across his gilded polycarbonate breastplate. The helicopter fled to a safe distance.

"Bravo," Brigid called from the shadows of the housing. "You're a natural born politician, Kane."

He turned to her with a wounded look. "Isn't that rather a harsh judgment on a friend?"

The entry door to the pyramid's depths blew outward like a cork from a bottle.

Chapter 32

Huitzilopochtli slew joyously. Sword whirling through armor and flesh as air, he waded through a final knot of defenders and stepped gingerly into the festive hall across shards of armaglass blown in by RPGs.

"Die, monster!" A knight of the Quetzal charged him, shield up and sword raised.

White teeth glared from a black-painted face in a fearsome grin. Huitzilopochtli swept his sword transversely down, right to left. The black glass shards hit the knight's forearm midway up from his sword hand. His hand jumped free on a spume of scarlet.

Huitzilopochtli's flat backhand struck the man at the level of his eyes. The whole top of his head was sliced off. Half-decapitated, the body hurtled past and fell outside into the watery light.

Huitzilopochtli trembled in ecstasy as he imbibed the man's life force. There was something about doing it in the hot blood of combat, something about triumphing, dominating, destroying that made it all the sweeter and the keener. Mere sacrifice could not compare.

A brave man, Huitzilopochtli thought, worthy of his flowery sacrifice. He flicked his brawny wrist to clear his sword of gore and clots of brain.

When we have crushed these dogs, he promised himself, I'll institute sacrifice in the form of gladiatorial combat as I've wanted to for so long. Both Tezcatlipoca and their mother opposed the idea. Coatlicue thought it might send the wrong message, encouraging mortals to fight gods—even though, as Huitzilopochtli tried to point out to her, they'd always lose. Tezcatlipoca offered many eloquent reasons, but Huitzilopochtli had long decided his brother objected to the idea because he thought it was trite.

Stalking through the now abandoned commissary with the hot blood of the hunt practically boiling in his veins, Huitzilopochtli cursed his brother for a coward for demurring from this raid. Or something worse. His jaguar knights had not been conspicuous in the hottest fighting these past few days, either. Huitzilopochtli's own eagle knights had been more than happy to grab for the glory, as was their divine master. But now it came to Huitzilopochtli that the cunning Tezcatlipoca might be scheming against him, hoping Huitzilopochtli and Quetzalcoatl would exhaust their resources battling each other, leaving the survivor—who naturally would be Huitzilopochtli—weakened and vulnerable.

He felt a tingling sensation at his left hip. Scowling, he stopped and reached into the pouch of cured human hide that rode there, coming up with a polished disk of obsidian just larger than the palm of his hand. "Yes?" he barked at it.

Coatlicue's face appeared in the mirror. Her jade eyes were wide. "My son! You must return at once! Talocan is under attack. The interloper Tonatiuh stands upon the top of the pyramid, calling you out! He has challenged you before the cameras of our own news service."

Fury surged within the war god. The insolence! How dare they do to him what he was so incisively doing to them? "I'll come as soon as I can gather my forces."

"No! There is no time. You must come at once and face this foreigner alone. Or all we have worked for is lost!"

He wanted to argue, but found himself peering at a blank planchet of glass. Grinding his teeth in rage, he thrust the now quiescent mirror back into its pouch.

"Get me a helicopter," he snarled at his escorts. "Now!"

DOWN IN THE PYRAMID, the well-shaped hand of Coatlicue, which even in the flush of her first youth, when she had been known and well feared as Felicidad Mendoza, had been both feminine and strong as many men's, descended, holding the mirror. But what reached the bottom of the arm's arc was a wire-muscled, dark-skinned, very masculine hand.

Attached to the other end of that arm, Tezcatlipoca the shape-changing god smiled a private smile.

"CHOPPERS INBOUND from the north!" Domi sang out. Her words were instantly overridden by a shrill wail emanating from the shattered doorway.

The door had missed the two Quetzalcoatl knights on guard when it flew out and over the black altar to bounce down the stairs. They raised their plasma rifles.

The wail stopped, only to blast forth again. The knights' screams mingled with the terrifying sound as blood squirted from their ears. Then they were shattered as if by a high-velocity blast wave.

Brigid grabbed Lakesh by his aspect's brawny upper biceps and whirled him out of the tiny pavilion. "Find cover," she rapped as the sound faded again. "I'll handle this!"

"Why, certainly it's wise of you to preserve my own wisdom for future service—" He moved with alacrity out and around the side of the structure as a figure stepped forth.

"So you're the *bolilla* bitch they picked to be the new Chalchihuitlicue," she said.

"And you are Felicidad Mendoza," said Brigid. "Rather well-preserved, for a woman your age."

KANE LOOKED UP as a ruby beam cracked over his head, so low that the top two inches of the tallest feather of his helmet were snipped off and floated down before his face like a leaf. A second pulsed at once.

Three black shapes had appeared, streaking like arrows for the pyramid. The lead ship's nose came up and it drifted, almost slowly, to the level of the following two, which were stepped above it. Then it banked to starboard.

The disk of its main rotor intersected that of its right-hand wingman. Both instantly shattered into sprays of black splinters. The two gunships, now basically fast-moving bricks, descended into the fog.

A fractional second later two flame spheres sprouted through the thick white blanket, rolled upward on stalks of black smoke.

"Oh, yeah," Domi sang out. "Two for the price of one! I *meant* to do that."

Smoke puffed beneath the left-hand element's starboard stub wing. "Missile launch!" Grant yelled.

It was immediately apparent that instead of a volley of 57 mm rockets, the launch was a solitary—which almost certainly meant a big antitank guided missile with a hefty shaped-charge warhead. It spiraled toward the altar, drawing a corkscrew of smoke.

Kane threw up his sword and loosed a solar flare. It missed.

"Everybody get behind me!" he shouted. He summoned forth the energy of the burning geomagnetic lines, dumped it into the Sun shield, raised the blazing disk before him.

The missile struck.

EMERALD EYES MET eyes of jade, locked. Two beautiful red-headed woman, one with hair like a slow-motion fall of Hawaiian lava, the other whose hair resembled fine copper wire, stared at each other with pure essence of rage. If looks could kill…

They'd cancel each other out, apparently. "Your death gaze is stronger than I would have thought," Coatlicue grudged. "The traitor Marroquín chose well, it seems."

"Well, you are giving me a hell of a headache."

"Enough female bonding down there," Domi called, out of sight on the roof. "Duck!"

An ear-imploding explosion made Brigid crouch and half turn from sheerest reflex.

THE SUN GOD let the mighty muscles of his legs flex as shock absorbers. He rocked back as a fireball erupted on the front of his Sun shield. Flame and shockwaves fanned outward, safely missing Tonatiuh and his comrades.

"Show-off," Grant said.

The surviving chopper's gunner might have been stunned by his mighty rocket's spectacular noneffect. He did not do the obvious thing and sweep the pyramid's apex with his chin gun, as Poncha had. He did nothing at all as his pilot let the chopper's momentum carry it forward right over the giant structure.

As it did, Grant whipped up his plasma rifle and blasted the aircraft in the belly.

The hurtling gunship began to come apart around an expanding yellow glare. Itzapapalotl yowled in alarm. Then the helicopter swept beyond her and blew up.

"Cutting that pretty close, weren't you?" Kane asked. Grant shrugged.

"Brigid's in trouble," Domi shouted.

BRIGID HEARD Coatlicue scream behind her and knew at once the mother-goddess was not crying out in terror. A wave of sound smashed her like a wag. Something twisted her body from within, trying to tear each and every molecule in her body away from the others.

She spun and straightened. Her headdress was ripped from her head. Her hair streamed out behind her like rocket exhaust. The light cloth she had wrapped around her breasts disintegrated.

But investiture with the self-perpetuating energy pattern known as Chalchihuitlicue, the lady of the jade skirt, had given Brigid super-human strength and durability as it had her companions.

But it had its limits. Her eyes stung and watered. Her lungs could not suck in air no matter how she strained. She couldn't long withstand Coatlicue's murder scream.

Nor could she draw sufficient moisture down from the clouds, nor up from the lake deep beneath the city, to use as a weapon against the other goddess. Too much energy and concentration were required literally to hold her together.

But Brigid was Brigid, as well as Chalchihuitlicue. Her greatest strength was still her mind. She saw a chance and reached out with the power of her demon rider....

Coatlicue's wail rose to a crescendo, then cut off, died in a dry, strangling squawk.

Coatlicue's eyes snapped open. Then they shriveled

within the orbits of her skull. Her eyelids caved in, then tautened, turning the consistency of parchment.

The fingers of Coatlicue's raised hands began to diminish and wrinkle like raisins. Her full breasts withered, as did her thighs.

But her belly was swelling, swelling, not just to the front but outward in all directions. Like a balloon being pumped full of water.

Which burst. Water exploded in all directions. The mother of the gods collapsed into a pile of dehydrated tissue stretched over skull and bones.

"Quick thinking, Baptiste," Kane said.

Brigid turned, smiled faintly, brushed at a lock of hair that had fallen into her eyes. "I need to sit down," she said weakly. She tottered toward the altar.

"Not there, Brigid," Domi called down from her roof. "You don't want that stuff on you."

Brigid nodded and slumped down to the platform.

Domi turned her face to the sky. "You think Huitzilopochtli was in one of those Deathbirds we just wasted?"

"We aren't that lucky," Grant said.

Quetzalcoatl stepped around the corner of the stone pavilion built over the now open entrance. "You have all performed brilliantly," he said. "But my new…associate assures me that Huitzilopochtli will unquestionably take up Tonatiuh's challenge."

"He's sure gonna be pissed when he sees what you did to his mom," Domi said.

Quetzalcoatl knelt beside Chalchihuitlicue. "Brigid! Darling Brigid, are you all right?"

She raised her head. He recoiled. Her eyes were like bezels of blood in which were set emerald irises.

"I'm afraid more of her force got through than I thought,

Dr. Lakesh," she said apologetically. "I'm afraid I might be…hemorrhaging…."

Blood gushed from her mouth. Her head fell to the side.

Chapter 33

"Baptiste!" Kane roared. He lunged toward her.

Grant interposed himself. "You can't help her, Kane. Let the man do his thing."

Tonatiuh glared in fury at the mortal who had presumed to interfere with him. "Back off the trigger, here, big guy," Grant said. "It's me. Your partner. Grant, remember?"

With a spasm of will Kane asserted himself over his demon riders. He nodded convulsively. "You're right."

But his *anam-chara* lay on her back as if lifeless, blood streaming from her nose and ears, as well as her mouth. It ran like tears from her eyes, which stared without blinking at the ceiling of cloud, which seemed to be breaking up. Domi began to cry.

A Quetzal knight shouted, "My lords! Look above you!"

Kane looked up. A black dot had appeared below the clouds. It rapidly grew larger, taking on the shape of a man with splayed-out limbs. The distance-muted rotor chop of a helicopter hidden in the clouds fell like rain.

The figure rolled into a ball, then at the instant before impact straightened with its feet below it. It hit the top of the black altar.

The black granite slab split straight across with a cannon-shot crack and a golden flash.

Huitzilopochtli straightened, great-muscled legs straddling the split, grinning malevolently down from his black-painted face. He wore a skirt of gold plates, a golden helmet with a high side-to-side crest, flat sandals laced high up his shins. He carried shield and sword similar to Tonatiuh's, with his symbol painted on the front of his buckler.

"So you thought to challenge the primary god of war," he said. "Yes, I speak English out of regard to your gringo ears. My mother, the goddess Coatlicue, taught me. Where is she?"

Grant nodded toward the heap of parchment-covered bones. "That's her. Her moisturizer broke down on her."

Huitzilopochtli turned and his eyes bulged from his blackened face. "Tactful, Grant," Kane said quietly out the side of his mouth.

His partner shrugged. "Never said I was a diplomat."

A steam-whistle sound broke from Huitzilopochtli. He raised his arms to the sky, muscles bulging in fury.

"You shall pay with your blood and souls!" he roared. "I shall take your hearts and burn them as sacrifice to my mother Coatlicue. Except for you, Tonatiuh—when I have done with you, there shall be but one Sun god remaining, and it shall be the god of war."

"Let's all jump him at once," Grant muttered. "Bet he can't take us all."

"No good," said Kane. "If I welch on the challenge, the whole populace turns against Quetzalcoatl—which means all of us. And even if we got away with our skins, you're the only one who'd still be alive come sunup tomorrow."

He stepped forward. "You get your chance to make good your boast, Left Hand Hummingbird," he declared in a ringing voice. "But if I win, it's over. Quetzalcoatl will be restored to his full place."

Huitzilopochtli's face seemed carved of stone as he glowered down upon his rival. Then it cracked in a brutal smile. "My brother, who fears to show his face even now, would probably make his peace with you quickly enough were you to defeat me. But that will never happen. Prepare!"

"Everybody!" Kane swept his arm around the platform. "Off! Give us room here."

Lakesh, still in his Quetzalcoatl aspect, stood up bearing Brigid's limp body in his arms. He strode to the side of the platform and hopped down to the next step of the pyramid. Kane set his jaw. Grant was right: he could do nothing for her but beat Huitzilopochtli—and hope.

Eyes wide in bloodless faces, the remaining knights backed away and clambered down. Grant laid his hand on Kane's shoulder where it was left bare by his breastplate, squeezed once hard, then turned and climbed down to the next level himself.

Kane's companions could just see over the platform's edge. Domi pulled herself up to sit cross-legged on her roof, still in Itzapapalotl form. "Good luck, Kane," she called softly.

Huitzilopochtli jumped down to stand facing Kane across the broken black altar. He bared his teeth. "He will need much more than luck. Are you ready, Tonatiuh?"

"I am."

"Then we begin."

Kane's sword still swung from his right wrist by its thong. He let it. Instead, he stretched his arm toward the war god and curled his fingers and thumb.

His Sin Eater pounded into his hand and erupted in a yard-long muzzle flame and a loud ripping snarl.

Huitzilopochtli rocked his weight back slightly on his heels as bullets hit him full in the center of his bare, great-muscled chest. They flashed into brief incandescence as Kane dumped the whole magazine against the war god.

The slide locked back on an empty box. The silence was startling. After a beat Huitzilopochtli laughed.

"What do you play at, Sun god? You must know I am enveloped by a field of invincibility. Your foolish bullets barely tickled."

"Try another magazine," said Kane, who had reloaded from his pouch.

Huitzilopochtli's smile never twitched a micron as Kane blasted him with twenty more rounds. "My patience wears thin, gringo," the war god said as the second mag ran dry.

Kane let the wep snap back into the holster strapped to his forearm. Then with a quick movement of his arm he flipped the hilt of his sword up into his right fist.

"Then see how you like this," he said. He straightened his arm toward Huitzilopochtli and sent his solar flare leaping forth.

Huitzilopochtli just got his own shield interposed as Tonatiuh launched his bolt. Superheated plasma surrounded him in a brilliant nimbus.

The watchers, knowing how the solar flare drained Tonatiuh's energy, expected the beam to wink out. It did not. Nor did it penetrate Huitzilopochtli's own personal form-fitting force screen.

The war god leaned forward and began to stride into the beam, leaning as if he were forcing his way against the blast of a hose. Step by step he waded up the roaring jet. The hard stone of the platform melted and ran before and beneath his sandaled feet as he came on.

"Kane!" Grant shouted above the noise. "What the hell do you think you're doing?"

The flare flickered, once, twice, then went out. Kane staggered, caught himself.

"Drained your batteries, did you, Sun god?" Huitzilopochtli asked tauntingly.

Slowly a smile stretched itself above Kane's vertical bar of beard. "Pretty much. And yours, too, I bet."

His sword whipped in a backhand stroke for Huitzilopochtli's muscle-wedge of a neck. Inhumanly fast as he was, the war god barely managed to lean back out of harm's way as the obsidian blades sang past.

Huitzilopochtli straightened. Tonatiuh stepped back. The war god smiled.

Then his heavy, handsome, black-painted features crumpled into a frown. He let his own volcanic glass sword hang from its thong, raised his hand to his left cheek, touched it lightly.

When he dropped his hand, the fingertips glistened with red wetness.

"Looks like we got us a little more level playing field, here," Kane said. "No projectile weps, no magic shields. Just us, *mano y mano.*"

"That's *mano a mano,* you ignorant prick!" Huitzilopochtli roared. He launched a ferocious overhead swing.

Kane stopped it with his shield. The impact flung him back five yards through the air. He sat down hard on the very rim of the platform.

Huitzilopochtli rushed him. Kane leaped aside and up, getting his feet beneath him—and aiming a cut at Huitzilopochtli's unprotected right side.

But Huitzilopochtli was supernaturally good, as well as fast. Before he either took the cut or rushed headlong off the top of the pyramid he whirled aside, went to one knee.

"Well done," he said. "Not good enough, but better than I thought you'd do."

"You, too," Kane said.

Huitzilopochtli laughed. The two men crab-stepped cautiously back toward the broken altar, away from the edge. When they neared the stone slab, Huitzilopochtli launched a furious attack.

As blows rained on his shield Kane soon realized the war god was faster, stronger and better than he was. It wasn't a heartening combination.

He managed to survive the first wild volley with no more cost than having his plumes cut off at a bias a hand span above his head, not a loss that bothered him. He managed to take a couple of cracks of his own, which either clacked off the rim of Huitzilopochtli's shield or missed clean. It was a moral victory; Huitzilopochtli plainly intended not to give him a chance to get off any shots at all.

They drew apart. Kane was panting like a locomotive but gratified to see his adversary breathing through an open mouth as well. His Tonatiuh-persona and Don Pedro yammered like a flock of magpies in Kane's skull. He did his best to ignore them. They weren't war gods, either.

If this deadly duel was going to be won, it would be won by Kane. Which meant Mag rules.

Which brought it all into focus.

He began to circle to his right. A few sideways steps, being careful not to cross his feet—which would have drawn a charge and at the very least would have made him trip over himself and go down—brought the altar between them.

"Clever," Huitzilopochtli said. "Do you really think that will keep my blades from finding your flesh?"

No, but it will keep you from knocking me down with a charge. Kane said nothing.

Huitzilopochtli leaped up onto the altar, hacking down at Kane's head. Kane flung his shield up in time, crouched and swung for the war god's ankles. Huitzilopochtli leaped

over the blow. As Kane cocked his sword back for a follow-up shot, Huitzilopochtli touched down and slashed
back. Kane felt a sting along his right forearm.

He jumped back. It took a heartbeat to steel himself to
glance at his arm, fearing to see parted muscles bunched
up at forearm and the inside of his elbow; those volcanic-
glass blades would slice to bone as readily as they'd cut
through skin. It registered that he still gripped his own wep
even as he looked to see a thin line of blood drawn transversely across his arm, just beginning to bead and run.

Huitzilopochtli jumped down on Kane's side of the altar.
They exchanged a quick series of blows, at the end of which
Kane was bleeding from a slash across the bridge of his nose
that burned as if Huitzilopochtli's blades had been dipped
in acid, and another on the deltoid muscle of his shield arm.

Blades weren't Kane's favorite medium of social inter-
action. But he knew a thing or two about a knife fight. One
of which was that it just took a few little cuts to start a
fighter bleeding enough to weaken quickly.

Huitzilopochtli was grinning at him, though his eyes
were dark marbles of hate sunk well back in his skull. He's
playing with me, Kane realized.

He heard his friends calling encouragement. He hoped
somebody was keeping an eye on the open entry to the
pyramid, just in case Tezcatlipoca decided to poke his nose
out. He couldn't let himself waste much thought on it.
Time was not on his side; the trickle of blood running
down his left arm reminded him of the fact.

It was time to take a serious gamble.

He feinted at Huitzilopochtli's head to bring the war
god's guard up. Their shields clashed together. Kane thrust
with all the strength of his legs and back.

Huitzilopochtli pushed back. For a moment they glared

at each other, sweating and straining over their shield rims. Inevitably, Huitzilopochtli's greater strength began to tell. Kane felt himself being driven inexorably back.

He sprang back. With all his strength and intention focused on thrusting forward, Huitzilopochtli overbalanced. At the same time, his shield, with nothing to push against suddenly, opened outward like a gate.

Kane already had a horizontal cut whistling on its way at sternum level.

With his superb training and godlike reflexes the war god didn't seriously stumble, nor was he open long. He caught himself in time to throw his upper body back out of harm's way.

Had he been able to gut the big son of a bitch then and there, Kane would not have complained. Instead, as intended, his black glass blades kissed the leather shield strap inside Huitzilopochtli's left forearm. It only nicked the smooth brown skin—but the strap parted, causing the shield to come loose.

Huitzilopochtli stepped back. He still gripped another strap, but the buckler wanted to flop, difficult to control. With a snarl he threw it spinning away—then seized the haft of his sword with both hands and launched his most furious attack yet, great smashing, sweeping blows that flurried in with impossible speed.

Kane gave way step by step. There was no thought of attacking now; it took everything he had just to keep his own shield between that howling glass-edged sword and his tender flesh. He tried to take each hack with his shield angled, to prevent the war god from hitting it dead-on.

But he couldn't avert it forever. Huitzilopochtli landed a stroke full force and fully perpendicular to the plane of Kane's shield. Metal-sheathed polycarbonate or not, the shield split right in two. Only by luck, and the fact that he was already backing up a half step, saved Kane from having his arm severed or shattered by the blow. As it was, his left forearm was numbed—and his right heel fetched up against the side of the stone pavilion.

Roaring his triumph, Huitzilopochtli aimed a shot from over his shoulder that might cleave even a god from crown to navel.

Chapter 34

Kane ducked right.

Huitzilopochtli embedded his sword in the stone of the doorjamb.

Without hesitation Kane launched himself into Huitzilopochtli's midriff in a clumsy but fierce tackle. Stuck tight, the glass-bladed sword was wrenched from Huitzilopochtli's hand as the war god was driven onto his back with Kane full length atop him. The lanyard parted with a twang.

It could have been good luck or bad that brought Kane's right hand, and hence his own sword, behind Huitzilopochtli's back. Had the wep been edge-up their combined weights coming down on it would have chopped the war god's spine neatly in two between the fifth and sixth dorsal vertebrae. Instead the blade lay flat. Their weight trapped it as neatly beneath him.

Kane brought up his legs, trying to get on his knees with thighs around Huitzilopochtli's waist. Stronger though the war god was, their strengths weren't that incommensurate. He was nowhere near strong enough to throw Kane off from the classic mount position.

Huitzilopochtli head-butted him. Kane lowered his head so that their helmets clashed. Again polycarbonate gave way to superhuman strength. Both gilded helmets split.

With a bellow and a heave of his whole body,

Huitzilopochtli threw Kane off him. The thong around
Kane's right wrist broke, leaving the sword behind. His
back slammed against the black altar. Huitzilopochtli jackknifed to his feet, but facing away from his opponent. By
the time he turned, Kane was on his feet, wiping blood
from his cut nose with the back of his hand.

They stood facing each other, Huitzilopochtli a great
raging tiger without stripes, Kane a lean gray wolf.

Huitzilopochtli attacked with a wild looping right to the
head that was almost a haymaker. Kane ducked, then
stepped into him with his left leg, driving a right cross to
his midsection and following it at once with a brutal hook
to the short ribs.

Huitzilopochtli glided back. His lips were closed but
still smiling. Fists raised, he came on.

Still leading with his left, Kane jabbed him twice in the
right eye. Huitzilopochtli backed off, the lid already puffing.

I'm the better boxer, Kane thought. But the war god was
probably more experienced with wrestling—it went right
with the whole Mexican masked-wrestler motif Brigid had
told him about. Which meant he was at least prepared
when Huitzilopochtli lunged. He thought the war god
might shoot on him, dive low for a takedown, and readied
the classic riposte, which was basically to stay fairly upright and just push him face first into the stone platform
by the shoulders. Instead Huitzilopochtli just put his head
down, meaning he got his weight lower than Kane's by the
time they hit.

Which meant he instantly drove Kane bicycling backward. Kane grabbed both gigantic biceps, sat down a little too hard, saw sparks as his tailbone slammed, then he
rolled back, put a sandal into Huitzilopochtli's flat gut and
threw him into the side of the stairway housing.

The war god recovered far quicker than Kane imagined possible. The haft of his own sword jutted temptingly near to hand, but Huitzilopochtli was too canny to squander an opportunity trying to jimmy it loose. He rushed Kane, storming punches into his head and face as the other god got to one knee.

Kane went into a turtle, bringing up both forearms to try to block the sledgehammer hits. Huitzilopochtli raised his right hand high overhead, prepping a hammer-fist blow that would either stave in the back of Kane's head or snap his neck. Kane took advantage of the lull to push out a not very potent straight right punch.

Not very potent, but it hit Huitzilopochtli's exposed solar plexus. The war god *whoofed* and backpedaled. Kane had bought the space he needed to get his legs under him again, and did.

His right eye was sealed, not by a direct hit but by a cut opened in the brow above; blood was pouring into the socket and already starting to congeal there, effectively gluing shut his lid. Kane lacked time even to try to wipe it clear because Huitzilopochtli was on him again.

Kane struck twice wildly, felt his fists strike. Then Huitzilopochtli had him by the upper arms. Kane returned the favor. This time Kane's center of gravity was lower, giving him better leverage to resist the war god's pushing.

But rather than trying to drive him back, Huitzilopochtli let his arms flex slightly, then shoved upward. Kane's center of gravity stayed low, but his head rose. His clear eye met both of Huitzilopochtli's.

It was like an ice pick stabbed through to the brain. A black explosion filled Kane's skull. Pain shot straight down his spine and arms.

Tonatiuh saved him then. It was the real Sun god, not

Kane, who in less than an eye blink sought and found the fiery lines. Perhaps it helped that at that instant the sun broke through beneath the overcast and sent red rays slanting across pyramid and plaza. Kane's energy had been drained away in draining Huitzilopochtli's, and he had had no chance to recharge. But the Sun god knew his own powers well, and stopped the blackness from overwhelming Kane.

He could see, fuzzily. The war god's eyes were flashed and mad. "I too have a death gaze, Sun god," he said, his voice barely showing strain. "Now I drink your life, accept your flowery sacrifice to myself. And next I will claim your friends' lives!"

Kane's skull throbbed as if his brain were swelling. *I cannot resist his gaze much longer!* Tonatiuh wailed within his mind.

"That's…okay," Kane grunted aloud. "Because where gods fail…Mags…*prevail.*"

He brought his right knee up hard into Huitzilopochtli's balls.

The old Adam betrayed the war god then. Gagging, Huitzilopochtli doubled over in all too human fashion— into a brutal punch that was more shovel-hook than uppercut from Kane's god-hard fist against Huitzilopochtli's broad chin.

Huitzilopochtli's head snapped back. Kane raised his right leg, turned his hip over and pistoned a thrusting side-kick into Huitzilopochtli's midsection. The war god staggered back, gagging, reached behind himself and came around with a snub-nosed revolver in his right hand.

And Kane, who had snatched up his own dropped sword, planted it with a log-splitting sound smack in the center of Huitzilopochtli's chest.

Huitzilopochtli bellowed. He dropped his handblaster, a 5-shot titanium Taurus 445 in .45 Colt. The war god's cry of mortal agony went on and on, louder and louder, until white dust began to fly from the face of the stone pavilion and Chalchihuitlicue's fog bank to be blown away from the pyramid base.

But if his cry had the force and volume of his departed mother's scream, it lacked its disintegrating properties. Unfazed, Kane wrenched the weapon from the war god's chest and threw it away. Then with hands back to back he plunged his fingers into the red wound gaping like a vertical mouth in Huitzilopochtli's chest, and shoved him back until the backs of his legs struck the altar. Then he bore the war god down upon his own altar, and with a sound like an oak tree splintering pried open Huitzilopochtli's rib cage with his own bare hands.

He reached into the now cavernous yawn of the stricken god's chest and wrapped his hand around his heart. It continued to beat strongly. He smiled, then, and prepared to wrench it from Huitzilopochtli's chest.

And from behind a voice cried, "Stop!"

Kane froze. Such was his rage that he thought no force on Earth could keep him from carrying out his vengeance vow.

He was wrong. The voice of a dead man could.

Still gripping the heart, Kane looked over his shoulder. Dr. Marroquín stood a few paces behind.

"How the hell did you get here?" Kane demanded.

Marroquín held up his hand. The disk of his miniature Smoking Mirror flashed a reflection of the sun's rays like the blood that now covered the front of Kane's face and breastplate like new skin. "The same way I escaped from the stricken helicopter," he said calmly. "This very useful device also allows me to teleport. Rather in the manner of Dr. Lakesh's clever interphasers. Now, please, Lord Tonatiuh—friend Kane. Let go. Do not slay Huitzil-opochtli."

"Why not?"

"It would disrupt the order of things within the valley too greatly. We have our victory—the power of the two is broken. They can no longer resist Quetzalcoatl's return—not now, when all Tenochtitlán has seen how you have bested the war god, and even claimed his heart."

"But it's mine. And I do claim it." The fury had begun to ebb within him. At the same time he neither knew whether it was Kane who said that or Tonatiuh, nor did he care.

"Please," the whitecoat said. His face looked more than grave. It looked…worried.

"He's right, Kane," Lakesh called. "We've won, my friend. Your victory is immaculate."

Huitzilopochtli was fully unconscious now. The beating of his heart seemed all but imperceptibly to weaken.

"What about Tezcatlipoca? What do you think he'll say?"

Marroquín smiled thinly. "I believe I can assure you he will assent."

"And what makes you think that?"

"Kane!"

Kane turned. He let go of his victim's heart.

"Baptiste?"

She stood beside Quetzalcoatl on the step down from the platform. "Lakesh healed me. Quetzalcoatl. I—I'm fine, now, if just a little shaky."

"Let me take him," Marroquín said. Kane looked back to him with a frown. Was the renegade scientist pleading? "Please."

"What makes you think you can carry him?" Kane demanded.

"The same thing that makes him so sure Tezcatlipoca will agree to terms," Brigid called. "That's not Marroquín, Kane."

Dr. Marroquín gave a little sigh. "Oh, I'm Marroquín, all right, Lady Precious Green," he said, shaking his oddly tonsured head and smiling. "At least, I'm the only Marroquín you've known."

He *changed*. The contours Kane associated with Dr. Marroquín blurred, flowed. Grew taller. And then a dark-skinned man a little shorter than him stood facing him, clad in a loincloth. He was leanly muscled, and handsome in a hawklike way.

"I am Tezcatlipoca, as your astute Dr. Baptiste divined," he said. "And now as god to god I beg your mercy for my brother."

"How about mercy for you, since you seem to be the ranking bad guy right about now?" Grant demanded.

"As I have said, I am the one you believed was Marroquín. I brought you here and changed the four of you. You have given me what I want, and if you will allow me to see to Huitzilopochtli, I will see that you receive all that I have promised you."

"Why should we trust you?" Kane asked.

"If you will consult your colleague's eidetic memory, you will learn that I am also a god of justice. In various guises I tempt men to do ill, and then punish them if they do so—or reward them if they behave virtuously. A distasteful pastime to you, perhaps—but Lady Chalchihuitlicue will attest that my adherence to justice is scrupulous."

"That is what the legend says," Brigid said. "And, down here, anyway, the legends all seem to be true."

Kane took a deep breath and stood aside.

Tezcatlipoca walked past him with an unself-consciously regal bearing utterly unlike Marroquín's. Tezcatlipoca took up Huitzilopochtli in his sinewy arms, turned his face upon the setting sun and bore his stricken brother down into the pyramid from which they had jointly ruled Tenochtitlán.

Epilogue

It was night in the conversation-space high up in the institute's main building. The afternoon's battle had not touched it. The buffet had been replenished, but only Domi was able to eat. The others slumped on chairs and sofas and tried to stay awake.

"The original Dr. Marroquín," said Tezcatlipoca, back in the guise of the man of whom he spoke, "suffered an unfortunate accident while experimenting in the Black House some time prior to his apparent defection. Such were the levels and nature of the energies involved that his body was instantly and tracelessly disintegrated—only by exhaustive analysis of sensor readings from the lab was I able to discover that much. As it happened, I found it convenient that the good doctor should carry on, or be seen to. So I employed my shape-changing skills—along with some old-fashioned stage magic and the odd falsification of records."

"An accident." Brigid didn't try not to sound arch.

Tezcatlipoca laughed. It was an engaging laugh. No doubt about it.

"I won't insult your intelligence by attempting to convince you that I would be incapable of arranging for the violent dissociation of the poor doctor's component atoms. I've done much worse. Let it pass—it's only barely relevant."

Teresa and Ernesto were present, as well. They sat side by side on one of the couches. The young hybrid woman stared at her father, in the guise of the man she had come to think of as a father, with an admixture of fascination and loathing.

"I'm curious," Brigid said. "The artifact in the basement. Is it—?"

"A very good replica of the true and original Smoking Mirror, capable of most, but not all of its functions." The false whitecoat waved a self-deprecating hand. "Not even I have been able to plumb all of the genuine article's mysteries."

"What makes you think your—this Huitzilopochtli character will abide by the new arrangement?" Grant asked.

"Fait accompli, mostly. All of Tenochtitlán saw him fall to the hand of Tonatiuh. All Tenochtitlán saw Tezcatlipoca and Quetzalcoatl mount the top of the Pyramid of the Gods side by side to announce the restoration of the triumvirate. Even with his powers of recuperation, even with the restorative power of the life-vats, Huitzilopochtli will be many days recovering from his injuries. The new order will be firmly in place by then."

He sipped from a mug of *chocolatl*. "And also because of our mother's death. You need feel no concern, Dr. Baptiste. I shall mourn my mother in my own way and in my own time. I loved her, but I bear you no animus for killing her. It was a necessary outcome. One I contrived.

"Huitzilopochtli was—is—the weaker willed of the two of us. He was too susceptible to Coatlicue's sway. It was she who truly became addicted to sacrifice—that is, to ever more and greater mass sacrifices. She encouraged that addiction in my brother. In both of us. It is not easy to resist, as those of you who bear Tonatiuh, Chalchihuitlicue and Itzapapalotl can attest from having drunk in lives in battle. But I successfully resisted it."

"You've taken many lives in sacrifice," Teresa said with venom.

He held up a hand. "Peace. It is true. I do not deny taking sacrifices. I do deny that my appetite for them became a need as overwhelming as it did for Huitzilopochtli and Coatlicue.

"Along with his blood addiction, our mother encouraged my brother in his incipient megalomania. After they—we—drove Quetzalcoatl out thirty years ago, they began to aggrandize themselves. Not just at my expense, but that of Tenochtitlán's economy and the stability of the whole valley, as the other city-states began to groan under their exactions. Which was why, some two years ago, I decided balance must be restored. Which meant Quetzalcoatl must be returned to share power. And so I set in train the events that culminated here this day."

He set down his mug. "And so, my guests, you will be restored to your former estates, as promised. You must spend one final night in the vats—your own exertions have weakened you too greatly to survive the change without recovery."

Kane looked to Brigid. They shuddered.

"What will you do for a Quetzalcoatl?" Grant asked.

"We will find an appropriate candidate. We have some short period of grace, during which the plumed serpent can be said to be closeted for meditation, or even tending to the healing his great foe Huitzilopochtli—and also finalizing details of the new regime. And the new Quetzalcoatl will enjoy something more of a grace period himself, time to learn his persona and powers without having to be thrown directly into a steaming cauldron. I salute you, by the way, Dr. Lakesh—like your friends, you performed admirably."

Lakesh nodded and smiled. "Thank you very much,

Lord Tezcatlipoca. That's very gracious of you. And yet I wonder, might we be being perhaps a trifle hasty in this desire to return to our former selves?"

"With all due respect to the Sun god and his pals," Kane said, "the sooner I have my head to myself the better."

"Kane speaks for me," Brigid said. "Chalchihuitlicue isn't quite as ferocious as Tonatiuh. But there's plenty about her I find…unsettling. And the thought of spending even another second in one of those hybrid blood-baths— I'm sorry, Teresa!—makes my skin crawl."

"You need not apologize to me," Teresa said almost inaudibly, staring down at the floor between her feet. "I am what I am."

"You are a very intelligent and brave young woman," Brigid said.

Lakesh stood. He was Lakesh in appearance now; none of them had an aspect on, except their host. "I can certainly understand how you feel, dearest Brigid. And the estimable Kane, as well. I myself most assuredly share your distaste for the methods required to sustain us in our present elevated level of existence. But perhaps my duty lies in continuing to sacrifice my qualms in the interests of the great cause we all serve. There is much to be learned as the feathered serpent, and certainly, with his powers, I can do much to bring our goals closer within reach."

Kane and Brigid were both staring at him. "We're not going back to Cerberus without you, Doc," Kane said. "I thought we all agreed on that."

"Well, to be sure. Yet you young people are so eager to relinquish your powers—that is, resume your normal lives. Perhaps you can precede me back while I stay on a bit longer…."

"You need to let go, Doctor," Brigid said. Her voice was low but edgy.

"All of us go together or none of us goes," Kane said. "And as it happens, we're all going."

"What Kane and Brigid are too tactful to tell you, Doc," Grant said, "but *I'm* not, is—no way do we leave you the only god in the bunch. That's just not going to happen."

Lakesh sat back down. He looked to Domi, who was just polishing off a turkey leg, bones and all. "Domi, darling one, you are less—how shall I say?—oppressed by the burden you bear than the others. Surely you understand, surely you can explain to them how I feel?"

She smiled at him, licked her fingers and wiped them on her white smock. Then she stood and came toward him, moving with the sinister feline grace of Itzapapalotl.

"I like being a goddess," she almost purred. "I like being the obsidian butterfly. We've got a lot in common, you know—you do know. The blood stuff doesn't bother me the way it does Kane and Brigid. The urges don't bother me."

Lakesh turned his head this way and that as she stalked behind his chair, trying to follow her with his eyes. She got right behind him, leaned over him—and took her aspect upon her.

"I *like* this. I like jolt, too. If I do too much of either, it'll take me over. And I won't let that happen."

She reached around, hooked a taloned forefinger under his chin and lifted his face toward hers. "Like Brigid said, like we all say, let it go. You haven't really got a choice."

For a moment Lakesh looked as if he would get angry. Kane saw the skin beneath his chin dimple at a sudden increase of pressure from the needlelike claw-tip.

"Oh, very well," Lakesh said peevishly. "I cannot afford to stay away from Cerberus too long, in any event."

The obsidian butterfly smiled. And was Domi again.

THE FIVE OF THEM stood together in the Ceberus control center, staring at a large vid display. It showed real-time overhead imaging of Tenochtitlán, partially obscured by a broken overcast.

"Doesn't seem real, does it?" Grant said in a quiet rumble.

"You don't know the half of it," Domi said. "You never were a god."

"Nope. Just good old Grant. And I'm damn glad."

"Not that staying 'just good old Grant' slowed you up much," Kane added.

"I wonder," Brigid said, "how Ernesto is going to adjust to the role of the plumed serpent?"

"I'm sure the Quetzalcoatl entity will bring him along gently and in due course," Lakesh said with a certain waspishness.

He went to his favorite chair and sat. Then he swiveled to face the others. "Back there in the institute, you—you all were practically threatening me, to get me to relinquish Quetzalcoatl."

"We were," Kane agreed.

"But surely—surely you would never have done anything overt to me?"

"Why, Doctor," Brigid said, "I'm surprised at you. Haven't you learned better than to ask questions you don't really want to know the answer to?"

DEATH LANDS®

Separation

*Available June 2004
at your favorite retail outlet.*

The group makes its way to a remote island in hopes of finding brief sanctuary. Instead, they are captured by an isolated tribe of descendants of African slaves from pre–Civil War days. When they declare Mildred Wyeth "free" from her white masters, it is a twist of fate that ultimately leads the battle-hardened medic to question where her true loyalties lie. Will she side with Ryan, J. B. Dix and those with whom she has forged a bond of trust and friendship…or with the people of her own blood?

Readers won't want to miss this exciting new title of the SuperBolan series!

Don Pendleton's **Mack Bolan**

Zero Option

Zero Platform is about to become the first orbiting weapons system operated by human/machine interface. Its command center has been razed to the ground, but the person willing to become the first human prototype of bio-cybernetic engineering survived the attack. Now Doug Buchanan is running for his life, a wanted man on three fronts: by America's enemies determined to destroy Zero's capabilities, by traitors inside Washington plotting a hostile takeover of the U.S. government and by the only individual who can save Buchanan—and America—from the unthinkable.

Available July 2004 at your favorite retail outlet.

Take
2 explosive books
plus a
mystery bonus
FREE